A
ROGUE'S
COMPANY

Also by Allison Montclair

The Right Sort of Man
A Royal Affair

A ROGUE'S COMPANY

ALLISON MONTCLAIR

MINOTAUR BOOKS
NEW YORK

Published in the United States by Minotaur Books, an imprint of St. Martin's Publishing Group

A ROGUE'S COMPANY. Copyright © 2021 by Allison Montclair. All rights reserved. Printed in the United States of America. For information, address St. Martin's Publishing Group, 120 Broadway, New York, NY 10271.

www.minotaurbooks.com

THE HAUNTING OF THE DESKS. Copyright © 2021 by Allison Montclair

Excerpt from *The Unkept Woman* copyright © 2022 by Allison Montclair

The Library of Congress has cataloged the hardcover edition as follows:

Names: Montclair, Allison, author.
Title: A rogue's company / Allison Montclair.
Description: First Edition. | New York : Minotaur Books, 2021. |
   Series: Sparks & Bainbridge mystery ; 3 |
Identifiers: LCCN 2020056397 | ISBN 9781250750327 (hardcover) |
   ISBN 9781250750334 (ebook)
Subjects: GSAFD: Mystery fiction.
Classification: LCC PS3613.O54757 R64 2021 | DDC 813/.6—dc23
LC record available at https://lccn.loc.gov/2020056397

ISBN 978-1-250-84815-4 (trade paperback)

Our books may be purchased in bulk for promotional, educational, or business use. Please contact your local bookseller or the Macmillan Corporate and Premium Sales Department at 1-800-221-7945, extension 5442, or by email at MacmillanSpecialMarkets@macmillan.com.

First Minotaur Books Trade Paperback Edition: 2022

10 9 8 7 6 5 4 3 2 1

TO ADRIANA, OUR NEW DAUGHTER-IN-LAW,

FOR THE JOY SHE HAS BROUGHT TO OUR FAMILY

ACKNOWLEDGMENTS

In addition to sources cited in their previous works, the author has consulted books and articles by W. E. Fairbairn, Peter Fryer, Veronica Chincoli, Stanley Jackson, Alexander John Hanna, Colin Black, Francis L. Coleman, Janie Hampton, and Eugene Braunwald. Tom Abraham, Kayleigh Simpson, and Sarah Broadhurst of the Zoological Society of London answered zoo-related questions, and Dr. Naomi Botkin reviewed the cardiology and was satisfied with it.

The author takes responsibility for all errors made. However, before confronting them with said errors, please bear in mind that they have now read two books on British military martial arts, so perhaps you should reconsider.

It goes without saying that a woman should always know how to protect herself.

—W. E. FAIRBAIRN,
HANDS OFF!: SELF-DEFENSE FOR WOMEN, 1942

PROLOGUE

I t is said that the first naval conflict of what was then called the Great War took place far removed from the main European theatres. The British maintained a solitary gunboat, the HMS *Gwendolen,* on Lake Nyasa. The *Gwendolen* patrolled the western coast of the lake, although the British regarded the entirety of the lake as theirs since it had been rediscovered and named by David Livingstone during his wanderings. On August 4, 1914, the captain of the *Gwendolen*, a man named Rhoades, received orders to attack the *Hermann von Wissman*, the only German gunboat on the lake, which patrolled the eastern shores bordering German East Africa. Captain Rhoades went in search of the boat, helmed by a Captain Berndt and named for a German explorer from the previous century who raised funds to purchase it for the laudable purpose of combatting the enslavement of the locals by Arab traders. Ten days later, the British located the unsuspecting German gunboat docked for repairs at the slip at Sphinxhafen, named by the Germans not for the great Egyptian wonder far to the north but for a series of peculiarly sphinx-like rocks that jutted out of the water. The locals, who were there long before the Germans, called the port Liuli. The lone gunner on the *Gwendolen*, whose full name is lost to history but who was believed to be a Scotsman named Jock, fired four shells from a distance of approximately two thousand yards, the last of which further disabled the already disabled ship.

Captain Rhoades knew Captain Berndt. They had met on social occasions many times on both shores, and had in fact brought their vessels together for Christmas celebrations the previous year, each crew coming aboard the other's ship to share meals. Rhoades was privately glad that he caught his newly created enemy's ship in repairs rather than afloat, and hoped that the loss of life had been minimal.

The Scottish gunner, on the other hand, was pleased with his accuracy and the requirement of only four shells to complete the mission. This was no matter of stereotypical national frugality. He knew that a war of this magnitude in faraway Europe would mean scarce replenishment of dwindling ammunition in Africa, and he wanted to make what he had last as long as he could.

Great Britain had been at war with Germany for precisely ten days. The Great Naval Battle of Lake Nyasa did not end it.

Nothing of great moment happened on the lake during World War II, and Great Britain's naval triumph had long been forgotten by the time the steamship *Vitya* was loading up for its journey from Monkey Bay at the southern end of the lake to Karonga near the northern end, about 380 miles by water. The *Vitya* was an old sternwheeler and could hold 250 passengers comfortably, but comfort was never a concern for its owners, who were quite happy to cram as many paying customers onto the benches belowdecks as they possibly could.

They were in luck this trip. A large contingent of Ismaili Muslims was traveling north, intending to continue on to Dar es Salaam to celebrate the upcoming Diamond Jubilee celebrations for the Aga Khan. Most of them had never traveled outside their villages before, much less been on a steamship, so there was an air of festive excitement and lively chatter as they boarded.

This excitement was not shared by the captain and his chief officer, who had been making the round trip twice a week for many years. The captain took the time to speak with a tea planter he knew who was returning home with his wife, while his chief personally escorted the only other white passengers, a trio of English schoolteachers on holiday from their postings in Tanganyika, to their cabins, marking the youngest and prettiest one as a possibility for a shipboard dalliance during his few hours off. The whites, having checked in, immediately repaired to the small bar on the upper deck to exchange small talk and bemoan the humidity.

The Ismailis were not the only passengers belowdecks, of course. There was the usual mix—miners coming home after years spent underground at Roan Antelope, Nkasa, and the rest of the workings in the Northern Rhodesia copper belt; a cluster of askari wearing the uniforms of the King's African Rifles; a handful of missionaries from competing churches talking shop in English and Chinyanja; and so forth.

There was a young couple in their late twenties who kept to themselves. A casual observer might have mistaken them for husband and wife, given the solicitous attentions the man paid towards her, but a more perspicacious viewer would have spotted the similarity in their features and correctly guessed that they were brother and sister. They spoke softly in Chitumbuka, for they were of the Tumbuka people.

The more perspicacious viewer, if a polite soul, would not have eavesdropped on their conversation, because it was clear that she had been weeping.

"I wish I could go back to our village," she said, looking away from the lake.

"That's the first place they'll come looking for you, Bay," he said.

"But these people you are taking me to—I don't know them. They don't know our language."

"I know them, I trust them," he said. "And they speak English well."

"Tell me the truth, Kon," she asked. "Are you taking me north to spare me the shame I am bringing the family?"

"I am taking you north because you will be safe there," he said. "You have nothing to be ashamed of. I am your big brother. It is my responsibility to look after you. I am sorry that I have been derelict in my duties."

"You have nothing to apologise for," she said, smiling at him though the tears were falling again. "This was all my doing. How long will I stay there?"

"As long as it takes," he said. "I have already written Younger Brother, and will join him as soon as we get you settled. Knowing him, he will have a solution for the situation before I even arrive."

"He is the smart one," she said. "I pray that he is not in over his head there."

"He is an excellent swimmer in all situations," Kondanani reassured her.

"Unlike me," she said, looking at the old steamer dubiously.

"Come on," he said, urging her forward. "The sooner we get you there, the sooner I can get to Dar es Salaam."

He handed their tickets to the crewman who pointed them towards a stairwell leading them belowdecks.

They were lucky—they found two spots on a bench against the hull away from the boiler room, so that they could continue to talk without shouting. All around them, people claimed as much space as they could, only reluctantly removing their belongings from the seats next to them when it became clear that the boat had been overbooked. Latecomers plopped themselves down in the aisles, grumbling when they had to let others walk by or over them to use the already beleaguered lavatories at either end.

"How long must we endure this?" asked Bayenkhu.

"Thirty-eight hours," he replied. "That's from when we leave."

But the boat stayed docked in Monkey Bay for another two hours.

"No weather report?" the captain asked the chief.

"Telegraph's down up north," he replied.

The captain looked at the skies immediately ahead. They were clear enough, but he knew that could change in minutes.

"Well, whatever comes, we'll bull our way through," he said, patting the wheel. "Let's go. Cast off! Slow ahead, starboard rudder five degrees."

"Slow ahead, starboard rudder five degrees," repeated the helmsman.

The *Vitya* edged away from the dock, the great wheels turning slowly at first. Once they were clear, the captain gave the order to bring them to half until they were safely out of the bay. The passengers on deck cheered and waved kerchiefs to those remaining on shore.

The cheers could be heard down below, even with the rise in the churning noise of the engines. Bayenkhu leaned wearily into her brother, who draped his arm around her and held her close.

They ate fruit that they had brought from a cart at the docks, and shared a canteen of water that they needed to make last for the entire trip. The lake was choppy, and the rise and fall of the boat had them both feeling queasy. They each risked a perilous journey to the lavatory, stepping gingerly through the unlucky souls who were now lying in the aisles, not caring whom they inconvenienced.

She fell asleep, nestled against him. He was feeling restless. The boat was bouncing harder, and he could hear the rain now pounding against the hull outside and thunder crashing.

Despite that, he craved fresh air. And he needed to smoke.

"Bay, I'm going up to the deck for a cigarette," he said. "I'll be back."

She murmured something unintelligible in reply, and he carefully eased his arm from where she had pinned it against the wall and got to his feet. She leaned down into the cloth bag that held her belongings and embraced it like a lost friend. He smiled sadly, seeing in repose the face of the once innocent girl who had come to trouble his life and chase after him everywhere he went.

Until the time came for him to leave. And then she left, too.

He went up top. Sheets of rain poured down from the sky, and the flashes of lightning only revealed waves higher than he thought a lake could have. The boat was pitching in every direction, the wheels continuing to churn to his right. He turned towards the cabins to shield his matches and managed to light a cigarette on the second try. He sucked in the smoke gratefully—his nerves had been more rattled than he realised. He turned to gaze out over the water.

Then there was a loud thump from below, and the boat lurched to starboard. To his horror, the great wheels slowed to a halt. The ship continued to roll inexorably on its side. He clutched at a doorknob and tried to haul his way back to the stairs, screaming, "Bayenkhu!"

But the winds blew his words away, and there was already screaming coming from below.

He could see the top deck looming over him, and made a desperate unsteady dash to the railing. He dove out as far as he could and plunged through the lake's roiling surface, kicking hard to carry himself away. When he came up, he turned to look back.

There was only the stern of the ship, pointing towards the sky.

Then there was nothing.

"Bayenkhu!" he shouted again.

There were other shouts. Other names hurled into the air.

A broken board floated by and he grabbed it, wrapping his arm around it for added buoyancy. The waves sent him up and down. He could not say how long the storm lasted, but eventually it ceased and the waves calmed.

"Bayenkhu!" he screamed into the darkness.

No one replied. No one called his name.

"Bayenkhu!" he tried one more time.

"Who's there?" came a man's voice from nearby. "Do you have a boat?"

"I have a piece of wood," he said.

There was a pause.

"Will you share it?" came the other voice.

"I am coming," he said.

He kicked his way towards the man, who turned out to be an askari soldier. He grabbed on to the other end of the board.

"Thank you," he said.

"Will they know on land?" asked Kondanani. "Do you think there was a distress call sent?"

"I don't know," said the soldier. "It happened so fast."

"We should try for the shore," said Kondanani.

"West is closer," said the soldier.

They looked up. There were no stars to guide them, but a faint glimmer was visible behind them.

Sunrise.

They kicked away in the opposite direction, as did others who had made it out in time.

He felt the tears forming, and willed himself to keep from crying.

I will give no more water to this lake, he thought.

It was a seven-mile swim before they reached the coast at Florence Bay. They crawled the last few feet and collapsed. Kondanani looked back out to the lake, which in the sun looked peaceful and calm.

I'm sorry, Sister, he thought. I failed you. I promise that I won't fail this final task.

CHAPTER 1

The tram trundled down from the Vauxhall Bridge and screeched reluctantly to a halt, pausing long enough to allow two women to jump down to the pavement. They waved to the conductor as it left, then looked around at their surroundings. The short brunette got her bearings while consulting a set of directions scribbled on a torn envelope. The tall blonde carried a small valise. She looked in all directions, avidly surveying every building, every person, even the piles of rubble waiting to be collected from the bomb sites.

"So this is Lambeth," said Gwen.

"This is Lambeth," confirmed Iris. "You've been in Lambeth before, haven't you?"

"I've been through Lambeth," said Gwen. "On the way to Brixton Prison and, goodness, I'm saying that like it's a normal thing. But I've never actually set foot in Lambeth proper. Should I be doing the Lambeth Walk?"

"Please don't," said Iris. "You have too much of the Mayfair touch to pull it off. And thanks for sticking that tune in my head. This way."

"I liked *Me and My Girl*," said Gwen wistfully as they walked along the Thames. "I thought Lupino Lane was terrifically funny. We saw it in '37, not long after it opened."

"We?"

"Ronnie and I, of course," said Gwen. "One of our earlier dates. What 'we' did you think I meant?"

"You just recounted a memory of him without starting to tear up," observed Iris.

"I did, didn't I?" exclaimed Gwen in surprise. "I'll have to tell Dr. Milford. That's—I was going to say progress, or something. I don't know if it is."

"If your goal is to reclaim your life so you can start living it again, then it's progress," said Iris.

"As is today's adventure," said Gwen. "How much farther is he?"

"About five minutes walk," said Iris, glancing at her directions. "Five for me, anyway. About three for you if you seize the bit."

"Thank you for setting us up," said Gwen. "And for coming with me."

"Of course," said Iris, smiling up at her. "I wouldn't dream of you meeting him without me there. Consider me your chaperone."

"I scarcely need one at my advanced age."

"You're a reputable young blue-blooded widow heading into a seedy neighborhood to meet a strange man. What will your in-laws think?"

"They will think nothing," declared Gwen. "Because I don't plan to tell them about it."

"But if it ever comes out, you have me as a witness to your respectability."

"There isn't anything respectable about this," said Gwen. "Not in the circles I travel in."

"Times are changing," said Iris. "You're changing with them."

They walked up Lambeth Road. The railroad ran alongside them, raised above the neighborhood, cutting off the view of the river. The broad arches supporting the track bed provided homes to warehouses and the odd commercial establishment.

"Will he like me, do you think?" asked Gwen. "Will I like him?"

"I don't know," said Iris. "Liking isn't really the point, is it?"

"It's just that I've never been this—"

Gwen hesitated.

"Go on," said Iris.

"This—physical with a man. With anyone."

"It's going to be a hot and sweaty experience," said Iris.

"And I've never really had that. Is he—is he a brute?"

"He has to be a brutish sort to do what he does," said Iris. "But he's disciplined."

"A disciplined brute," said Gwen. "I've never encountered anyone like that."

"You were never in the army," said Iris. "Two arches over from the Fitzroy Lodge, he said, which is coming up. Glad to see they've found some new digs."

"Who are they?"

"A boxing club. They were bombed out during the Blitz. Just opened the new location. Ah, there it is!"

MACAULAY'S MARTIAL ARTS, read the sign. ORIENTAL COMBAT TECHNIQUES. FITNESS TRAINING. SELF-DEFENSE COURSES FOR MEN AND WOMEN. A group of photographs taped to the window showed men wearing white cotton jackets belted over drawstring trousers grappling with each other. One in particular was featured throwing other men over his shoulder or sending them to the mats with force so fierce that it was evident even in the frozen moments of the photographs. In the center, the man stood at attention in a British Army uniform. Underneath, a caption read: "As taught by former Master Sergeant Gerald Macaulay, His Majesty's Army."

"That's him?" asked Gwen.

"That's him," said Iris. "Are you ready?"

"Library skills and martial arts," said Gwen. "That's what I wanted to learn from you."

"And we've already been to the library," said Iris. "In you go, soldier."

She opened the door and they went inside.

There was no anteroom, although a desk sat in the front corner for whatever business matters needed to be conducted. A large square mat covered most of the interior, while around the periphery were punchbags, mostly heavy but some speed. In the rear stood several thick wooden poles with small crosspieces fixed at various heights and angles.

A man was bouncing lightly on his feet in front of one of the heavy bags. He was wearing an undershirt over white drawstring pants, the matching jacket draped over a nearby folding chair. He suddenly spun, his right foot connecting high on the bag with a resounding thud, sending it swinging to the left. Before it swung back, he spun the other way, his left foot striking it equally hard.

"Really, Gerry, what did that poor bag ever do to you?" said Sparks as they walked towards him.

"Hello, Sparks," he said, picking his jacket off the chair and putting it on, securing it with a black cloth belt. "This is the woman we spoke about, I take it?"

"She is. Master Sergeant Macaulay, may I present Mrs. Gwendolyn Bainbridge, my friend and business associate."

"How do you do?" said Macaulay, holding out his hand.

"How do you do?" Mrs. Bainbridge replied, looking at it before shaking it.

He caught the look.

"Not what you expected?" he asked.

"I thought there might be some form of bowing involved," she said. "I didn't expect a handshake."

"If you were undertaking a full course in one of the disciplines, then there would be more adherence to tradition," he said. "But you're here for the short-term self-defense course, so we won't bother. Grab a chair and let's talk."

He grabbed his chair and straddled it, resting his forearms on the back. Mrs. Bainbridge took another from against the wall and sat upon it properly, while Sparks sat on the desk and watched.

"Before we get you involved in all this, we have to talk about why you're here," said Macaulay.

"I wish to be able to defend myself against attack," said Mrs. Bainbridge. "As a woman should. As anyone should."

"That's all well and good," said Macaulay. "But how far are you willing to go?"

"How far? How do you mean?"

"The techniques I teach are the same we taught the lads for the war," he said. "No-nonsense, kill or be killed, hand-to-hand combat. The war is over, at least it is here, but the techniques aren't toned down for civilian life. So my question is, are you willing to learn skills that could lead you to killing a man?"

She looked over at Sparks, who gave her no help. She turned back to Macaulay.

"If he were a man deserving of it, then yes," she said.

"So if he grabbed your purse, for example."

"No."

"If he placed his hand on your knee in the cinema?"

"I wouldn't kill a man for that. I might slap him."

"What would you kill a man for?"

"If my life was threatened, of course. Or that of someone I cared for."

"Would you do it to protect a complete stranger?"

"I suppose that I would," said Mrs. Bainbridge, considering. "Assuming I knew the wrong and right of it."

"Ah, that's the trick, isn't it? Peacetime life is more complicated than wartime, and so are the choices."

"Wartime was plenty complicated for me, thank you very much," said Mrs. Bainbridge. "Let us proceed."

"Next order of business is the paperwork," he said, standing and walking over to the desk. He looked at Sparks sternly. "Have you decided to take up a new career as a paperweight, Sparks?"

"No."

"Then move your arse. Sit on a chair like a normal human being."

"No one's ever called me normal before," said Sparks, jumping down. "These are strange days."

He plucked a form from a pile on the desk, then crossed out one item and checked two more.

"You're signing up for ten lessons," he said as he came back over. "Normally five pounds, but I'm waiving the fee as we discussed on the phone. That part is crossed out. I need you to initial the checked parts."

"What's this one?" asked Mrs. Bainbridge, glancing over it. "I agree to waive any claims for physical injury? That's a possibility?"

"Tell her, Sparks," said Macaulay.

"You will get hurt," said Sparks. "You will feel pain."

"Can you handle pain, Mrs. Bainbridge?" asked Macaulay.

"Have you ever given birth, Master Sergeant Macaulay?" she replied.

"Afraid not," he said, smiling for the first time. "And it's Mr. Macaulay now."

She signed the contract. He handed her the carbon, which she folded carefully and placed in her bag.

"Very good," she said. "Now, where do I change?"

"Change? Change into what?"

"I brought along my exercise togs," she said, holding up her valise. "Is there a room?"

"Mrs. Bainbridge, you've just been attacked and dragged into a dark alley by some ruffian who intends to have his way with you," said Macaulay. "Do you expect to say, 'Wait a moment, I am going to fight you, but I have to change first'?"

"Well, no, that's ridiculous," said Mrs. Bainbridge.

"You're going to learn to defend yourself in everyday circumstances," he said. "Wearing everyday clothing."

"Then next time, I'll wear something I don't mind getting mussed," she said. "But since I wasn't told that, I am going to get out of my nice new government-approved Utility suit and wear my exercise togs. Where do I change?"

"There's a lav in the back," he said, pointing.

"Thank you," she said.

Macaulay and Sparks watched as she walked to the back of the room and disappeared.

"Where on earth did you find that one?" asked Macaulay.

"Met her at a wedding," said Sparks. "We hit it off. Decided to go into business together."

"When I heard you had set up shop with another woman, I figured you found someone like you. But she's nothing like you, is she?"

"There is no one like me," declared Sparks. "When I die, the species will go entirely extinct."

"Seriously, Sparks. Do you think she's up to this?"

"Don't underestimate her, Gerry. We've been through a couple of tight spots together, and she's come through with flying colours. My worry is that she can be reckless. She almost got us both killed one time. That's why I brought her here."

"Reckless and self-destructive," said Macaulay. "Sounds like another woman I once trained. I was wrong, you have found a kindred spirit."

"Maybe. But I want her to be better at it."

"You'll have to tell me how starting a marriage bureau got you into a couple of tight spots."

"Trouble finds me wherever I go," said Sparks gloomily. "But you knew that already."

"I did. Ah, here comes milady."

Mrs. Bainbridge emerged wearing a pale blue cotton blouse over a pair of baggy black shorts. She carried her suit draped over her arm.

"Tennis, anyone?" muttered Macaulay.

"I brought my plimsolls," she said as she approached, holding up a pair with a blue and red tartan pattern. "Will those do?"

"Regular shoes, if you don't mind," said Macaulay. "There are attacks you will be making with them, so you need to feel the balance."

"It sounds like dancing," said Mrs. Bainbridge, draping her suit over a chair. "All right, I'm ready."

"The system you are going to learn is based on one developed by Major W. E. Fairbairn, who was my boss when I was with the Shanghai Municipal Police," he began. "He put it together from a combination of jiu-jitsu, Chinese boxing, and down-and-dirty street fighting. He called it Defendu, which he thought sounded Oriental, but I think just comes across as silly."

"One second," interrupted Sparks. "Your necklace, darling."

"Oh, Lord, thank you," said Mrs. Bainbridge as she removed it. "Hold my pearls whilst I get pummeled, would you?"

"I suppose you have a practise necklace you can wear," commented Macaulay.

"Nothing that goes with this outfit. Sorry, there will be no more interruptions. Please continue."

"We will have ten lessons," he said. "In each, I will teach you one basic strike and one response to a hold. I expect you to practise during the week in between, then we review and move on to the next. Clear?"

"Clear, sir."

"One last thing. You're a married woman."

"I was," she said, blinking for a moment.

"If you're a widow, my condolences. If you're divorced, my con-

gratulations. My point is that this is a course for women defending themselves primarily from assaults by men, and I will be using
the word 'testicles' more than once during your training. I assume
from your marital status that you are familiar with the word and
know where they are located."

"I am and I do," said Mrs. Bainbridge. "I fear, however, for my
friend, Miss Sparks. She is but a maid and innocent in the ways of
men. She might faint."

The snort this elicited from Sparks was profoundly gratifying,
as was the smirk on Macaulay's face.

"Very good," he said. "Come meet your opponent."

He led her to one of the heavy bags, on which the outline of a
man had been drawn with a marker pen.

"This here fellow is Sidney," he said.

"How do you do, Sidney?" Mrs. Bainbridge greeted him

"Sidney is a nasty piece of work," said Macaulay. "He's taller
than you, he's heavier than you, and he's stronger than you. He
wants to do unspeakable things to you, and then go off and do
them to some other unsuspecting woman. But you have one great
advantage over him right now."

"What's that?"

"You're a woman, and he isn't expecting a woman to fight back.
That gives you the element of surprise, which will exist up until the
moment you attack. Which means that your first move has to be
fast, unexpected, and effective."

He stood in front of the bag. Suddenly, his right arm shot up
and forward, the heel of his hand connecting just below the chin
on the drawing.

"The chin jab," said Macaulay. "If you're facing your opponent,
it's the first and most effective thing you can do. Hard to defend
against because of the short distance involved, and if he does pull
back enough to slip the blow, you continue straight to your sec-
ondary target."

"Which is?"

Macaulay turned back to Sidney and repeated the strike, this time with his left. He slowed it down just long enough for her to observe his extended fingers stop at the eyes.

"The chin strike will stun him and throw him back and off balance," he said. "Miss the chin, you can still blind him."

"Temporarily, I hope."

"Maybe permanently," said Macaulay. "We don't much care about Sidney's future at the moment."

"Oh," said Mrs. Bainbridge.

"Come up and give it a go," he said, stepping aside.

She stood in front of the heavy bag and looked at the drawing, feeling mildly ridiculous. Then she pulled her arm back.

"Stop," commanded Macaulay immediately. "What is your advantage again?"

"The element of surprise?"

"Correct. And you just lost it by pulling back your arm. Strike from where your arms rest normally."

"But won't I lose power?"

"Not that much, and the advantage gained is worth the trade-off. Arms at your sides. Now, strike!"

She shoved her arm upwards clumsily, smacking the bag with her full palm.

"Keep your fingers back, hit the point of the chin with the heel of the palm. Again."

She struck, this time landing with just the heel.

"Better," he said. "Here. Slowly, very slowly, try it on me. Stop when it touches my chin."

She faced him. His eyes bored into her own. She looked down at her hands for a moment. He shook his head.

"They're at the end of your arms where they always are," he said. "Never look away from me. Strike."

She kept her eyes on his and moved. At the last moment, her

hand came into her view, coming to a halt below his chin. He leaned forward and rested his chin on her palm.

"Got the idea now?"

"I think so."

"Back to Sidney. Right!"

She struck.

"Left!"

"I'm right-handed."

"And if that hand is unavailable for any reason?"

"Like encumbered by my bag?"

"Like broken or held and this is your last bleedin' chance to live. Left!"

She struck with her left, much more weakly.

"Again. Better. Now, go for the eyes."

She quailed for a moment, visualising the outcome.

"No," he said immediately. "You've committed to the blow. Sidney is onto your game now. You've missed his chin, and if you don't hit his eyes on the follow-through, you're dead and your child is an orphan."

Little Ronnie, she thought, and she followed through, her fingers gouging at the dots inside the ovals.

"That was harsh," she said.

"It's a harsh world," he replied. "You're here because you've stopped pretending that it isn't. Right. Right. Left. Left. Right. Eyes. Left. Eyes. Good. Now, you've set him back on his heels. He's unfocused, stunned, and wide open for the follow-up. Remember that word Sparks doesn't know?"

"Quite well."

"Your knee, straight up into them. It should be immediately after the chin jab, one two. Speed, speed, speed, Mrs. Bainbridge."

"Which knee?"

"Whichever leg your balance is on, use the other one. Right jab, follow with the knee. Go!"

She jabbed up, stepped into the bag and slammed her knee into it.

"Again. Mean it!"

She repeated it.

"Faster! One two!"

She struck the bag over and over, her breathing getting ragged, the fury building within her.

"Harder!"

A scream she didn't know she had erupted from within her as she rammed her knee into Sidney. If he had been real, the prospect of his producing little Sidneys would have been gravely in doubt.

"Good," said Macaulay, nodding. "Catch your breath for a moment. What was happening with that scream?"

"I'm not sure," she gasped, bending over to rest her hands on her knees. "I felt—"

"Go on," he encouraged her.

Sparks watched her friend's face intently, her own concealing her concern.

"Anger. No, rage. Sorry about the noise."

"Don't be. If this happened in real life, that scream would be one of your weapons. Scream bloody murder, lass. You'll startle him, you might scare him off, and you might get help. Now, the rage—that's a useful thing if you can get it under control. It gives you strength. It gives you speed. But it clouds your judgment, and that can lead you to make mistakes, and mistakes in a fight can be fatal."

"So all I have to do is master it, and everything will be bright and breezy."

"I never said it would be simple to do. But it can be done."

"How?"

"Practise, for a start. When the physical becomes automatic, the body will remember. Ready for the second half?"

"I think so," she said, straightening up.

"Close your eyes," he instructed her. "Deep breath. In for ten. Hold for ten. Release for ten. Do that again."

She did, then opened her eyes and nodded.

"Better, thanks. What hold will I be breaking today?"

"Lady's choice. Where would you like to start?"

"How about when I'm grabbed from behind?"

"There's five different ways to be grabbed from behind. Choose one."

"Oh, dear. I haven't considered it thoroughly, have I? How about the arm around the neck?"

"Excellent. Come over to the mat."

They walked to the center of the room. He stood directly in front of her, then turned away.

"Arm around my neck, doesn't matter which," he said. "We'll do this slowly."

We're dancing, she thought. We're only dancing.

And she stepped up and slipped her arm around the throat of a man she had just met.

"Your immediate objective is to get him to loosen the hold before you lose consciousness," he said. "Your way of accomplishing that is to cause him severe pain as quickly as possible. Which means the testicles. Man's best friends and his worst enemy. All right?"

"Yes."

"If you have room to get a hand behind you, grab and squeeze, or grab and pull."

"And if there is not enough room?"

"The shins, Mrs. Bainbridge. Heel of your shoe up as high as you can get, then scrape down hard and finish with the heel to the middle of his foot. Ever bark your shin on a low table?"

"Yes. Very painful."

"Multiply that by a factor of ten. He'll loosen his hold. Then you do this."

He brought his right arm across hers and grabbed her wrist.

"I'm going to do this slowly. Presumably the arm has loosened from the pain. You turn to the left while stepping back on your right foot—"

Slowly, inexorably, he turned inside her grip.

"You grab the wrist with the other hand and keep turning, twisting it downwards. Either he follows it down or it breaks."

She followed it down, then saw that she was coming face-to-face, or face-to-foot, with his boot.

"That's the finale," he said. "Kick to the face. This should all happen extremely fast. Got it?"

"I have the moves," she said, rubbing her wrist as he released her. "I don't have the speed."

"Again, that comes with practise. It should be second nature. Let's have you try it. We'll skip the pain part—you can save that for Sidney."

"Poor Sidney," she murmured.

He stepped behind her and put his arm around her neck.

She was suddenly acutely aware of the flimsiness of the cotton fabric of her tennis outfit as he pressed against her.

Dancing. Only dancing, she thought.

"Right, my grip has loosened. Go."

She grabbed his wrist and turned, then joined her other hand to the grip.

"Good," he said. "Force me down."

She did.

"That will really work on a man who's stronger than me?" she asked, raising her foot towards his face.

"No man likes pain. You move fast, then down he goes. You've had some dance training, I take it?"

"Yes."

"Don't kick like a bloody ballerina. You want to break his damn nose."

"More like a cancan girl," suggested Sparks.

"Once again, but with the left this time," he said.

They resumed their positions. He yoked his left arm around her and pressed against her back.

The body remembers.

Standing on the balcony at their hotel in Rome on their honeymoon in the middle of the night, him daring her to stand naked in the cool air for anyone to see if they knew to look up. Ronnie coming up behind her . . .

"Anytime you're ready, Mrs. Bainbridge," said Macaulay.

Jolted back to reality, she grabbed his wrist with her left and turned the other way, performing the sequence but mirrored. She kicked up hard this time, only to have her ankle caught in his free hand before it connected with his face.

"That kick's coming along," he said drily. "Let's leave it out for now. I've had this nose broken enough for one lifetime."

"I'm terribly sorry," she said.

"Never apologise for doing a thing right," he said. "Again."

They worked on it for twenty minutes, then he took her back to Sidney and placed her with her back to him.

"I'll call out testicles, shins, or head butt, and you react accordingly. Shin!"

She scraped her heel down the heavy bag.

"Stomp his foot like you're squashing a cockroach!" he barked.

"I've never squashed a cockroach."

"No, I suppose you have someone do that for you. Shin!"

She squashed the imaginary cockroach, wincing as the shock waves reverberated through her leg.

"That hurt, didn't it?" he asked.

She nodded.

"I guarantee it hurt him a whole lot more. Head butt!"

She knocked the back of her head against the bag.

"No love taps. Head butt!"

This time, she felt the reverberations inside her skull.

"And after I've given myself a concussion, what do I do?" she asked, rubbing her head.

"You finish him off and stagger away," he said. "Testicles!"

She pounded her fist behind her.

"Nothing to grab, is there?" she observed.

"You were on target, at least," he said. "Shin!"

They continued in this manner until her time was up.

"Good first lesson," he said. "Make sure you practise. Got a heavy bag at home?"

"I honestly have no idea," she gasped.

"Well, you can always prop a mattress against the wall. Take a breather."

"Thank God," she said, sagging to the floor.

"Very good, Gerry," said Sparks, pulling a form and a notepad from her bag. "Now, it's our turn to administer the torture. Here's our contract. Note that our five-pound fee has been waived in exchange for your lessons with Mrs. Bainbridge."

"Three cheers for the barter economy," said Mrs. Bainbridge, sitting with her back against Sidney.

"Sign this, and The Right Sort Marriage Bureau will make its best efforts to find you a suitable partner. Note carefully that we are not waiving the twenty-pound bounty should we be successful and you end up marrying one of our other clients."

"I couldn't trade that for more lessons?" he asked, glancing over the contract.

"Let's see if I'm still alive after the first ten, then we can negotiate," said Mrs. Bainbridge. "Please note that you are waiving any claims for emotional injury."

"That happens, does it?"

"All is fair in love and Defendu," said Sparks. "Press hard when you sign so the carbon comes through."

He signed. She signed underneath, gave him the copy, then folded the original and replaced it in her bag.

"Right," she said, opening her notepad. "Let's get the basics, then we'll get to the rest of it."

She went through his background, then looked over the notepad at him.

"Who are you searching for, Gerry?" she asked. "In your heart of hearts?"

"Ah, the organ I'm not supposed to have," he said, grinning ruefully. "I've been spending the better part of my life beating people up or teaching other people how to do it."

"Are you looking for someone interested in what you do? A fellow fighter?"

"Or the opposite?" asked Mrs. Bainbridge, who had regained her wind enough to focus on her instructor's face.

"The opposite," he replied. "I became what I am because there were opportunities available, then the war happened and my expertise was needed more than ever. Now, it's not, and thank God for that, but I want to finally settle down with someone who—"

He hesitated

"Who what, Gerry?" prompted Sparks.

"Who I can be gentle with," he said shyly. "I want to take care of someone."

"And for her to take care of you?" asked Mrs. Bainbridge.

"I can take care of myself," he said quickly. Then he shook his head. "Yeah, that's the problem with me, isn't it? I would like to come home to someone where we can spoil each other rotten at the end of the day."

"There are women who would like that very much," said Mrs. Bainbridge.

"But there's another thing," he said, "and this may narrow the field. She'd have to be willing to leave England."

"You're leaving?" exclaimed Sparks in dismay. "Not going back to Shanghai, surely?"

"No, that place is over and done with," he said. "No future in it for the likes of me. I was thinking Africa. One of the Rhodesias."

"Really? Why there?"

"It's a place where an Englishman can start over and do very well very quickly," he said. "Living's cheap, and some mates of mine are already set up working security for the mining operations and such. They could use a trainer."

"How soon would you be going?" asked Sparks.

"Next year, if I make the jump," he said. "I'm giving this place six more months to take off, and then we shall see."

"So we have a narrowed field and a deadline," said Mrs. Bainbridge, getting unsteadily to her feet. "We'll get to work, Mr. Macaulay. And we'd be happy to let our female friends know about this place. I do offer a suggestion, though."

"Yes?"

"Install a changing room," she said, gathering up her suit. "The ladies prefer it. Some have more delicate sensibilities than I have. Back in a jiffy."

"She's not on the market, is she?" asked Macaulay as she trotted off.

"Item seven in your contract," said Sparks. "We agree not to date our clients. And she wouldn't want to take her son out of London, anyway."

"Pity. Fancy going a few rounds while we wait?"

"Thanks, Gerry, but I don't want to spoil my makeup."

"Keeping up with your practising?"

"Oh, yes," said Sparks, a glint in her eye. "And I've got to put my skills to the test a few times lately."

"Successfully, I take it."

"I'm alive and unbruised, thanks very much. And I mean it about the thanks. You taught me well."

"Still carry that pigsticker in your bag?"

"You know it."

Mrs. Bainbridge returned, properly suited although her hair was in a rare state of upheaval. Iris looked up at it, then silently reached into her handbag, pulled out a dark blue beret, and handed it to her.

"Oh, dear," said Mrs. Bainbridge. "Is it as bad as all that?"

"If it's any consolation, Sidney's looks far worse."

"That's no consolation at all," said Mrs. Bainbridge, placing the beret on her head. "There. I am fit to be seen in public. Mr. Macaulay, this was most educational. I look forward to next week's session, and hope that my recently inflicted brain damage won't adversely affect my ability to find you a suitable match."

"Luckily, you've got Sparks with you," he said, shaking her hand.

"I am most fortunate in that," said Mrs. Bainbridge. "Good day."

A man coming in held the door for them as they left, then stared after them admiringly.

"Good on you," he said to Macaulay. "Who are the birds?"

"The tall one's a new client," said Macaulay. "Taking self-defense lessons."

"Give me her name and number before she's finished, I beg you."

"Not a chance."

"How about the petite stunner by her side? She taking the course, too?"

"Former student," said Macaulay.

"Any good?"

"The best."

"But you could take her, right?"

"Oh, I could," said Macaulay. "But there's not many men in England who can say that."

* * *

"Well?" asked Iris as they walked to their stop. "How did you like it?"

"It was oddly therapeutic," said Gwen. "More fodder for Dr. Milford to chew on."

"Yes, I was wondering where that scream came from. Your power increased when you did it."

"I thought screaming would be part of the technique," said Gwen. "You never did when you were learning?"

"Early on," said Iris. "But when I trained with Macaulay, we were taught to be silent when we—well, when we engaged. At what or whom were you screaming?"

"All of the evil and sadness in the world."

The tram arrived, and they climbed to the upper deck.

"Be specific," persisted Iris when they had taken their seats.

"We received a cable. My father-in-law is due back from East Africa."

"Ah. And he knows about the decision not to send your son to his handpicked school, where generations of male Bainbridges were warped at an early age."

"Carolyne wrote him about it, but we haven't heard anything back from him on the topic."

"It was amazing that you got her to come round. Maybe she'll continue to back you."

"It will be regarded as mutiny belowdecks," said Gwen. "They both have legal custody of Little Ronnie while I'm still a ward of the court, so she was within her rights to act, but once he's home, Lord Bainbridge will be assertive, and she will submit as she always does. I almost wish he had stayed down there. If he pushes it, I may have to resort to litigation, and I'm not certain that's the best idea."

"If it were me, I'd go to war."

"But it's not you, and I'm not the only one whose happiness is at stake. The problem with war is that there are casualties. Mr. Macaulay was right—peacetime is more complicated."

"Speaking of Gerry, any immediate thoughts of a match? Romantic match, I should say, not an opponent on the mat."

"My ears are still ringing from bumping heads with poor Sidney, and I want to be at my desk with my box of file cards so I won't miss any possibilities."

"Fair enough. I'll get Saundra to type up my notes first thing. How lovely to say something like that! We have a secretary! And a second office!"

"Which we need to finish painting," added Gwen. "Shall we do that this Saturday?"

"I'm free. Here's your stop. See you in the morning. The world must be peopled!"

"The world must be peopled," said Gwen.

She gave her partner a wave as she reached the stairs, then climbed down to the street.

She walked the rest of the way to Kensington, stopping in front of a storefront window to brush her hair as best she could.

How was your afternoon, Gwen? she thought. Well, Iris set me up with a strange man, I changed into a skimpy outfit, we were intensely physical for almost an hour, and now my hair's a complete mess.

Yes, that would go over well at home.

Home.

The place where she lived at the mercy of her in-laws until she could successfully challenge them for custody of her son, which she couldn't do until Dr. Milford certified her as competent again. Never mind that she was successfully running a business—which was an activity Lord Bainbridge's antiquated circle would consider evidence of instability in a woman, anyway. But the world continued to consider her sanity suspect because she lacked sufficient

British stoicism to keep calm and carry on after the love of her life died for his country, and now she was about to go to battle over the education of their six-year-old son.

Nine more lessons, and she could go to battle properly prepared.

She turned onto their street and came to the front door of the Bainbridge house. Before she could pull out her key, the door opened and Lord Bainbridge stood there, regarding her with disdain.

"Harold, how good to see you," she said in what she hoped was a pleasant tone. "I trust that you had a comfortable journey."

"Gwendolyn. You're late."

Jab to the chin, she thought. Eye gouge. Knee to the testicles.

"What's this nonsense about Ronald not attending St. Frideswide's?" he asked coldly.

No, she thought.

Not yet.

CHAPTER 2

He looked tired, thought Gwen. Tired and angry. Not a good combination under any circumstances, but particularly not a good one for this first reunion. She had hoped that they could have hid behind polite pleasantries before it became time to exchange blows.

Lord Bainbridge was not a tall person, which had been a surprise to Gwen when they had first met. Ronnie was a fine, young sapling of a man, tall enough to look directly into Gwen's eyes when they danced despite her heels, and the introduction to his middling shrub of a father had been startling. Ronnie's height made more sense when she met his mother who, though not approaching Gwen's five foot eleven, still towered over her husband and from all reports came from a family whose men could have stood in for ship masts.

Lord Bainbridge resented his wife's physical superiority, and made certain that their portrait, which hung menacingly in the front parlour, had her seated with him standing behind her, resting his hands on the back of a chair that must have been chosen to make him look taller. A regular high-backed chair would have given him the appearance of a large, unfriendly hand puppet.

This tactic of arranging his surroundings for his benefit carried into other aspects of his life. Every pose, every position in any given room, was meticulously calculated to display him at his best. Gwen had underestimated his pettiness, or suppressed that aspect in her memory while he had been away for so long, so now there they stood, he with the benefits of higher ground and a blocked doorway. Gwen, a soldier's wife and daughter, was chagrined over being caught at such a strategic disadvantage.

"I apologise for my tardiness, Harold," she said. "Would you mind if I came in before we continue this conversation? I have no interest either in scandalising the neighbours or entertaining the passersby."

He stepped back reluctantly, and she walked by him into the entry hall.

"When did you get in?" she asked.

"You haven't answered my question," he said.

"No, I haven't. The subject is still awake and within earshot. I have had a long and difficult day, and I am famished. We are going to sit down to dinner as a family, reunited for the first time in several months, and maintain civility in front of my son—"

"Why are you late?"

"I am taking a physical fitness class," she said.

"Whatever for?"

"So that I may be physically fit, of course. Now that I am a working woman with a desk job, I need to do something to stay in shape."

"Why? Planning to sink your hooks into another wealthy boy now that my son is dead and gone?"

"How dare you!" she said, the colour rising in her cheeks. "You of all people should know how much I loved Ronnie."

"I of all people know how much he was worth."

"And you think that's why I married him."

"I do."

"And why, then, do you think he married me?"

"Because you were a good-looking girl and he was young and besotted."

"You think so little of your only son."

She saw him go dead behind his eyes for a moment.

"What I think of him no longer matters," he said. "What matters is how to handle my grandson."

"My son. Harold, Ronnie left behind a letter—"

"So my wife wrote me. Hinting that he did not wish his son to attend St. Frideswide's."

"Not hinting. Stating directly. As much as one can shout vehemently in a letter, that's what he did."

"No matter now. He's dead, you're a lunatic, and—"

"Stop," she ordered him.

"How dare you tell me what to do in my own—"

"I said stop!" she whispered urgently, lowering her voice and glancing up and over his shoulder.

A small boy with blond curly hair was standing at the top of the stairs.

"Mummy!" he cried joyfully. "Grandfather is back from Africa! Isn't that wonderful?"

"Yes, it is wonderful," said Gwen, stepping around Lord Bainbridge as her son flew down the steps. "Don't run!"

He stopped midway, then came down the rest with exaggerated slowness, lifting his knee high into the air with each step. On the last, he jumped into Gwen's open arms, and she lifted him high, then sat him on her hip and turned to face her father-in-law.

"Are you happy to have your grandfather home again?" she asked Ronnie.

"Oh, yes," he said. "And Grandmother is happy, too. We've missed him so much, haven't we?"

"We have," said Gwen. "Has he told you any stories about Africa yet?"

"Not yet. I want to hear about the crocodiles. Did you see any crocodiles, Grandfather?"

Lord Bainbridge looked back and forth between mother and son, then forced a smile onto his face.

"As a matter of fact, I did," he said. "Fortunately, they were resting. They were tired."

"Why were they tired?"

"They had just finished eating."

"Oooh!" cried Ronnie. "What did they eat?"

"A water buffalo that had neglected to be watchful, and was dragged under as a result," he said.

"Sounds dreadful," said Gwen.

"Perfectly dreadful," said Ronnie. "I want to hear all about it."

"Well, why don't you take Grandfather into the parlour while I get changed for dinner, and he will tell you all about it. Won't you, Harold?"

"Well, if you insist, young man," he said. "But don't tell your grandmother. She would disapprove."

"I won't," Ronnie promised him seriously, slithering out of her grasp. "Come, Grandfather."

He grabbed the older man's hand and tugged. Lord Bainbridge let himself be pulled out of the entryway, but not before shooting Gwen a withering glance.

She ignored it and walked up the stairway to the first floor.

"Thank you for rescuing me, my darling boy," she whispered as she entered her room. "I'll see if I can do the same for you."

She changed into an evening gown, then pressed a button on her dressing table. A short while after, Millie, the upstairs maid, appeared in the doorway. She took one glance at Gwen's hair, gave her a look of dismay, and grabbed a brush from the table.

"What on earth have you done to it, Mrs. Bainbridge?" she asked, attacking it with a will. "Was there a tornado in Mayfair that we didn't hear about?"

"It's a long story. Was there a tornado downstairs that I need to hear about?"

"Oh, goodness! Lord Bainbridge showed up unexpectedly while we were still getting the house ready, and he was terribly angry. Everything was at sixes and sevens. Lady Bainbridge was out at the Hibberts, Mr. Percival was in his shirtsleeves, can you believe it? Albert was absolutely flummoxed that no one had called him to pick up His Lordship."

"But his cable said he was arriving tomorrow. Surely he understood what a commotion he would be making by coming in a day early."

"I think he expected the place to be exactly the same as when he left it."

"And the people, too. How has Lady Bainbridge been taking his return?"

"I think— Well, I shouldn't be saying this."

"Then say it."

"She's been sneaking off to fortify herself, if you take my meaning."

"I do," said Gwen. "I wouldn't mind a dram of fortification myself. But I don't want things to get out of hand on his first night back. Let me see."

Millie held a hand mirror behind her head as Gwen examined her reflection in the large mirror.

"Very good," she pronounced. "The rats will have to seek elsewhere for a nest. Thank you, Millie."

The dinner gong rang from below.

"Wish me luck, Millie," said Gwen. "I may need it."

"Good luck, miss," said Millie, picking up her suit to hang in the closet. "Do you want me to wash what's in the valise?"

"If you would, I'd be grateful."

"Oh, did you play tennis today?" asked Millie as she opened it.

"No, just an exercise class I've started taking."

"Good for you, miss. Maybe you could get Her Ladyship to go."

"That would be a picture," said Gwen. "Thank you, Millie."

She went downstairs, paused before entering the dining room, then steeled herself and forced a smile onto her face.

The table in the dining room was made of a deep, rich mahogany, a pair of split pedestals bearing the brunt of its weight, with thick, elaborately carved legs at the corners, vines and leaves descending into lion-head feet, the lions roaring silently at the feet of the diners. Ronnie, when he was younger, would crawl around them and roar back. When fully extended, it could seat twenty-four, but it was currently available for ten, its shortest length, the extra leaves stored away in the attic.

There were four for dinner on this particular night, crowding the center as if keeping balance in a lifeboat. Lord Bainbridge and Lady Bainbridge sat on the side by the entryways, while Gwen and Ronnie sat across from them next to the large windows which looked out onto the side garden. Ronnie rarely ate in the dining room, and was excited and awed. He had been scrubbed extra thoroughly by Agnes, who had taken the time to emphasise proper manners and good behaviour. He sat on a cushion placed on one of the regular high-backed chairs and viewed his grandparents, who dressed for dinner as they always did, as if they had stepped out of an illustrated book from the previous century.

Lady Bainbridge had taken a great deal of time preparing her appearance for dinner, Gwen observed. More than she did for her evenings out. Her powder was subtle and smooth, for a change, instead of the garish, almost Kabuki-like masks that she applied to present to society. She sat rigidly at the table with her husband seated next to her, seemingly unable to turn her neck to view him, although her eyes shot frequently in his direction whenever he spoke, and more often when he was silent.

She had Percival, the butler, bring up two bottles of the '28

Gruaud-Larose to celebrate Lord Bainbridge's return. Lord Bainbridge eyed the wine dubiously, took a sip, then nodded. Percival poured glasses for the two ladies and Lord Bainbridge.

Ronnie, who had a glass of milk, watched the process with fascination.

"May I have a taste?" he asked.

"Not until you're much older," replied his mother.

"Nonsense," said Lord Bainbridge. "Give the boy a glass. It's my first night back."

"But Harold, he's only six," protested Gwen.

"He's got to learn what good wine tastes like," said Lord Bainbridge. "Percival, a glass for Ronald."

"It's Ronnie," said Ronnie.

"At the table, amongst decent company, you will be referred to by your given name," said Lord Bainbridge. "You are going to be Lord Ronald Bainbridge someday. Best start acting like it now."

"He's too young," insisted Gwen.

"I am his guardian. This is my house. Hold your glass with one hand, Ronald."

Ronnie looked at his mother uncertainly, then slowly picked up the goblet that Percival placed by his plate. The butler remained expressionless, but Gwen sensed his disapproval.

"Now, I am going to make a toast," said Lord Bainbridge. "We stand for toasts, Ronald."

They stood, Ronnie taking care not to spill his glass.

"To the King, long may he reign over us in health and prosperity," said Lord Bainbridge.

"To the King," said the others in muted tones.

Lord Bainbridge sipped his wine, savouring it. Lady Bainbridge drained half of hers.

Gwen, sipping slowly from hers, watched her son take a taste from his glass. He swirled it around in his mouth experimentally, his eyes narrowing, then swallowed.

"It's sweet, then it's not sweet," he said. "May I drink my milk now?"

"You must make a toast," said Lord Bainbridge. "It's your first. Make it a good one."

"That's easy," said Ronnie.

He held his glass up.

"To Mummy!" he cried.

Despite her dismay at the proceedings, Gwen couldn't help smiling.

"Thank you, my darling boy," she said.

"To Gwendolyn," said Lady Bainbridge, drinking. Then she turned to her husband, who hadn't moved. "Well?"

"To Gwendolyn," he said, finally raising the glass to his lips.

He didn't drink to me much, thought Gwen. But at least he drank.

Lord Bainbridge did not enjoy the soup, a vichyssoise sweetened with sherry. The chicken, roasted with fennel, met with his approval, however.

"We don't get fennel in the Rhodesias," he said, digging in heartily. "No one grows it, for some reason. Never occurred to me that I would miss it until tonight. Delicious. I should take a bag of seed with me when I go back."

"You're going back?" exclaimed Lady Bainbridge. "But you've only just returned."

"Oh, stop mewling. I will go back at some point, don't know when. Have to keep a firm hand on the tiller, otherwise the whole bloody mess will founder."

"Could you tell Ronnie about some of the foods you ate there that we don't have?" asked Gwen politely.

"Did you eat crocodile?" asked Ronnie.

"Don't be nonsensical, Ronald," said his grandmother.

"In point of fact, I did eat it once when I was a young man, tooling around the Rhodesias, looking for green rocks. One of the lads shot a croc that had crept into camp, and we fried it up as a lark."

"What did it taste like?"

"Like the strangest chicken you've ever had. Like a chicken had mated with a fish. It needed sauce badly, but we weren't traveling with sauce, needless to say."

"Why were you looking for green rocks?"

"Those are the ones with copper in them. You find a place with green rocks, you claim it and start digging."

"Is that what you did?"

"Again, when I was a young man. Before I met your grand-mother."

"Oh. Did you ever go to Africa, Grandmother?"

"Briefly," said Lady Bainbridge with a shudder. "I couldn't stand the place. Terrible heat, and all of those mosquitoes."

"She lasted a year, perhaps less," said Lord Bainbridge. "Put her foot down finally, and the old man died, so back to England we went."

"May I go with you when you go next time?" asked Ronnie.

"We shall see," said Lord Bainbridge, smiling at his grandson. "It's a very long trip."

"Even with airplanes?"

"Even with airplanes. I had to take four different airplanes to come home, and two trains before that."

"That sounds lovely," sighed Ronnie. "Would you come with me to Africa, Mummy?"

"I'd love to, dearest," said Gwen. "But I do have my work, you know. I can't simply abandon Iris for two months."

"It really takes two of you to run that place?" asked Lord Bain-bridge. "How hard can it be?"

"Hard enough that we've expanded into the office next door and hired a full-time secretary-receptionist," replied Gwen.

"Yet all you do is shuffle index cards and tell people to meet for tea," scoffed Lord Bainbridge.

"The selection of the pairings requires a great deal more than that," said Gwen. "We interview extensively and discuss each potential match at length before sending out our letters, and our methods are sound. We've accounted for nine weddings and seven confirmed engagements to date."

"And one murder, I heard," said Lord Bainbridge.

"Please don't mention that in front of Ronnie," said Gwen.

"I knew about it already," said Ronnie gleefully. "Mummy and Iris caught the murderer!"

"How did you know about that?" asked Gwen, turning to him in dismay.

"I heard Grandmother talking about it to Lady Merrifield," said Ronnie.

"Oh, dear," said Lady Bainbridge.

"You know what I've said about listening at doors," said Gwen sternly.

"I didn't mean to, but they were talking very loudly," said Ronnie.

"That sounds like your grandmother," said Lord Bainbridge. "Well, if you're so tied up with this trifling nonsense that you cannot accompany your child on holiday, then maybe I'll take him to Africa myself."

"Hooray!" cried Ronnie.

"Depending on how well he does at St. Frideswide's," continued Lord Bainbridge, smiling across the table at them.

"St. Frideswide's?" asked Ronnie in confusion. "But I'm supposed to go to school here. I'm starting in two weeks."

"Change of plans," said Lord Bainbridge. "Now, finish up, then off to bed with you."

There was custard for dessert.

It is difficult to eat custard when one is suppressing a full-throated scream, thought Gwen. She managed to choke it down.

Ronnie finished his, then looked across the table.

"May I say good night now?" he asked.

"You haven't finished your wine," said Lord Bainbridge.

"I don't want to," said Ronnie.

"You asked for wine. The proper thing to do, having asked for it, is to finish it. Otherwise, you are insulting your hostess who provided it."

"Harold, don't bring me into this," said Lady Bainbridge softly.

"But—" started Ronnie.

"Finish your wine, boy."

"Harold, please don't—" protested Gwen.

"I said finish it!" shouted Lord Bainbridge.

There was silence at the table, a terrible silence that extended through the entire house. Then Ronnie lifted his goblet and drank the remainder. He set it down, looking queasy.

"May I go now?" he asked.

"You may," said Lord Bainbridge. "Good night, Ronald."

"Mummy will be up to say good night," whispered Gwen. "Go to Agnes, Ronnie."

He left the table and trudged away.

"That was wrong," said Gwen.

"He has to learn table manners if he is to dine in the great houses of England," said Lord Bainbridge. "No time like the present. I will be taking charge of him more now that I'm back. Good Lord, he does pester one with questions, doesn't he? If I knew he liked crocodiles so much, I would have brought one back for him to play with."

"About his school—" began Gwen.

"He's going to St. Frideswide's. I will make the arrangements in the morning."

"But we were going to discuss it."

"We just did," said Lord Bainbridge, pushing his chair back and standing up. "I'm going to the club, Percival. Have Albert bring the Rolls-Royce around."

"What?" exclaimed Lady Bainbridge. "Tonight? It's your first night back."

"And they haven't seen me there since I left," said Lord Bainbridge. "Don't wait up for me."

He strode out of the room. Lady Bainbridge turned to watch him, almost choking in her shock. Then she turned back and poured herself another glass of wine.

"First night back," she muttered. "You would think—"

Then she stopped, remembering that Gwen was still at the table.

"I'm so sorry, Carolyne," said Gwen.

"Away for six months, and more concerned with putting in an appearance at that damned club than being with his wife," she fumed.

"He'll come around," said Gwen. "It's his way."

"Oh, I know his ways," said Lady Bainbridge. "I've known them long before you—well, let's put an end to this discussion. I am going to bed. I will say good night to you, Gwendolyn."

"Good night, Carolyne," said Gwen.

She watched as Lady Bainbridge downed her wine in two quick gulps, then rose unsteadily to her feet and walked out of the room, wobbling slightly. Then she turned back.

"That letter from my son," she said. "Do you have it somewhere safe?"

"I do."

"Put it somewhere safer. I don't want Harold to get hold of it."

"I will, Carolyne."

Her mother-in-law nodded brusquely, then staggered off to bed.

Poor thing, thought Gwen.

Then she realised that she had never thought that about Carolyne before in her life.

Her own goblet was still a third full. She looked it, then left it sitting on the table, the remainder untouched.

* * *

The man with the binoculars watched her leave the room. He was standing by the barberries that separated the Bainbridge property from the one to the right, a pair of hedge clippers in his other hand which, when anyone appeared, he freely applied to what was becoming an excessively well-trimmed shrub.

Only four at dinner, he noted. One servant, probably the butler. One chauffeur, although he spotted two cars in the garage at the rear. Presumably a cook somewhere, and someone watching the child.

The rich were incapable of raising their own, he thought with a scowl.

He had caught glimpses of other servants passing by windows, but couldn't get an accurate count. Couldn't be too many, given the smallness of the family.

No gardener.

That might be a way in, he thought, gripping the clippers tightly for a moment.

To his surprise, a car engine started up, then the Rolls came to the front of the driveway and stopped. The chauffeur got out and held the door as Lord Bainbridge strode angrily out of the house.

The man slipped the binoculars inside his jacket pocket and casually walked towards where he had left his motorcycle, pausing to lop off a stray twig here and there as he did.

I really should be charging them, he thought.

As the Rolls drove past, he quickly tossed the clippers into the rear basket of the motorcycle and climbed on, donning his helmet and goggles as he did. Then he kicked it into life and followed the Rolls.

Gwen went up the stairs to say good night to Ronnie. Agnes was standing outside his room, looking in with a worried expression.

"Is everything all right?" asked Gwen.

"He's asleep," said Agnes. "He wanted to go straight to bed. No playtime, no drawing, no book. And he was out like a lamp the moment his head hit the pillow. I was worried he might be ill, but there's no fever and he seems fine otherwise."

"He had wine with dinner," said Gwen. "Lord Bainbridge made him drink an entire glass."

"He never!" said Agnes in horror. "What on earth for?"

"To teach a lesson at the table, I presume."

"How horrid," shuddered Agnes. "He's only six. And Lord Bainbridge wants to pack him off to St. Frideswide's. Can't we do anything?"

"I don't know," said Gwen. "Ronnie's grandparents have custody of him until a court decides that I am capable of managing my life again."

"But you are. Completely capable. It's nonsense to say otherwise."

"I was hoping to avoid a legal battle."

"I will fight on your side, Mrs. Bainbridge," said Agnes fervently. "Any testimony that I may provide to keep Ronnie from that terrible place will be freely and wholeheartedly given."

"Thank you, Agnes," said Gwen, taking her hand for a moment. "I'm going to kiss him good night. I will see you tomorrow."

"Good night, Mrs. Bainbridge."

Agnes left for her room, and Gwen softly opened the door to Ronnie's room.

He lay on his bed, his head away from the doorway. She entered and sat on the bed next to him, gently stroking his hair. He murmured something she couldn't make out, then settled back into sleep. She leaned over and kissed his cheek.

"Stay resolute and strong, my darling boy," she whispered. "Mummy will protect you. She's made a poor job of it lately, but she will step up. I promise you."

She gave him one last kiss, then crept out of the room, closing the door behind her.

She felt restless. She wandered into the playroom, where Ronnie's latest picture of the continuing adventures of Sir Oswald the Narwhal sat half-finished on the small easel set up in one corner. He had become enamored of narwhals after seeing one in the British Museum in June, and had created Sir Oswald, who fought Nazis and had adventures in places real narwhals were not known to inhabit.

The current episode seemed to place Sir Oswald in a jungle, if Gwen was able to interpret the scenery correctly. And there! Lurking in the depths of a pond—could that be a crocodile?

Be careful, Sir Oswald, thought Gwen. One never knows what dangers one will find in strange lands.

She took a deep breath and wandered aimlessly about the room, looking at previous pictures. Ronnie's improving, she noted with pride. Gets his artistic ability from me, I suppose.

"Did you paint?" she had asked Ronnie when he first showed her his childhood playroom.

"Oh, I was rubbish at painting and drawing." He laughed. "I kept at it, but it was hopeless. When I came home from St. Frideswide's after my first year there, I wanted to burn every scrap and every doodle. Then I found out Pater had already done it. He disapproved of artistic tendencies in children. Or at least in boys."

"How terrible! Even if you didn't like them, he shouldn't have done that."

"Oh, I agree," said Ronnie. "He wanted me to be the manliest of men. Shooting, riding, boxing, all of it."

"Did you?"

"I liked boxing even less than I liked drawing," said Ronnie, gazing up at where a sturdy metal hook was set into a corner of the ceiling.

"Didn't like getting hit?"

"Didn't like hitting," he said shortly. "Didn't like hurting other boys for no reason. I was good at it, I'm sorry to say. Won the school

title one year. Pater came up to cheer me on. It was the only time he
visited me in the eight years I was there."

"*I promise never to hit you,*" *Gwen said solemnly.*

"*Even if I deserve it?*"

"*You never will,*" *she said, kissing him.*

And he never did, thought Gwen. Although he must have over-
come his aversion to hurting people when he went off to war.

But war is different. And it ended up killing him, so what did it
matter anymore?

Lord knows she felt like hitting someone at that moment.

She looked up at where the hook still hung, bolted firmly into
the ceiling.

I wonder, she thought.

The Rolls drove east until it reached a destination in Fitzrovia.
Lord Bainbridge got out and walked up a short set of steps to a
white building across from a private park. The man on the motorcycle glimpsed a black man in a white uniform with golden buttons open the door to admit him. Then the door shut.

He parked his motorcycle, then walked casually down the street
until he came to the alley that bordered the rear of the white building. As he reached it, another black man wearing a chef's uniform
came out of a door into the alley, reached into his apron pocket,
and pulled out a pack of cigarettes. He looked up suspiciously as
the first man approached, then relaxed as he saw him holding up a
cigarette of his own.

"Got a light?" the man asked the chef.

"Sure," said the chef, flicking a Stormgard lighter and holding
it towards him.

"*Natotela,*" said the man as he lit his cigarette.

"You speak Chibemba?" asked the chef.

"Some. Not my first tongue. Tell me, friend—are they hiring in
there?"

"Nah, they're full up right now," said the chef. "You know how it is. Just get demobbed?"

"Two weeks ago. Things are tough."

"Sorry," shrugged the chef. "Tell you what. Give me your number, I give you a call if anything opens up."

"That would be appreciated," said the man.

He took a drag on his cigarette, let it out.

"So who owns that fancy Rolls?" he asked.

Gwen walked quietly through the hallways and up flights of stairs until she reached the attic. This had been a place of refuge for her husband when he was a child, a secret sanctuary where he could read his adventure books and build his model airplanes. Where, as a grown man, he had proposed to Gwen, and where, just a few short months ago, she had found his letter, now safely stored in a metal box of keepsakes behind a loosened panel in her closet.

She pulled the chain, turning on the lights and scanning the dusty room for the item she thought might be stowed away amidst the old pieces of furniture and steamer trunks.

There it was, lying forlornly on its side. The heavy bag that once swung from the hook in the playroom ceiling, fiercely awaiting all challengers.

She walked over to inspect it. It was dusty enough, God knows, she thought, and much too large for her to wrestle back down to the playroom by herself. Nor did she want to alert the household to her new obsession. It would be one more bit of ammunition for the attacks against her should Harold continue to maintain his position on her sanity.

She would have to leave it here, but at least she had something at home to practise upon.

She looked again at the dust collecting on it, then at the inadequacy of her handkerchief and the fineness of her evening frock.

"*Do you expect to say, 'Wait a moment, I am going to fight you, but I have to change first'?*" Macaulay's voice sounded in her head.

"I will fight you in normal clothing in due time," she said to the bag. "But I'm wearing a Schiaparelli. Avert your eyes, please."

She removed her gown and draped it carefully over a chair, taking care to wipe it off first. She turned back to the heavy bag.

"Now, rise, sir, from that semirecumbent position," she said, squatting by it.

She managed to get both arms around its midsection, then wrestled it to the vertical. That simple action brought rivulets of sweat running down her body, which mingled efficiently with the dust coating the bag to form nasty grey stringy bits that clung to her skin. She sighed, then lugged it over to rest against a wooden post holding up a roof beam. She stepped back and looked at it in satisfaction.

The bag sagged towards her as if executing a bow, then continued the movement as gravity dictated, toppling onto the floor.

Gwen gave it her fiercest glare, but there was no reaction from the bag.

"You're getting back at me for how I treated your friend Sidney this afternoon," she said sternly. "Well, I won't have that. You are going to stand up straight so that I may practise my Defendu."

She hauled it upright, then kept it pinned against the post with one hand while reaching for a chair to prop against it. The bag held steady. She glanced around, and saw a roll of twine someone had thoughtfully left on a table. Although she doubted they had left it for the exact purpose of securing an abandoned heavy bag to an attic post, she didn't think anyone would mind if she appropriated it for that task. She took a step towards the table. Behind her, the bag immediately fell back down.

"Every time you do that it makes me want to hurt you even more," she muttered, grabbing the twine.

She grabbed the bag and shoved it vehemently against the post, then quickly wrapped a length of twine around the middle and tied it with a knot her Girl Guides leader once taught her. The bag bent over as if it were contemplating its navel, but the twine held. She tied another length around the top, then stepped back and looked at her handiwork with satisfaction.

"As you can see, I have prevailed," she informed it. "You are my prisoner, and I am going to inflict upon you as much pain as an inanimate object may withstand. Beg for mercy all you like. There will be none."

She stood in front of the bag. Then her left hand shot forward into where she thought its chin would be.

A cloud of dust shot out in all directions, much of it finding a new home inside her nostrils. She sneezed violently several times and searched in vain for her handkerchief, finally wiping her nose on her bare arm. She stared at the bag in chagrin.

"This isn't over," she said grimly. "I will return tomorrow with a cleaning rag and remove every last bit of dust you have left."

She brushed as much of the grime off her as she could, then pulled on her evening gown. She turned back and held up an index finger in warning.

"And then I shall thrash you, Lord Bainbridge," she said.

With that, she stormed out of the attic.

CHAPTER 3

"First night back, and he's already set the entire household on edge," said Gwen, pacing about the office, pausing to stare at a section of the wall that they had yet to repaint, examining the cracks and pits that years of neglect had left for them to fix.

"Including you, I see," said Iris.

"Oh, I was on edge long before this," said Gwen. "Well beyond it, according to the doctors and the judge. But lately I thought I was handling everything just fine. Then my father-in-law shows up a day early, and I'm ready to take all of my Veronal with a champagne chaser."

"Save some," advised Iris. "It's hard to get right now. So's the Veronal."

"First night back, and he goes to his club. To his club! Can you imagine that? Poor Carolyne!"

"Did I just hear you express sympathy for the woman who has made your life a living hell for the last two years?"

"She's still a woman, Iris," said Gwen. "I never thought I would say this, but she's a woman, she's been without her husband for six months, and I think she had certain—expectations over what their first night back together would be like."

"Oh," said Iris. "Poor old biddy."

"She's not an old biddy. She's somewhere north of fifty and she was clearly hoping—well, hopes were dashed for her last night as much as anyone, I should think."

"Serves her right," declared Iris.

"How would you have felt if whatever his name was had returned from whatever secret mission he was on and not bothered to swing by your flat?"

"That would have depended on how insistent his wife was on having first innings," said Iris. "I was usually the dessert course on his menu. Occasionally an hors d'oeuvre, if I was fortunate."

"But you remained loyal despite never attaining entrée status, at least for a while. What if he decided to skip the meal entirely? How would you have felt?"

"Murderous. And, now that we've overindulged in this metaphor, ravenous. Shall we have an early lunch today?"

"I am too keyed up to eat. What is it about men and their clubs? Don't they have any consideration?"

"Which one is it?"

"The Livingstone Club. It's for old and not so old Africa hands."

"Ah. Over on Bedford Square."

"Do you know it?"

"I have been there on occasion."

"But it's for men," said Gwen, puzzled.

"And their guests," said Iris.

"I see. So you were a guest."

"On occasion."

"What were the occasions?" asked Gwen suspiciously.

"I am sure I don't remember," said Iris, stretching languidly in her chair. "How are you feeling physically today after your first Defendu lesson? Did you practise?"

"I feel sore in places where I've never felt sore before," said Gwen. "And yes, I practised, if struggling to set up a dust-covered heavy bag counts."

"I will give it to you. What did you name it?"

"How did you know that I did?"

"Because you name all the objects in your immediate vicinity, and because everyone names their heavy bag for extra motivation. Let me guess—you called him Harold."

"Lord Bainbridge, if you please," said Gwen. "We must give him his due. Like Lord Bainbridge, on the dusty side, but unlike Lord Bainbridge, surprisingly flexible."

"And where is the second Lord Bainbridge now?"

"Where he should be—tied to a post in the attic."

"My dear Gwendolyn! You are demonstrating some shocking new proclivities. Dr. Milford will have a field day with you this week."

"I do need to speak with him desperately," said Gwen.

"About what?"

"About having me declared legally competent. I can't wait any longer now that Harold has returned. I need to regain custody of Ronnie before he's sent off to that terrible boarding school."

"We're seeing Dr. Milford tomorrow," said Iris. "Can you hold out that long?"

"I can hold out," said Gwen. "But Harold is already making arrangements for Ronnie. And he's furious with Carolyne for not making them before."

"What may I do to help?" asked Iris. "Should I put in a word to Archie? Have some of his boys pay Lord Bainbridge a visit and work him over?"

"Tempting," said Gwen. "But counterproductive. He would only dig in his heels further."

"Would you like me to compromise him and give you the photographs for blackmail?"

"That is awfully kind of you," said Gwen. "But I care for you too much to subject you to that. Honestly, the mental image you've just conjured has taken me further away from any desire for lunch."

"Excuse me," said Mrs. Billington, knocking lightly on the door.

When they were still only in one office and living from one new client fee to the next, they had once invented an imaginary secretary whom they dubbed Miss Betsy. In their minds, she was a prim, efficient, no-nonsense type who would go on typing even if some late-to-the-party V-2s were landing all about the block.

Saundra Billington was no Miss Betsy, although she typed well enough and was sufficiently efficient for their needs. She was a plump brunette in her late thirties, with a husband who worked as an electrician for the railway and a pair of noisy adolescent boys whom she was happy to abandon during the day. She was neither prim nor no-nonsense, however, and after six years of typing correspondence for the Royal Army, she was delighted to be in an office working for women, and even more delighted to hear all the tales of lonely hearts, broken troths, and blighted romance that came through her door seeking remedy.

"I'm Cupid's secretary," she would brag to her husband. "The ladies send me out for a fresh quiver of arrows whenever they run out. Let me tell you about the bloke who walked in today."

But that conversation would take place later that night. At the moment, it was Mrs. Billington herself who was aquiver, ready to burst with the information she was about to impart.

"We have a potential client. A walk-in. I've taken down his basics."

"Excellent," said Sparks as Mrs. Billington came forward with the forms.

"What is it?" asked Mrs. Bainbridge.

"What is what?" asked Mrs. Billington, trying and failing to suppress a sly smile.

"You've come in rather than buzz us on the intercom," noted Mrs. Bainbridge, "and you're dying to tell us something. So, tell us."

Mrs. Billington peeked out into the hallway, then closed the office door.

"He's an African!" she whispered excitedly.

"Really?" asked Sparks. "From where, specifically?"

"Nyasaland," said Mrs. Billington, pointing it out on the form. "That's one of ours, isn't it?"

"It is," said Mrs. Bainbridge. "Very well. Give us a few minutes to review his information, then we'll buzz you."

"You don't need me to take notes?" asked Mrs. Billington eagerly.

"No," said Sparks firmly.

"Thank you for offering," added Mrs. Bainbridge, noting the look of disappointment on their secretary's face.

"Very good, ladies," she said, opening the door and returning to her office.

Iris and Gwen waited until she was out of earshot. Then Iris got up and softly closed the door again.

"We should discuss this," she said, returning to her seat.

"Yes, we should," agreed Gwen as she glanced over the form. "We haven't thought this through enough."

"We haven't needed to. All of our clientele to date have been British."

"He's British," pointed out Gwen. "Let's not mince words. All of our clientele have been white. The subject of matching other races has never been an issue before."

"Is it an issue now?" asked Iris.

"Interesting that you're asking me that question," said Gwen. "You seem to think I'd be more likely to have some problem with this than you."

"How many Africans have you met in the elevated circles in which you've circulated?"

"None. And you? I supposed there were some at Cambridge when you were there."

"Yes, and you could count them on one hand. No women at all. I hear there are two now. Just started a year ago, God help them.

It was hard enough being a woman in that place. I can't imagine what it's like being female and black there."

"So, we have little experience dealing with people of his culture," said Gwen. "More important, we have no female clients of African descent."

"Nor do we have any Caribbeans," said Iris. "Nor, for that matter, any Arabians, Indians, Chinese, Malays, or anyone with skin darker than mine. Why would he come to us? I should think he would have better connections to the local African community than we do."

"You have none currently?"

"I knew this lovely jazz violinist from Portuguese East Africa, but he died in the Blitz. Nobody from when I was in the army—my group was focused on the European theatre."

"So if we take him on, what do we do? Do we advertise?"

"It might be worth it to expand our clientele."

"And where? Is there a particular newspaper that caters to that community? A particular neighbourhood where they live? I really have no idea."

"Soho, I should think."

"Then we should ask Sally for advice. He lives there. He knows it better than either of us."

"That is the beginning of a plan," said Iris.

"There is still the problem of the initial interview," said Gwen, looking troubled. "We can't use our usual patter. It would be deceptive to promise him dozens of possibilities when we have none."

"I think we should be up front about that before he commits," said Iris. "A man should know the value of what he's paying for. Thinking about it, perhaps we should waive the initial fee until we have more African clients."

"I disagree," said Gwen. "That would be treating him differently than our other clients. I would be open to the idea of refunding it later if we have no success, but that shouldn't be part of the contract, nor should we tell him we'd be willing to do that in advance. It would be bad for business if we told an international client that we were not willing to put in the same efforts for him as we do for our local ones."

"International," said Iris thoughtfully. "That's a better euphemism than most."

"And we shall apply it to all future clients not born here," declared Gwen. "Even the French. Especially the French."

"Why the French?"

"Who is more not English than the French? And they live so close by, yet refuse to be like us."

"Fine, international for all not born in the British Isles. Oh— what about Canadians? And Australians? And especially the Americans? They're strange, but they're not really foreign."

"Still not from here," said Gwen. "I am going to be strictly parochial about this. Now let us meet our new international client."

Iris buzzed the intercom.

"Mrs. Billington, bring Mr. Daile over, would you please?"

"Certainly, Miss Sparks."

"Is that how it's pronounced?" asked Gwen. "Rhymes with mail?"

"We must ask him," said Iris.

A moment later, there was a soft knock.

"Come in," said Sparks.

He certainly was darker than Sparks, a medium brown-skinned man about five ten. He was clean-shaven and dressed in a grey demob suit that had been meticulously maintained. He smiled as Mrs. Bainbridge came around her desk to shake his hand.

"How do you do, Mr. Daile?" she said. "I am Mrs. Gwendolyn Bainbridge, and this is my partner, Miss Iris Sparks. Welcome to The Right Sort Marriage Bureau. Am I pronouncing your name correctly?"

"It is actually Dah-ee-lay," he said. "I answer to Daile, of course, given how the English always believe the last 'E' is silent. How do you do, Mrs. Bainbridge and Miss Sparks? Simon Daile. I am honoured to make your acquaintance."

"But you're Scottish!" exclaimed Mrs. Bainbridge. "I mean, you speak like a Scotsman. I wasn't expecting that."

"It startles all the English people I meet," he said, laughing. "My first schooling, and the source of my English, came at the missionary school run by the Free Church of Scotland, and until I traveled here, I thought that was how all the English spoke. It was very difficult to understand people when I first came to London."

"I'm surprised you didn't go to Edinburgh or Glasgow, then," commented Sparks. "Forgive my curiosity, but does Daile mean anything in particular in your language?"

"It means one who dwells in the thicket, and my native language, if you will forgive me for anticipating your next question, is called Chitumbuka. Since you bring it up—I know what sparks are, and I know what a bridge is. What is a bain, Mrs. Bainbridge, and how were your ancestors named for it?"

"There is a very short river called the Bain in Yorkshire," said Mrs. Bainbridge as she indicated for him to take a seat. "No idea what it means or why it was called that. I suppose someone built a bridge over it once upon a time, and everyone from there was called Bainbridge by everyone else after that. That's how names go, isn't it? I acquired the name when I married into the family, so I cannot tell you any more."

"I have heard that name before," said Mr. Daile. "Are you related to the Bainbridges of Bainbridge, Limited? They own tea and coffee plantations in my country."

"Yes," said Mrs. Bainbridge. "Lord Harold Bainbridge is my father-in-law."

"Then you will be a lady someday," said Mr. Daile. "How surprising to find you doing this type of work. Or any kind of work."

"I won't rise to the title, unfortunately," said Mrs. Bainbridge. "My husband was killed in battle."

"My sympathies," he said, nodding respectfully.

"What brought you to England, Mr. Daile?" asked Sparks.

"I came to further my education," he said. "The missionaries arranged for a scholarship, and I was intending to learn advanced agricultural techniques that I could then bring back to improve the lives of the farmers in Nyasaland."

"Oh, did you go to Royal Ag?" asked Sparks. "I know a few people who were there at that time."

"No, alas," Daile replied. "The missionaries had an arrangement with Harper Adams College, so that is where I went."

"I am not familiar with it," said Sparks.

"I am," said Mrs. Bainbridge. "It's in Shropshire somewhere, isn't it?"

"In the village of Edgmond, yes," said Daile, pleased. "A very small school, with only two hundred or so students. I'm surprised that a great lady like you would know of it."

"Our groundskeeper's son went there when I was young," said Mrs. Bainbridge. "First in their family to attain any form of higher education. They were tremendously proud. We all were."

"When was he there?" asked Daile.

"Let me think. It would have been in the late twenties, so before your time, I should imagine. When were you there?"

"I matriculated in 1938. I completed my first year, worked on a farm during the summer, and was a month into my second year when the war began. I enlisted straightaway."

"Bravo," said Sparks, glancing at the form. "Royal Navy, I see. And you were demobbed recently?"

"Three months ago," he said.

"Thank you for your service," said Mrs. Bainbridge. "Were you overseas much?"

"For most of the war," he said.

"See any action?" asked Sparks.

"Saw none, heard plenty," he said, grimacing slightly. "The day I got out of training, they took one look at me and said, 'You must be used to hot places, laddie,' then sent me down to the boiler room. I was a stoker for the rest of the war. I never fired a single shot in anger or otherwise."

"Dear me, how awful," said Mrs. Bainbridge. "But you survived."

"I did, thank the Lord."

"And now you are going back to school?"

"Things are somewhat in confusion on that point," he said ruefully. "The missionaries had lost track of me, and the one who had originally obtained my funding is in retirement somewhere in Burma. It is not certain that they will be giving me any assistance at this point. Until they do, I am working as a gardener in London."

"Not exactly what you were trained for," commented Sparks. "Flowers and topiary are a far cry from farming."

"Not as far as all that," said Daile. "I am still getting plants to grow and defending them from attack from land and air by enemies large and small. The techniques I learn here are ones I may eventually be able to teach back home."

"Is that your ultimate goal?" asked Mrs. Bainbridge. "To return to Nyasaland?"

"I do not know," he confessed. "I have been away for so long, and by the time I complete my education, it will be more than ten years away, which is why I have been contemplating remaining in England."

"Interesting," said Sparks. "Is that why you have come to us? Because you are thinking of settling down?"

"It is," he said.

"You see," began Mrs. Bainbridge, glancing over to Sparks, who nodded slightly, "this is a relatively new venture with a small-ish clientele. We are expanding, of course, but we wish to speak plainly to you. We currently have no one who is not of English descent. We would, should you choose to go forward with your application, embark upon a search for suitable candidates, but as I am sure you know—"

He raised a hand to interrupt her.

"I have no objections to being connected to an Englishwoman," he said. "As long as she is a good Christian with proper values and willing to lead a rural life, whether in England, Scotland, or indeed, anywhere my fortunes take me."

Mrs. Bainbridge blinked for a moment.

"Well, that opens up possibilities," said Sparks brightly, stepping into the breach. "And gives us some limitations. A willingness to travel will discourage some, encourage others. The same is true for good Christian values."

"Is it indeed?" he asked. "I would have hoped that those would be encouraging for everyone."

"If they were, we wouldn't have spent the last seven years fighting each other," said Sparks. "But there are many who still carry those values and hopes, and I hope that we shall be able to find one of them for you. Let's continue: Age range?"

Sparks peppered him with questions and, to her relief, her partner quickly rejoined the conversation.

"Right," said Sparks when they had finished. "We have enough for now. We may reach you at this address and telephone?"

"The telephone is for my landlady," he said. "I would prefer that you contact me by mail. I don't want to be a bother to her."

"Very thoughtful of you," said Mrs. Bainbridge. "May I ask you one more question?"

"Certainly, Mrs. Bainbridge."

"What do you miss the most about your home?"

He appeared surprised by the question. Then his eyes grew soft and a smile spread across his face.

"The fruit," he said. "The fresh fruit. Mangos, pawpaws, avocado pears, bananas—I cannot remember the last time I had any of them. The taste of a mango, Mrs. Bainbridge, freshly picked with the juice running down your chin—I would go home for that alone."

"I haven't seen a banana since before the war," said Mrs. Bainbridge wistfully. "I can barely remember what they taste like. And I don't think I've ever tried any of those others."

"Maybe someday you will see my country," he said. "Take a tour of your family's holdings."

"I've had the coffee," she said. "It's rather good. As for the tea— I'm an oolong girl, and that's that."

"Very good," he said. "I am very excited to have begun this adventure. Oh—isn't there a payment?"

"There is," said Sparks. "Five pounds, and we're off to the races."

"I beg your pardon?"

"It means we get to work," she said hastily.

Oh, Lord, thought Sparks. Did I just say "races"?

"I hope that I do not present too much of a challenge," he said as he turned over the fee.

"Everyone is a challenge in his own way," said Mrs. Bainbridge. "If people were easily matched, they wouldn't need us."

"Very true," he said. "I look forward to the results of your search. Good morning, ladies."

"Good morning," said Mrs. Bainbridge.

They waited for his footsteps to fade away down the staircase, then Iris got up and closed the door again. Gwen immediately buried her face in her hands.

"We still haven't thought this through enough," she said, her voice muffled.

"No, we haven't," agreed Iris.

"I feel quite foolish," said Gwen. "I assumed that he would be just as narrow-minded as I am. How do we go about this?"

"Let's start by trying to match him from the women we already have available," suggested Iris.

"But none of them would be expecting to meet someone . . . international," said Gwen. "Do we take that into account? We've never asked anyone about racial preferences."

"Nor has anyone mentioned any," pointed out Iris. "Some have declared themselves about the Irish. For that matter, some of the Irish have declared themselves about the English."

"But I assumed that everyone who walked through our doors previously was expecting to be matched with someone white," said Gwen. "Didn't you?"

"I did," said Iris.

"And if we simply have him show up for a date with no—"

"No what?" asked Iris as Gwen hesitated. "Were you about to say 'warning'?"

"No notice," said Gwen. "Yes, that sounds weak."

"What sort of notice do you propose?"

"Ask the ones we set him up with beforehand, I suppose," said Gwen. "I can't think of any other solution."

"Very well. But this doesn't solve the larger problem."

"No, it doesn't. Maybe we have to add racial preferences to our interview questions."

"Or not, and let the chips fall where they may."

"We'll lose business if we do that, Iris. You know that, I know that."

"No, I don't know that," said Iris. "This isn't the States. There are no laws here keeping anyone from marrying anyone else."

"No laws, just centuries of class discrimination."

"And colonisation, and subjugation—"

"Hold on," protested Gwen. "All I want to do is marry off

lonely people, not debate the checkered history of our glorious Empire."

"Yet the forces of history will be marshaled against us—if we let them."

"You're making this into a crusade."

"I'm opposed to crusades," said Iris. "We have not had to address these issues before because we were working safely inside our little bubble. Now, we do have to address them, and I want to handle it correctly."

"Which means we pair up Mr. Daile without regard to colour," said Gwen.

"Yes."

"And we expand our advertising to the international community. Or perhaps I should say communities."

"Yes. Can you handle this change in your views?"

"I am not changing anything," declared Gwen. "I've just never had the chance to put my views into practise."

"So you think."

"And you think that I am failing miserably." said Gwen.

"Not miserably. But you were raised in a society based upon prejudice, and it's dragging you down. Look at our literature. Try to find an English author who doesn't inveigh against Jews or Blacks—"

"Jane Austen."

"All right, I'll give you Austen, although I vaguely recall that there is a swipe at Jews somewhere in *Northanger Abbey*. It might have been a specific character flaw in whoever said it. My point is that we are shaped by where and how we grew up, and it is up to us to reject our upbringing."

"Easy for you."

"Easier for me because I was raised by a progressive mum."

"Well, let's put our upbringing and ideal selves to the test," said

Gwen. "Let's see if we come up with any of the same candidates. Are you ready?"

"I am," said Iris, reaching for her index box with the female clients.

They began riffling through their cards, pausing occasionally.

"Stop," said Gwen abruptly.

"What? Have you found one so soon?"

"It's not that," said Gwen miserably. "There's something bothering me."

"What?"

"You know how I have this tendency to read people."

"I would call it more of a gift than a tendency."

"Well, I've always taken a small amount of pride in being able to do that," said Gwen. "And I was reading Mr. Daile while he was talking to us, and the bothersome thing is that I realised that whatever this is, a tendency or an ability or a gift, it's been based exclusively on being raised by and growing up around British people. British, and whoever was around when I was in finishing school in Geneva. So, Europeans. Whites. And I don't know if it's of any value outside of that world."

"Did something about Mr. Daile trigger something?"

"Something did," said Gwen. "And now I don't know if that was a genuine reaction, or ingrained prejudice, or what."

"What did you read in him?"

"I think he lied to us."

"About?"

"About most of it. Maybe all of it. I think he did come here to study, and he was in the navy, but all the rest— No, I'm a horrible human being like everyone else in the posh world I was born into. Forget I said anything."

"You are not a horrible human being, and I still trust your instincts," said Iris. "So why, if you're correct, would he come here and lie to us? And invest five pounds and commit to going on dates that we arrange?"

"I don't know," said Gwen. "Fine, it's my own stupidity at work. Ignore it. Let's find him someone."

"Fine," said Iris, turning back to her index cards.

She flipped through several, then pulled five from the box. She laid them out in front of her like a tarot deck, then removed two and put them back in the box. She studied the remaining three, then put them in order.

"Done," she said.

Gwen was still staring at her box.

"Have you even begun to look?" asked Iris irritably.

"I'm sorry," said Gwen. "Give me a few more minutes."

"Take as long as you need," said Iris. "I'm going to work on Gerry Macaulay while you do."

"Maybe I should do him first," said Gwen.

"Now you're stalling," said Iris. "I will send you to bed without dinner if you do not apply your skills to Mr. Daile's case."

"Threatening me never helps," said Gwen as she halfheartedly began riffling through her cards with her thumb.

"You need to look at them, dear," said Iris. "You're not performing a magic trick."

Gwen pulled a card from the box and slapped it down on the table.

"I don't need to read them," she snapped. "I have them memorised."

She pulled out two more, then stacked them and turned to Iris.

"You go first," she said.

"Very well," said Iris. "Constance Pettiford. A minister's daughter, so there's your good Christian values. Her father is dead, her mother is living with her older brother, so she has no home life tying her down should travel be warranted. Quiet woman."

"Too quiet," said Gwen. "On the timid side, in fact. This might be too much of a leap for her."

"Because he's—"

"Because he may want to settle outside of England."

"Fine. Your turn."

"Amanda Courtland. Traveled extensively, served in the Pacific Theatre as a radio operator, has a sense of adventure."

"Interesting. Here's my second: Petulia Longley. Finds London overbearing, takes solace by singing in her church choir—"

"Anne Tilsworth. Mountain climber, trekker, horsewoman—"

"Let me interject a comment," said Iris.

"Go ahead."

"First, you interrupted me, which you never do."

"I apologise," said Gwen.

"Second, I am already seeing a pattern. I am emphasising the religious angle because I feel that's the most important. You are picking out our more daring ladies, without any regard to their spiritual sides."

"Because I think he's a liar," said Gwen. "And I don't consider lying a Christian value."

"May I make a suggestion?"

"Am I going to like it?"

"Probably not," said Iris. "Take the rest of the day off."

"What?" exclaimed Gwen indignantly. "Whatever for?"

"To sort yourself out," said Iris. "You're not on your game. Go home, play with your son, beat up Lord Harold the Second, and come back tomorrow for a fresh start."

"While you send our church mice out with this man."

"I will not send anyone out with anyone until you come back tomorrow in a more agreeable mood. Now, go home. I mean it."

Without saying anything, Gwen stood up, grabbed her hat from the coat tree, and walked out.

Iris stared at her last candidate, then put the cards back in the box.

Dammit, Gwen, she thought. Now you have me doubting him.

She reached for their telephone and dialed a number. A man answered on the first ring.

"Sally, it's Sparks," she said. "What are you doing right now?"

CHAPTER 4

Iris came into the reception office and handed a letter to Mrs. Billington.

"Could you do me a favour and find the address for Harper Adams College, Village of Edgmond, Shropshire, then address an envelope and mail this, please?"

"Of course," said Mrs. Billington, glancing at it. "Checking up on the new client, are we? I thought he was wrong the moment he walked in."

"Not at all," said Iris. "We sometimes verify background information."

"All right, if you say so," said Mrs. Billington. "Why this particular time?"

"Call it curiosity, and leave it at that. Mrs. Bainbridge left early, and I need to go investigate something—"

"About Mr. Daile?" asked Mrs. Billington eagerly.

"For business in general," said Iris firmly. "I'm locking our office, so if I don't return by five, close up shop, would you?"

"And our clients?"

"Make appointments, take down the basics. The usual."

"You don't want me to interview them?"

"No. That's our job."

"Fine," said Mrs. Billington. "Have a good investigation."

"Thanks," said Iris as she left.

Then she poked her head back inside.

"And don't go messing with our file boxes," she warned her. "I've booby-trapped them. With explosives."

"You didn't!"

"Well, not explosives," Iris conceded. "But I will know, so leave them alone."

"Yes, Miss Sparks," said Mrs. Billington, trying to keep the disappointment from her face.

Salvatore Danielli, aspiring playwright, wartime saboteur, and casual and inadvertent nemesis to furniture built for smaller men, had been Iris's friend since their days at Cambridge together. He had taken a flat in Soho that gave him easy access to any number of freelance jobs that kept him afloat while he attempted to write the Next Big Thing before someone else wrote it, in which case he would have to write the Big Thing After That.

Soho was a neighborhood of cheap rents and few questions asked, which meant that it was populated largely by actors, artists, writers, musicians, drunkards, immigrants, and London's pettier scammers, who also considered themselves actors and artists. At any given moment of the day or night, there was a throng of people hustling from gig to gig or bar to bar, while connoisseurs of foreign foods and unsuspecting marks flocked in to find delicacies unavailable elsewhere in London, whether comestible or human.

Iris, having already fended off propositions from two American sailors and an inebriated businessman seeking an afternoon's adventure, arrived safely at Sally's building and pressed the buzzer for his flat. A moment later, he stuck his head out the window and bellowed, "Coming!" then disappeared from view. She heard what sounded like a brontosaurus galumphing down the stairs. The door opened and Sally stepped onto the sidewalk and looked down at her.

"You are supposed to be working, Sparks," he said sternly. "You told me that you were a proper working woman with a job with a desk and an office, and that you could not come out to play as you used to do."

"We have two offices and three desks," Iris corrected him. "I am working. Sometimes my work takes me into the field."

"Soho is not a field," he said, looking around.

"You need a haircut," she observed. "At least, those portions hanging down where I can see them are getting quite shaggy. I assume the top is equally unkempt."

"I supposed it is," he said, feeling it under his trilby. "Thank God you came. I might have been mistaken for a bohemian if it had got any longer."

"You're a writer and you're poor—aren't those the necessary qualifications?"

"No, because I intend to be a rich writer," said Sally. "Therefore not a bohemian, merely delusional. Shall we take the tour? I'd offer you my arm, but you'd have to be constantly jumping up and down to reach it."

"The casual cruelty of the tall to the short," sighed Iris. "I could swing from it while we walk. Maybe do some chin-ups."

"We could put together an act. 'The Strongman and the Sociopath.'"

"Which one am I again?"

"Do I really have to explain it to you?"

She stepped forward and hugged him, her cheek against his chest.

"Thanks for doing this," she said. "Was I interrupting anything crucial?"

"A translation," he said. "An Italian novel about despair. It was all too effective. I was ready to throw myself out the window, but I might have got stuck like Winnie-the-Pooh in the rabbit hole, and that would have been mortifying. I was desperate for a break, so your call was quite opportune."

"How are the rewrites on *The Margate Affair* going?" she asked, releasing him.

"I'm letting it stew for the nonce. I had reached the point of wanting to make an actual stew out of the manuscript and ingesting it, so I've set it aside until I'm able to look at it again without nausea."

"Keep at it," urged Iris. "I really think it has promise."

"Promises are easily made, and more easily broken, in my experience," he said. "So. What's going on?"

"We have a new client," she said. "From Nyasaland."

"Who is looking for a bride from old stock in the old country to bring back to the plantation to live a life under parasols and mosquito netting."

"Not exactly," said Iris. "He's of actual Nyasan descent, if that's the correct adjective. He speaks Chitumbuka, which I've never heard of before today, and a lovely, Scots-inflected English."

"An African African," said Sally. "Missionary? Student? Soldier?"

"Educated by the first, yes to the second, and sailor, not soldier."

"And you need to find him a female of similar background?"

"Not necessarily," said Iris. "But it got me curious about where one would find African expats hanging about in London. If we're going to start taking on international clients, then we need to know where to recruit."

"Because matching up single, stuffy, socially awkward, emotionally stunted, reticent English people was not enough of a challenge," said Sally. "On to the foreign lovelorn."

"As long as they pay us in pounds," said Iris. "Lead on, Macduff!"

"Don't misquote Shakespeare," moaned Sally. "You know how it irritates me. Right, follow me."

"Where are we going?"

"A couple of spots," he said as they walked. "The key to locating any foreign community is to find where they eat. Unfortunately, the local African population has not reached the threshold level of sustaining their own restaurants, unless one counts Moroccan or Egyptian cuisine."

"I doubt that one could even make a go of a new place with some form of African menu," she said. "You can't get the fresh ingredients. You should have heard our client rhapsodise about the fruit. So, no restaurants. Any clubs in particular?"

"The Troc used to be the place for the old Africa hands, but not the actual Africans. In any case, it's become more of a hangout for variety stars and agents. Quite tedious. The International would have been a likely place, but they were bombed out. They just reopened near Piccadilly, but they're drawing a Mayfair crowd now. You'd fit right in. Do you know Frisco? He's still running the place when he's not bouncing across to Paris."

"I do know Frisco. I can speak with him myself. Where else?"

They walked down Shaftesbury Avenue, passing by the saxophone shop. Someone inside was playing American-style bebop, the notes flying frenetically about like a disrupted flock of starlings. They paused to listen for a moment, then strolled on. Sally glanced across the street at a long boarded-up location.

"That used to be a restaurant called Mastricola's," he said gloomily. "Remember it?"

"I ate there once or twice with my mum. Good Italian place."

"It was run by my second cousin Eduardo and his wife, Lucia. Wonderful cooks, lovely people. Then came the anti-Fascist riots, and too many rocks through the windows. They closed down. Their son died fighting for the Royal Army in Burma."

"I'm sorry."

"Wasn't your fault. It's perverse of me to live in Soho when so much of that sort of thing happened here. But it's affordable and I'm near the theatre district. I'm even picking up some television work. Mostly stage managing, but some occasional bit parts."

"Really? I'd watch you, but I can't afford a set."

"It's amazing how they can take a man of my size and reduce him to fit in a screen slightly larger than a paperback novel. I suspect witchcraft is involved. Right, let's turn on Dean, and I'll take you to our first stop."

They went north, then west on Old Compton Street.

"There," said Sally, pointing to a newspaper and magazine shop on the right. "Moroni's. Ever been?"

"Never have. What is it?"

"Newspapers and magazines from everywhere, and everyone who came here from everywhere goes to Moroni's to find out what's happening back home. And to meet other people from back home. See there?"

A trio of workmen were speaking loudly in some Slavic tongue, gesticulating rapidly as they did.

"Serbian is my guess," said Iris. "Might be talking about politics, might be talking about football. Don't speak it. Does Moroni's carry African newspapers?"

"If anyone does, it would be them," said Sally as they got nearer. "Want to go inside?"

Iris peered in to see towering displays of magazines on both walls. Further back were collections of health and art magazines whose interest was devoted to the health of beautiful, minimally clad young women and the artistic depictions thereof. Beyond, in the back, were stacks of yellow-backed novels whose titles she could not read from the sidewalk but whose nature she could guess at.

"I'll pass for now, thank you," she said. "If I'm ever in need of pornography, I know where to go."

"Oh, there are much better places for pornography," said Sally. "Two on the next street. But the main thing about Moroni's is this."

He pointed to a bulletin board in the window, covered with torn, handwritten notices with telephone numbers or postal boxes at the bottom of each. "Drum kit for sale—call . . ." "Waiter needed—knowledge of Chinese essential—call . . ." "Quick, on the spot mending . . ." "Have you seen this child? Call . . ." "Gentleman's gentleman available . . ." And so forth.

"A handbill from The Right Sort Marriage Bureau would fit in nicely, don't you think?" commented Sally.

"It would indeed," said Iris. "Thanks for the tip. What's the next place?"

"Well, if one is looking specifically for people from Africa, then there is one spot where you can find them hanging about on their breaks."

"Their breaks? Their breaks from what?"

"You'll see."

They walked back to Dean Street, then headed north.

"How is Gwen doing?" he asked. "How did she react to having the new client?"

"With the best of intentions."

"Oh, dear. Was she very awkward?"

"I'm certain Mr. Daile was aware of it, but she was trying so hard to be fair-minded that I think he forgave her in the end."

"She is very forgivable."

"Isn't she? People are always forgiving Gwen. It's infuriating. Why, when I look back at my brief existence on this planet, and all the things that I've done to people, the lack of forgiveness on the parts of my enemies—hell, my friends—has been very disappointing."

"I've forgiven you," said Sally. "Practically on a daily basis."

"Which is why you are my best friend," said Iris. "Drop that arm down, why don't you, and I'll cling to your wrist. It's the best we can do."

They drew some stares from other passersby, staring at the giant and the petite brunette holding on to him like a child to her dad.

"What a spectacle we must make," said Iris, shooting a withering glance at one gawking woman.

"Nonsense," said Sally. "They probably think you're just another Soho key-rattler with her latest."

"Lovely," said Iris.

"Nice of Gwen to hold down the fort so you could step out with me."

"Actually, our girl Friday is manning the ramparts as we speak. Gwen had to leave early."

"Is she all right?"

"Her father-in-law came home sooner than expected and is reasserting himself as lord of the manor. The specific bone of contention is over Little Ronnie's schooling."

"She will prevail," declared Sally. "She's stronger than she thinks."

"Do you think so? I don't believe any of us is as strong as we think, much less stronger. She's being buffeted about. She should get out of that house and take her son with her."

"Why won't she?"

Iris glanced up at her friend.

"There are legal aspects that I'm not at liberty to discuss," she said reluctantly. "Please understand, darling. You are my closest friend, but she is also my friend, and my partner, and there are things that I have been told in confidence."

"And I thought there would never be any secrets between us," he said. "What can I do to help?"

"The same thing you do for me, darling. Be a friend to her."

"The easiest task you have ever given me," he said.

"I hope I haven't been too demanding."

"Well, no murders this month, so that's a start," he said.

"August isn't over."

"Stop, you'll draw the attention of the Evil Eye."

"Superstitious, Sally? I never would have dreamed."

"My grandmothers both warned me about that one when I was a child, and I can never shake it. I've gone to Cambridge, abandoned the Church, and fought a war that destroyed most of my remaining beliefs, but the Evil Eye has stuck with me through thick and thin."

"You're unusually depressed today. That's normally my role in our relationship."

"Yet you're more chipper than I've seen you in ages. Shockingly so, in fact. And you've only been seeing that psychiatrist for six weeks. Please share whatever he's prescribing you."

"So far, we're still in the talking stages."

"Then how do you account for this ridiculously good mood?"

"Well, let's see. I have a new boyfriend—"

"Who is a gangster."

"But a nice gangster, at least to me. I'm drinking less, which may be cause or may be effect."

"I've noticed that. You're certainly drinking less than you did in our university days."

"Well, it would be hard to drink more than I did then, wouldn't it? God, it's amazing that I still have a liver, given that period of my life. So there is that. And I think getting rid of Andrew was the healthiest step I've taken in recent memory."

"I agree. He was never going to divorce his wife and marry you."

"Most importantly, The Right Sort is doing well. Three months ago, I was living from week to week, and now I can see my way clear all the way through New Year's Eve. Of course, it helps that the flat is paid for through then, so there's one positive benefit of having been someone's mistress."

"Where will you go when it runs out?"

"I'll cross that bridge when I come to it. Speaking of which—where are we going? We are no longer in Soho."

"You'll see. It isn't much further."

They were in Fitzrovia, now walking east. Iris had a sudden sinking feeling.

"We're not going where I think we're going, are we?" she asked.

"Depends," he said. "You wanted to find expats from Africa in large quantities. There is no better location—"

"Damn you," she said. "I hate this place."

They had come to the southeast corner of Bedford Square, a private park with a spiked iron fence encircling it. But that wasn't Sally's destination or the source of Iris's ire. Facing the western end of the park was a white, three-story Georgian town house, nestled between the Architectural Association and some newer brick affairs. A discreet bronze plaque to the left of the doorway announced the presence of the Livingstone Club.

"So you know it," said Sally.

She walked in on Cardwell's arm, wearing a short black frock that showed a lot of leg and even more shoulder. She giggled as he greeted Henri, the maitre d', whose white uniform with golden buttons set off the darkness of his complexion.

"Good to see you, lad," said Cardwell, clapping him on the back. "Got our table ready?"

"Of course, sir," said Henri, his English tinged with a mix of French and something else she couldn't identify. "Please follow me."

He led them into the dining room, whose walls were covered with oblong masks painted in black with red and white features, spears festooned with long, colourful feathers, and trophy heads of gazelles, antelope, kudus, lions, and other unfortunate victims of British bloodlust.

"Oh, how lovely!" she exclaimed, leaning into Cardwell and looking around, wide-eyed. "You are such a dear for bringing me here."

"And you're such a dear for accepting this old hunter's invitation," he replied, squeezing her shoulder. He bent down to whisper in her ear. "Our quarry is at four o'clock."

"I have him," she whispered back, then she giggled again and swatted his hand away. "Now, now, William. Behave or you won't get dessert."

"What will you have to start, my dear?" he asked as Henri held her chair.

"Chenin blanc, if they have it," she said.

"Do you?" asked Cardwell.

"We do," said Henri. "May I suggest the '37 Huet Vouvray?"

"Capital, Henri."

"And for you, sir?"

"Whisky," said Cardwell. "You know what I like."

Henri bowed, and left. A waiter appeared shortly after with their drinks. Cardwell downed his immediately.

"Another!" he bellowed. "Keep them coming."

He pointed to a gazelle head mounted over a window to his right.

"See that?" he asked. "One of mine. Brought him down with one shot in mid-bound!"

"Well done," said Sparks. "I wish all bounders were treated so."

"Jolly good," he roared as another tumbler of whisky appeared. He drank it quickly.

A man sitting behind him near the window caught her glance as Cardwell's head was tilted back. She rolled her eyes for a moment, and he smiled sympathetically.

Hook set, she thought. Reel him in slowly.

Cardwell spun tale after tale of big-game hunting while knocking back more and more whisky. Towards the end, the pace of his monologue began to flag. Then his chin slowly lowered to his chest and he began to snore softly.

"William?" said Sparks. "William! Wake up!"

Cardwell continued to snore.

"Damn it," sighed Sparks.

She looked around the room, her eyes settling on the gentleman who had glanced at her before.

"Excuse me," she said softly. "Could I trouble you for some assistance? I need to get him to his car. I think he's done for the night."

"Certainly," said the man, taking his napkin off and placing it on his seat.

He came forward, and they each took an arm and managed to get Cardwell to his feet.

"There were three of them," muttered Cardwell as they walked him to the entrance.

"Three what, darling?" asked Sparks as Henri went outside to flag Cardwell's car.

But Cardwell only murmured something unintelligible.

"It was probably elephants," said Sparks. "He always finishes with the one about the elephants. I could tell it to myself at this point."

The car came up, and they wrestled him into the backseat. Then Sparks closed the door and waved to the driver.

"Aren't you going with him?" asked the gentleman who had assisted her.

"I'm afraid it would cause rather an uproar if I showed up at his actual home," said Sparks.

"I see," said the man.

"At least I got most of the meal this time," she said. "I was hoping he'd make it through dessert before he passed out. I hear they do a lovely trifle here."

"If you are still hungry," offered the gentleman, "and not, shall we say, beholden to your—friend."

"Oh, I think I'm done with him," said Sparks, turning to him with a smile. "Any man who can't hold his liquor long enough to spend an evening with me isn't worth my while."

"Then let me prove myself worthy," said the man, offering his arm. "My name is Carlos Rodriquez Osorio."

"Mary McTague," said Sparks, taking his arm. "A pleasure to meet you."

And she allowed him to take her inside.

"Yes, I know it," said Iris to Sally, feeling far less chipper than before.

"Then you know that the serving staff are all Africans," said Sally. "Allows the old boys to reminisce in proper patronising fashion, then sleep it off in the rooms upstairs. Now, come this way."

He led her one block west, then stopped at the corner and nodded to the north.

"This is Morwell Street," he said. "Essentially the back alley for the buildings fronting the park. See those gents down there?"

She saw a group of black men chatting in the alley, smoking cigarettes. They wore the uniforms of the Livingstone Club, unbuttoned in the August heat. The bits of conversation that drifted towards her were in English, with different accents.

"They come from everywhere, and they get stuck waiting on the same old white men who treated them so badly back home," she said.

"I suppose they'd rather be treated badly here with a decent salary," said Sally. "Anyhow, that's where you can find them in bulk. Unless you have someone who can get you in the front door."

She thought of Cardwell. He had disappeared after the war, leaving a note at his desk with the two words, "Heading south."

"Not at the moment," she said. "But it might be more useful taking the back-door approach."

"Probably," agreed Sally. "One other path that strikes me is contacting some of the political clubs. You know, the Pan-African types and the student unions."

"We've tried to avoid politics at The Right Sort," said Iris. "We don't want to be associated with any viewpoint to the exclusion of others. Besides, I don't think it's the most useful marker for matching people."

"Really? That surprises me. Why not?"

"Because people who think similarly enjoy others who think similarly, and people who think dissimilarly enjoy the arguments. Either way, the affiliations generally don't help in the winnowing, and asking about them takes up an extraordinary amount of time in the interviews. Still, as a place to send a flyer—maybe the League of Coloured People might have a bulletin board. My sense is they're the widest-ranging in terms of membership. The student unions are mostly male."

"I wouldn't know," confessed Sally. "I never really knew anyone in any of them."

Iris noticed that the cluster of waiters had stopped talking and was looking at the two of them with suspicion.

"We should move on," she said.

"All right," he said, and they walked back towards Soho.

"Did you know that the club also has a tunnel in the cellar connecting it to that building across Morwell?" asked Iris.

"No, I didn't know that," said Sally, looking at her curiously. "What's in that building?"

"More bedrooms," said Iris. "A place of secrets."

"How do you know about that?" asked Sally. "Or don't I want to know the answer?"

"It was the scene of a crime once," said Iris. "Hey, there's a pub over there."

"So there is," said Sally.

"Shall we attempt to re-create our university days?"

"You've been doing so well," said Sally. "I'm not sure I want to be responsible for the decline of your morals."

"I'm buying," said Iris.

"Well, in that case . . ."

CHAPTER 5

G wen arrived home and let herself in rather than disturb Percival. As she closed the door, she could hear Lord Bainbridge from somewhere towards the rear of the house. She couldn't make out the words, but his voice was raised and in full harangue.

She walked towards the noise, stepping lightly so as not to alert him. Gradually she heard a woman's voice, interjecting softly and tearfully.

"But there isn't enough time, Lord Bainbridge," she protested. "I can't do that with only two days' notice."

It was Prudence, their cook, which meant that Lord Bainbridge was in the kitchen. Gwen knew she shouldn't eavesdrop, but she liked Prudence and was concerned. She crept closer to hear better.

"You have a job, woman," said Lord Bainbridge. "One job, and it is to provide good meals for this family and whomever else I choose to invite. Most of the time, it requires little of you, and it's clear that you feel that my extended absence allowed you to take whatever liberties and shortcuts you fancied to minimise your responsibilities. Well, your days of loafing about are over. You put together a top-notch meal for my guests Friday night, or you will be given the chop Saturday morning."

"But the ingredients, Lord Bainbridge," protested Prudence.

"I couldn't possibly get that many chickens. There's rationing and laws and such."

"You do whatever you have to do. Am I understood?"

"Yes, Lord Bainbridge," she said.

Gwen heard him storm out of the kitchen. Quickly, she ducked into the boot room, waiting until he had passed into the front of the house. She emerged to hear Prudence weeping. She went into the kitchen to find her slumped at the table, her face in her palms.

"Prudence, what can I do to help?" asked Gwen, squeezing the other woman's shoulder gently.

"Oh, Mrs. Bainbridge," said Prudence, hastily getting to her feet and wiping her eyes on her sleeves. "How much did you hear?"

"Enough."

"He thinks he's in Africa, where there are no shortages and he has entire farms waiting to supply him," said Prudence. "He's acting like the war never happened to this house. Oh, God—I'm sorry! I don't mean that. Poor Master Ronald! Of course, the war hit us terribly, especially you."

"No, it's all right," said Gwen. "What if we pooled all our coupons? Would that get us enough for Friday?"

"I don't think so, and I don't even know where to purchase that many chickens," said Prudence. "Even on the black market—"

She stopped, a mixture of hope and fear dawning on her face.

"Mrs. Bainbridge, what about your friend?" she asked hesitantly.

"My friend?"

"The others on the staff said you got mixed up in something recently that involved— No, it's asking too much."

"No, it isn't," said Gwen. "It may be expensive."

"I'll talk to Mr. Percival about that," said Prudence. "He keeps emergency funds."

"This does sound like an emergency," said Gwen. "I'll make a call."

"I'm so sorry, Mrs. Bainbridge," said Prudence, starting to sob. "I shouldn't be asking you to do anything like this. He shouldn't be making us do it. I swear, I'm one scream short of stuffing his chicken with—well, I don't want to say."

"I wouldn't do that, Prudence," said Gwen, smiling. "We must not give in to our baser impulses, no matter how gratifying the results. Tell me what you need."

"There are going to be eight guests," said Prudence. "Plus the three of you. Little Ronnie will take his dinner with us."

"Oh, dear," said Gwen. "I didn't realise that I was to be on display. Good to know—I'll wear the appropriate uniform."

She left Prudence to dig through her recipes. To her dismay, Harold was shouting again, this time in the front of the house.

"If I choose to go to the club, then I will go to the bloody club!"

"But Harold, we've barely had a moment together."

It was Lady Bainbridge, whose voice was rising to match her husband's.

"We will have a moment together when I want a moment together," he said. "There are men at the club I need to see."

"Why can't you meet them at your office?"

"Because they aren't at my office. There are arrangements to be made that do not concern you but are vital to the success of the company, and those may only be done at the club."

"But dinner—"

"Will be far superior there than the fare I have had here."

Gwen ventured cautiously forward until she could get a glimpse of them facing each other in the entrance hall.

"Do you know what it was like staying here while you were gone?" asked Lady Bainbridge. "Wondering if you were safe? You could have been crushed in a cave-in, or shot in a riot, or bitten by a tsetse fly, or drowned in a steamship like those poor people in Lake Nyasa—"

"No more!" shouted Lord Bainbridge, turning white with anger. "Albert?"

"Sir?" came the chauffeur's voice.

"Is the car ready?"

"It is, sir."

"Then I shall be off. Don't wait up."

Gwen heard the front door open and close. A moment later, she heard the Rolls's engine roar to life, then recede into the distance. A motorcycle started up somewhere down the street.

She stepped into the entrance hall. Lady Bainbridge was staring at the door, almost shredding the handkerchief clutched in her hand.

"Carolyne? Are you all right?" asked Gwen.

"Six months away," she said without turning. "Six months I remained here, playing my part, never protesting. Fortunes must be tended to, wherever they are. We live on the leavings, and are expected to be grateful. It would be churlish to be anything else, wouldn't it?"

"He has no right to treat you like this."

"He has every right," said Lady Bainbridge. "Every right, every power. That's the injustice of it. If I had any courage, I would— No, I won't say it. I am going to change. I will see you at dinner."

She trudged up the stairs, turning halfway to look back at Gwen.

"He has never needed me," she said. "He has never put me ahead of his business. Not once."

Then she continued up and went to her rooms.

Silence fell on the Bainbridge House. Not the silence of emptiness, but the silence of people holding their tongues, staying out of sight, not even daring to breathe loudly lest they incur the wrath of the lord of the manor, whose tyranny reigned even when he was no longer present.

Dinner on Friday evening will be agonising, thought Gwen. Perhaps she could feign illness and beg out of it.

But that would leave Carolyne without an ally at the table.

Good Lord! Had it come to that? That she would step forward to help a woman who had been the scourge of her own existence for so long? Carolyne was a bully who wielded her power over the household like a slave driver with a whip. But like so many bullies, she was bullied herself, and what was happening to her was unjust.

Empathy, thought Gwen with a sigh. Too damn much of it at times. I should dig deep and be more selfish. But first—the chickens.

She pulled her address book from her bag, then turned to the S's. There it was: "A. Spelling."

It was a Stepney Green number. She went to the downstairs telephone and dialed it.

"Yeah," answered a gruff voice.

"I would like to speak to Mr. Spelling, please," she said.

"Would you now? And 'oo are you and 'ow'd you get this number?"

"It's Mrs. Bainbridge," she said. "Miss Sparks's friend. Mr. Spelling knows me."

"'Ang on."

There was a muffled conversation, then another man came to the telephone.

"Mrs. Bainbridge," said Archie. "What an unexpected surprise. Is Sparks all right then?"

"Yes, Miss Sparks is fine," said Gwen.

"Then this is even more of a surprise," said Archie. "To what do I owe the pleasure?"

"I'm afraid I need some help from you in your professional capacity," said Gwen.

"Is that right? In which aspect would you be requiring assistance?"

"We are having a dinner party Friday night . . ."

"I'm taking this is not an invitation."

"Unfortunately, no. We need to obtain chickens, and I was wondering—"

"If I knew a man who 'ad a few to spare."

"Precisely. I'm sorry to be asking, but—"

"But you're a blue blood who doesn't associate with black marketeers unless push comes to shove, and now it 'as."

"I suppose it appears that way," said Gwen.

"Oh, more than appears, Mrs. Bainbridge. There you are, Sparks's friend and business associate, and 'ere I am, another friend of 'ers, 'ose done you a favour or two not too far in the past, and the first time you ever call me directly is for chickens."

"I'm sorry, Mr. Spelling."

"You 'aven't even brought yourself to callin' me Archie, 'ave you?"

"I will, Archie. Please understand, your world is very new to me."

"Our worlds are closer than you think, Mrs. Bainbridge. The aristocracy and the underworld are connected in ways you don't know."

"Archie, I am very sorry to be calling you for the first time on business," said Gwen. "I wouldn't have done so, but it's to save our cook's job. My father-in-law is being ridiculous and peremptory, and I will do what I can to help the poor woman."

"Well, that's better, then," said Archie, sounding mollified.

"And it would otherwise be awkward for me to be calling my best friend's boyfriend, don't you think?"

"She calls me 'er boyfriend?" said Archie.

"That's been the recent practise," said Gwen.

"That's the best news I've 'ad all week," said Archie. "Right, 'ow many chickens?"

"Enough to feed eleven," said Gwen.

"Since you're a 'Friend of Archie,' you get the friendly discount. Your cook lady better 'ave the cash on 'and when the delivery comes."

"She will," promised Gwen. "How much should she have?"

He named a price that made her wince and wonder how much he'd charge someone he didn't like.

"Thank you, Archie," she said. "I will call sometime just for the two of us to chat."

"It would be an honour and a privilege, Mrs. Bainbridge," said Archie.

"Do call me Gwen from now on."

"I will do that, Gwen," said Archie. "Regards to Sparks."

She hung up, then brought the news to Prudence, who burst into tears and clutched her hand for an uncomfortably long moment. Gwen finally managed to disengage and went upstairs in search of her son.

Ronnie wasn't in his room. She found him in the playroom, his crayons scattered about the floor as he worked intently on a drawing.

"Hello, my darling boy," she said, sitting on the floor next to him and planting a kiss on the top of his head. "Is this your latest creation?"

"It's Sir Oswald," he replied.

"So I see. What is his latest feat of derring-do?"

"He's in Africa," said Ronnie. "He's helping a water buffalo escape from a crocodile."

"Ah. Very brave of him. Crocodiles are very dangerous."

"I'm making it for Grandfather," said Ronnie.

"A 'Welcome Home' gift. He will be delighted."

"He was fighting with Grandmother," said Ronnie. "A lot. I could hear them from here."

"I'm sorry if that upset you," said Gwen. "I hope Agnes was able to comfort you while Mummy was at work."

"Agnes is upset, too," said Ronnie.

"Oh?" said Gwen, her heart suddenly racing. "Why is Agnes upset?"

"She wouldn't say," said Ronnie. "Are we eating at the big table again tonight? Do I have to dress up? I don't like dressing up just to eat. I worry about spilling on my good clothes."

"We'll be eating at the regular table," said Gwen. "You're fine as you are."

"Will Grandfather be there?"

"Not tonight, dearest. He'll be coming home after your bedtime. You may give him your gift in the morning."

"All right," said Ronnie. "I have to finish it. Maybe if he likes it, he won't send me away."

She didn't know what to say to that.

"Do you know where Agnes is right now?" she asked.

"I think she's in her room."

"I'm going to check in on her," said Gwen. "I will see you at dinner."

She kissed him again. He ignored her and continued working on his picture.

The door to Agnes's room was closed. She knocked softly. A moment later, it opened and Agnes stood before her, her normally cheerful countenance gone. In its place was a portrait of grief. Her eyes were puffy, and the tear streaks were evident through her makeup.

"What happened?" Gwen asked immediately. "Tell me."

"He gave me my notice," said Agnes.

"No! When?"

"Not half an hour ago," said Agnes.

"Let me come in," said Gwen. "Talk to me."

Agnes opened the door wider to admit her, then closed it behind her.

"You can have the chair," she said, sitting on her narrow bed with her legs drawn up.

Gwen sat by the dressing table.

"I know the job wasn't to be forever," said Agnes, wiping her eyes with her handkerchief. "But I thought once you had recovered that you'd put him in school in London, so I could still take him and pick him up after while you were at your office. I know all about the custody situation, of course, but you've seemed so well lately. I didn't think there would be any troubles, especially once Lady Bainbridge started coming around. But then Lord Bainbridge came home . . ."

She started to cry.

"Two days!" she wailed. "Not even two days, and the first words he said to me were 'you're gone.' Not even a thank-you for all I've done. He's going to send your beautiful boy to that brutal school and he'll never be the same. Oh, Mrs. Bainbridge—I could strangle that man! Not for me, but for Little Ronnie!"

"I'm trying to keep him here," said Gwen. "I'll petition the court if I have to. Please, don't distress yourself on our account. I'll think of something."

"You have to hurry, Mrs. Bainbridge," said Agnes urgently, reaching over to clutch her hand. "They'll be starting the autumn term in less than two weeks."

"I'm seeing my psychiatrist tomorrow," said Gwen. "I've been doing well. If I can get him to sign off on my competence, then I can go to the court straightaway. I promise you, this will work out."

"But if it doesn't . . ."

"Be strong for now," said Gwen. "And please—don't let Ronnie know anything about this. He already knows something upset you."

"I'm sorry," said Agnes, drawing a deep breath. "I'll just fix my face up and get him ready for dinner. The trouble is he's very astute for such a young boy. I think he gets that from you."

"It's a curse sometimes," sighed Gwen.

She left Agnes. It was not yet four o'clock, which meant there would be ample time before dinner. She had wanted to get her mind off work by coming home. Now, home had provided her more than enough to fret over. She wanted nothing more than to retreat somewhere and get her mind off her problems. To change out of her suit—

Her suit. It was one of her older wartime Utility outfits, an everyday cream-coloured jacket-and-skirt combination with little ornamentation that took the bare minimum of coupons when she had purchased it. Just the thing she needed.

She found the maid's closet and removed a metal pail and a rag. Then she went to the lavatory and filled the bucket with water. She lugged it to the steps to the attic, making certain that she was unobserved, then climbed up through the trapdoor and closed it after her.

The heavy bag was where she had left it. She dipped the rag in the bucket and wiped away the dust from the surface, revealing the original reddish brown colour underneath. She continued until the bag was completely clean. She stepped back to observe her handiwork.

"Well, Lord Bainbridge, we meet again," she said. "You may appear pristine now, but I know the truth about your unseemly past. You think you got the better of me."

Then she hit him with a left jab.

"No more," she said.

"He's succeeded in antagonising most of the women in the household," Gwen complained the next morning. "Maybe all of them. I haven't talked to the housekeeper or the maids, but it wouldn't surprise me if he had peeved them off as well by now."

"Probably got to them first," speculated Iris. "Then worked his way up the ladder to his wife."

"There are hints of mutiny in the ranks," said Gwen. "I heard veiled threats of homicide from no less than three different women in the space of an hour. If we get organised, there could be a reen-actment of the maenads in *The Bacchae*."

"I hope your son has been spared his wrath."

"That may have been the worst of it," said Gwen sadly. "He had worked for hours making a picture for him as a gift. The latest in his Sir Oswald series. It showed him in Africa, fighting an evil crocodile to save a water buffalo."

"What happened?"

"He gave it to Harold this morning. His grandfather looks at it, then says, 'What is that supposed to be?' 'A crocodile, Grand-father.' 'And this?' 'A water buffalo. And that's a narwhal.' Then Harold says, 'Ridiculous. There aren't any narwhals anywhere near Africa. And they can't go on land. This is nonsense. Tell your gov-erness to instill some actual knowledge in that little head of yours.' And he crumples up the picture and throws it in the wastepaper basket! Ronnie was inconsolable. I finally had to leave him with Agnes, and she was crying harder than he was."

"That's it," said Iris grimly. "If nobody else kills your father-in-law, I shall."

"Well, you can't just yet. We've all committed to a dinner party tomorrow night."

"Oh? Who are the guests?"

"I think men he does business with, but I don't know the exact guest list. I don't have much in the way of contact with the board of Bainbridge, Limited. They were all at the wedding, of course, but since then—"

"Aren't you a board member?"

"What?"

"You. A member of the board of Bainbridge, Limited. Ronnie was, wasn't he?"

"I suppose so, but—"

"You inherited his shares of the company."

"Which are in the control of my legal guardian," said Gwen. "Until the court deems me fit to run my finances again."

"Idiotic," said Iris. "Here you are, comanaging your own business, solving the occasional murder on the side—"

"Which I cannot bring to the court as evidence of my sanity."

"—and yet your fortunes are being administered by a group of men, and you have no say in how they are doing it. You deserve a seat at the table, guardian or no."

"What do I know about munitions factories and copper mines?"

"What you know about anything. Learn about them, so when you assert yourself, you will be listened to."

"They won't take me seriously," objected Gwen. "They've all been doing this for years."

"And I bet they knew nothing when they started, either," said Iris. "They probably all inherited their seats from their families."

"You're very insistent this morning," observed Gwen. "Very well, I'll start studying smelting and things that go bang, but I don't have time before this dinner takes place. Oh, I should tell you—I spoke with Archie yesterday."

"Archie? My Archie?"

"Yes. I needed a supplier for chickens for the dinner so Prudence wouldn't get the sack. I hope you don't mind."

"Why would I mind? I'd be happier if you were more accepting of him and his friends."

"'Friends,' Iris? They're criminals."

"Yes, but they've been good to us, haven't they?"

"Because we paid them."

"You enjoyed going out to that club with everyone last month."

"We were celebrating our triumph. I was still giddy with it."

"You danced with several of them."

"Extremely giddy. But I'm not as used to socialising with the criminal element as you seem to be."

"I didn't grow up in the underworld, despite what you may

think," said Iris. "My acquaintance with it came during the war. Men with skills beyond the pale became very useful."

"Is that when you learned to pick locks?"

"Ah, no, that was at boarding school," confessed Iris. "We had a club. In any case, you shouldn't be overly judgmental. We both know criminals. Yours are just at a higher level than mine."

"What are you saying?"

"Archie's lads work on a much smaller scale than Bainbridge, Limited. Your father-in-law and his cronies loot and plunder entire nations."

"They're businessmen, Iris. The comparison is unfair. You might as well say that you and I are exploiting lonely people for financial gain."

"That thought does cross my mind occasionally," admitted Iris. "The differences are that we are trying to help them, we charge a fair rate, and we aren't treating our employees shabbily in the process."

"Employee, singular. But what are you driving at?"

"Miners, plantation workers, all the men doing the real labour while your father-in-law reaps the benefits."

"That's how things work in the real world."

"And that includes paying the African workers less than the whites, doesn't it?"

Gwen didn't respond.

"Doesn't it?" persisted Iris. "You must be aware of that. You've been part of that family for over seven years."

"It was something Ronnie and I talked about," said Gwen guiltily. "He was hoping to make changes once the war was over and he could take his rightful place at the board. But now, he's gone."

"Then I hope you carry on his good intentions," said Iris.

"I won't even have the opportunity if I can't be certified competent again," said Gwen. "I am going to speak with Dr. Milford about that tonight."

"If he needs my input—"

"He thinks you're crazy, too."

"So he knows his stuff," Iris said with a grin. "But you're much further along in the cure than I am."

"I hope so," said Gwen. "I don't know what to do otherwise."

"Keep taking out your frustrations on the second Lord Bainbridge. How is that going?"

"I cleaned him up and gave him a good pasting yesterday. The chin jab is coming along nicely, if I do say so myself."

"Good. And the defense to the neck hold?"

"I don't feel as proficient in that," said Gwen. "It's fine when I have my back to the bag and go after the shin or the, um . . ."

"Testicles," prompted Iris.

"Yes, those," said Gwen, blushing. "But the wrist grab and turn feel like I'm dancing without a partner. It's all theoretically fine until you actually get out on the floor. And I can't very well ask one of the servants to be my willing victim."

"I bet Millie would if you threw her an extra bob or two," said Iris.

"But I don't want to damage Millie," said Gwen. "She does my hair so well. I don't suppose you could give it a go."

"Stand up," said Iris, coming out in front of her desk.

Gwen joined her. Iris walked around her, looking at her critically.

"You've got nine or ten inches on me," she said. "I can't reach your neck at the right angle unless I stand on a chair."

"Well, I guess that's—" said Gwen, then she stopped as Iris grabbed the guest chair and placed it behind her. "Are you sure about this?"

"Just don't complete the turn," said Iris, stepping onto the chair. "Or I'll end up riding pickaback. Step into the yoke, milady."

Gwen backed into her. Iris wrapped her arm around her neck.

"No head butts," she warned her. "Or I will hurt you."

"No head butts," agreed Gwen. "A scrape down the imaginary shin like thus, and grab!"

She stamped her foot, grabbed Iris's wrist, and began the turn, stopping immediately.

"That was good," said Iris. "Now, speed it up."

Gwen tried it a few more times.

"Could you switch to the other arm?" she asked.

"Certainly."

This time, Gwen turned further than she had from the other direction, lifting Iris off the chair.

"Whee!" cried Iris. Then "Oh!"

Lord Bainbridge stood in their doorway, looking at them in disdain. The two women looked back at him, Iris still clinging to Gwen's back, her feet dangling.

"Is this what you consider running a business?" he asked acerbically.

"What are you doing here?" asked Gwen as Iris hurriedly slid to the floor.

"I was curious to see whether this was a going concern or another symptom of your self-indulgent madness," he said.

"We had a break," said Gwen. "Iris was helping me practise."

"Practise what? I can't think of anything looking like what I just saw that doesn't verge on immorality or illegality."

"That physical fitness course I told you I was taking? It's a self-defense course," said Gwen.

"Iris was playing my attacker."

"I see," said Lord Bainbridge, smirking slightly. "And I assume Miss Sparks is taking the course with you."

"I've already taken it," said Iris, looking him steadily in the eye. "Would you like to test me?"

"I'll pass, thank you," said Lord Bainbridge.

He stepped into the office, looking around. His gaze was immediately drawn to the unpainted wall.

"Interesting colour scheme," he noted.

"We just took over the second office recently," said Gwen. "We'll be finishing the painting this Saturday."

"You will be painting? You? Yourself?"

"Me, myself, and Iris. It's cheaper if we do it ourselves."

"And we're doing a much better job of it this time," added Iris. "The first office could use another coat, honestly."

"Maybe you could hire yourselves out for the added money," said Lord Bainbridge. "I doubt you have much coming in as it stands."

"We're doing all right," said Gwen.

"Really? Show me your books."

"No."

"No?" he said, his eyebrows rising. "Did you say no to me?"

"I did."

"I bet you don't even keep books properly," he scoffed.

"I keep the books. I keep them very well, thank you. But you have no right to see them, and I choose not to show them to you."

"May I remind you that you are still a ward of the court, and under legal guardianship?"

"You don't have to remind me," said Gwen. "Although it appears to give you great pleasure to do so at every possible opportunity. But you are not my guardian."

"He reports to me."

"That's his business. If he comes in and demands to see them, I will have no choice but to show them to him. I don't think he's much of an expert on bookkeeping, though."

"And you are."

"I've learned," said Gwen. "We've been in business for six months now. Our clientele is expanding daily, and we've done well enough to expand to a second office and hire our first employee."

"With whom we will have to address letting ruffians from the street stroll into our office without warning," said Iris.

"I am no ruffian," he thundered.

"We'll have to disagree on that point," said Iris. "Now, if you would like to continue this conversation, please make an appointment with Mrs. Billington. We may have an open slot for you next week sometime. If not, there's always 1947."

"You dare speak to me like that," he said, turning to her. "Don't forget, I know about you, Miss Sparks."

"Not everything," said Iris. "The things you don't know would chill your bones to the marrow. But I tell you what—if you'd like to see our books, we'll make an arrangement with you as fellow businesspeople."

"What arrangement?" he asked warily.

"You show us your books, and we'll show you ours," she said. "Sound fair?"

"Congratulations, Gwen," he said. "You've found the right partner. When this all comes crashing down, don't come crying to me for help."

"You're the last person I would go to," said Gwen. "Now, I'm certain you have better things to be doing with your time than wasting ours. I will see you at dinner."

He sniffed, then turned and walked out.

"I withdraw my offer to compromise him," said Iris, listening as his footsteps receded down the stairwell.

"Understandable," said Gwen.

"I still might kill him."

"You can't. We have that dinner party on Friday."

"Saturday, then."

"We're painting the office Saturday."

"Right," sighed Iris. "Blast."

CHAPTER 6

Mrs. Bainbridge, how are we today?" asked Dr. Milford, motioning her to one of the seats in front of his desk.

"It has been an agitating week, to say the least," she replied.

"Has it?" he asked, taking the other seat to face her. "Tell me."

"Before we go into it, I need to ask you a favour," she said. "It's urgent."

"Go on."

"I began therapy as a requirement of the court," she began.

"And because you needed it," he reminded her.

"Yes, of course," she said. "And I promise that I will continue with you even after I have been declared competent. But Lord Bainbridge has returned from Africa, and he won't listen to us about keeping Ronnie in London for his education. He insists on sending him away to that terrible boarding school, and the term starts in two weeks."

"I see. And the favour?"

"I need to regain custody of Ronnie as quickly as possible. I need the court to declare me competent, and I need you to sign off on that. Will you?"

He looked at her for a long moment, steepling his fingers in front of his chest.

"I am afraid that I cannot do that as yet," he said finally.

"But I've made progress!" she protested. "You can't say that I haven't."

"You have."

"Or that I'm not capable of running my own business."

"You are."

"Or that I present any kind of threat to myself or others."

He was silent.

"Do I?" she asked, her voice faltering.

"Last month, you related to me a tale of an adventure you had just been through," he said. "A tale so amazing, so beyond normal everyday experience, that I would have concluded it to be the product of a disordered mind had it not been confirmed in every detail by Miss Sparks. And even after hearing her, I haven't entirely ruled out the possibility of folie à deux."

"But it happened. Every last word of it."

"Very well. And one thing that happened in the course of it is that you threatened a man with a loaded gun."

"Which he had been using to threaten us!" protested Gwen.

"Yet once you had him bound and secured, you pointed it at him and threatened to pull the trigger."

"We needed information from him. I wasn't actually going to shoot him. It was an act. I was playing."

"Are you saying that the thought never crossed your mind? To put a bullet in, say, his leg, or somewhere else nonfatal?"

She hesitated. He shook his head immediately.

"And you want me to declare you to be safe enough to be entrusted with the custody of a child," he said. "I'm sorry, Mrs. Bainbridge. You still have work to do."

"There is an entire population of Englishmen who have shot enemies in combat recently," she pointed out.

"And the ones who shot unarmed prisoners were court-martialed, or should have been," he replied. "Nor did the rest escape the experience unscathed. There are several in the waiting room even now, as I'm sure you have noticed. Now, let's get to work, Mrs. Bainbridge."

"And when my son has been sufficiently traumatised by that school, I'll bring him to you for treatment, shall I?" she asked bitterly.

"Tell me about your week," he said.

Gwen came out looking more agitated than she had been going in. Iris started to say something, but Gwen gave a quick, small shake of her head.

"Miss Sparks, the doctor will see you now," said the receptionist without looking up from her magazine.

Sparks walked through the door, glancing behind her at Gwen, who sat on a chair by the wall, staring into space.

"You're not going to help her?" she asked as soon as the door closed behind her.

Dr. Milford pointed to the seat in front of his desk.

"But she needs to—"

"Sit down, Miss Sparks," said Dr. Milford.

She sat.

"First, I never discuss what happens with my patients with anyone," he said. "Especially other patients."

"But—"

"Second, you're deflecting."

"Very well," she said, fuming. "I thought focusing on someone other than myself was a sign that I was rising above my narcissistic tendencies, but fine, let's talk about me."

He leaned back in his chair and looked at her.

"Well?" she said after thirty seconds had gone by.

"Well what?"

"Aren't you going to start?"

"You're the self-diagnosed narcissist," he said. "Go ahead and talk about yourself."

"Would you like to hear about yesterday's drinking binge?"

"Yes, I would."

"I had cut back to high moderation over the last few weeks," she said. "No morning bracers, only one polite glass at lunch, sometimes not even that. Then yesterday I went walking with an old friend, and we wound up in a pub. Things get fuzzy after that."

"So it was the old friend's fault."

"No, no," said Iris. "It wasn't Sally. If anything, Sally's the one who rescued me back when I was hell-bent on drowning myself in a butt of malmsey. He was in a blue mood yesterday, so I took him to a pub to change the colour."

"So it was straight-up altruism on your part, nothing else."

Iris sighed.

"Of course there was something else," she said. "Some bad memories came bubbling up."

"Memories of what?"

Iris looked down at her lap, debating within herself. Dr. Milford waited.

"Right," said Iris, not meeting his gaze. "I've never told anyone the full story. This comes under the Official Secrets Act portion of our confidential arrangement."

"Acknowledged," said Dr. Milford.

"The memories of that particular area of London are tied up with something that happened a few years back," said Iris. "During the war."

"Go on."

"I had been loaned out to a counterintelligence operation after my debacle during parachute training. No, after my screaming refusal to ever step foot on a plane again after my debacle during parachute training."

"What was the operation?"

"To feed false information to a known Fascist sympathiser," she said. "And to turn him if we could compromise him sufficiently."

"And how were you to do that?"

"Do you know what a honeytrap is, Doctor?"

"I can guess, but tell me."

"It's a seduction."

"And in this honeytrap, you were—"

"The honeypot. Our first meeting was an 'accidental' encounter at the Livingstone Club. I went in ostensibly as the flirty girl in the War Office who just happened to have access to various invasion schemes."

"And you seduced someone."

"Well, the classic approach is to allow them to think they are seducing you. It's so much more satisfactory to their ego. Listen to me, telling you about egos. You know all about them, don't you, Doctor Freud?"

"A fair amount. And was the operation a success?"

"Initially. After a suitable exchange of banter and courtship, I allowed him to take the virtue that I never had in the first place. And along we went for a while, me blabbing away about war plans that were carefully constructed to misdirect the enemy."

"And then?"

"And then he figured it out. I don't know if I slipped up, or if someone else gave me away. He attacked me."

"That must have been—"

"And I killed him."

"Ah," said Dr. Milford.

They both were silent.

"It was self-defense," he said finally.

"That's what they called it," she said.

"What do you call it?"

"I know how to defend myself," she said. "I am very good at

defending myself. There were several ways in which I could have done so in that moment without killing him. Instead, I panicked and stabbed him."

"What was he doing when you did?"

"He had his hands around my throat and was trying to choke me."

"Then your actions were still justifiable."

"Oh, they were justifiable," she said. "In war, in espionage—even in a regular court of law, should the case ever have made it into a regular court of law. I would have been exonerated. My superiors were satisfied with my performance in the field, and that was all that mattered."

"Was it?"

"That's what I kept telling myself. You see, I volunteered for this tawdry mission. They needed someone who was willing to—oh, hell, who was shameless. The other girls were too pristine, or genteel, or something, and I wanted to show I would go all out for the war effort, especially having failed so miserably in my first attempt."

"Who were the other girls?"

"Blue bloods, mostly. They were recruited for their brains and a facility for languages, and just like in Cambridge, I was the diamond in the rough. But I was a party girl par excellence."

"Even though you were engaged at that point."

"Even though I was engaged," she said. "Maybe especially because I was engaged. And of course, that's how Mike caught me, mid-mission, in a romantic tête-à-tête with a dashing Spaniard, and all I could do was brush him off and maintain my cover. The look on his face . . ."

She stopped, the tears coming abruptly. She scrambled for her handkerchief, mopping her cheeks.

"I've always wondered if I killed Carlos because I was angry at my superiors for letting me destroy my engagement. Or—"

"Or?" he prompted her.

"Or if I needed to destroy everything to punish myself for making that happen," she concluded.

"Or?"

"There is no other 'or,'" she said, looking at him for the first time since she began telling the tale. "Or is there? What 'or' should I be mining?"

"Let's see," he said. "You've mixed in sex, death, class resentment, betrayal, and guilt all in one story, and you wonder why you feel conflicted?"

"Goodness," she said. "And I didn't even mention my absent, alcoholic father. Is there any hope for me?"

"Always. Why do you think you won't absolve yourself when every institution in society would?"

"Because those are merely the collective opinions of the majorities in control."

"And you don't like to be controlled, even if it's to your benefit. Do you, Miss Sparks?"

"I thrive on chaos," she said wearily. "That's my life."

"Would marrying Mike have given you a sense of order? Would it have given you freedom from being controlled?"

"Our courtship took place during the Blitz, if that provides you with any useful context."

"Say life had gone otherwise. Say you had turned down the honeytrap assignment, lived through the rest of the war as a competent, unadventurous staffer of some kind, and finished up by marrying Mike. Would you be happy now?"

"Happiness is overrated."

"Content? At peace?"

"We'll never know, will we?"

"No, we won't," he said. "You live the life you have now, with the singular history that led up to it. You killed a man. It sounds like he was a good candidate for an early end, no matter whether it was you who did it or someone else."

"Are you condoning murder?"

"Justifiable homicide in defense of self and country. Accept the world's judgment in this."

"But the world is also judging me harshly in many other areas of my life."

"Then change those areas. Or change the world. But in this one instance, forgive yourself."

"Any bright ideas for how I go about doing that, Doctor Freud?"

"What triggered the memories?"

"They're never far from the surface."

"Then what triggered the drinking binge?"

"Um," said Iris, trying to remember the exact sequence. "I think it was seeing the Livingstone Club again. That's where it started. I've managed to avoid the place up until yesterday."

"Go back there. It's a building. Confront it. Stare it down fiercely, and it will crumble before you. There's a nice, soothing park across from it, as I recall. That should provide you some emotional support."

"It's private. Fenced and gated."

"Well, then—"

"But I could pick the lock and break in," said Iris, perking up.

"I cannot give you permission to act upon that impulse," he said, smiling for the first time.

"Fortunately, you don't control my impulses," said Iris, smiling back.

When Iris came out, Gwen's outward composure had been restored. Her eyes, however, told a different story. Without saying anything, the two women left the anteroom and walked out onto Harley Street.

"You've been crying," observed Gwen. "Let me fix that for you."

Iris stood obediently while Gwen took her handkerchief and smoothed out the tracks on her cheeks.

Like I'm a child with my mum again, she thought, looking up at the tall woman bending over her. There's comfort in that.

"In all the time we've known each other, I've never seen you cry," commented Gwen as they began to walk. "Not once. Usually I'm the one blubbering away at a moment's notice, leaking salty rivulets onto the good furniture."

"I thought the chair felt soggy when I sat on it," said Iris. "Are you up to drinks and cake?"

"Not today," said Gwen. "I'm not in the right post-therapy mood for self-indulgence."

"Neither am I, now that you mention it. Until tomorrow, then."

"Until tomorrow."

Gwen walked back to Kensington, her feet automatically following her regular route while her mind lurched about, seeking remedies for her troubles. The suggestions it provided to her ran towards murdering her father-in-law and disposing of his body in a variety of lurid methods, some less amusing than others.

Maybe I am dangerous, she thought.

The idea did not displease her.

As she turned onto her street, she noticed a gardener trimming the hedges in front of one of the houses on the opposite side. He was black, and her thoughts turned to Mr. Daile.

Now, now, Gwen, she admonished herself. Just because he is of the same colour and profession doesn't mean . . .

But the gardener saw her looking at him. As she drew nearer, he smiled broadly and lifted his cap. It was Mr. Daile.

"Mrs. Bainbridge, it is you!" he exclaimed in delight. "I thought it might be you, but then I thought, 'No, Simon, just because you see a tall, blond English lady doesn't mean she's the same tall, blond English lady,' but it is you! How did you know I was working here? Have you come with news of a potential match for me already?"

"Hardly, Mr. Daile," she said. "I had no idea you were working in this vicinity."

"Then what brings you here?"

"I live here. Across the street in Number Eleven."

"No! How extraordinary!" he said, laughing. "Such an immense city, and we encounter each other like this."

"Are you the Stillmans' gardener now?"

"No, I work for a service," he said, replacing his cap. "Very few London houses have full-time gardeners anymore. I trim the hedges, cut the grass, then move on to the next one. Do you have a gardener at Number Eleven?"

"Not since before the war, I'm afraid," said Gwen. "The house in the country has four, I think, but all we grow here are vegetables and herbs like good patriotic Londoners should."

"Have you a hothouse?"

"We do. I'd love for us to get in some flowers again."

"That will be a sign that the war is truly over," he said. He glanced at his watch. "It appears that I have reached the end of today's labours. I'll have to return tomorrow. It was an unexpected pleasure, Mrs. Bainbridge."

He peeled off his work gloves and held out his hand. She shook it. He walked over to where a motorcycle was parked by the side of the road and placed his shears, cap, and gloves in a basket on the back that had rakes and a hoe sticking up from it, a red streamer tied to the latter.

"Is that yours?" she asked. "I thought I heard a motorcycle around here."

"My baby," he said, patting it proudly. "A 1933 Royal Enfield. I bought it when I came to Harper Adams, and it waited patiently under a tarpaulin in a shed there until I returned. It was a joyous reunion."

He traded his cap for a leather helmet, straddled the seat, and pulled down his goggles.

"Very dashing, don't you think?" he said. "Maybe I will wear them for my first date."

"I'll add that to your information," said Gwen. "We have a few girls who would fancy riding on that."

"Perfect," he said. "I look forward to meeting them. Good day, Mrs. Bainbridge."

He started the engine, paused as a dark blue Rolls-Royce Wraith pulled out into the street, then drove away.

Small world indeed, thought Gwen. But not that small.

She couldn't shake the sense that he was spying on her.

She walked inside, and Percival met her in the entry hall.

"Was that my father-in-law leaving as I came up?" she asked.

"Yes, Mrs. Bainbridge. He is going to his club."

"Were there any scenes before he left?"

"I'm sure I don't know what you mean, Mrs. Bainbridge."

"I mean, Percival, does anyone here need comforting from me at the moment? Start with my son, then work your way through the household."

"There were no incidents, Mrs. Bainbridge," he said in a low tone. "I cannot say that comfort would be unwelcome in some quarters."

"Thank you, Percival," she said, removing her hat. "I'll make the rounds."

Iris awoke early on Friday morning and made herself some oatmeal, sprinkling a precious teaspoon of sugar on it as an end-of-the-week treat. She eyed the whisky bottle with longing, but left it untouched.

The weather was already uncomfortably hot. She had sweated through the night, so she rubbed herself down with a wet washcloth, then dressed in a light blue rayon suit, adding a jabot collar for a touch of frill. She chose her brightest red lipstick, then walked out to face her enemy.

It wasn't very far out of the way from her flat in Marylebone to the Livingstone Club. Fitzrovia was the neighbourhood adjacent to the east. She walked south on Welbeck, then turned left on Wigmore Street. The sun was just up, and the milkmen and bakery lorries were making their deliveries. There was not much automobile traffic otherwise, petrol supplies being what they were. Other pedestrians were headed to tube and bus stops, mostly going south. Iris kept a brisk pace, swinging her arms occasionally to loosen herself up, and in less than fifteen minutes arrived at Tottenham Court Road.

Right here, left on Bayley, straight on to the private park, and break in, she thought. Use the protective cover of the foliage to come within a safe distance of your target. Bravely stare it down from behind a bush. Then see if you can walk to Mayfair without dashing into the nearest pub.

Fortunately, no pubs would be open that time of morning.

Although there was one not-so-legal joint she knew of . . .

Courage, Iris.

She went south, then turned left on Bayley.

It's only a building, she thought. It has neither tongue nor memory. There is no reason—

A man standing at the entrance to Morwell Street saw her and looked at her in surprise. Her immediate impulse was to turn on her heel and run, but he had already recognised her. There was nothing for it but to brazen it out.

"Sparks," said Detective Sergeant Michael Kinsey. "What on earth are you doing here this time of morning? Or anywhere this time of morning?"

"Taking my constitutional on the way to work," said Sparks. "It's the new me. Hello, Mike. Or should I address you formally, Detective Sergeant? Are you working, Detective Sergeant Mike? Or moonlighting as a watchman?"

"Working," said Kinsey.

"Ah. What sort of case? Oh!"

A pair of constables emerged from the street, carrying a stretcher. On it, a sheet covered a body.

"Sorry you had to see that," said Kinsey, glancing at it as they placed it in a waiting lorry.

"Murder?"

"Pending the autopsy and official pronouncement at the inquest, yes," said Kinsey.

"And is your boss here as well?"

"Detective Superintendent Parham has been and gone," said Kinsey. "Leaving me behind to do the hard work."

"Tell him I said hello."

"I will," said Kinsey. "He told me that you and Mrs. Bainbridge solved another murder or two while I was away. He was reluctantly impressed."

"Not enough to offer me a job, but that's all right," said Sparks.

"Would you want to work there? You've never been one for following orders."

"True enough. My goodness, I can't believe anyone would murder anyone in this neighbourhood. It's so déclassé."

"You're a snob, Sparks," said Kinsey. "Murder goes everywhere. Anyhow, he wasn't killed here. Someone wrapped his body in a blanket and dumped it after the fact. There's no blood splatter from the bullets—"

"He was shot?"

"Twice."

"And nobody heard anything?"

"Nobody called it in. The porter at the Livingstone Club found him when he was bringing in the dustbins."

"Who was the poor sod?"

"We don't know yet. No wallet, no ident card of any kind."

"A robbery, perhaps?"

"Maybe, but my instincts say no. He was searched too thoroughly, and a robber wouldn't take the trouble to drag him here. Plus, he was a largish bloke—it would have taken more than one man to do it—what? Why are you smiling like that?"

"I've forgotten how much fun it is to hear you talk shop," said Sparks. "You really are meant for this work, Mike."

"Thanks. You once told me it was the worst pillow talk ever, as I recall."

"I was teasing, and you knew that," said Sparks. "But it's especially nice to hear you talk like that to me now. It makes me feel as if you've forgiven me finally."

"I've put many things behind that were in the past, Sparks," he said. "I'm a married man now, aren't I?"

"You are indeed. And congratulations. How was the wedding?"

"Smallish. Teddy was my best man, both families attended, not too many friends. We honeymooned at Cornwall."

"Never been there, but I hear it's lovely. Well, I should leave you to this. What's next?"

"I'm waiting for the photographer to come back with a picture of his face for me to start showing around," said Kinsey. "Thought I'd start with the staff at the Livingstone Club."

"Why them?"

"Well, he was black, wasn't he? Oh, you didn't see him. Black, looked African to me as opposed to Caribbean or American, although that's as far as my expertise in distinguishing national origins goes. His suit wasn't English-made, although there weren't any labels to say where it came from."

"That's odd. Removed to throw you off?"

"Maybe. So I'll start with the African expats. It's not a large community. Someone might know him. Or at least be able to narrow down where he came from."

"Good luck. I'd best be getting to the office. It was nice to see you, despite the circumstances."

"Yes, it's not the job for casual socialising," he said. "Funny see-

ing you around here. Got me thinking that this is the neighbourhood where that Spanish fellow I had seen you with used to live.
The one who turned up dead in the alley in Brixton."

"Is it?" asked Sparks, willing herself to remain cool. "I never
knew exactly where that was."

"You put things in the past behind, too, eh?"

"I'm working on it. The past is getting bigger all the time."

"That case was never solved," said Mike, giving her a hard look.
"Maybe we'll catch a break in it someday. It's bound to happen."

"It's bound to," she said lightly. "Maybe the murderer will return to the scene of the crime."

"Only the stupid ones do that," he said.

"I wouldn't know. See you around, Detective Sergeant."

"Goodbye, Sparks."

She walked on towards the park, forcing herself not to look back
at him. It wasn't until she made the turn and was safely out of his
sight that she allowed herself to start breathing hard, pausing by
the park fence to hold on to one of the wrought-iron bars until she
could bring her nerves back under control.

It wasn't until she was in Mayfair that she realised she had
never once looked at the damn club.

"Good morning," said Gwen as she came in, unpinning her hat
and placing it on the coatrack by Iris's. "And a happy Friday to
you."

"Is it a happy one for you?" asked Iris. "Tonight's the dinner
party, isn't it?"

"Yes," said Gwen. "Hopefully, the chicken fairy will swoop in
in ample time for Prudence to marinate. Apart from that, all I have
to do is show up in a nice frock, make pretty small talk, and try not
to look as bored as I'll feel."

"Sounds dreadful."

"Are you going out with Archie tonight?"

"No. He has something going on tonight, and I've learned not to ask for details. I'll stay home, wash my hair, and curl up with a book and a tumbler."

Gwen sat down at her desk and glanced at her letters, then placed them back, a troubled look on her face.

"What's bothering you?" asked Iris.

"How do you feel about coincidences?" asked Gwen. "Accidental encounters between people who would be unlikely to meet in a city this large?"

"How on earth did you know?" exclaimed Iris.

"Know what?"

"About my running into— Wait, are you talking about yourself?"

"I was trying to."

"Sorry, sorry, I had a coincidence of my own, coincidentally, but tell me about yours."

"Mr. Daile," said Gwen. "I saw him."

"Where?"

"Clipping a hedge down the block from our home."

"Really? Did you speak to him?"

"Of course. He claimed to be as surprised as I was. He thought I was coming to relay the name of his first date from The Right Sort."

"Maybe we should try that for select clients. Make it part of a deluxe package, complete with heralds with trumpets tootling the news to the lucky recipients."

"We can barely afford a secretary, and you want to bring trumpets into it?"

"We could do it once for a publicity stunt. Invite the press. I think it would be worth the investment."

"I'll think about it," said Gwen. "Here's the problem: I don't think Mr. Daile was telling the truth about why he was there, and that makes twice in two encounters. What's disturbing is that he's now been at both my place of business and my home."

"It's not that much of a stretch. You live in a neighbourhood that has gardens galore."

"I think he's stalking me, Iris."

"Why would he want to do that?"

"That's what troubles me. I can't think of any connection between us, unless it's something to do with my father-in-law."

"He did know about the Bainbridge holdings."

"But Bainbridge, Limited, is a major name in that part of the world. Am I to assume that every African I meet has something to do with Harold?"

"You were looking for possible explanations. That may be one."

"It's my ridiculous upbringing making me like this," said Gwen fretfully. "How long do you think it will be before we get a response from your letter to his university?"

"With luck, maybe Monday or Tuesday. Do you think he's dangerous?"

"I didn't have that sense of him," said Gwen. "Although those shears looked rather menacing. I was quite relieved I wasn't a hedge."

"Very well. Let's keep his marital prospects on hold until we get that letter. Now, I must tell you that I, too, have had a random encounter of cosmic proportions on the way to work this morning. None other than Detective Ex!"

"Really? You ran into Mike Kinsey? Where?"

"He was investigating a murder. The body was found on Morwell Street."

"In Fitzrovia?"

"The same."

"How shocking. Who was killed?"

"They don't know yet. Some poor African fellow—"

She stopped, and they looked at each other.

"You don't suppose—" began Gwen.

"That it was our Mr. Daile?" finished Iris. "That would be stretching coincidence beyond its breaking point."

They looked at each other some more.

"Of course, it wouldn't hurt to call and make sure he's all right," said Gwen, digging through her file box. "I'll get his number."

She handed the card over.

"Odd," Iris said as she dialed. "I have the feeling I know that number from somewhere. Hello? I'm trying to reach Mr. Simon Daile. He gave us this number. Are you his landlady? How do you do? Is he in?"

She listened for a moment while Gwen tried unsuccessfully to pick up the response on the other end of the line.

"He did? Of course, it would be that time. No, it's nothing urgent. Please let him know that Miss Sparks called from the agency with a question. He could call me back on Monday. That's fine. Thank you."

She hung up.

"Well?" asked Gwen.

"Mr. Daile left for work at eight fifteen this morning," she said. "The body I saw was already dead by then."

"I'm glad he's all right," said Gwen with a sigh of relief.

"A minute ago, you thought he was stalking you. Now, you're happy he's alive."

"Apart from the stalking and the lying, he seems a nice enough person," said Gwen. "I certainly don't want to see him dead."

"I may turn an ankle keeping up with all your changes in direction," said Iris. "Silly, us both wondering if it was him. A black man is killed in London, and we automatically wonder if it's the one black man we've met recently."

"Honestly, given our recent history it's refreshing to hear about a murder without us being involved in some fashion," said Gwen.

"Odd that you were in Fitzrovia this morning. Morwell Street. That's behind the Livingstone Club?"

"Yes."

"What prompted you to go there?"

"I decided to take a different route to work for a change," said Iris. "Well, better get started on the day."

That's the second lie she's told me this week, thought Gwen.

But she dropped it and went back to her letters.

CHAPTER 7

Friday afternoons were normally a slow crawl towards the anticipated weekends for the ladies of The Right Sort. This one, however, raced by too quickly for Gwen, who was dreading the evening dinner. Iris, normally a chatterbox, was surprisingly quiet.

"Tomorrow, we paint, and you'll tell me all about it," she said, giving Gwen a quick hug before they parted at the end of the day.

"If I'm still alive, and not in jail," said Gwen.

"If the latter, call me straightaway," said Iris. "If the former—well, tell me anyway."

There was no sign of Mr. Daile when Gwen reached her street. She gave a sigh of relief, then wrestled her conscience two falls out of three over her self-condemnation. Rather than letting herself in through the front door, she walked down the driveway to the delivery entrance and slipped into the kitchen.

Prudence looked up in surprise and momentary fear, then relaxed when she saw who it was.

"Did the delivery come in time?" asked Gwen, feeling as if she were speaking in code.

"It did, bless 'em for being men of their word," said Prudence, stepping back to reveal a large copper roasting pan filled with chickens. "I felt like a criminal. I should have met them at the docks in the dead of night."

"That would have been more appropriate," agreed Gwen. "Has Lord Bainbridge come home?"

"He has, and he's more snappish than ever, if you can imagine such a thing. You'll be lucky he doesn't bite your head clean off."

"Well, if he does, there will be one less place at the table," said Gwen. "Where is Lady Bainbridge?"

"Preparing for dinner," said Prudence with a quick tilt of her hand and head, miming a bottle.

"Oh, dear," sighed Gwen. "I was hoping to get home before she started. I mustn't keep you any longer. Good luck."

"To us all," said Prudence, clasping her hands in front of her in a brief prayer.

Gwen left her and walked to the front of the house, where she heard her son's voice from the direction of the dining room. She found him sitting on a chair, watching intently as Percival operated a metal crank inserted into a mechanism under the long table.

"Hello, my darling boy," she said, crouching by Ronnie's side. "What are we watching?"

"Percival is showing me how he makes the table longer," said Ronnie. "I've never seen it before. Have you?"

He stared in fascination as the two halves of the table were inexorably forced apart, revealing two long, thick metal bars with spiral threading running lengthwise underneath.

"I never have," said Gwen. "It's rather clever. It's like turning a screw, isn't it, Percival?"

"It is, madam," said Percival.

"Is it very difficult to do?" asked Ronnie.

"Would you like to try?" asked Percival, smiling at him.

"May I?"

"If your mother permits."

"Of course, Percival," said Gwen.

"Very well, Master Ronald," said Percival, beckoning to the boy. "It takes two hands. It's rather stiff in its workings, I'm afraid. It's been quite some time since we've had a large enough party to require extending it. Fortunately, we will only need room enough for the one leaf. Put your hands on each end—perfect. Now, turn it anticlockwise."

Ronnie exerted his full strength on the handles of the crank, as if he were opening a hatch in the hull of a submarine. Slowly, the gap in the table expanded by another inch.

"I did it!" he crowed.

"Well done!" applauded his mother. "How strong you are getting!"

"Would you like to do some more?" asked Percival. "I would be grateful for your assistance."

"Oh, yes!" said Ronnie, grunting with the effort.

Percival glanced at Gwen and nodded slightly to his right. Curious, she joined him in the corner of the room while he watched Ronnie work.

"I had to retrieve the table leaf from where it was stored, Mrs. Bainbridge," he said significantly.

"Oh?" replied Gwen. "Where was that?"

"In the attic," said Percival.

"Ah."

"Where I noticed something unusual."

"Did you?"

"Yes, Mrs. Bainbridge," he said. "Your late husband's old heavy bag had somehow gotten up from where it had been stowed and tied itself to a post."

"My goodness."

"This sheds some light on some peculiar noises reported by the staff."

"Really? What noises?"

"Priscilla thought some large animal had got in there, and was prowling around. Nell, being a more impressionable woman than perhaps would be practical for service, is convinced that we have a ghost. Do you have any opinions on the matter, Mrs. Bainbridge?"

"I would say Priscilla is closer to the mark than Nell," said Gwen.

"I agree," said Percival. "May I reassure them that there is nothing to worry about?"

"I would be grateful if you did, Percival."

"And, in exchange, would you accept my taking the occasional turn during my free moments?" asked Percival. "I used to box in my younger days. I could use the exercise."

"Of course, Percival," said Gwen. "I am glad that that poor, abandoned thing has been restored to its rightful purpose."

"Indeed, Mrs. Bainbridge."

"While I have you here, Percival, could you tell me the guest list for tonight? I need to know what conversation to prepare. And avoid."

"Of course, Mrs. Bainbridge. Most of them are from the board of directors for Bainbridge, Limited. Lord Morrison, Otis Burleigh, Alexander Birch, Hilary McIntyre, and Townsend Phillips. Mr. Burleigh's son, Stephen will be attending, and a gentleman with whom I am not familiar, Walter Prendergast."

"So munitions, railways, and copper," said Gwen. "And nod politely during the ranting about Atlee."

"I think you are on the right track, Mrs. Bainbridge," he said. "Very good, Master Ronald, I think that should be enough. Let's put the leaf in and close it up again. Will you grab that other end for me?"

Ronnie, flushed with the triumph of his efforts, ran eagerly to take one end of the leaf. Percival took the other.

"One, two, three," said the butler, and the two heaved it up.

"It's heavy," panted Ronnie. "I don't know if I can hold it for very long."

"Allow me," said Percival, sliding one hand towards the middle of the leaf.

He lifted it effortlessly from the boy's grasp and lowered it into the center of the table, sliding it until the edges lined up.

"Now, do you think you can turn the crank the other way until the pieces meet up?"

"Oh, yes," said Ronnie, scooting under the table.

"Ronnie, when you're finished, go find Agnes," said Gwen. "I am going up to dress for dinner. And don't forget to thank Percival."

"Thank you, Percival," came Ronnie's voice from under the table as the ends began to close on the leaf.

"You're very welcome, young sir," said Percival with a smile. "And thank you for all that you've done."

"You're welcome."

"My thanks as well, Percival," said Gwen.

"Always a pleasure, Mrs. Bainbridge," said Percival.

I never knew how strong Percival was, she thought as she went upstairs to change.

She made her selection carefully. Something to look nice in for the male assemblage, but not so much that she was showing off. She especially had to make certain that she wouldn't outshine Carolyne. She ended up choosing a light blue gown with chiffon sleeves that puffed up over her shoulders, and augmented it with a double strand of pearls which Carolyne had given her for her first birthday after the wedding. She thought it would send a message of support to her beleaguered mother-in-law.

She knocked on Lady Bainbridge's door before going downstairs. Her mother-in-law opened it and immediately assessed Gwen's wardrobe.

"That will do," Lady Bainbridge said, approving without smiling. She was wearing her silk kimono while Millie hovered behind her, powder puff at the ready. If the layers of makeup were any indication, Carolyne was halfway to grand dragon mode.

Gwen caught a whiff of sherry, but gave no indication that any-thing was unusual about that. And nothing was, considering.

"I thought I would go down to be available to greet our guests," said Gwen. "Is there anything you need?"

"Explosives would be thoughtful," said Lady Bainbridge.

"Don't go turning into Guy Fawkes," said Gwen. "Prudence has been working very hard to prepare this dinner. We wouldn't want to disappoint her by blowing up the place before the main course."

"Very well," said Lady Bainbridge. "I will behave for Prudence's sake. I will come down in due course. At least there will be none of those vapid tittering wives to contend with."

"Small consolation, but consolation nevertheless," agreed Gwen. "I will see you downstairs, Carolyne."

And make a good entrance, she added silently.

She descended to find her father-in-law pacing the foyer, a tum-bler in his hand. He glanced up at her irritably, giving her frock a cursory glance and nod.

"I expected you five minutes ago," he said.

"Has anyone arrived?"

"No, but they should be here shortly."

"Is there anything you wish to say to me beforehand?"

"Don't bring up that wretched business of yours," he said. "I won't have the dinner conversation bogged down by trivialities."

At least he's calling it a business, she thought, nettled.

She went into the front parlour where a small bar had been set up, a footman hired for the evening standing at the ready behind it.

"May I offer you anything, madam?" he asked.

She was tempted to dive right into a gin and tonic, but shook her head. It was going to be a very long evening, and she needed to pace herself.

The bell rang, and Lord Bainbridge strode into the room to stand imperiously by the fireplace. Gwen stood at the other side, her hands folded in front of her.

Percival answered the door, then appeared at the parlour entrance.

"Lord Morrison, milord," he said.

Thomas Morrison was her father-in-law's oldest friend, and second to him in power at Bainbridge, Limited. Gwen smiled as he strode into the room, as energetic a man at sixty-five as any of her friends in their twenties, his hair still mostly black, graying at the sides. He was wearing an evening jacket that fit him more snugly at the waist than it should have, but he looked ready to take the dance floor for anything, provided the music predated the Great War.

"Harold, m'boy!" he boomed, stepping up to seize Lord Bainbridge's hand. "You've had some time in the sun, I see! Thought you had left the prospecting to the younger set after all these years! Gwendolyn, you are as lovely as ever."

"Thank you, Lord Morrison," she said. "It is good to see you again."

"Glad to see you out and about, eh?" he replied. "She looks the very peak, doesn't she, Harold? I say, that rest did you wonders."

Rest, she thought. Is that what they're calling it?

"I needed it," she said. "Things had got quite exhausting."

"Well, we expect to see you making the rounds again, m'dear," he said. "Too much light to be under a bushel, eh?"

"You're too kind," she said.

I've been out and about for nearly a year, she thought. Thanks for noticing.

"Mr. Otis Burleigh and Mr. Stephen Burleigh," Percival announced as two more guests entered the room.

"Good evening, Harold," said the elder Burleigh, a portly, florid man in his late fifties. "You know my son, of course."

"Of course," said Lord Bainbridge, shaking their hands. "Good to see you again, lad. Glad you made it home safe."

"Thank you, Lord Bainbridge," said the younger Burleigh.

A more pronounced contrast could not have been made between father and son, thought Gwen. The younger was lean as a whippet. Not bad-looking. Nice brown hair and quite a decent mustache. He was tanned, almost weathered, and his eyes were older than his face, something she saw regularly in the young men who had been away for the duration of the war.

He turned to face her, and the eyes grew young again.

"A privilege to see you again, Mrs. Bainbridge," he said, taking her hand between his. "We met briefly at your wedding, although I doubt you would remember me with all of the guests. Weddings are so overwhelming, aren't they? I have never really had the pleasure of knowing you, but I knew Ronnie growing up. I was so sorry to hear about him. He was the very best of men. I hope you have recovered."

"I have, thank you," said Gwen. "Not fully, perhaps never fully, but I can face the world, more or less."

"The world is fortunate to have you back in it," he said.

"Mr. Alexander Birch and Mr. Hilary McIntyre," announced Percival.

"You must greet your guests," said Stephen, releasing her hand. "I hope we shall speak more tonight."

"I would be delighted," said Gwen, finding to her surprise that she meant it.

And he's not wearing a ring, she thought.

As she turned to greet the new arrivals, she noticed Lord Bainbridge watching her. She looked away immediately.

She tried and failed to pick Stephen Burleigh's face out from the sea of happiness that floated through her memories of her wedding. She thought she would pore over the album later.

Lord. It had been ages since she had done that. Would she be able to handle it?

Someone was saying something to her.

"I beg your pardon," she said. "I was somewhere else for a moment."

"I was saying nice to meet you," said a man she didn't know. "Prendergast. Walter Prendergast."

He fell in age somewhere between the board members and the younger Burleigh, a powerfully built man with a craggy face, with a robust, full brown beard and leaden grey eyes that at the moment were giving her an up-and-down assessment that was brutal in its directness.

"How do you do, Mr. Prendergast?" she replied, shaking his hand. "Mrs. Gwendolyn Bainbridge."

"Knew that," he said. "You're too young to be the wife. Though there's plenty of girls your age who've roped in older fools."

"Those women may prove to be the foolish ones in the long run," she said.

"Depends on the girl," he said. "Perfectly rational financial decision. Decide you're in it for the money, and you won't be disappointed as long as the money holds out. It's the ones who go in for love who wind up miserable."

"You've never been married, I take it," she said.

"I haven't turned fool yet," he said. "You're not drinking. What would you like?"

Might as well get started, she thought.

"A gin and tonic, please," she replied.

"Be right back."

She watched him walk to the bar. Something about his mien made the hired footman snap to attention as he took his order. She glanced around the room to see her father-in-law watching her keenly, then Prendergast recaptured her attention as he returned with her drink.

"Cheers," he said as he handed it to her and raised his own glass.

"Cheers," she replied. "What are you drinking?"

"Water," he said. "Like to keep my wits about me in a strange home. You'd rather dull yours down, I see."

"It's a social occasion. I don't need to be on guard here."

"Is that so?" he asked. "Home is where you need to be on guard the most, in my experience."

You are not wrong, she thought.

"You're the one who was 'away,' aren't you?" he asked abruptly.

"Meaning?" she asked, flustered by the direct question.

"Meaning 'away,' for a vague and mysterious purpose," he said. "Usually when the aristocracy uses the word, it's prison, an asylum, or off having the wrong man's baby. Which was it for you? You don't seem the convict type."

"You see, that's where you're wrong," said Gwen. "I was in prison."

"Were you?" he asked, his eyes widening. "For what?"

"I killed a man," she replied coolly.

"Why?"

"For asking too many personal questions," she said. "I must attend to our other guests. Enjoy your dinner."

She left him as he guffawed in appreciation.

Townsend Phillips was the last to arrive as apparently was usual for him, given the good-natured gibes of the others. He was in the midst of profuse apologies to Lord Bainbridge when Percival appeared in the doorway and cleared his throat. The assemblage turned to face him.

"Lady Carolyne Bainbridge," he said, and she stepped into the doorway, pausing to take in the room and to allow the room to take her in as well.

Millie had brought some measure of restraint to the makeup, which was now starkly dramatic without succumbing to the macabre. Lady Bainbridge wore a dark green brocaded jacket over a lighter green silk gown with a triple rope of pearls linked by an oblong piece of jade set in silver filigree. Despite the smallness of the gathering, she chose to wear a tiara which continued the green theme with emeralds alternating with diamonds.

And that's her second-best tiara, thought Gwen, mentally applauding her mother-in-law. Only she, her husband, and I know that, but she's letting him know that she's not making the top-drawer effort for this lot.

"Gentlemen, welcome to our home," she said with a grand outward gesture of her arms. "It is wonderful to have us all back together."

"Carolyne, you look positively ravishing," said Lord Morrison, stepping forward to kiss her hand. "As lovely as the day we first met."

"You are as incapable of seeing reality as ever, Tom," said Lady Bainbridge. "Which is why you will always be welcome here."

A lesser woman might have simpered, thought Gwen, watching with reluctant admiration as Lady Bainbridge made the rounds of greetings. Even Prendergast seemed impressed with the performance, bowing from the waist upon their introduction.

A muted gong sounded from the dining room.

"To dinner, gentlemen," she said. "Tom, would you do me the honour?"

"Of course," said Lord Morrison, offering his arm.

The older Burleigh offered his to Gwen, and they walked through to the dining room.

"My first chance to speak with you," he murmured. "Lucky to be next in seniority for a change. Not enough ladies to go around."

"I would have wished for more," said Gwen. "How is your wife?"

"Taken to bed with a cold, unfortunately," he said.

"Then we've spared her a night of social misery," said Gwen. "Please give her my best wishes for a speedy recovery."

"I will do so."

"How is business?"

"Oh, I don't want to bore you with that," he said with a rueful smile.

"On the contrary, I have taken an interest in business affairs lately," she said. "Now that my father-in-law has returned, I expect to hear much more about them."

"Has he spoken about his trip?" asked Burleigh.

"Not much," said Gwen. "He's been off to his club practically every evening."

"Has he? Well, that's Harold for you," said Burleigh, chuckling. "And here we are. Looks like I'll be sitting next to you. I hope I prove to be less of a bore than usual."

"Don't be silly," said Gwen. "I am delighted to have your company, Mr. Burleigh."

She stood at her place between Burleigh and, to her slight dismay, Mr. Prendergast, and waited for Lady Bainbridge to be seated. Then they took their seats.

Given the imbalance of the sexes, Gwen was placed in the middle of the side by the windows, opposite her mother-in-law. Lord Bainbridge presided at the head of the table.

Percival and the hired footman circled the table, pouring the first round of wine. Then Lord Bainbridge stood, his glass raised.

"Gentlemen, I lift a glass to our good fortune," he said. "To the survival, nay, the flourishing of Bainbridge, Limited, after a long period of global distress. To peace, but not so much of it that we don't continue our lucrative relationship with His Majesty's armed forces."

"To Bainbridge, Limited, and Lord Bainbridge!" echoed Lord Morrison.

"To Bainbridge, Limited!" the men joined in.

Gwen did not add her voice to that toast. Noticeably, neither did Lady Bainbridge.

If this were one of those mystery movies from the thirties, mused Gwen, the murder would happen now. A toast replete with hidden meanings, the downing of the wine, then the headlong collapse onto the table, surrounded by suspects. She took a cautious sip from her glass, casting a glance at her father-in-law as he drank his.

Lord Bainbridge survived the toast. So did everyone else.

Perhaps the soup will do him in, she thought as it was served, trying not to be too hopeful about it.

"You were married to the son," said Prendergast.

Gwen, in mid-spoonful, managed not to choke before dabbing at her mouth with her napkin.

"Yes," she said. "Ronald Bainbridge."

"Who was an only child."

"Yes."

"So your boy will be the next Lord Bainbridge," he concluded.

"God willing, and in the fullness of time," she replied. "We're none of us in any hurry for that to happen. Little Ronnie is six."

"You, on the other hand, are a grown woman."

"Your powers of observation do you credit, Mr. Prendergast," she said, letting a hint of acid seep into her tone.

"So why are you never at the board meetings?" he asked.

"I beg your pardon?" she said, startled.

"Your husband's dead, presumably you inherited," said Prendergast. "Your husband got hold of a share equal to his father's when he inherited his uncle's share. Unless he passed it directly on to your child, and I doubt he was thoughtless enough to do so, you now own that share. So why are you never at the meetings?"

"I believe there is a representative—"

"That Parson fellow. I know the man. A spineless worm. He reports to you, does he?"

"Well—"

"Didn't think so. Don't understand that one bit. You, unlike him, have a spine, from what little I have observed tonight. So I ask you again, why haven't you—"

"Walter, stop pestering the poor girl," said Burleigh from her right. "This is a dinner party, not a deposition."

"The problem is I don't know what I'm getting into," said Prendergast, undeterred. "I know about you, Burleigh. I know about Bainbridge, and Morrison, and the rest of you, but I don't know about her. They've kept her out of sight, which is why I came tonight. I wanted to see where she fits into all of this."

"She is sitting next to you," said Gwen quietly. "She will decide where she fits in due course, but she is not interested in discussing it in present company."

"The present company is also the company," said Prendergast. "You don't know what you're—"

"Walter, she said she isn't discussing it," said Burleigh sharply. "I know that you think your lack of social standing gives you the freedom to exhibit poor behaviour in decent society, but good manners are good manners, even for people of your upbringing."

"Oh, I know all about behaviour, and manners, and society, Burleigh," said Prendergast. "I might be purchasing a title one of these days, and the manners and the manor to go with it. Then you may come sup with me."

"If I accept your invitation, and it is highly unlikely that I shall, then you may speak to a lady however you like in your mythical palace," said Burleigh. "But you will not be rude to one in my presence. Now, finish your soup and try not to slurp while you do so."

Prendergast, with an exaggerated gesture, brought a spoonful to his mouth and ate it silently.

"You'll forgive me if I direct my conversation to Mr. Burleigh for the moment," said Gwen sweetly.

"Do what you like," said Prendergast.

"This is proving to be a strained evening," she said to Burleigh. "I am very glad you are sitting with me."

"The pleasure is mine," he said. "Although I would have preferred for Stephen's sake that they had placed the two of you together."

"Are you looking to pair us up, Mr. Burleigh?"

"I'm always looking to pair him up, as any good parent would," said Burleigh. "But he's been in the doldrums ever since—well, he had a rough go of it during the war, and a sympathetic ear from a lovely woman will always lighten the burden."

"I'll be sure to pay him some attention after dinner," said Gwen.

"I would be grateful. And you needn't concern yourself with my attempts at matchmaking. I understand you've become quite the expert on that."

"Professionally speaking, I have," said Gwen. "But I'd rather talk of your business than mine."

They were interrupted as the chickens, having traveled from parts unknown by means clandestine, finally reached their ultimate destination.

Perhaps it will be now, Gwen thought idly, glancing at her father-in-law as he dug in. The vengeance of Prudence!

But the main course followed its predecessors at the table into the collective maw of Bainbridge, Limited, and guests with no discernible homicidal effect. Quite the contrary, given their reception.

"Truly marvelous chicken Provençal," enthused Birch. "As good as what they serve at Au Petit Savoyard."

"I agree," said Phillips. "My compliments to your cook. How on earth did you manage to get so much chicken of this quality?"

"Ask me no questions and I'll tell you no lies," laughed Lord Bainbridge. "I engaged in some, shall we say, unsanctioned transactions. When it comes to my friends, gentlemen, I will neither admit to any obstacle nor spare any expense."

Swine, thought Gwen contemptuously. Taking credit where none was due. She was of a mind to reveal the true source of the main course, but held her tongue.

Electrocution! That would be the most suitable method for the head of Bainbridge, Limited. A clever arrangement of wires, and somewhere under the table, a hidden button would be pressed, a hideous buzzing sound would be heard, sparks flying everywhere—

"You're off into the ether again, Mrs. Bainbridge," commented Prendergast.

"I was musing on all of the interesting uses to which copper may be put," said Gwen. "Appropriate for this gathering, don't you think?"

"What was that bit about matchmaking?"

"A sideline of mine. Nothing that would interest you. Tell me, Mr. Prendergast—what is your connection to the present company? I've not heard your name before."

"I'm a man with money who's looking to make more," he replied. "I'm looking into diversification. Munitions are a growth market. Things that explode will always be valued."

"As my husband found out to his everlasting detriment," said Gwen. "Or were you already aware of that?"

He had the good grace to look stricken.

"Forgive me," he said, his tone subdued for the first time. "I didn't know the details. All I knew was that he died in combat. I don't mean to make light of it."

"The circumstances of his death might even have been considered retribution of sorts," she continued. "I've sometimes considered that, and wondered if his father ever made that connection."

"Lord Bainbridge never discussed him?"

"Not with me," said Gwen. "Well, this is not the best topic for a dinner party. Let's see: Hobbies? Sports? Films? Music?"

"None, no, no and no," he replied.

"So it's all about finances with you," she said. "How very single-minded."

The plates were cleared.

"Harold, did you hear about the poor fellow at the Livingstone Club?" asked Birch.

"I did," said Lord Bainbridge curtly. "And he wasn't at the club, Sandy."

"Well, behind it, then," said Birch.

"What's this?" asked McIntyre.

"They found a body in the alley, or somewhere," said Birch. "Someone shot him. Thought he might have been one of the staff."

"How horrid!" exclaimed Lady Bainbridge.

"He wasn't one of the staff," snapped Lord Bainbridge. "What does it matter where he was found?"

Why is he so upset? wondered Gwen. Just because a random event might cast aspersions on his beloved club?

Lord Bainbridge caught her looking at him and immediately brought his expression into something more bland.

"Maybe you should set your daughter-in-law on the case," said Phillips, noticing the exchange of glances.

"Why her?" asked Prendergast, looking at her curiously.

"Well, she solved a murder, didn't she?" replied Phillips with a high whinny of a laugh.

"What on earth do you mean by that?"

"A month or so ago, wasn't it, Mrs. Bainbridge?"

"Yes," said Gwen. "I prefer not to discuss it."

"I'd like to hear more," said Prendergast.

"It's not an acceptable discussion for the dinner table," said Gwen.

"I agree," said Lord Bainbridge. "Nor is this murder. It had nothing to do with the club other than coincidental proximity. Let's move on to happier topics."

She was grateful for the change. She sat back and listened as Lord Morrison recounted the old story of his and Lord Bainbridge's first time in Africa together.

"Thought it would be a lark when we went, didn't we, Harold?" he said. "A boys' adventure, right out of university. I was miserable from the start, but you took to it like the proverbial duck, didn't you? Clumping about in the wilds for weeks at a time while I sat in the one bar that had a working generator and an ice machine they had humped over God knows how many miles of muddy road. Of course, I picked up something from the ice, young fool that I was. Your insides were made of sterner stuff."

"I caught my share," said Lord Bainbridge. "I just didn't mewl about it the way you did."

"Or you did, but no one could hear it over my piteous cries," said Morrison, laughing. "So, there I lay in a cheap room with mosquito netting so tattered a vulture could have flown through to peck at my near-corpse, and in dashes one of the boys you had taken when you went off exploring. Didn't speak a word of English, and I hadn't the foggiest notion of what fool language he was rattling off, but I caught the word 'Harold,' so I motioned for him to calm down. He takes a deep breath and says something that almost sounded like English. He kept repeating it, and I finally sorted it out. 'Green rocks,' he was saying. And then he pulls a stone out of his pocket with glorious veins of malachite ore running through it. Turned out to be the biggest copper find since Davey stumbled onto Broken Hill."

"Pure luck," said Lord Bainbridge. "Had to make certain the locals weren't seeding the area with the rocks to lure in English money. But they were oblivious to what lay under their feet. We were able to peg that area for a song."

He always looked so wistful when that story was told, thought Gwen. Nothing else brought that expression to his face. It must have been the happiest time of his life. And it was forty years ago.

She often wondered if her happiest times were all behind her. Then she remembered her son, and smiled.

A sorbet was served for dessert, and then Lord Bainbridge rose.

"Gentlemen, I invite you to join me in the library. I have brought back cigars cured and rolled at the family plantation, with some brandy that I think you will appreciate. My dear, I beg your indulgence for abandoning you."

"I am happy to escape the smoke," said Lady Bainbridge. "I bid you good evening, gentlemen. Please keep the windows open, Harold."

"I will," he promised.

Gwen followed the gathering out, then stopped as someone tapped her on the shoulder. It was Stephen Burleigh.

"I am begging you as the only other young person here, please keep me out of that library," he whispered.

"Follow me," she whispered back.

She led him to the front parlour, where they sat on a sofa together. Percival being occupied in the library, it was left to the hired footman to look after him. After bringing them two glasses of cordial, he retreated a discreet distance away.

"You don't look much like your father," commented Gwen. "I've been trying to summon up your image from my memories of the wedding, but without success."

"I used to look very like him," said Stephen.

"But he's so—stout."

"Downright rotund," he said, grinning. "As was I back then."

"Were you? One would never suspect it."

"Well," he said, sipping his cordial, "four years in a Japanese prison camp and two with malaria will have that effect."

"Oh, my God," she said. "Forgive me. I had no idea."

"Nothing to forgive, Mrs. Bainbridge," he said. "I was one of the lucky ones. I made it out."

"Are you enjoying yourself tonight?" she asked. "Is that even a thing one can ask?"

"There are moments," he replied. "I'm getting myself used to all this again."

"What's the hardest part?"

"The chatter," he said. "It all sounds so meaningless. I have no idea if any of them has any genuine feelings for each other, except for Morrison and your father-in-law. They go back."

"How long have you been back in London?"

"A month," he said. "Caught a transport back from Burma the moment I was well enough to stagger from the infirmary on my own two feet."

She put her hand on his for a moment. He shivered at the touch, then smiled quickly to cover his embarrassment.

"So sorry," he said. "I can't always control my reactions nowadays."

"Quite all right," she assured him. "Was that where you spent your war? In Burma?"

"Yes. Got caught by the Japs in the retreat when they blew up the only bridge on our escape route, and that was the end of my war. Strange to be back in London, seeing all the people going about their normal business, walking by the gaping holes where the bombs hit without even looking."

"What do you intend to do?"

"Oh, Father is grooming me to take his place on the board at Bainbridge," he said. "I suppose I'll have to. Can't think of anything more tedious, unless it's hearing him talk about it."

"I think he's rather nice," said Gwen.

"He's all right," Stephen conceded. "Incessant droning on about money, copper, guns, and so forth, when he's not reminiscing about big-game hunting. He wants me to take over so he can trot off to Kenya and bag another lion because the billiards room doesn't have one yet."

"I am sure you'll be a worthy addition to the board," said Gwen.

"Well, I'm much happier sitting here with you, Mrs. Bainbridge," he said. "So much nicer than being in a meeting with that lot."

"Meeting? What meeting?"

"It's an informal board thing tonight," said Stephen. "I cannot tell you how happy I was to see you here. At least there would be one person I could—"

"I'm sorry," said Gwen, rising to her feet. "I think I need to see what's going on."

"What?" he exclaimed, following her. "I don't understand. Can't we just—"

She walked rapidly through the house to the library door, which was closed. There were muffled male voices on the other side, and the telltale aroma of cigar smoke was already seeping into the hallway.

Without bothering to knock, Gwen opened the door and entered the library. The men were standing down at one end by a sideboard with a crystal decanter of brandy, puffing away while gesticulating with their free hands.

". . . and that note is coming due," Prendergast was saying. "I want to know—"

He stopped as he noticed the others staring at Gwen. He turned to look at her, his expression a mixture of surprise and appreciativeness.

"Forgive the intrusion, gentlemen," she said, forcing herself to keep her voice from shaking. "I understand that this is a board meeting. As a principal shareholder, I should like to be present."

There was a pause, then Lord Bainbridge stepped forward.

"I would like to speak with you outside," he said quietly.

"But—"

"Now."

Something in his expression made her blench. He nodded towards the door, and she retreated into the hallway. He followed her, then saw Stephen standing there, looking aghast.

"Inside," ordered Lord Bainbridge.

"But—" protested Stephen.

"Not a word more," said Lord Bainbridge.

Stephen gave Gwen a sympathetic but helpless glance, then went into the library. Lord Bainbridge closed the door behind him, then turned back to Gwen, his face livid.

"How dare you embarrass me like that in front of the board," he said hoarsely. "What did you think you were doing?"

"I have a right—"

"No," he interrupted. "You do not have any rights here. You have a legal guardian who sees to your rights, and he, in your interests and more importantly for the protection of my grandson, has ceded all financial matters to me. I am in charge of your rights, and I will not have you traipsing into territories you don't understand and are not qualified to handle. You have no rights in this company or in this family that do not belong to me, and I will deal with them as I think is best. Now, unless you want to be thrown out of this house and go slinking back to live with your brother in Tewkesbury, I strongly recommend that you end this reckless behaviour. I will give your apologies to our guests. Good night."

With that, he went back into the library, shutting the door in her face, leaving only the traces of cigar smoke in his wake.

CHAPTER 8

"He did what?" exclaimed Iris as they went down to the basement.

"He threatened to throw me out of the house," said Gwen.

"Can he do that? Legally?"

"I don't know. I suppose he can, as long as they have custody of Ronnie."

Iris sorted through several keys on a ring, selected one and opened the door to the storeroom. Gwen, who by now was entirely accustomed to Iris having keys she shouldn't have, merely peered over her shoulder into the gloom.

"How Mr. MacPherson ever finds things in this mess, I'll never know," she commented. "We should clean it up and organise it sometime when he isn't around. He'll think it was the fairies."

"Then he'd never be able to find anything in here again," said Iris as she pulled the chain for the overhead bulb. "Ah. There it is. Grab the other end, would you?"

They carefully eased a stepladder from its resting place between stacks of decaying cardboard boxes and carried it out.

"I am impressed that you went in there in the first place," said Iris as they went up the flights of steps to their office. "Unusually confrontational for you."

"Dr. Milford will have a high old time with it," said Gwen. "I owe it to having you as an examplar in my life."

"How much of Bainbridge, Limited, do you own?"

"I don't know."

"Why not?"

"Because Ronnie and I never discussed the details," said Gwen. "And when—"

She stopped. Iris looked back down the rungs of the ladder to see her friend fighting back tears.

"Ronnie was killed, I was sent to hospital, then to the sanatorium," said Gwen, speaking as calmly as she could. "I wasn't present for the reading of the will, and when I finally was released and met with Mr. Parson, I was still on a chemical cosh and not really absorbing the details of whatever perfunctory explanation he gave me. And I was primarily concerned with my son."

"But since then—"

"Since then, I've spent so much time trying to regain control of my life that I've never really looked at what I was getting control of. I tried to speak with Mr. Parson again, but he won't give me the pleasure of an audience until the court deems me competent."

"It keeps coming back to that, doesn't it? All right, we're here."

She unlocked the door to their office, then they brought the ladder in. They had already brought in the paint cans, rollers, brushes, and drop cloths. There was the right wall to do, and the side of the front wall to the right of the doorway.

"I need to get my painting togs on," said Gwen, picking up a small valise from the table. "Oh, my son will be joining us for an hour."

"Will he? How delightful! How did you get the in-laws to agree to that?"

"They don't know," said Gwen. "Agnes is taking him to the zoo, but she needed some time to sign up with a placement agency."

"Maybe he could help us."

"I've packed his smock, just in case," said Gwen. "Be right back."

Iris spread the drop cloths at the base of the walls, then draped another over her desk. As she did, she heard the rapid clattering of small feet running up the stairs, followed by a more measured set. A moment later, Ronnie burst through the doorway.

"Hello, Iris!" he cried in delight.

"Hello, my favourite young man in all of London," she replied, coming over to shake his hand. "Welcome to The Right Sort Marriage Bureau."

Agnes appeared behind him, looking frazzled.

"I wasn't expecting so many steps," she gasped.

"You get used to them," said Iris. "Mrs. Bainbridge is changing. If you are satisfied with my bona fides, I will happily watch Ronnie for the next few minutes so you can go."

"Thank you so much," said Agnes. "I'll be back within the hour. Ronnie, don't you get one speck of paint on yourself, all right?"

"Yes, Agnes," promised Ronnie.

She smiled anxiously, then took a deep breath and began the return trip to the street.

"Well, now that you're here, let me give you the grand tour," said Iris. "This is where Mummy and I work. That's her desk."

"It's enormous!" said Ronnie, staring at the massive mahogany partner's desk, one of a matched pair that were already in the office when the two women expanded the business.

"It is," she agreed. "I have one just like it hiding under that drop cloth. We think they've been here since the beginning of time. They probably had to construct the building around them."

"There's my picture!" he exclaimed excitedly, pointing to a crayon drawing in a frame on the wall by his mother's desk. In it, a narwhal in a top hat was sitting in a theatre, watching a yellow-haired woman on a stage playing Puss in Boots.

"Indeed it is," said Iris. "Sir Oswald the Narwhal at a panto, I understand. I adore that picture. I'll have you know that you are the only artist we have hanging on these walls."

"Gosh!"

"Now, come with me and I will show you the other office."

She led him out into the hallway to their original room. There was only one desk in it, the one with the four rickety legs that had been Iris's when they had started up, but was now where Mrs. Billington held sway. Gwen's desk, which had been missing a leg, had been sold to a used furniture shop, and the copy of *The Forsyte Saga* which had propped it up had been returned to the Bainbridge family library from whence it had been appropriated for that more useful purpose. A decent leather sofa sat by one wall, with side tables laden with magazines at both ends. Framed photographs of wedding couples alongside newspaper announcements hung on the walls, along with testimonials from the happy clients.

"Those are all people who have gotten married because we introduced them to each other," said Iris.

"That's nice," said Ronnie, who was more interested in inspecting the wall itself. "Did you and Mum paint this room, too?"

"Yes. Why?"

"You did a better job in the other one," he pronounced.

"We're getting better at it," said Iris.

They went back to the newer office. Gwen had returned, wearing a pair of grey overalls over an old muslin blouse that was permanently splattered with green paint. She had wrapped a scarf around her hair to protect it.

"Well, my darling boy, how do I look?" she said, twirling.

"Like a man," he said. "I've never seen you wear pants."

"It's very Katharine Hepburn," said Iris.

"Except she wears stylish lady's trousers, and I look like someone ready to paint an office," said Gwen. "Ronnie, why don't you sit at Mummy's desk and draw while Iris and Mummy set up? You may put your smock on and help when we're ready."

"All right," said Ronnie, retrieving his knapsack.

He climbed onto Gwen's chair and removed a drawing pad and a small box of Atlas Crayons. He spilled its contents onto the blotter, then opened up his pad.

"I'm going to make a picture for Iris," he announced.

"Hooray!" exclaimed Iris. "I can't wait to see it. Is that a new box of crayons?"

"Yes," he said. "Grandfather bought them for me."

He stared at the eight crayons, his brow furrowed in concentration. Then he selected the black one and went to work. Iris turned to see Gwen watching her son with a beatific expression that almost glowed from within.

"I'll take right, you take left," said Iris, pouring the paint into a pair of roller trays.

They began with the corners, edging them neatly with the brushes, taking turns with the stepladder.

"It would make sense for me to do the top edge and you the bottom," said Gwen.

"You never miss an opportunity to bring up the height difference, do you?"

"You are both tiny creatures, and should not be making comparisons," said Sally's voice from the doorway.

Ronnie looked up from the desk, and his eyes grew big. They had to for him to take in the enormity of the man filling the doorway.

"Sally!" said Gwen in surprise. "How wonderful! What brings you here today?"

"Rumour has it that you were forced to resort to manual labour," he said, coming into the office. "I came to spectate and make helpful comments from across the room. And to bring you sustenance."

He held up a bag from which the smell of freshly baked crumpets wafted to mingle with the paint fumes.

"You are a dear," said Gwen. "Sally, I don't believe you've met my son, Ronnie."

"I don't believe I have," said Sally, walking towards Iris with his hand proffered. "How do you do? Delighted to make your acquaintance."

"She meant me," squealed Ronnie, giggling.

"Well, of course she did," said Sally, turning to peer at him like he was a specimen in a case. "That makes so much more sense. I'm Salvatore Danielli, but call me Sally."

"Hello. I'm Ronnie."

They shook hands solemnly.

"You're the biggest man I've even seen!" said Ronnie, looking up at him in awe.

"Ronnie," protested his mother. "That's not polite."

"No, no, he speaks the truth," said Sally. "The truth should always be spoken by children. Yes, I am the biggest man you've ever seen. The interesting thing is I am not the biggest man I have ever seen."

"There are bigger?"

"Oh, yes," said Sally. "Even in England. Well, Scotland. I once met a fellow there who was seven foot eight. He had to go outside to change his hat."

"Wow!" said Ronnie. "Is it fun being so tall?"

"Fun," Sally repeated thoughtfully. "Such an interesting question. There are times when it's fun, and times when it's an inconvenience. Do you know what I've never been able to do?"

"What?" asked Ronnie.

"Touch the ceiling," said Sally, reaching up and missing by six inches. "But I bet you can."

"How can I when I'm shorter than you?" asked Ronnie.

"May I?" asked Sally, glancing at Gwen.

"Of course."

Sally squatted down, put his hands on Ronnie's waist, and lifted him into the air.

"Reach for the skies, pardner!" he said, and Ronnie raised his arms up until he could press both palms against the ceiling.

"I did it!" he shouted in glee.

"Nicely done," said Sally, putting him back down. "Now, show me what you're working on. Is that the legendary Sir Oswald?"

"Yes."

"I thought so. What dangerous adventure is he up to this time?"

"He's getting married," said Ronnie, pointing to what was clearly meant to be a little church, outside of which stood a narwhal wearing a top hat and somehow holding a bouquet of flowers.

"No adventure more dangerous than that," said Sally, pulling up Iris's chair and sitting next to him. "That's why we cowardly men come to your mother to arrange it. Have a crumpet, miniature human, and tell me all about Sir Oswald. Who is he going to marry?"

"Iris," said Ronnie, grabbing a brown crayon. "I'm going to make her hair first."

"Congratulations!" Sally said to Iris. "Start those swimming lessons right away. He'll want you to live in his underwater palace."

"I'll strap a sword to my nose," said Iris. "I want to fit in with the family."

"Are you married?" Ronnie asked Sally.

"I am not," said Sally.

"Why not?"

"Don't pester people about marriage, Ronnie," said Gwen. "You know better."

"Would she have to be tall like you?" asked Ronnie, ignoring her.

"Not at all," said Sally. "Any height will do, so long as she loves me and I love her."

"I told you to stop, Ronnie," repeated Gwen with a touch more steel in her voice. "Now, you'd best finish your drawing before Agnes gets back."

He did, and the grown-ups pronounced it wonderful. Then he donned his smock, took off his shoes and socks, and was allowed to daub the center of the wall while the ladies took a crumpet break.

"Such a pleasure to watch a real artist at work," Sally commented. "He's doing a better job than both of you."

"Said the man who sat and ate crumpets," said Iris.

"I'm being helpful," protested Sally. "Hey! You missed a spot!"

"Where?" asked Ronnie in alarm.

Sally walked up and pointed to an area just below the ceiling. Ronnie looked up at it, then at Sally, and grinned. Sally picked him up.

"Hold your arm absolutely still," he whispered.

Ronnie complied, and Sally moved him up and down, Ronnie's brush leaving a trail of green on the wall.

"That should do it," said Sally. "And this must be Agnes, if I'm not mistaken."

"My goodness, Ronnie," said Agnes, laughing as she came into the room. "You've turned into a giant paintbrush."

"Everything go all right?" asked Gwen.

"As well as it could," said Agnes. "Thank you for the reference. Get your shoes and socks back on, young man. There is an entire zoo full of creatures impatiently awaiting your arrival."

"I made a picture for Iris," said Ronnie.

"Did you? Ah, Sir Oswald is getting married, I see. Is that Miss Iris he's getting married to?"

"Yes."

"I thought he might," said Agnes, winking at Iris. "You talk about her so often."

"Goodbye, Iris and Sally," he said. "I had a lovely time."

"We will see each other soon, I hope," said Iris.

"Now, have a wonderful time and mind Agnes," said Gwen, giving him a kiss. "Thank you so much for all your help."

"Bye, Mummy!"

They listened to the downwards clattering, then the door opening and closing.

"I want you to know, Sparks, that I do approve of mixed marriages," said Sally. "Including those of the interspecies variety, although I worry about which faith the pups will be brought up in."

"I am going to have this framed," said Iris, holding the picture up. "It will be placed opposite yours, so we— Oh, hello. I'm sorry, we aren't having business hours today."

"That's all right," said the man at the door. "It's Mrs. Bainbridge I've come to see."

"Mr. Prendergast?" said Gwen in surprise, acutely aware of her paint-splattered appearance. "What on earth are you doing here?"

"I called at the house, and they said you were at your office," he said. "Catchy name, The Right Sort. Full marks for that. Can't say I think much of having the office this many floors up."

"Excuse me, I don't mean to be rude, but what is this all about?" said Iris.

"He was at the dinner last night," said Gwen. "This is Walter Prendergast. Mr. Prendergast, this is my partner, Miss Iris Sparks, and our friend, Mr. Salvatore Danielli."

"How do you do?" said Prendergast. "Mrs. Bainbridge, I would like to speak with you. Is there somewhere we could go?"

"To speak about what?" asked Gwen.

"A private matter that I believe will be of some importance to you."

"Shouldn't one of us be present?" asked Sally.

"You want to observe the social niceties," said Prendergast. "Good for you. I, on the other hand, don't give a damn about them. Mrs. Bainbridge will be perfectly safe in my company, but this must be a conversation between her and me."

"I can take him into the other office," said Gwen. "I'll be fine."

"All right," said Iris. "Don't forget what Gerry said the other day."

"I won't," said Gwen, grabbing her keys from her bag. "Come with me, please."

"Gerry?" asked Sally after they left.

"Macaulay," said Iris. "She started self-defense training this week."

"I feel infinitely better knowing that," said Sally.

Iris lifted the corner of the drop cloth from her desk, opened the bottom drawer, and pulled out two glasses.

"Want one?" she asked.

"Please."

She handed him one, and they stood by the wall, placing the glass bottoms against it so they could listen to the conversation on the other side.

Gwen let Prendergast into the office, turned on the ceiling light, and motioned him to the sofa. She took Mrs. Billington's chair behind the desk.

"That big Italian fellow a boyfriend?" asked Prendergast.

"He's English," she said. "And that's none of your business."

"He's very protective of you."

"Should I ever have need of protection, he would be quite good at it," she said. "We are alone, Mr. Prendergast. What is it that you have come to say?"

"To the point, excellent," he said, placing his hands on his thighs with a quick double-tapping gesture. "Last night, you barged into a meeting you were not meant to be in, got yourself summarily removed by your father-in-law, and didn't come back. He returned after a few minutes, looking splenetic, and begged pardon for your behaviour, mentioning you were not fully in possession of your faculties, to which the old boys commenced tut-tutting. One of them murmured to me about your stay in a sanatorium in sympathetic tones that failed to conceal his glee."

"Did he?" said Gwen, her fury rising. "And have you come to have another viewing of the crazy lady? Are you wondering why they haven't locked me in the attic with Mrs. Rochester?"

"Mrs. Bainbridge, I am no psychiatrist," said Prendergast. "I am here because you struck me as being as far from lunacy as one could possibly be. I am here because I want to know what really happened last night, and why."

"Why is it any concern of yours?"

"Good, good," he said, double-tapping his hands on his thighs again. "I am in possession of information that I suspect may be of use to you. Interest to you, certainly, but whether it will lead you to take action or not, I cannot say. I am in a quandary as a result. Two quandaries, in fact, and I am not sure how to proceed, which is of interest to me because I have always been a man of certainty."

"How can you always be certain about things?"

"Because I don't make decisions until I am," he said. "If I am uncertain, then I learn everything I can until I reach a state of absolute knowledge. Then, only then, will I act. So, I have come to you and am suddenly stymied. Tongue-tied, you might say."

"You have been nothing of the kind," said Gwen.

"This, this is all a preamble," he said. "How much do you know about Bainbridge, Limited? Of its organisation?"

"I know that it's a limited partnership, that the principal partners are my father-in-law and, I suppose, myself."

"Yourself, exactly," he said. "Know thyself, Mrs. Bainbridge, and all may be revealed."

"If you seek to enlighten me, Mr. Prendergast, you must first tell me your interest in all this."

"I am an investor, Mrs. Bainbridge. Shortly before your father-in-law's last visit to East Africa, I made a sizable short-term loan to Bainbridge, Limited, two percent over market terms against twenty percent of the shares, equally distributed by all partners."

"I was never a party to that."

"Oh, but you were. You see, Bainbridge, Limited, was started up by Lord Bainbridge's father. Forty percent went to each of his sons, and four percent apiece to the five old men at the table last night. It was a very intelligent setup. If the brothers banded together, they could make decisions for the company. If they disagreed, then one of them would have to get the support of at least three of the lesser partners—"

"Which would add up to a fifty-two percent majority," concluded Gwen.

"Precisely. But with you non compos mentis, your guardian acts on your behalf. And he, being a ninny and unwilling to take the time to learn the business, ceded control of your shares to your father-in-law. Which means that Lord Bainbridge now has complete control of the company. How do you feel about that, Mrs. Bainbridge?"

"Are you trying to stir me up, Mr. Prendergast? Is that why you came?"

"There's the first quandary, Mrs. Bainbridge," he said. "I have conflicting interests in the situation now, and there is nothing I can do or say that can't have ulterior motives attributed. It might be in my best interests to renew the terms of the loan, or take my shares and join the company. Or to demand payment in cash and get out of it entirely. As long as Lord Bainbridge controls your shares, he'll have the majority even if I come in for twenty percent, and I don't like having one man control my fate. Do you?"

"Not particularly. So you want me to step up and take charge of my portion."

"That might be against my interests as well," he said, smiling oddly. "Although with my twenty percent and your reduced share—"

"Which would be thirty-two percent."

"Yes. We could team up for control."

"And you want that."

"I don't know," he confessed. "Africa's getting dicey. They had a railway strike in Northern Rhodesia last month that set back copper profits considerably. The peacetime economy is volatile, and I haven't even mentioned the biggest threat of all."

"Which is?"

"The end of the British Empire, Mrs. Bainbridge," he said. "The Indian subcontinent will be lost inside a year, and all the African colonies may take inspiration from that. If they decide to nationalise, well, God save the pound."

"I see. But you must want me to act, because why else would you be telling me all this?"

"Because you barged in through that door last night," he said. "When I found out what Lord Bainbridge was doing to you it didn't sit well with me. Not at all. You have more spine than anyone in that room last night, and the immorality of it all offended me."

"Oh," said Gwen. "I guess I'm surprised that you would place that sense of . . . injustice, I suppose, over your financial interests."

"So am I, Mrs. Bainbridge, so am I," he said. "It's completely out of step with my life hitherto. And I don't blame you for not trusting my motives even now."

"I didn't say that."

"You don't have to. You're a sensible woman, and a sensible woman would be right in wondering what I'm up to. Which leads to my other quandary."

"Yes, you mentioned there was something else. What is it?"

"When you came through that door, Mrs. Bainbridge, full of fire and determination, I felt like I had been struck by a thunderbolt," he said. "And there lies the predicament. I want to ask you out to dinner, Mrs. Bainbridge. A series of dinners, in fact, with an eye towards learning everything I can about you until I reach a state of absolute knowledge, and then can make a decision. But I can't do that because you would quite rightfully suspect that I may only be trying to gain control of your shares through an entirely despicable means, and I don't want you to think that of me. So, Mrs. Bainbridge, it may be necessary to accept my payment to Bainbridge, Limited in cash and get out so that there will be no financial conflicts and I can ask you out freely."

It had all come out in a rapid-fire burst, and by the time he was finished, his hands were practically drumming a tattoo on his thighs. He took note of them, grimaced, and let them fall quietly to his sides.

"I would like to know, Mrs. Bainbridge, before I take such drastic actions, if you would agree to that?"

"Agree to dinner, Mr. Prendergast?"

"To dinner, and the further investigation of other possibilities."

Her heart was pounding. She didn't know if it was because of the suddenness of his request, or her fury at her father-in-law. She had tried reading Prendergast while he spoke, but she couldn't tell what his motives were.

She suspected it was because he didn't understand them himself.

"Mr. Prendergast, I don't know how to answer you," she said, not unkindly. "There are other complications in my life of which you are unaware, and until they are resolved, I am afraid I cannot accept."

"If I can help in some way—"

"You cannot," she said quickly. "Thank you for offering, but I have to take care of them myself."

"Very well," he said, rising to his feet. "I hope that I haven't distressed you unduly."

"Not unduly," she said, coming around the desk to lead him out. "Thank you. Thank you for explaining things to me."

"What action will you take?"

"Would it be advisable for me to tell you?"

He smiled and took her hand for a moment.

"Good," he said. "Very good."

He relinquished it and went down the stairs.

She watched him go, then locked the door behind her and went back into the other office. Iris was busy running the roller over the last section of wall while Sally sat at Gwen's desk, studying Ronnie's drawing.

"How much did you hear?" asked Gwen.

"Are you accusing us of listening at the keyhole?" asked Iris, her eyes wide and offended.

"The keyhole, or with a glass to the wall," said Gwen.

"Would we do such a thing?" asked Sally.

"You're both spies. Of course you would."

"We've retired from espionage, remember?" said Iris.

"And I was more of a saboteur," said Sally. "I'd more likely blow a hole through the wall than put a glass to it."

"Right," said Gwen wearily. "Would you mind finishing up? I'm going home."

"Gwen," said Iris, but her partner was off to the lavatory, valise in hand.

She didn't return to the office, choosing to take the steps directly. As she reached the landing below, she heard Sally's voice from behind her. She looked up to see him at the railing.

"Gwen, he's not right for you," he said quietly.

"So you were listening."

"I wanted to make sure you were all right," he said. "I'm your protector, remember? You said so yourself."

"I said you would be a good one if I needed one," said Gwen. "I don't need protecting at the moment. By either of you. Goodbye, Sally."

He watched until she was out of sight, then went back into the office. Iris was studiously painting.

"That was ill-advised," she said, not looking at him.

"I don't recall hearing any advice before I did it," he replied.

"Would you have taken it?"

"Maybe. Probably not. Any crumpets left?"

"Finish them," said Iris.

Gwen turned onto her street in Kensington, oblivious to the wave
and smile of Mr. Daile as she passed him trimming another hedge.
As she reached the front door of the house, she heard a motorcar
start up from somewhere in the rear.

No, she thought, and walked quickly over to the driveway and
took a position in the center.

Rolls-Royce made only 492 Wraiths before shifting production
to the war effort. Lord Bainbridge owned one of them, a Prussian
blue beauty with leather upholstery and a hand-polished burled
mahogany dashboard. It was this car that now hurtled towards
Gwen, the Spirit of Ecstasy perched on top of the hood, her silver
wings streaming behind, her expression more grim than ecstatic
as she came face-to-face with the Fury of the driveway. The Wraith
braked to a stop inches from Gwen, its engine pulsating in a series
of roars.

Gwen stood her ground, fixing her gaze on the two occupants
of the car.

Albert finally leaned out the window.

"Mrs. Bainbridge, he needs to go to the club," he said. "Would
you mind getting out of the way?"

"Not until I speak with him," she replied.

"I don't think—" he began.

She strode to the rear passenger door and tugged on the handle. It was locked. Lord Bainbridge sat in the rear seat puffing on a
cigar and staring at her through the open window with mounting
rage.

"I have no time for this, Gwendolyn," he said.

"Make time," she answered.

"Drive, Albert."

Before she even thought about what she was doing, she stepped onto the running board, clinging to the window frame. The Rolls lurched forward, then stopped as Albert realised she was there.

"Don't make a scene!" barked Lord Bainbridge.

"Let me in, and a scene won't be made," she snapped.

"Sir, we're going to be late," said Albert.

Lord Bainbridge looked at his watch, then Gwen, then came to a decision.

"Get in," he said.

She reached in to unlock the door, then opened it and sat down next to him. The car leapt forward before she had completely closed the door. Somewhere behind them, she heard a motorcycle start up.

"If this is about your behaviour last night, then I have nothing to say," said Lord Bainbridge, looking out his window.

"This is about your behaviour," she said. "Last night, last week, and for the last two years."

"My behaviour? My behaviour has been impeccable."

"Your treatment of me has been odious. I've known that. I've forced myself to live with it. But now I'm beginning to think it's been illegal as well."

This caused him to turn and look at her, his expression speculative. Albert turned north on the Hyde Park cut through.

"Illegal in what sense?" asked Lord Bainbridge as they crossed the Serpentine.

"In manipulating my status in court so that you could take control of my shares in Bainbridge, Limited, and run the company unfettered."

"Ronnie's share."

"*My* share, as you damn well know."

"Which is being managed for you by a caretaker—"

"By a toady who licks your boot as it presses him flat."

"The tone of your voice does not help your case," he said. "If anything, your conduct now, not to mention last night, only adds grist to the legal mill when it comes to the determination of your competence."

"I have been competent. I have been more than competent. I have run a business, I have sorted through affairs of great complexity, and I can call upon witnesses from Scotland Yard and—"

She was about to mention the Palace, but that was still a matter about which she had to maintain secrecy.

"And from amongst our clientele," she finished lamely.

"But can you call a psychiatrist to attest to it?" he asked.

"You needn't have declared me incompetent on a permanent basis," she said. "You could have waited."

"In order for us to take care of my grandson—"

"My son!" she shouted. "My son, my son, my son!"

"Please, Mrs. Bainbridge," called Albert. "I'm trying to drive here."

They had emerged from the park and were heading north.

"I'm sorry, Albert," she said, lowering her voice.

"That's fine, Mrs. Bainbridge," he said as they reached Marylebone Road. He paused to observe the traffic, then eased the Wraith onto the eastbound side.

"As I said, once I was released, and receiving care from Dr. Milford, there was no call for you to deny me custody. There are plenty of women receiving care who can still be good mothers. But if you allowed me that, then you would have had to give up your dictatorial control of the company, wouldn't you?"

"I am not going to dignify that—"

"Please stop cloaking this tawdry business in fancy phrases. As long as you had put it in terms of guarding my child, I could persuade myself, just barely, that you had his interests at heart, and I could forgive you. But to find out that the entire time you have put me through this misery for money! It's—"

"Sir, brace yourself!" shouted Albert.

A lorry cut in front of the Wraith. Albert jammed on the brakes, throwing the two passengers violently forward.

A car pulled up directly behind them, cutting off their retreat. Three men emerged from the car as did another from the back of the lorry, hat brims pulled low over their faces, large kerchiefs tied over their mouths.

It might have looked absurd, thought Gwen as she watched them approach. Were it not for the guns.

"I can't drive us out, sir," said Albert.

"Stay calm," said Lord Bainbridge. "Let's see what this is all about."

The men fanned out around the car. One put a gun through the window to Albert's head.

"Keys," he said.

Albert shut off the engine and handed them over.

"Right," said one behind him, pointing his gun at Lord Bainbridge. "You. Out of the car. You're coming with us."

"What is the meaning of this?" blustered Lord Bainbridge.

"You 'eard me. Out of the car, and be quick about it."

"Oi!" said a young man peering through Gwen's window. "'E's got a bird with 'im."

"What?" said the man by Lord Bainbridge.

The young man straightened to bring his head above the roof level.

"A lady," he called across the car. "I thought 'e wasn't supposed to 'ave no one with 'im."

Can't reach his chin, thought Gwen. Can't reach his testicles, either.

But that's a lovely wide tie he has on.

Her hand shot out towards his chest and got a firm grip on his tie. Then she pulled with all her might.

Caught off guard and off balance, he fell towards the Rolls, his face smacking into the edge of the roof with a satisfying thunk. Stunned, he sagged downwards, bringing his face in line with Gwen's window.

There it is, she thought.

She jabbed forward with her right. It slid off the kerchief covering his face, but she managed to poke him in the left eye before raking her nails back down his cheek, drawing blood and tearing the kerchief away. He screamed, clutching his free hand to his eye.

He is young, she thought as she grabbed her door handle. She shoved the door open, toppling him backwards. She hurtled out the door after him, reaching for his gun.

Then she froze as another gun was cocked just behind her ear.

"That's enough of that, missy," said a man.

She stared down at the young man below her.

"My face!" he blubbered, still writhing in pain. "Look what she did to it!"

"Yeah, and she got a right sweet look at it, didn't she?" said the man behind her. "Which complicates things."

He lifted his gun, then brought it down sharply.

And the world rushed away from her.

CHAPTER 9

The Rolls turned in to the driveway and lurched to a stop. Albert emerged and staggered to the front door, clutching his head with one hand and a scrap of paper with the other. He went through the door into the entryway.

"Verger!" he yelled. "Verger, where are you?"

Percival appeared from the dining room.

"Albert, stop yelling this instant," he said. "Lady Bainbridge is at home."

"Get her," said Albert. "Something's happened."

"What do you mean? You know she was planning to—"

"She'll be canceling her plans, Verger. Get her down quickly, and ask Prudence if she'd make an ice pack for me."

"Albert, what—"

"We were attacked. Waylaid. They took His Lordship."

"Took? Took how?"

"Kidnapped, man. Get Her Ladyship down, no time to waste. I don't want to keep repeating everything."

Percival made for the steps.

"And Verger," called Albert. "No bloody police."

"But—"

"Life or death. They said so."

He went into the front parlour and sat down heavily.

Lady Bainbridge came down with Percival a minute later, her dressing gown wrapped around the beginnings of her evening apparel. Albert stood quickly, wincing as the pain shot through his head.

"What happened?" she asked, sitting and motioning for him to do the same.

"We were cut off by a lorry on Marylebone Street," he said. "Men came out. Armed men, their faces covered."

"Dear God!"

"They took him, Lady Bainbridge," he said. "Threw him into the back of the lorry, conked me with a pistol to slow me down, and threw this note onto my lap."

"And you did nothing?"

"What do you mean, I did nothing? I beg your pardon, Your Ladyship, but they had guns. Mrs. Bainbridge tried to put up a fight—"

"Wait. Are you saying Gwendolyn was with you? What was she doing there?"

"She wanted to talk to Lord Bainbridge about something, and they were going at it something fierce when the rest happened."

"But you said she put up a fight? Gwendolyn?"

"She went at the fellow on her side. Took him down proper, too, but one of the others—"

He hesitated.

"What happened to her?" asked Lady Bainbridge softly.

"He hit her. She went down like a sack of meal. Then they took her, too."

"Oh, no," she whispered. "Do you think— Will she be all right?"

"I don't know, Lady Bainbridge. She shouldn't have tried."

"She did more than you did. What then?"

"They took the keys to the Rolls. One of them threw them in the rear, then handed me the note and said, 'Give it to the wife.

No police. We have a man inside, and we'll know in ten minutes if you call them. It won't go well for your boss if that happens.' Then he whacks me once to make his point, and by the time my head cleared, they were gone. I came straight here."

"Give me the note," she ordered.

He handed it to her.

"Lady Bainbridge," interjected Percival.

"What?"

"I was going to say put gloves on," he said. "In case there are fingerprints. But you already have the note."

"Utter nonsense," she huffed. "Albert, you've read it, I take it?"

"I have, milady," said Albert.

"'No police,'" she read. "'We'll call with our demands. Be ready to pay.' Pay? Will they want very much? Does anyone have any idea what ransom costs nowadays?"

"I am afraid this is entirely out of my experience, milady," said Percival.

"Wasn't the Carstairs' son kidnapped? What did they pay?"

"That was twenty-five years ago, milady, and I don't know the details."

"Prices have probably gone up since then," she mused distractedly. "Call the Nevilles and cancel for me. Say I've taken ill or something. Money. It's Saturday night. Even if I have enough, I cannot get at it until Monday morning when the banks reopen. You don't suppose they could open up just for me on a Sunday?"

"I would doubt it, milady."

"I wish I knew of someone who could give me advice on all this," she said. "There must be someone we know with experience in criminal matters—"

She stopped, her face rapidly going through a series of expressions of increasing distaste.

"Percival," she said. "I need you to find me a telephone number."

* * *

Iris stood barefoot in front of the sofa in her living room, running through her stretches before commencing the Defendu routine. She had let them slide for a while, but with alcohol playing a lesser part in her life, she decided to be more regimented with her martial arts skills. She had deployed them successfully a few times in the past months, but in retrospect had relied more on the element of surprise than actual superiority of technique. Watching Gerry work with Gwen reminded her of how much she needed to get back into it.

And it gave her something to do on a Saturday night when her gangster boyfriend was busy, gallivanting about with the lads, as gangsters did, on some task Archie said she was better off not knowing about.

She had not anticipated that a relationship with Archie Spelling would be just as secretive and elusive as her previous relationship, an affair she had carried on with a married operative from the Service. Yet here she was, home alone on a Saturday night again, a disgrace to the sisterhood of party girls. A tin of kippers waited on her tiny kitchen counter, next to a bottle of whisky that was nearing the end of its brief but illustrious reign.

She emptied her mind, her hands dangling at her sides. Strike from stillness. Complete the blow before you've finished the thought.

Her right hand thrust forward, palm out. She pulled it back and repeated the motion. Then the left.

Don't think. Don't remember. Don't wonder why you, who prided yourself on your quickness and powers of observation, completely missed the signs that your best friend had suddenly manifested feelings towards your other best friend, and that could only lead to disaster.

She brought her palms together, inhaled slowly, and let the breath out. Then she kicked high and low, low and high, left foot, right.

Were Sally and Gwen a pair she would have matched professionally? He was too tall for her, of course. He was too tall for every woman, come to think of it, but given Gwen's height, he was less too tall with her.

But height didn't matter, thought the short girl as she threw a combination of punches and kicks that would have leveled a man of any size before he knew what hit him. Sally said so himself. Right in front of Gwen and her child.

Why a disaster, Iris? You adore them both. Why wouldn't they be perfectly suitable as a couple?

Is it because you fear losing your only two real friends to each other? Or were you, who had for years spurned all greater possibilities with Sally so as to keep him as a friend, now jealous because he had finally turned his attentions elsewhere?

So much for rising above my narcissistic tendencies, Dr. Milford.

She flipped an imaginary assailant over her shoulder and stomped his imaginary trachea.

And how does Archie fit into this picture? You don't bring Gwen and Sally along when you're out on the town with him. You wouldn't want them along. Their disapproval would only drag you down.

Stop thinking, damn it.

"Discipline, Sparks!" shouted Gerry. *"Be as reckless as you want in every other aspect of your existence, but when you fight, you will be disciplined. Or you will die."*

Or kill someone you shouldn't, she thought.

The telephone jangled her out of her lack of concentration.

"Miss Sparks?" came an unfamiliar man's voice.

"Who is this?" she replied.

"Please hold for Lady Bainbridge."

"What?"

But there was no immediate reply, just some muffled tones on the other end. Then a woman spoke.

"Miss Sparks, this is Lady Carolyne Bainbridge," came a voice that she had heard once before in her life. Only this time, the tone was less haughty.

"Is Gwen all right?" Iris asked immediately.

"How—how did you know about Gwen?" exclaimed Lady Bainbridge.

"Why else would you be calling me? You and your husband detest me, which is difficult on short acquaintance. Detesting me usually requires time and a broken engagement. What happened? And why are you calling, and not your husband?"

"It's about both of them. Gwen and my husband."

Iris had a fleeting thought that she meant something else about Gwen and Lord Bainbridge, but rejected it as soon as it took form.

"I have sent Albert to pick you up," continued Lady Bainbridge. "He will fill you in. Pack an overnight bag."

"Why?"

"Because I expect you will need to be here overnight. Maybe two nights. Albert should be waiting for you in the Rolls outside your flat. I will see you shortly."

"Will a formal frock be needed?" asked Iris, but the connection was severed before she finished the question.

Guess not, she thought. Gwen, what is happening?

She came out of her building to see a Rolls-Royce Wraith parked in front. A uniformed chauffeur got out and opened the rear door for her. She walked up to him and stopped.

"Miss Sparks?" he asked.

"Yes. May I see some identification, please?"

"Excuse me?" he exclaimed, his offense evident.

"A girl can't be too careful getting into strange cars," she said. "Even when they're as nice as this one. Identification, please."

He pulled out his wallet and extracted his ident card. She

looked at it closely, then handed it back. As she did, she noticed the angry bruise and the crusted blood on the side of his head.

"Who did that to you?" she asked.

"I'll tell you all about it while we're driving," he said, motioning to the door.

She tossed her valise onto the seat, then turned back to him.

"I'll drive," she said. "You're not looking at all well."

"Miss Sparks, I can't let you do that."

"I am not setting foot inside that car if you're behind the wheel. You need to see a doctor."

"I'll be fine."

She stepped quickly around him and plopped herself down behind the wheel. She looked up at him with pity.

"No one will know," she said, patting the passenger seat. "Get in."

He hesitated, then closed the rear door and came around to the front passenger side and got in next to her.

"I've been driving that family nigh on thirty-five years," he said, looking around in wonder. "In all that time, I've never sat on this side."

"What a treat it must be," she said, adjusting the mirror. "Tell me what on earth all the fuss is about?"

"It's Lord Bainbridge and Mrs. Bainbridge," he said. "They've been kidnapped."

If he was expecting an outcry of some sort, he was disappointed. She merely nodded slightly, looking straight ahead as she absorbed the information. Only the clenching of her hands on the steering wheel revealed any emotion.

"Right," she said. "Details. Where did it happen?"

"On Marylebone Street," he said. "Eastbound."

She put the Wraith in gear.

"We'll go there first," she said. "Tell me everything."

It was a five-minute drive from her flat on Welbeck Street. She let him talk uninterrupted. When they got to the spot on Maryle-bone, she pulled over and got out of the car, glancing around.

There was a dark green wooden fence to her left, screening the street from a construction site. She tried to remember what had been there before, but couldn't. Another memory erased by the Blitz.

"Good choice for an abduction," she commented. "No witnesses on this side."

She squatted at the kerb, looking for tire tracks, but the street was clean.

"Did you get a plate number?" she asked. "For either the lorry or the car?"

"I'm afraid not, Miss Sparks," said Albert. "I was looking at the guns, mostly, and then the one bloke hit me and I wasn't thinking about much after that."

"You said there were four men?"

"Yes. Three from the car, one from the lorry."

"And she took them on," she said, shaking her head in wonder. "Idiot."

She stood and gazed down the road.

"They headed east. Could you see whether they kept going, or if they turned off on Edgeware?"

"Sorry, Miss Sparks. I'm of no help to you there."

"They could be anywhere," she mused. "We could try checking hospitals for the injured one, but they're probably lying low. All right, let's get you to Kensington."

She got back in and made a series of turns until they were heading in the right direction.

"Where'd a girl like you learn to drive?" asked Albert.

"A girl like me? I got behind the wheel of more than a few cars with more than a few boys too drunk to drive. I may have been too drunk to drive myself on some of those occasions, but we all survived somehow. Then in the war—motor pool for a while. I got to drive a tank once."

"Goodness, Miss Sparks. How did you accomplish that?"

"For a lark. I had a cousin in the 27th Armoured. I was visiting him in Newmarket when he was in training, and he snuck me into an M3 Stuart. I like this much better, I must say."

"Nice cousin, breaking regulations for you like that."

"Yes, he was," she said softly. "He didn't make it off the beach at Sword."

"Sorry."

They drove on in silence. As she approached the street in Kensington, he motioned for her to pull over.

"I appreciate the break," he said. "But I have to be the one bringing you here, banged up or not."

"I am willing to risk you driving the last block," she said.

He got out and held the rear door for her. She got in. He closed it, sat in the driver's seat, and readjusted the mirror.

"That's better," he said, patting the steering wheel.

He pulled the car up to the garage in back, and insisted on carrying her valise over her protests. They went in through the kitchen.

Apparently, I am a tradeswoman, she thought. Where's the ceremony?

Percival was waiting in the hall outside the kitchen.

"Good evening, Miss Sparks," he said, taking the valise from Albert. "I will show you to your room."

"Thank you, Percival, but I would rather be taken straight to Lady Bainbridge."

"Very good, Miss Sparks. She is in the library. Please follow me."

Iris had been in the Bainbridge town house only once before and had never seen the library. Her first glance was at the books, which were locked away in giant cabinets and had the look of having never been read since they were collected. She spotted a few that she immediately wanted to peruse.

"I know that look," came a woman's voice from the end of the room. "I was a passionate reader when I was your age."

Lady Bainbridge was sitting on one of a matched pair of armchairs by the fireplace, which was unlit. A blue-and-white delft porcelain tea service was laid out. She motioned to the other chair. Iris sat down.

She didn't offer to shake hands, thought Iris.

"Tea?" asked Lady Bainbridge. "Or something stronger? Would you prefer sherry? Or shall we go straight for the whisky?"

"As much as I enjoy whisky, I would like to keep my head clear while my friend is in danger," said Iris. "Let's stick to tea. We can have a proper binge when it's over. Why have you asked me here? Why not call the police?"

Lady Bainbridge handed her the note. Iris read it quickly, then again more slowly.

"Do you think they're telling the truth about having a man inside Scotland Yard?" asked Lady Bainbridge as she poured the tea.

"It depends on the gang," said Iris. "This was a very well planned and executed job, so they may very well have access to someone there. However, I do know some people at the Yard I would absolutely trust if you want me to bring them in."

"Would you take that risk?" asked Lady Bainbridge.

"For your husband, yes," said Iris. "But not for Gwen."

"I didn't think so," said Lady Bainbridge. "What should we do?"

"You haven't heard from anyone yet?"

Lady Bainbridge shook her head.

"Let's say they want some astronomical figure," said Iris. "Fifty thousand pounds. Could you get it?"

"Possibly," said Lady Bainbridge. "I may have to sell one or two pieces of jewelry."

"How long would that take you?"

"A day, at least. And I couldn't do anything until Monday."

"On the one hand, that buys us some time," mused Iris. "On the other—well, I hope they're patient kidnappers. The longer things take, the more likely they'll want to cut their losses."

"Meaning kill Harold and Gwen," said Lady Bainbridge.

"Meaning exactly that," said Iris. "Why did you want me involved?"

"I couldn't go to the police," Lady Bainbridge replied. "It occurred to me that you might have alternate resources."

"Such as?"

"Such as whoever supplied us with black market chickens."

"You think he has something to do with this?" Iris asked indignantly, getting to her feet. "If that's the case, then you can send me home, Lady Bainbridge. My friends may be thieves and ruffians, but they do have certain standards."

"Please, sit down," said Lady Bainbridge. "I meant to say he might be able to advise us on how to proceed. I would assume that he has some knowledge in this area. And I take it that he is a friend of Gwendolyn's, as well as being your—friend."

"You can say 'boyfriend,'" said Iris, sitting down again. "God, that sounds so adolescent. 'Gentleman friend' might send him into a fit of laughing. But yes, he may know people who know people. I will give him a ring. Who in the household knows what has happened?"

"Only Percival and Albert."

"Could you call them both in, please?"

Lady Bainbridge pressed a button by the fireplace. A moment later, Percival knocked and entered.

"Yes, Lady Bainbridge?"

"Fetch Albert, would you?" she ordered.

He returned a minute later with the chauffeur, who now had an ice bag pressed to his head. Lady Bainbridge motioned for them both to approach.

"Go ahead," she said to Iris.

"Right now, we're keeping this matter quiet," said Iris. "I am going to ask the two of you not to mention it to any of the other servants. We need to create stories to satisfy them should they ask. Lord Bainbridge could be staying in town at his club, I suppose. What shall we do about Gwen?"

"She could be visiting a friend," suggested Percival.

"Without saying goodbye to Ronnie? Well, that may be the best we can do on short notice. An emergency of some kind. As for my presence here—"

"I've taken the liberty of putting you in a guest room in a hallway that is otherwise unoccupied," said Percival. "That should minimise contact with the staff."

"Where can I operate with some privacy and a telephone?"

"Lord Bainbridge's office," said Lady Bainbridge.

"Excuse me, madam, but he doesn't like other people going in there," said Percival.

"Well, he's not likely to be complaining about it now, is he?" snapped Lady Bainbridge. "Show Miss Sparks to his office. And make up a tray for her."

"What would you like, Miss Sparks?" asked Percival.

"Anything that isn't tinned kippers," said Iris. "And a pot of hot coffee. It may be a long night. One more thing, gentlemen, while you're both here."

"Yes, Miss Sparks?"

"This wasn't a spur-of-the-moment job. They knew Lord Bainbridge's routine. It took planning, which means they either had someone inside or were keeping watch on his movements. Anyone you'd suspect from the household staff?"

"All of them have been employed here for years," said Percival. "I would not suspect any of them."

"Have you noticed anyone watching the house?"

"No," said Percival.

"Well," said Albert hesitantly. "There's that gardener. You know the one. The black fellow. Showed up a few days ago."

"I can't say I've noticed any such," said Percival.

"That's 'cause you don't go outside much," said Albert. "I've seen him down the street. He always seems to be clipping someone's hedge when we go out. And I could have sworn I saw him on a motorcycle behind us once or twice."

"How did you know it was him?"

"I saw the motorcycle parked with his gardening kit," said Albert. "An old Royal Enfield. Can't be too many of those with people looking like him riding about."

"Was he following you today?" asked Iris.

"Couldn't say. I was distracted by the goings-on between Lord Bainbridge and Mrs. Bainbridge."

"Well, I'll keep it in mind. Now, would you be so kind as to show me to Lord Bainbridge's office, Percival? I'll pitch camp for the evening."

"Very good, Miss Sparks."

"What are you going to do?" asked Lady Bainbridge.

"Phone my friend, for starters. After that, I shall take a deep breath and think. So far, it's all been questions and reactions."

"What should I be doing?" asked Lady Bainbridge.

"Figure out how you'll pay the ransom," said Iris. "Is the phone in Lord Bainbridge's office also the house phone?"

"No. It's a number he uses only for business matters."

"Then if the kidnappers call the house phone, send someone to bring me in on the line. And tell them you can't get the money until Monday."

"Very well. Miss Sparks, I need not remind you that this is all confidential."

Yet you just did, thought Iris.

"Don't worry," she said. "I'm good with secrets. Good evening, Lady Bainbridge."

Percival led her to a door on the other side of the house, then unlocked it.

"Is this always locked?" asked Iris as he showed her in.

"Whenever he is not in it," replied Percival. "The maid only cleans it when he or I are present."

"Any booby traps for the uninitiated?"

"He would never do any such thing," said Percival.

"I would," said Iris.

It was not a large room. A rolltop desk with cubbyholes on either side was set against the wall opposite the door. A red leather-bound chair, worn with use, sat in front of it. Walnut bookcases stood against the wall to the right. Next to the chair was a small table, apparently for holding trays for meals. A small valise sat in the corner, festooned with shipping tags. Of immediate importance was a brass-plated telephone on a stand, the current directories on a shelf below it.

"This will do nicely," said Iris.

She thought she saw Percival twitch in disapproval as she sat in Lord Bainbridge's chair.

"I will fetch your supper," he said. "It will have to be cold. Otherwise, I would have to get the cook involved."

"And that would lead to questions," said Iris. "That's fine. It will no doubt be better than what the evening held for me before. Close the door behind you, please."

"Of course, Miss Sparks."

He left. She waited, then crossed silently to the door and opened it to see him receding down the hall. Satisfied that she was secure, she closed the door, and resumed her place at the desk. She removed her address book from her bag, found the number she wanted, and dialed. A man answered.

"Hello, Eggy. Is that you?" she asked. "It's Sparks. How's the jaw doing? Still? Have you tried cold compresses? I know, I know, it was a serious wallop. I told you you were dropping your left. Yes, I'm sure you'll get him next time. Listen, I need to talk to Archie. I know he's not with you, but you're the one he told me to call if there was any kind of an emergency, and I'm afraid I have one. No, I'm not at home. Let me give you the number here. Write it down, Eggy. Yes, I trust your memory, only I saw you singing nursery rhymes after you went down for the count. Are you ready? It's NOBle Three—"

She had him repeat it back to her, then hung up. There was a knock at the door, and Percival returned with a tray of cold cuts, cheese, and pickles.

"The coffee should be ready momentarily, Miss Sparks," he said, placing it on the side table. "Press that button there if you need me for anything else."

"Thank you, Percival," she said.

He nodded, turned to leave, then turned back.

"How bad is it, do you think?" he asked.

"If it was just him, my guess is it would be even odds of survival," she said. "But Gwen was taken because she saw one of their faces, from what Albert told me. She's the one in real danger."

"I see," said Percival, his shoulders sagging slightly. "I hope your efforts prove effective, Miss Sparks."

"You and me both," she said.

He nodded again and left.

And now we wait, she thought. Gwen, what did you get yourself into this time?

Gwen was swimming in a sea of ink, unable to determine where the surface was. A giant octopus chased her, its eyes glowing, its fangs—

Did octopuses have fangs? Or was it octopi? She wasn't certain. It might depend on the species. She would have to ask Ronnie.

She kicked forward, but she wasn't in her element, and her pursuer was. It gained on her with every step.

Not step, she thought. It was an octopus. Which would explain all the ink. Or was that squids? Ronnie would know that, too. Ronnie was—

A tentacle caught her by the ankle. Then another. She couldn't get away. More and more tentacles wrapped around her body, pinioning her arms to her sides as the creature drew her inexorably toward its gaping maw. She screamed.

And woke.

And screamed again.

She couldn't see. She couldn't move, ropes wrapped around her, tightly tied. She was on her back on a cot, and more ropes secured her so she couldn't even roll off it. She struggled against them to no avail, mewling noises spewing helplessly from her.

"Gwen," came Lord Bainbridge's voice. "Calm yourself, or they'll gag you."

"Wha–what?" she stammered. "Where am I? What's happening?"

"I don't know where we are," he said. "We've been kidnapped."

"Oh, thank God!"

"What on earth? How could that possibly be your response to this?"

"I thought for a moment I was back in the sanatorium," she said, starting to sob. "That they had me in restraints again."

"They did that to you," he said softly. "I had no idea."

"Why would you?" she asked bitterly. "You never came there. You never brought Ronnie. Not once."

"It would have been a terrible thing for him to see his mother like that."

"And you were too sensitive for the experience as well, were you?"

"Gwen, this is hardly the time or place for this."

"No, no, it isn't," she said, taking deep breaths. "My head hurts. Someone hit me."

"Yes."

"What's the hour?"

"Eight thirty-five."

"Still Saturday?"

"Still Saturday."

"What do they want?"

"Ransom. For me."

"How much?"

"Forty-five thousand."

"Will you pay?"

"I can't pay anything from here. I'm in the same position as you, tied up and blindfolded. It will have to be Carolyne's doing."

"The way you've treated her this past week, you'll be lucky if she pays," she said.

"There's no call for that," he said.

"No, there isn't," she said. "I'm sorry. What about me?"

"What about you?"

"Did they ask for any payment for me? Or am I just a throw-in?"

He didn't answer.

"What is it?" she asked. "What are you not telling me?"

"From what I understand, you present them with a problem," he said.

"What kind of a problem?"

"You've become a witness. You saw the face of the young lad, which means you're a threat to them."

"Oh. That doesn't sound promising."

"I have been trying to persuade them that you are an unreliable woman whose sanity is questionable, and whatever limited powers of observation you possess would have been adversely affected by the blow to your head."

"The sad part is I think you believe every word of that," she said.

"You went on the offensive when confronted with several armed men," he said. "That was remarkably unintelligent of you. What were you thinking?"

"I was thinking that someone was threatening one of my family," she said. "I protect my own."

"You consider me family? Even though you despise me?"

"You are my husband's father and my son's grandfather. Of course you're my family. And I don't despise you, although I find your behaviour has been despicable."

"Yet you were willing to risk your life for me."

"I don't know if I analysed the situation to that extent," she confessed. "I saw an opening. I went for it."

"What would have been the next step had his partner not intervened?"

"I had the man down. I was going to grab his gun."

"And hold him hostage?"

"Or start blasting away," she said. "I know how to use a pistol."

"You're insane," he said.

"So I've heard. I've been working on it."

She made another attempt to loosen her bonds with the same result.

"They know what they're about with these ropes," she said. "We'll have to come up with something else."

"Something else? For what?"

"For the escape plan, of course."

"Insane," he muttered.

CHAPTER 10

It was getting late. Iris was feeling cooped up. A cherrywood, Dutch-style clock ticked away on the mantel, its merry chimes on the hour and half hour catching her off guard every time, while its silver three-quarter-phase moon peeped coyly over the top of the clock face. She wondered if its concealed eye was winking at her. She didn't want to wait a week to find out.

Percival returned to collect her dinner tray and wind the clock with a brass key that he removed from a cunningly concealed drawer in its base.

"How is Lady Bainbridge holding up?" asked Iris.

"She has progressed to the whisky portion of her evening," he said. "Would you like any?"

"No, thank you, and please don't tempt me again. How did the cover story go with the rest of the staff?"

"Concern as to Mrs. Bainbridge's friend, especially on the part of Master Ronald," he said. "He's a sweet lad."

"He is indeed. How about the reaction to Lord Bainbridge's absence?"

"I would characterise it overall as relief," he said.

"Not surprising, given what I've heard since his return," she said. "I'm waiting for a call at this number. I don't know when it will be."

"Then I shall bring you a blanket and pillow, should you need to kip down here."

"That would be most appreciated. What time do you normally turn in?"

"When Lord Bainbridge comes home," said Percival. "Tonight, I will remain awake until both you and Lady Bainbridge have retired for the evening. You'll need me to show you to your room at some point."

"Yes, I will. Thank you, Percival."

He left, closing the door. She was shut in again. She paced the office, stopping to contemplate the photographs on the bookcases. There was the young Harold Bainbridge, not yet a lord, posing in a mine entrance with another young white man, both wearing miner's helmets. There he was again, a rifle slung over his shoulder, one foot on the body of a cheetah. And again, now in the present day, standing in front of a stately brick home, flanked by a dozen African men, women, and children. More photographs, she guessed taken by Lord Bainbridge himself, showed the landscapes—rivers, endless seas of grass, fields of tobacco, jungles.

He was a good photographer, she conceded reluctantly. And the noticeable feature of the pictures showing him was that he was smiling, something she had never seen him do in her own encounters with him.

One shot in particular drew her attention: Lord Bainbridge in his thirties, his arm draped around a young boy of eight or nine whose face she recognised immediately. Ronald, Lord Bainbridge's son. Gwen's first Ronnie, the love of her life. The boy looked excited to be wherever they were. Iris would have been, too, had she had a chance to travel to Africa at that age. She would have been constantly running about, collecting butterflies and beetles, being chased after by the servants until she could run no more.

There was something missing, she thought as she looked around.

There were no pictures of Lady Bainbridge. Or of Gwen. Not even the wedding photos.

Not even one of his grandson.

This room was where Lord Bainbridge came to be alone, and he wanted no thoughts of the living members of his family interrupting him.

Well, maybe they were inside the rolltop desk, hidden from her inquisitive gaze. She tugged at the cover experimentally, but it was locked. She could pick the lock, of course, but that would have been an imposition, given her role there tonight.

Still, she had nothing better to do, she thought, idly reaching for her bag where her lock picks were ever at the ready.

No, Iris. Think some more about the problem at hand.

The African photographs put her in mind of Mr. Daile and his promotion from suitor to suspect. She wondered if his appearance at The Right Sort was part of a plan to gain access to Lord Bainbridge through Gwen. His work as a gardener could very well be a ruse. If that was the case, then maybe she needed to track him down.

Only she couldn't, not while she was needed at the Bainbridge house.

Sally, she thought. As soon as I hear from Archie, I'll get Sally on Daile detail. Sally would do anything for me.

Or was that no longer the case?

Speaking of cases, there was that valise sitting off in the corner. She wandered over to inspect the shipping tags. How long does it take to fly from Northern Rhodesia? she wondered. It would be quicker now that the Mediterranean route was safe again. She flipped through the tags, retracing the journey. Trains from the

Copperbelt to Lusaka, then BOAC in a series of hops, Lusaka to Nairobi to Khartoum to Cairo. Then across to Rome and home to London on Sunday. Three days of travel overall.

She shuddered at the thought of voluntarily taking that many flights. There was not enough copper and tobacco in the world to make her get on an airplane once, much less five times in one trip.

That's why I'll never be a magnate, she thought. A copper magnate! With the power to attract. Well, she already had that, and it never gave her anything but trouble, didn't it?

She picked up the valise and hefted it experimentally. It felt empty. She shook it. Nothing rattled.

Not yours, Iris, she admonished herself. Don't go poking into things that don't concern you.

She opened it anyway. It was empty.

She didn't know what she expected to find. It was the effect of her being in someone else's room with too much time to kill. She looked longingly at the locked desk.

Then the telephone rang.

She answered before the second ring.

"Sparks, is that you?" came Archie with so much concern in his voice that she clasped the handset to her bosom for a moment.

"It is. Thank you for calling, Archie. I know I'm interrupting something, but this is an emergency."

"NOBle is a Kensington exchange," he said. "You 'anging about with the Royals again?"

"Hardly. I'm at the Bainbridge house."

"They let you in?"

"Yes."

"Front door or back?"

"Back. It's not a social call."

"What's going on?"

"It's Gwen, Archie. She's been kidnapped, along with Lord Bainbridge."

There was silence at the other end of the line.

"When?" he finally asked.

"This afternoon. Cut off by a lorry on Marylebone Street, then boxed in with a second car. Four armed men, plus a pair of drivers, I'm guessing."

"Any ransom calls?"

"Not yet, but they left a note saying there would be. I'm surprised and more than a little worried that they haven't called yet. I'm thinking adding Gwen to the mix threw off their plan."

"Why did they take 'er?"

"She was in the car by chance. The chauffeur said she went at one of them, and they knocked her out and carried her off."

"Gwen attacked someone? Are we talking about the same Gwen?"

"It wasn't the best idea," said Iris. "So Lady Bainbridge brought me here and asked me to call you."

"She knows about me?"

"Not in great detail."

"And what does 'er Ladyship want from me?"

"Advice, she said. She's never been in this situation before."

"And she thinks I 'ave? Do you think I do snatchings?"

"Emphatically not, and I told her as much. But she thought you might have ears in places we don't, and know how these things work. And reading between the lines, since she can't go to the police, if there are any other lines of communication you might know of."

There was a long pause.

"What you've just asked is beyond the boundaries of our relationship," Archie said slowly. "Far beyond. I don't pry into your war 'istory, you don't pry into my business, and we get along fine."

"I know, I know, darling," said Iris. "And if it was just Lord Bainbridge, I wouldn't dream of getting involved. But it's Gwen, and for her, I would risk everything."

"Even me."

"Even you. And to put that in perspective, I adore you."

"'Adore' is a nice word. But do you love me, Sparks?"

"Oh God, Archie," she said. "I don't know if I can say that word, or if I'll ever be able to say that word. I don't know if I can even think it to myself. I'm too damaged and bitter to let myself love or be loved."

"Well, then I suppose I'll 'ave to settle for being adored," said Archie. "It's more than I expect out of life at this point. I'll make some calls, Sparks. See what I can find out. No guarantees."

"Thank you, Archie," said Iris, wanting to weep. "I'll make you a guarantee. I will—"

"Don't cheapen it, Sparks," said Archie, cutting her off. "I'm doing this for you, and for Gwen. No conditions. I won't know anything until tomorrow, most likely. I'll call you at this number."

He hung up.

Stupid girl, she thought. All you had to do was say you loved him. It's an easy enough thing to say. You've lied about far worse things many times. Even said that word to a few men before.

Two who she promised to marry. One who she killed.

Maybe that was why she was afraid to say it out loud. It meant the end of things.

I will run away when this is over, she thought glumly. I will take that valise, pack my smalls and my weapons, and steal away to Africa. I will find out what happened to old Cardwell when he cracked and went south. I will have mad adventures, and become the mystery woman who vanished into thin air, leaving behind only a whiff of scandal, brimstone, and regret.

Maybe they'll let me into the Livingstone Club as a member when I'm done with it all, she thought, contemplating the valise and all of its tags, each telling a story.

Wait.

Sunday. Lord Bainbridge returned to London on Sunday.

Hadn't Gwen said he came back a day before he was expected? And she said that on Tuesday, so he would have made his entrance on Monday.

But the luggage tags said he came home Sunday.

She sat down at the desk, elbows on the edge, and rested her chin in her hands, thinking. Then she reached into her bag, pulled out a small, foldable London bus map, and spread it out in front of her.

Archie stared at his telephone, then grabbed a small black book from inside his coat.

"What's up, Arch?" asked Reg.

"I'm going to the zoo tomorrow," said Archie. "Set it up."

"Right," said Reg, leaving the room immediately.

Archie's book was filled with telephone numbers, but not a single name. Only he knew to whom they belonged. He dialed one.

"Corny, it's Archie Spelling," he said. "Tell Manfred lions at noon. Yeah, thanks."

He hung up, then looked up another number.

"It's Archie Spelling," he said when it was answered. "Monkeys at twelve thirty, all right?"

He hung up, then started cursing under his breath.

"Oi!" shouted Gwen. "Oi! Is anyone about?"

"Stop it!" hissed Lord Bainbridge. "You'll only get them angry."

"You want to stop me, come over here and stop me," said Gwen. "Oh, right, you're bound and blindfolded. Give all the orders you like. Oi! Guard! Mister Guard, I need to talk to you!"

Footsteps approached. Then a key rattled in the lock, and she heard a door open.

"Getting knocked on the head doesn't quiet you down much, does it?" said a man.

"Are you the one in charge?" asked Gwen.

"I'm in charge of you right now," he replied. "And if you keep barking like that, I'll stuff a sock in your mouth and you can shut up or choke to death. It don't matter to me which."

"Listen," said Gwen. "I don't know how much prior experience you've had with tying up women, but there comes a point where one needs the lavatory. Rather desperately."

"I've seen what you can do when your claws are unleashed. You can stay right where you are."

"Please, I'm begging you," she said. "I give you my word I won't try anything rash."

He considered the request for a moment.

"I'll be back," he said. "Don't go nowhere."

He closed and locked the door. Then the footsteps receded.

"And that's that," said Lord Bainbridge.

"No, he's coming back," said Gwen, listening intently. "And he's brought another man with him."

The key turned in the lock, the door opened, and two men stood over her. Then she heard a pistol being cocked. She flinched as she felt the muzzle touch her right temple.

"That's me with the gun," said the man who had come in before. "He's going to untie you. You are going to remain very still. The blindfold will not budge an inch. Understand me?"

"Perfectly," said Gwen. "Thank you, gentlemen."

"Oh, listen to 'er, all polite." The other man laughed as he loosened the knots. "All proper when she needs to be. Wasn't so proper before, were you?"

Her arms and hands tingled as the ropes came off. She wanted to rub them, but the gun was still at her head. She tried to hold back the tears, oddly grateful that the blindfold prevented the men from seeing them.

"Blindfold stays on," said the first man. "Get up."

She swung her legs over the side of the cot, felt for the floor with her feet, then stood, weaving as the blood rushed from her head. Neither of the men stepped forward to assist her. She bent at the waist, propping herself with her hands on her thighs, and breathed for a moment.

"You get sick 'ere, you're gonna 'ave to live with it," said the second man.

"I'll be fine," she said, straightening. "Which way do I go?"

One man seized her shoulder and pulled her roughly towards the door. He guided her into a hallway, then shoved her into the wall, pressing his gun to her head again, putting his mouth close to her ear.

"Nothing happens without me saying it happens," he said. "I was for dumping you in the river, just so you understand."

"I understand," she said. "Right or left?"

He pulled her to the right. She counted her steps as they walked. Twenty-three, then a right turn and fifteen more.

"Stop," he said. "There's a door on your left. When you go in, you can close it and take off the blindfold. Make it quick. I hear anything sounding like you're trying to pry something off for a weapon or tool, I shoot through the door and clean up whatever I find after. All right?"

"All right," she replied.

She was going to do just that, she thought in chagrin. Too obvious, Gwen.

She went in, closed the door behind her and pulled off the blindfold, blinking gratefully in the light of a single bulb that dangled from a chain overhead. It was a single cramped window-less water closet with no sink and nothing to indicate anything about the building she was in or its surroundings. Not even a single penciled message scribbled on the walls, obscene or otherwise.

But it was clean enough, she thought as she sat down, wiping her eyes with her sleeve. How lucky am I to have such neat kidnappers.

What would Iris do in this situation? Why would she even think Iris would know what to do in this situation? There were no locks to pick, and too many men with guns to fight her way out.

Iris would use her best weapon, thought Gwen. She would talk to them, charm them in spite of themselves, and find a way out somehow.

Gwen didn't know if she could talk her way out of it the same way. She wasn't accustomed to consorting with criminals—

Actually she was, come to think of it.

She finished, flushed, then replaced her blindfold.

"I'm ready," she called through the door. "Don't shoot, please."

She opened the door and stepped into the hallway.

"I want to speak to your boss," she said.

"How do you know that isn't me?" asked the first man.

"Because bosses don't waste time escorting prisoners to the WC," she replied.

"Why should he waste his time with you? What makes you so high and mighty?"

"Because I know some people of influence, and they will be quite angry if anything happens to me."

"Sure," laughed the second man. "I suppose a posh bird like you knows the king and queen personally."

"We've met, of course, but that's not who I am talking about."

"Look, duchess, or whatever you are, we don't care how 'igh and mighty your blue-blood friends are. They got no pull with us."

"I wasn't going high. Quite the opposite."

"Yeah?" The first man sniggered. "And whose name were you planning to drop to impress us?"

"Archie Spelling," she said.

There was an abrupt silence on the part of the two. Did she hear a slight, sudden inhalation by one? Did men gasp when they were surprised? She hoped so.

"Back to the room with you," said the first man.

Fifteen steps to the right, twenty-three to the left. A door opened. They led her back to the cot. She lay on it without being told, and they secured her. Then they left, closing the door behind them.

"You haven't escaped," observed Lord Bainbridge.

"Not yet," said Gwen.

"Hello?" said Sally.

"It's me," said Iris.

"Ah, good. I was hoping to apologise for my behaviour earlier. I rang you up at your flat, but no luck. I figured you must have been out on the town gangstering, knocking over a few banks or jewelry shops or whatever the two of you do when you get together."

"Apology accepted," said Iris. "Sally, I need your help."

"What? Just like that? A direct request, no playful badinage or taking the long way around? It must be serious."

"It's Gwen, Sally."

"What happened?" he asked, his tone immediately sober.

"She's been kidnapped, along with Lord Bainbridge."

"Right, on my way," he said. "Where am I going?"

"Nowhere yet," she said. "Let me bring you up to date."

When she was done, she could almost hear him thinking through the line.

"No ransom demand yet," he said. "I don't like that at all."

"Neither do I," she said. "Sally, I'm stuck here until further notice. I want you to keep an eye on Mr. Daile."

"Shall I pluck him away and interrogate him?"

"No," said Iris firmly. "I don't know for certain that he's involved, but neither can he be ruled out. I want to know where he goes when he's not clipping hedges."

"Done. Where do I find him, and what does he look like?"

"Damn, I can remember his number for some reason, but not the exact address. It's at the office. As for appearance—"

"That's too general to go on," he said when she was done describing Daile. "What if I end up following the wrong man?"

"I can't go with you, and there's no one else who would know—wait. Yes, there is. Mrs. Billington saw him. And you would need her to get the address from the office. I'm going to call her and tell her to meet you at The Right Sort."

"Are you going to tell her what this is all about?"

"No," said Iris. "I'll let her know it's advanced vetting for a marital prospect. She'll buy that. It will arouse her snooping instincts. I'll call you back after I've talked to her. Sit tight, darling. And thank you."

"Sadly, these are the best prospects I've had for a Saturday evening's entertainment in some time," he said. "I await your call."

Mrs. Billington was sitting on her sofa, listening to *Saturday Night at the Palais* on the Light Programme. Chips Chippindall was singing with Mrs. Wilf Hamer and Her Band from the Grafton Rooms in Liverpool, and she was wishing she were out dancing with Bertram somewhere. Or with anyone, so long as there was dancing involved. She was picturing the dance hall at Blackpool, the boys in their evening jackets, hair slicked back, her in a pink frock with flounces, all fluttery, some time in her teens, when the telephone rang. She answered, expecting it to be another incessant complaint from her sister about being left home by her husband yet again on a Saturday night. Mrs. Billington was in much the same straits, Bertram being out shooting billiards with the boys, but you didn't hear her complaining about it, did you?

But it wasn't her sister. It was her boss instead with a request. A request so unusual that it clearly meant Mrs. Billington was being taken more into their confidence, which pleased her no end. She hung up, then considered her outfit, finally complementing it with a long black scarf that she wrapped around her head and neck to make her look suitably mysterious. She took the memo pad from where it hung next to the telephone and jotted down: "Out on an undercover mission. Boys are in bed. Don't wait up!" She reviewed the message, then added two more exclamation points. Then she went out into the London evening, wearing a scarf that was altogether too warm for a Saturday night in August, to have a secret rendezvous with a giant.

Iris opened the door to the office and peered into the hallway. No sign of Percival. She closed her eyes and listened. No one was padding about upstairs. Somewhere, either in the servants' quarters or in a house elsewhere on the street, a radio was playing.

She removed her shoes and left them by the desk, then crept silently down the hall to the downstairs lav. She had been cooped up in the office forever, it seemed, but she wasn't able to risk the trip before. She took care of things, hoping no one upstairs would notice the flush. She washed up as silently as she was able, then slipped stealthily back to Lord Bainbridge's office. She reached for the door handle, then stopped.

Someone was inside. She could hear soft footsteps, then the sound of something hard landing on wood.

She opened the door. There was a small squeak of surprise. Ronnie stood by the desk, clad in light blue pajamas and tan moccasin slippers, on the verge of crying out in surprise and fear. Then he stopped as he saw Iris hold a finger to her lips.

"Hello, Ronnie," she whispered. "What are you doing up so late?"

"I was making a surprise for Grandfather," he whispered back. "What are you doing here?"

"Some business thing with your mummy," said Iris. "Your grandmother said I could use your grandfather's office since he was spending the night at the club."

"Where is Mummy?"

"Oh, didn't they tell you? She was visiting a friend who wasn't feeling well. She decided to stay the night."

"Which friend?"

"I don't know. I don't know all of her friends."

"Is Grandfather staying at the club because he's angry at me?" asked Ronnie, his eyes starting to water.

"Oh, no, no, no, darling," said Iris, quickly coming to kneel by him and give him a hug. "He goes there to spend time with his friends, and sometimes they have overnight parties."

"I didn't know grown-ups did that," said Ronnie. "So he's not angry at me?"

"I don't see how anyone could ever be angry with you," said Iris, letting him go. "Now tell me: What are you doing in here?"

"I heard the man at dinner telling a story about how Grandfather found some green rocks in Africa, and how happy he was," said Ronnie. "I thought if he found some green rocks here, it would make him happy again. So I made him some."

He held out his hand. On it rested a pair of rocks, painted a bright green. Another had been placed on the edge of the desk.

Oh my, thought Iris. This is how children break your heart forever.

"That is a lovely idea," she said. "I think it will make him very happy indeed. So you snuck down here to surprise him."

"Yes," said Ronnie. "I know I'm supposed to be in bed."

"I expect you'll be forgiven. I didn't know you were at the dinner last night. How very grown up you are getting!"

"I wasn't," Ronnie confessed. "I wanted to see what the table looked like when it was all laid out. It was very fancy. I didn't mean to listen, but they were talking about Africa, and I wanted to hear. Mummy says I'm not supposed to sneak around and listen to people's conversations. Did I do something bad?"

"I don't know if I'm the right person to answer that question," said Iris, feeling momentarily guilty about her eavesdropping earlier in the day. "If your mummy says you shouldn't, then you shouldn't."

"Oh," said Ronnie disconsolately. "I'll have to tell her, won't I? Do you think I'll be punished?"

"Always be honest with your mother," said Iris. "I wouldn't worry about being punished. It's a minor offense at best. Why, if I had been punished for every time I sneaked around as a child, I would never have been able to sit down again."

"All right," said Ronnie. "Could you get me a glass of warm milk?"

"Now, that is an excellent idea," said Iris. "Put the rocks on the desk, then we shall sneak into the kitchen together."

He put them next to the one that he had put there before she came in, then took her by the hand. They walked to the kitchen together.

Is this what it's like all the time? thought Iris as she got a bottle of milk from the refrigerator and poured some into a pan. I can take on a man twice my size, but I don't know if I'm strong enough to raise a child. There's no Defendu move to shield your heart from them.

She lit the burner and put the pan on the fire. Ronnie climbed onto a chair that was clearly his, allowing him to rest his elbows on the kitchen table while his feet dangled underneath.

"Should I also tell Mummy about listening to the argument Grandfather and the other man had about me?" he said.

"They had an argument about you?" asked Iris as she stirred the milk with a wooden spoon. "What about?"

"I don't know exactly," said Ronnie. "Grandfather owed him some money or something."

"And how did you come into it?"

"Grandfather said, 'You'll get paid, but if anything happens to him . . .' and the other man said, 'Nothing happens to the boy as long as you do what you're told. When the company is mine, we'll be quits.' What do you think it meant?"

Prendergast, thought Iris.

"I have no idea," she said. "But don't worry about it. Your grandfather will take care of it. Here you are. Careful, it's still hot."

"I thought he would be happy to be home," said Ronnie as she placed his glass in front of him.

"I'm certain he is, deep down," said Iris as she poured herself a glass and sat next to him. "And I'm sure he will be very happy with your surprise. Now, let's have a toast, shall we?"

"I know how to do that!" he said eagerly. "Can you do it with milk?"

"I don't see why not," said Iris, holding up her glass. "Go ahead."

Ronnie picked up his glass with an expression so serious that Iris almost laughed in spite of herself.

"To Mummy!" he said, clinking his glass against Iris's.

"Excellently done," said Iris. "To Mummy!"

And her safe return home, she added silently.

When they finished, she rinsed out the glasses and pan and left them in the drying rack. Then they walked upstairs, side by side, holding hands. She used her torch to help him find his way to his bed, then tucked him in.

"Good night, Iris," he whispered.

"Good night, dear," she said, leaning forward to kiss him on the forehead. "Dream of Sir Oswald. He'll guard you through the night."

"And you will, too, won't you?"

"I'll be right downstairs. But don't tell anyone I'm here. It's a secret."

"I won't," he promised sleepily.

She slipped out of the room, closing his door behind her.

Somewhere in the recesses of the house, a telephone rang.

CHAPTER 11

Iris ran down the main staircase to the hallway telephone. Percival was just putting down the handset.

"It's them," he mouthed.

He walked to the library door and knocked softly. Then waited. Then knocked again more loudly. There was no response. He opened the door.

"Oh, dear," he sighed. "You had better come help, Miss Sparks."

She walked quickly into the room behind him, then pulled up short. Lady Bainbridge was sitting in her chair by the fireplace, slumped to one side, snoring loudly. An open whisky bottle sat on the small table. Iris didn't know how full it had been earlier, but it was nearly empty now.

"Can you revive her when she's like this?" asked Iris.

"I usually send for a pair of maids," said Percival. "This will not be easy."

"Nor will it be useful," said Iris. "We don't know how she's going to react on the telephone."

"I don't suppose it would be worth your trying to imitate her," said Percival.

"I won't take that chance. They may have Lord Bainbridge there to confirm her voice. If he reacts the wrong way or they think it's the police—"

"No, you're correct," said Percival. "Forgive me, Lord, for what I'm about to do."

He took Lady Bainbridge by the shoulders and shook her gently. Then more roughly.

"Lady Bainbridge," he said loudly. "Lady Bainbridge! Wake up! They're calling!"

After several attempts, her eyes opened and focused unsteadily on Percival.

"What?" she said hoarsely.

"The abductors are on the telephone, milady," he said. "They wish to speak with you."

"Help me up," she said. "I'm not feeling well."

I'm not surprised, thought Iris, coming over to grab an arm.

Lady Bainbridge looked at her in puzzlement as she did.

"Who are you and what are you doing here?" she asked.

"Iris Sparks. You asked me to come help."

"Oh, yes," said Lady Bainbridge. "I remember. Harold's been kidnapped."

"Yes. And Gwen."

"And Gwen," repeated Lady Bainbridge as they maneuvered her through the doorway. "That's right, they got both of them. What were they doing together? You don't suppose she and Harold—"

"Not a chance," said Iris. "Suppress that thought until the end of eternity. Hold the telephone receiver so that I can listen in. Don't promise them anything. Remember that the banks don't open until Monday, so you'll need time."

"What if I don't want him back?" asked Lady Bainbridge.

"What?" exclaimed Iris.

"Just toying with the idea," she said, an unpleasant chuckle escaping her throat.

"Think about Gwen," said Iris. "They will kill her along with Lord Bainbridge. Think about Little Ronnie."

"Yes, Ronnie," said Lady Bainbridge, sniffling. "So like my Ronnie."

"And he needs his mother," said Iris. "So it's up to you to make sure he gets her back."

"A boy needs his mother," said Lady Bainbridge. "This phone? They called on the house telephone? How common!"

"Careful," whispered Iris. "They can hear us."

Lady Bainbridge looked at the telephone as if she had never seen one before. Iris motioned to her impatiently. She picked it up.

"Hello?"

"Lady Bainbridge, is it?" came a man's voice.

"This is she."

"Hold on a tick, Your Ladyship. Lord Hubby wants a word."

There was a moment's pause.

"Carolyne, are you there?" said Lord Bainbridge.

"I'm here, Harold," she said. "Are you all right?"

"I'm fine," he replied. "They are treating me civilly. Listen, darling—you must do exactly what they tell you. It's very serious."

"I will try," she said. "Harold, I need to know—"

"Me again," said the first voice. "Now, we know you haven't gone to the police. Keep it quiet or hubby winds up on the bottom of the river. And we don't want that, do we?"

Lady Bainbridge glanced over at Iris and Percival, who immediately shook their heads.

"No, we don't," she said.

"So you are going to get forty-five thousand quid together in cash. We'll call you in the morning—"

"Monday," prompted Iris in a whisper.

"That's impossible," she said. "I don't have anything like that about the house, and the banks don't open until Monday."

"You expect us to hold him that long?"

"Young man, if you had put any forethought into your planning, you would have taken this into account," she said huffily. "I cannot change the banking hours. If you want the money, you'll have to wait until Monday."

There was a pause on the other end. They were consulting, guessed Iris. She quickly pulled a small notepad and pencil from her bag and wrote "GWEN?" on a page. She held it up. Lady Bainbridge looked at it woozily, then nodded.

"All right, we'll call first thing Monday."

"Make it elevenish," she said. "I have to get there and back."

"Eleven, then."

"Actually, eleven thirty would be better," she said, considering. "The streets are very busy in that part of the city."

"Lady, I will slit his throat right now."

"Eleven thirty it is, then," she said firmly.

Iris waved her notepad frantically.

"And what about Gwendolyn?" asked Lady Bainbridge.

"What about her?"

"Is she safe?"

"For the moment."

"I expect her to remain so," said Lady Bainbridge.

"What do you care about her?"

"If she isn't returned along with my husband, then you get nothing," she said. "Do I make myself clear?"

"We'll call Monday at eleven thirty," said the man. "Have the money ready, or else."

There was a click as he hung up. Lady Bainbridge stared at the handset, then slowly replaced it on its cradle.

"Well done," said Iris.

"Darling," said Lady Bainbridge contemptuously. "He called me darling. He hasn't called me that in thirty years. I finally know what it takes for him to say it. Well, that's done. What should we do next?"

"I have put out some feelers in various directions," said Iris. "I won't have any results until tomorrow. You should go about your normal Sunday routine, although you should cancel any social engagements. Oh, and if I may, I would like to borrow Albert in the morning. I want to investigate something, and it would be quicker if he drove me."

"Albert drives us to church on Sundays," said Lady Bainbridge.

"Then he can drop you off and come back and fetch me. I expect we'll be back long before the end of services."

"Very well," said Lady Bainbridge. "Would you care for a nightcap before we turn in?"

"No, thank you, ma'am," said Iris regretfully.

"Then I shall bid you good night. Percival, fetch Millie for me and have her meet me in my room."

"Very good, milady," said Percival. "Miss Sparks, I will show you to your room now."

"Lead on, Percival," said Iris.

She followed him up the staircase. At the top, instead of turning right towards the family rooms, he turned left and brought her to a hallway leading to guest rooms.

"I've put you in the last one," he said, opening the door for her. "I thought you might want the privacy."

"And it puts me further out of earshot," she said, spying her valise. "This will suit me admirably, Percival, thank you."

"Not at all, Miss Sparks," he said. "And may I add, since Lady Bainbridge neglected to do so, thank you on behalf of the household."

"Let's see how it goes before you thank me, but I'm glad she asked for me. It would have been terrifying to learn about it and not be able to do anything. Good night, Percival."

He closed the door. She changed into a nightgown, brushed her teeth, and crawled into bed, too exhausted to move, too keyed up to fall asleep.

Forty-five thousand pounds, she thought, yawning. Such a strange number. Somehow she'd expected a rounder one. Some multiple of ten thousand. How did they come up with forty-five? There must have been some complex financial analysis known only to people in the abduction game. Calculation of risks versus rewards, compensation for the number of men involved, transportation costs, hideout rentals, food. Having Gwen as an unexpected second hostage must have thrown their estimates off, assuming they fed her.

Gwen would have a better idea of it. She was much better at finances than Iris.

She hoped Gwen was safe.

She hoped she was still alive.

Gwen heard multiple footsteps. Then the door was unlocked and she heard them lead Lord Bainbridge in.

"How did it go?" she asked.

"Shut it," said the man who she had dubbed First Gaoler in her mind.

He loosened her bonds.

"Stand up," he commanded her. "Blindfold stays on."

She sat up, paused and took a breath this time before getting to her feet. That seemed to prevent the wooziness she had felt before.

"Where am I going?" she asked.

The blow wasn't hard but it caught her off guard, the heel of his hand cuffing the side of her chin, sending her staggering.

"Here now!" protested Lord Bainbridge.

"I said shut it, and I meant it," said the man as he tied her hands in front of her. "Same goes for you. Let's go, duchess."

He shoved her into the hallway. This time, they went to the left. She counted forty-two paces before they turned in to another room.

No breeze, she noticed. That meant no open windows. They must have been belowground, wherever they were. No vibrations from traffic or trains. She thought she heard a deep-toned horn, possibly from a ship, sounding somewhere in the distance.

She smelled cheap colognes, more than one mixing together, combining with the stench of sweat and greasy food.

She bumped up against a table. Cups rattled in saucers.

"Watch it," said a new man's voice. "You almost spilled my tea. Give her a chair."

One was shoved up behind her, bumping against her calves.

"Sit," said the man.

She sat, half expecting someone to pull it out from under her, as if this whole frightening day had been only a series of cruel practical jokes.

"Tell me," said the man. "How does the posh daughter-in-law of a Kensington house know Archie Spelling?"

"We're friends," she said. "Very good friends. On a first-name basis, in fact."

"How did that happen?"

"My girlfriend and I needed stockings, and we were out of coupons. Someone who knew someone sent us to Archie, and one thing led to another."

"So you're Archie's girl now?"

"No. My friend is."

"If he passed you over for her, then she must be a looker in-deed," commented the man. "Or maybe he likes women who don't get violent."

If you only knew, thought Gwen.

"Of course, this might all be a load of tripe," continued the man. "Anyone could have picked Archie Spelling's name up from somewhere. So, answer me this, if you're such bosom buddies: Where does he go to drink with his lads?"

"The back room at Merle's. It's a pub on Wapping High Street."

"Yeah, we know about Merle's. Everyone knows about Merle's. So where does he go where everyone doesn't know about it? A good friend of Archie Spelling who is on a first-name basis would know that, wouldn't she?"

"She would," said Gwen, summoning up Iris's recountings of the place from her visits there. "You mean the private club he set up in the back of the warehouse on Wapping Wall. Down the block from the Prospect of Whitby?"

"Describe it."

"Bar at one end. Snooker table, card tables, pictures of chorus girls on the walls, dressed as one would expect a chorus girl on the wall to be dressed. Or undressed."

"Who sits at the front door?"

"Usually a man named Tony. Likes to play the ponies, that's how I remember his name. How am I doing?"

Two men got up from the table and moved some few feet away. There was a murmured conversation. Then they came back and sat down.

"You know him," said the man. "Which brings me to the next question. So what?"

"Look, I know that you're worried that I can identify one of you," she said quickly, trying to keep the desperation out of her voice. "I can tell you that I didn't get a good look, or that I have terrible memory for faces, or promise you my eternal silence, but I'm sure none of that matters to you."

"It doesn't," agreed the man.

"So what I propose is that Archie be my guarantor. Give me, I don't know what to call it, some professional courtesy or an employee discount or what have you. Let me go, on the condition that should I betray you in any way, Archie will personally see to my punishment. I know enough about him for that to be a substantial threat."

"But if you're a friend—"

"I don't think anyone is that good a friend to Archie that he won't put business first," said Gwen.

"Yeah, she knows him good," commented another man.

"I don't know," said the first man.

"Think about it," urged Gwen. "There is no need to make any of this worse than it already is, or frighten me more than you already have. I am more than suitably terrified. I'll be happy enough if I make it out of here alive and intact to not bother with seeking justice afterwards. And I should like something to eat and drink, please, while I'm making requests."

"What?"

"Well, I don't know how long you're planning to hold me, but I'm starving, I'm thirsty, and my head is splitting, thanks to whoever knocked me out."

"I think she's making a complaint to the management," said one of the other men, and his mates joined him in laughter.

"Get her a sandwich," said the man in charge. "Cup of water. We're short on tea here."

"Thank you," said Gwen. "May I ask how much my ransom is?"

"Your ransom? What makes you think you're worth anything?"

"That's rather insulting, isn't it?" asked Gwen.

A plate was placed in front of her.

"Go ahead," said the first man. "Eat."

"My wrists are tied," she pointed out.

"So?"

"Very well," she said, reaching forward with both hands.

She was able to get hold of the sandwich and raise it to her mouth. It contained a slice of a cheese that she couldn't identify and wasn't sure she wanted to identify. Nevertheless, it was food.

"I suppose there is a certain entertainment value in watching a woman eat while blindfolded and with her hands tied," she commented between bites.

"Oh, there is," agreed the first man. "We've been amused by everything here tonight, haven't we, lads?"

"Oh, yeah," said one of the others.

"Especially the part where you thought you could impress us with Archie Spelling," continued their leader. "That was a miscalculation on your part, duchess."

"How so?" asked Gwen, taking another bite.

"You assumed that all of us who run on the shady side of the street are in it together," said the first man. "That we have interests in common. You don't take into account the possibility that maybe we don't like each other. That maybe you landed in the middle of Archie Spelling's worst enemies, and bringing up his name is the worst idea you possibly could have had. That maybe it tips the balance in favour of leaving you with your throat slit under a trestle just to send him a message."

"If that were the case, I don't think you would have wasted a sandwich on me," said Gwen.

"Yeah, well, things are still up in the air," said the man. "We're waiting on some news. You've got another day."

"Then hurrah for me," she said. "In that case, may I have that glass of water? I'll take something stronger, if you have any."

She heard a cup land next to her plate, and guided her hands carefully until she got a firm grip on it. It was water. She gulped it greedily.

"One more thing to consider, duchess," said the man. "There's also the matter of recompense. The boy you went at may lose that eye, thanks to you."

"I am sorry for it," said Gwen.

"Oh, you're sorry, are you? Like that will bring his eye back?"

"I am sorry that you put him in a situation where I had to defend myself against him. I am sorry that he chose this particular profession, but he made that choice, not I. If he wants to play dangerous games, then he should expect to get hurt. So yes, I am sorry that I hurt him. And I would do it again."

"I suppose you would have shot the lot of us had you got the gun."

"What would you have done?"

"Take her back," he said wearily.

"Up," ordered First Gaoler from behind her.

She stood, and he led her out.

She had read in some cheap mystery that tensing one's body while being bound would create some useful give in the ropes, but the moment she tried, a gun was cocked and put to her head.

"You think we're stupid?" asked First Gaoler.

"Not at all," she said, relaxing her muscles.

They tied her extra tight after that, then closed and locked the door behind them.

"Well?" said Lord Bainbridge.

"I presented my credentials," said Gwen. "My bona fides have been verified."

"And?"

"And I won't know anything until tomorrow. But I will live that long, at least. I don't seem to be worth anything to them. Nothing like being kidnapped to show a woman her value in this world. I suppose I have you to thank for that."

"Me? Why me?"

"If you hadn't seized control of my shares, maybe they'd want ransom for me. And maybe I could pay it. But you like to keep me dependent on you, even in the worst situations."

She laughed suddenly.

"What on earth have you got to laugh about?" asked Lord Bainbridge.

"The oddest memory popped into my head," she replied. "A silly sketch Ronnie and I saw in a revue before we were married. This older gent has a beautiful daughter, and some Cockney lout asks him how much he wants for her. The older gent, marvelously huffy, says, 'Sir, my daughter is a virtuous woman. Her price is far above rubies.' And the Cockney says, 'Then tell me where Ruby lives. Maybe I can afford 'er.'"

"I cannot believe that you would remember that at a time like this."

"He sang such a funny song," she continued, ignoring him. "What was it? 'I Used To Date a Girl Who Wore Camouflage, But I'm Not Seeing 'er Anymore.' Ronnie would sing that to me at the most opportune times, and it always broke me up."

"You should stop this prattling and try to get some sleep."

"I can't," she said. "I'm scared, Harold. I'm scared that I have a concussion and will die if I don't stay awake. I'm scared that Ronnie will lose both his parents before his seventh birthday, both by violence, and that he will be scarred for life. I am scared that I won't see him grow up, or see what manner of man he becomes. I am scared that I will have no say in how he's raised, but I've been scared of that ever since I was in the sanatorium and found out you got custody of him. It nearly set my recovery back a year the day they informed me, did you know that?"

"I knew something about it," he said. "That there was some form of attempt at something foolish."

"Foolish is a poor word for it," she said. "I was in a haze of drugs and despair. They found me trying to hang myself with a bedsheet the night after I learned you had done it."

"We were only trying—"

"To take away my son. Tell me, dear father-in-law, was that to protect his interests or to seize full control of Bainbridge, Limited?"

"We're back to that, are we? Would you trust any answer I would give you?"

"We may both be dead within a day, Harold. There's no point in lying anymore."

"Gwen. We are both going to live. I promise you that we will come through this."

She was silent. Then he heard her crying softly.

"You see, that wasn't so hard," she said. "A reassurance to someone goes a long way."

"Even when it's a promise you don't know I can keep?"

"It's the kindness at the heart of it," she said. "It's the first kindness you've shown to me since before Ronnie died. And with that, I will try to sleep, Harold."

Mrs. Billington thought Sally wouldn't be hard to spot, given his size, but she was wrong. When she arrived outside of the building where The Right Sort kept its offices, he was nowhere to be seen. Then somehow he was by her side, and she never saw him coming. She almost screamed.

"That was startling," she said, catching her breath. "Must you sneak up on a person like that?"

"My apologies," said Sally. "Bad habit during peacetime. Let's get that address, shall we?"

She unlocked the front door of the building. She was about to reach for the light switch when Sally stopped her and produced a torch.

"I'd rather not attract unnecessary attention," he said.

"You're quite the spooky lad when you want to be," she commented as they headed up the stairs.

"Saturday night, closed office building in Mayfair," he said. "If the lights are on, the bobbies will want to know why we're here and not at a club somewhere."

"Is that where you would be right now if Miss Sparks hadn't called?" she asked.

"Depending on how sorry I was feeling for myself," he said. "I was on my sofa nursing a whisky and listening to the Light Programme, so I must have been feeling very sorry indeed."

She thought about asking him if he liked Chips Chippindall, but decided against it.

She unlocked the door to Gwen and Iris's office when they reached it.

"Keep the lights off?" she asked.

"Please," he said, shining his torch at Iris's desk.

On top were the sacred green metal file boxes, labeled "F" and "M." Mrs. Billington stepped to the desk, reached for the "M" box, then hesitated.

"What?" asked Sally.

"She made a joke the other day about leaving them booby-trapped," said Mrs. Billington. "It's silly, I know, but I feel nervous about touching them when she's not here."

Sally immediately moved to the desk.

"Get behind me, then stand absolutely still," he whispered urgently.

"What?"

"Do as I say, woman, or we're both done for!"

"Are you serious?"

"I've never been more serious in my life," he said grimly. "Get behind me if you want to live."

She scampered behind him, trying to peer behind his massive bulk. He shined his torch at the box, then quickly around the surface of the desk.

"Hmm," he said, pulling a pencil from his jacket. "Clever. Very clever indeed."

"What?" said Mrs. Billington as he poked about the desk around the box.

He tapped the top of the box with the pencil twice, then three times more. Then he opened it and shouted, "Boom!"

She nearly fainted.

Nothing happened.

"She was having you on," said Sally, turning to her with a grin. "So was I. I'm fairly certain Sparks doesn't have access to explosives. Not anymore, at least."

"You're a brute," she said, gasping. "A matched set of brutes, the pair of you."

"Let me get that address," he said, quickly thumbing through the cards. "Alphabetical, I assume. Ah, there we are."

He copied the address onto Iris's steno pad, then tore off the top sheet.

"It's in Bromley-by-Bow," he said.

"How are we going to get there?"

"I have a car," he said. "Let's go."

She locked up the office. Once outside, Sally led her to a black Jensen Wolseley Hornet two-seater and opened the door for her. She got in, then watched with fascination as he folded his body into the driver's seat.

"I had them modify the seat so I could fit my legs in," he said, noticing her stare. "I'd love a larger car, but I can afford this one. And given the limited petrol coupons, I rarely use it, so this will be fun."

Even with the modified seat, he had to bend awkwardly to bring his eyes in line with the windshield. Once the car pulled away from the kerb, however, he seemed comfortable in that position.

Bromley-by-Bow was by Bow, unsurprisingly, and on the western bank of the River Lea. The address turned out to be a two-storey brick building with a chemist's shop on the ground floor and rooms up above. A large, fading billboard on one side showed a healthy, rosy-cheeked maid to the left of a slogan proclaiming IT WOULD BE A MISTAKE TO MISS TAKING YOUR BOVRIL.

"My boys hate that stuff," said Mrs. Billington. "I told them it will make them big and strong."

"Qualities that are overrated, in my experience," said Sally. "That's the place. I am going to take a quick reccy to see if that motorcycle is parked in the vicinity. If you see our man, duck down. He might recognise you."

"Right. Should I blow the horn or anything?"

"No. I won't be long."

He opened the door, unfolded, and slipped away. She kept watch.

I'm on a stakeout, she thought excitedly. What would Bertram think?

Well, given she was out with a single man ten years her junior, she thought she might not want to tell Bertram all the pertinent details of her evening.

She watched Sally saunter by the chemist's shop and glance at the names on the attached boardinghouse. Then he disappeared down the block. Just as she was beginning to worry, he came up from behind the car and rejoined her.

"No Royal Enfield motorcycles in the vicinity," he reported. "Mr. Daile's name is not listed on the door, but that doesn't prove anything. A rented room is—"

"Why are we doing this, exactly?" asked Mrs. Billington.

"Vetting a potential husband," replied Sally.

"Do you often put candidates under surveillance like this?"

"More than you'd expect," returned Sally blithely. "Why, I once had to—"

"I'm not a stupid woman," said Mrs. Billington quietly. "Please don't insult me by treating me like one."

Sally was silent.

"Well?" she asked.

"There's something going on," he said. "It may involve Mr. Daile. Sparks wanted me to look into it."

"That was wonderfully vague," said Mrs. Billington. "Something criminal? Something dangerous?"

"You almost sound like you're hoping that it is," said Sally, glancing at her. "Yes. Yes to both. And I won't tell you anything else about it."

"Am I in danger right now?"

"This? Dangerous? Not at all," Sally said reassuringly. "This is gathering information. This is boringly safe."

"You have been in dangerous situations before, though," she said. "Haven't you?"

"There was a war. I was in it."

"And you don't like to talk about it."

"Not particularly."

"I know other men like that," she said. "All old before their time."

"That's comforting."

"Which of my employers do you fancy?" she asked, smiling at him.

"I'm sure I don't know what you're talking about," he said.

"You went to school with Miss Sparks, I know," she mused. "Old friends. Good friends. And you've stayed good friends without getting any further with it."

"You are starting to terrify me, Mrs. Billington."

"Yet you keep coming about, dropping everything at a moment's notice when they call," she continued, ignoring him. "I'm guessing it's Mrs. Bainbridge who's the main attraction now. Am I right?"

"I was mistaken," he said. "This is a very dangerous situation. And thank God, that's a motorcycle coming up to rescue me."

He plucked a pair of opera glasses from his pocket.

"Nice helmet," he observed. "Makes him look like a flier from the Great War. Take it off, laddie. Ah, there's the face. Is that him?"

He passed the opera glasses to Mrs. Billington.

"Yes," she said, looking through them. "That's Mr. Daile. What do we do now?"

"We do nothing," said Sally, taking them back. "My guess is that he's home for the evening from whatever he's been doing. Not gardening, certainly. He doesn't have any tools in his basket."

Mr. Daile entered the building. A minute later, a light went on in one of the upper windows. Sally put the glasses to his eyes as Mr. Daile sat at a desk by the window, visible from the street. Then he lowered them slowly.

"What's he doing?" asked Mrs. Billington.

"He's crying," said Sally.

CHAPTER 12

Iris woke as she heard a soft sound outside the door of her room. Resisting the urge to pull her knife from her bag, she got out of bed, padded to the door, and opened it cautiously.

A breakfast tray was on the floor before her. She picked it up and carried it to a small table by the window. Upon lifting the covers from the dishes, she found two slices of toast and, to her delight, a small pot of raspberry jam.

Glorious! she thought, spooning it greedily onto one of the slices. I wonder if they make it here, or bring it in from the country estate.

She bit into it, then let the sweetness spread through her before she even began chewing.

Good of them to share, she thought.

Then she realised they had extra rations this morning. Two of their household were missing.

This was Gwen's toast and jam she was eating.

It didn't taste so sweet now.

There was a small folded note wedged under the teapot. She opened it.

"'Albert will meet you at the garage at nine thirty,'" she read. "'Use the kitchen door. Percival.'"

I am still a secret, she thought.

She finished her breakfast and dressed. It was still early. She wanted to sneak down to the library and read the rarest volume they had, but that would not be permissible. She'd have to chivvy an invitation when all of this was done. Unless it all went horribly wrong and she became persona non grata for life.

She risked a peep out of her window, which was on the side of the house away from the driveway. A family came out of the house next door, dressed for church. A father, a mother, and two chattering girls that looked to be nine and eleven, if Iris was any judge, followed by a team of servants wearing their Sunday best. It would be a day off for the latter, she supposed.

Iris was not a churchgoer. Sunday mornings in her experience had become a time of hangovers and regrets. Lately, though, the combination of cutting down on her drinking with her reliance on gangsters' hours for her social fun had meant more and more Sunday mornings where she awoke alert and sober. She wondered if another foray into worship would fill the void.

Well, not this morning. She kicked her shoes off and went through her stretches and Defendu routine, barely avoiding knocking a vase off the table with a particularly energetic kick. By the time she was done, it was nine twenty. She put her shoes back on, touched up her makeup, grabbed her bag, and sneaked down the back stairs and out the kitchen door.

Albert was waiting for her by the Daimler. He tipped his hat and opened the rear door somewhat pointedly.

"How are you feeling today?" she asked.

"Much better, thanks," he said. "So I'll drive."

"I'll let you," she said, sliding onto the backseat. "Did Percival tell you where we're going?"

"Yes. The Livingstone Club. May I ask why?"

"It occurred to me that someone may have been monitoring Lord Bainbridge there," said Iris. "I want to make some enquiries, see what I can turn up."

"It doesn't open until noon."

"I'm not interested in what goes on during regular hours," said Iris. "It shouldn't take long. You'll be back in plenty of time."

She looked out the window moodily as he drove. He took a right on Kensington High Street and continued east. The road changed its last name every few blocks. Kensington High Street, Kensington Gore, then to the more prosaic Kensington Road.

Streets are like spies, she thought. They pass through where you live, changing identities according to local customs, and disappear without notice. She tried to remember what a gore was. Something topographical, vaguely triangular, but she couldn't help imagining the neighborhood steeped in blood every time she traveled through it. She wondered if anyone else made that connection, or if it had become just another name without meaning over time.

They skirted the south end of Hyde Park, continuing on Knightsbridge, a fine, upstanding name that made one feel safe from attack. At least from land, she thought, spotting a building still showing heavy bomb damage.

Knightsbridge led to Piccadilly, which gave way to Shaftesbury Avenue. Then, finally, they turned north on Charing Cross Road. Two more turns onto Adeline, and Bedford Square Park came into view.

"Turn left on Bedford Avenue, then pull over," Iris instructed Albert.

"But the entrance is on the next block up," he said.

"This is not a front-door sort of mission," said Iris. "There's a space. Grab it. I'll let myself out, if you don't mind."

"But—" protested Albert.

"Or even if you do," said Iris, getting out the moment the car came to a halt. "Back in a while. Get yourself some coffee if you like."

"Nothing's open around here," muttered Albert as he watched her walk to the entrance of Morwell Street.

She stood in front of it for a moment.

Just an alley, Sparks. Just a long narrow street with buildings looming on both sides, with the morning sun still low enough to put the whole thing in shadow.

I live in the shadows, she thought.

All right, Dr. Milford. I am finally going to face the building of my nightmares. Not face, exactly. I am bravely sneaking down the back alley of my nightmares. Does that count? By all reckoning, back alleys are even scarier, aren't they? I should get extra credit.

She started walking down Morwell.

On this side the backs of the buildings, having no need to present anything to the well-to-do passersby, abandoned any attempt to impress architecturally. Every single one of them showed a flat, unadorned wall pushed to the limits of the narrow sidewalk. It was Sunday, so the rubbish bins were out of sight. She could see all the way up to the exit onto Bayley Street, where the sun shone once again. No one else was there.

She walked quickly down the alley, slowing as she came to the rear of the Livingstone Club. There were two doors, one with the stenciled word DELIVERIES. She raised her hand to ring the bell—

She was running barefoot through the narrow hallway in the staff quarters, her slip all that covered her. She came to his room and managed to keep from pounding on it. She could only trust one man. She couldn't take a chance of waking the others. She rapped softly on the door. Nothing. She risked a louder knock, wanting to scream and put her fist through it. This time, she heard a rustling. Then Henri opened the door.

"Miss McTague?" he said in surprise. "But what—"

Then he stopped when he saw the blood.

"Sorry for the bother, Henri," she said. "I need to use your telephone. Rather desperately."

She stood frozen in front of the door, her hand hovering in front of the bell.

I've returned to the scene of the crime, Mike, she thought. I guess I'm one of the stupid ones after all.

She rang the bell.

Gwen woke and screamed. She couldn't move, she couldn't see, she was—

"Kidnapped," she said, gasping. "Right. Only kidnapped."

"Gwendolyn?" said Lord Bainbridge from across the room.

"Don't worry, disoriented, discombobulated, dis everything," she said. "I'll be right as rain in a moment, have no fear."

"Do you wake like this every morning?"

"Just the ones when I'm bound and blindfolded. Forgive me for being less than chirpy."

"Don't be ridiculous. You're holding up incredibly well under the circumstances."

"How are the circumstances?" she asked, struggling to get her breathing under control. "Any news?"

"They haven't been by yet," he said. "How's the head this morning?"

"Like a month's worth of hangovers crammed into one, applied with a rolling pin," she said. "But I slept, and I woke up again, so a jolly good start to the day. It's Sunday, isn't it?"

"It is."

"We're missing church," she said.

"I expect we'll be forgiven," he said.

"It may be my last day on earth. I should have liked to have gone."

He was silent.

"Harold, would you mind if I prayed?" she asked.

"Of course not."

"O Lord our heavenly Father, Almighty and everlasting God," she began, "who hast safely brought us to the beginning of this day, defend us in the same with thy mighty power, and grant that this day we fall into no sin, neither run into any kind of danger, but that all our doings may be ordered by thy governance, to do always that which is righteous in thy sight, through Jesus Christ our Lord. Amen."

She paused expectantly.

"No amen from you?" she asked.

"Sorry. Amen. I'm surprised you chose that one. We have run into danger in the extreme, prayer or no prayer."

"Yet we have lived another day," said Gwen. "I've learned to be grateful for every one I am given. And if this is to be my last—"

"Don't say that."

"If this is to be my last," she repeated firmly, "then I wish to end it well. Harold, I forgive you."

"What?"

"I forgive you. I don't understand what drove you to be the way you are, or how you came to hate me so. If it's because you thought I wasn't good enough for your son, please know that I loved him, and that he loved me."

"I know he did."

"And I know you faulted him for it."

Lord Bainbridge did not reply.

"You weren't happy when we dated, you weren't happy when we became engaged, and you weren't happy when we wed," she continued. "Then the war started, and happiness went away for all of us. But your personal melancholy—was all of it because of me? How did I cause it? Why did you despise me so?"

"I despised you because you cracked when he died," said Lord Bainbridge. "Because I thought you were weak. A weak, silly, spoiled woman had married my son, and the heir to the Bainbridge fortune was the product of this unfortunate union."

"I see," said Gwen. "Why didn't you see what I went through? I cracked because I loved Ronnie. Half of me was ripped away when he was killed. The question is not why I cracked. It's why you didn't. If you had loved him the way I did, and the way I love my son now, how could you not? He was your son, your only child. Did you ever love Carolyne like that? At any moment? In the beginning, perhaps?"

"That was a marriage based on—" He stopped.

"On what? On love at some point, surely? I know she loves you."

"Loved."

"Loves still. Or would love again, if you would only let her. I think it's why she drinks."

"She married me because she had to," said Lord Bainbridge. "Because there needed to be an heir, so my father called me home to make a match for me."

"Home from Africa."

"Yes. Because my brother was ill and had no children. He should have been Lord Bainbridge, not me. I could have gone on exploring, but the business needed me. The family needed me, I should say. They were one and the same, for all practical purposes. I came home, married Carolyne, and we had Ronald. Then my brother died."

"I never knew that was the sequence of events. Was there never any affection between Carolyne and you?"

"We convinced ourselves that there was. We were smothered in a soft cocoon of wealth and expectation. There was never enough air, but we were too young to realise that. That knowledge came later."

"Is that why you kept returning to Africa? Because you needed air?"

"You've never been. You would see what I saw. Which Carolyne couldn't. She wouldn't even try when she was there. Stayed inside the entire time, either the house or the club. It was just as stifling for her there as it is here."

"Why did you marry her if you were so incompatible?"

"Financial convenience. The merging of the families meant the merging of the fortunes. And the need for an heir, of course. No one trusted the cousins who would have been next in line."

"I suppose the financial convenience is paying off for you now, isn't it?

"We shall see."

"Say we come through this unscathed, only poorer. What then?"

"We soldier on."

"That's how you see your marriage? As a battlefield?"

"Appearances must be kept up. Appearances are what matters, for the good of the family. It's all for your son now."

"And this is what his life is to be? I never knew how literal the 'Limited' in Bainbridge, Limited, was meant to be. What if he wants to do something else?"

"He will see the sense of it as he matures. That's why I want to send him to St. Frideswide's. They will instruct him in his proper role and prepare him for its inevitability."

"You say 'mature' as if he were a bond that will pay you a dividend when he comes of age."

"Why else do we have children?"

"Because we want to create beings who will make the world a better place than we have made," said Gwen. "Your generation brought it to the brink of destruction, for which my generation has paid the price. I want my son to save it."

"Creating a son to save the world has generally not worked out so well for the son," said Lord Bainbridge. "There is precedent for that."

"I know that. Even though I'm missing church, I know that," said Gwen sadly. "But we'll only get it right if we keep trying."

"That knock on the head has turned you socialist, I see."

"Nonsense. I'm a businesswoman, Harold. We have started a new kind of enterprise, one that will be thriving long after Bainbridge, Limited, collapses on its rotten pilings. And my Ronnie will be free to do as he pleases and will do it brilliantly."

"You choose to fight me, then?"

"I have been fighting you all along," said Gwen. "Are you just realising it now?"

"People have fought me before," said Lord Bainbridge. "I have always prevailed."

"Men have fought you," she said. "Over matters of money. You are now confronted with a woman fighting for her son. You are overmatched, Harold."

"Brave words from a bound woman," he scoffed.

"Tell me about the dead man," she said. "The murdered African found by your club. What's your connection to him?"

"What?"

Sally pulled up to a space half a block down from Mr. Daile's lodgings and turned off the motor. They had kept their vigil the previous night until the light in his window went out, then stayed for another half hour just in case it was a ruse. Then Sally brought Mrs. Billington home, ignoring her protests. He slept fitfully, got up at five, and made a pot of coffee which he poured into a thermos. He tossed it into his rucksack along with his opera glasses, a sandwich he had prepared, and a few other items he thought might be useful.

The rucksack now occupied the seat where Mrs. Billington had sat the night before. It did not ask him any personal questions, which he found preferable.

He uncapped the thermos and poured himself a cup of coffee to keep him alert. At eight o'clock, right as he was downing his second cup, Mr. Daile came out and straddled his Royal Enfield. Sally tossed his cup into the rucksack and timed his ignition for the roar of the motorcycle to mask it. Mr. Daile pulled away. Sally gave him half a block's head start, then put his Hornet in gear and followed.

It wasn't a long trip. Mr. Daile drove west through Whitechapel, turned left onto Gracechurch, and headed toward the Thames. Sally was wondering if he was going to cross at London Bridge, but just before reaching it, Daile turned east again on Lower Thames and paralleled the river for some distance After passing the Westminster Bridge, he headed east again.

Are we meeting someone at the Mall? thought Sally as he maintained a decent distance behind him.

Then Daile made a series of turns, winding up at Eccleston Street by Buckingham Palace Road. He pulled his motorcycle over to the curb, parked, and walked into a grey gothic building on the southwest corner.

Sally parked where he could keep an eye on the motorcycle and waited a decent interval, then risked getting out. He sauntered over to the building where a sign was posted, showing photographs of the interior, including a large hall with pews.

ECCLESTON HALL, read the sign. SCRIPTURE GIFT MISSION. THE HALLS ARE AVAILABLE AT LOW CHARGES FOR APPROVED MEETINGS OF CHRISTIANS. TEAS CAN BE PROVIDED. FOR PARTICULARS APPLY TO SECRETARY. To the left was a schedule. At the moment, the hall was being occupied by the Free Presbyterian Church of Scotland.

Put in a good word for me, laddie, thought Sally. He walked back to his car, got in, and cranked down the windows. He poured himself another cup of coffee, pulled out his sandwich, and waited.

A porter Sparks didn't recognise opened the door and looked at her curiously. Women were only allowed in the Livingstone Club as guests, and those always came through the front.

"May I help you?" he asked in an accent that she placed from the southern part of the continent.

"I would like to speak to Monsieur Kouassi," she said.

"The club is closed," he said.

"I know," she said, "which is why I am here. Tell him Miss McTague needs to speak to him."

"I cannot disturb him at this hour," he said.

"Either you disturb him, or the police will disturb everybody," said Sparks. "Or would you like me to be more threatening? I can be."

"McTague, you said."

"Yes."

"I will see what I can do."

He closed the door. She heard it lock. She waited.

A few minutes later, she heard footsteps. Then the door opened, and the maître d' stood there, looking at her impassively. He was wearing ordinary grey slacks with a pair of black suspenders and a white undershirt.

"You're out of uniform, Henri," Iris observed.

"So are you," he said. "What do you want?"

"I need to ask you some questions."

"Do you? Interesting. The last time I set eyes on you, you and your mysterious friends were removing the body of one of our less savoury members under circumstances I am forbidden to discuss. Two days ago, another body is found not twenty feet from here, and now you are back."

"You're making me feel like an omen, Henri," said Iris. "Could we speak inside? I'm uncomfortable talking to you like this."

"Will the police be involved?"

"Not if I can help it."

"Can you help it?" he asked. "The last time, the incident was safely buried by whomever you worked for. I was told I could not ask who that was."

"And I can't tell you now," she said.

That was the point where he could call her bluff, she knew. She met his gaze steadily and watched to see if he would back down.

He did, stepping back and holding the door open for her to come inside.

"We will speak in my office," he said. "Come this way."

He led her through a room holding freestanding metal shelves of supplies. Somewhere off to her right she could hear kitchen sounds, snatches of different languages as preparations for luncheon took place. They walked quickly though the back hallways to a small office. Henri closed the door, then gestured for her to sit on a small wooden chair across from his desk.

"Make it quick," he said.

"You have a member named Harold Bainbridge, correct?"

"Lord Bainbridge is a long-standing member of the Livingstone Club," he replied.

"Lord Bainbridge returned home to his family from an extended trip reviewing his holdings in East Africa," said Sparks. "Since then, he has been off almost every night to come to the club. Is that correct?"

"Yes," said Henri. "Through Thursday evening. We haven't had the pleasure of his patronage since then."

"No doubt. Here's the interesting thing: Although he came home to his family Monday, he actually arrived in London on Sunday. Did he stay here?"

"He did not stay in the club Sunday," Henri said smoothly.

She didn't even need Gwen there to know that Henri was concealing something. She smiled.

"What about the special guest rooms?" she asked.

"Do you like secrets, Mary?" Carlos whispered in her ear, his lips lightly brushing the lobe.

"I adore secrets," she said, giggling.

"I am going to show you one," he said, guiding her to a stairway.

Instead of taking her up to one of the clubrooms, they went down into the basement.

"Are we allowed here?" she asked, wobbling slightly on her heels. "I mean, when there's no air raid?"

"Special guests are," he said, leading her to a plain, metal door with the word FACILITIES *stenciled on it. "When they are with a member with certain privileges."*

"Oooh, privileges," she burbled. "What sort of privileges?"

"*This key, for example,*" *he said, locating it on a ring.*

He turned it in the lock and opened the door. She peered inside to see a dark tunnel.

"*I'm not going in there,*" *she declared.* "*It doesn't look safe.*"

He flipped a switch, and a series of naked bulbs illuminated the tunnel which led, as she already had been briefed, under Morwell to the next building.

"*Safer now?*" *he asked, stepping in and holding out his hand.*

"*Will I be with you the whole time?*" *she asked.*

"*Of course.*"

"*Then not safe at all,*" *she said, placing her hand in his.* "*Show me your secrets.*"

Henri didn't answer.

"Come on, Henri," she persisted. "Did Lord Bainbridge take one of the special guest rooms last Sunday?"

"I fail to see what this has to do with your—operation," he said.

"We don't give a damn if he has a mistress or anything like that," she said. "But he's a munitions manufacturer with an international clientele, and there have been certain—irregularities."

"Irregularities?"

"I can't say more, Henri. But I wouldn't be here if national security wasn't at stake. Was he here last Sunday or not?"

"He was here," Henri admitted. "He took one of the special guest rooms. A suite, in fact."

"For how long?"

"He paid for a month."

"That long? That's unusual. Was he with anyone, or did you know of anyone else using the room?"

"He requested absolute privacy. Not even a charlady. And two sets of keys."

"So he did have someone else there," mused Sparks. "Any sign of the other person?"

"Whoever it was, if there was anyone, they did not use the tunnel," said Henri.

"Then they used the door to the Tottenham Court alley. Anyone see them come and go? Bring in meals and the like?"

"Our staff is instructed not to see anyone, not to notice anyone, and not to remember who they see and notice," said Henri.

"What about the dead man?" asked Sparks. "Anyone see him hanging about the place?"

"Not to my knowledge," said Henri.

"Well, then let's go take a look, shall we?" said Sparks, getting to her feet.

"You want to see the suite? What if Lord Bainbridge is there?"

"Henri, I can absolutely guarantee that he is elsewhere. Take me there."

He took a freshly laundered shirt from a drawer, slid his suspenders down, and donned it.

"All that for me?" she asked.

"I am escorting a solitary woman to the special guest rooms," he said, putting on a bow tie and jacket. "Reputations must be protected."

"I'm not worried about my reputation, Henri, but thanks for the thought."

"I was referring to mine, Miss McTague," he said, opening the office door. "Follow me, please."

He paused at the stairwell, listening for a moment, then beckoned to her. They descended the steps quickly and silently. He led her to the tunnel door, unlocked it, and turned on the lights.

"Any other rooms in use?" she asked as they walked through. "I don't want to bother the other members."

"Just one on a different storey," he said.

Her encounters with Carlos had taken place in room 2D. She hoped Lord Bainbridge had not taken the same room. She was already suppressing her screams coming in here, seeing a trail of blood droplets on the floor where there was none.

They came to the end of the tunnel, where Henri unlocked another door. It opened onto a stairwell. He took her up.

"Three-C," he said.

A small sigh of relief escaped her.

"Anything the matter?" he asked, hearing it.

"Just the prospect of climbing so many steps," she said. "Lead on."

The hall was short but richly carpeted. There were only four rooms off it; two on each side, separated far enough that noises couldn't be heard from one to the other.

As Sparks knew all too well.

Room 3C was on the far right. Henri pulled out his keys, then hesitated.

"What if someone is there?" he asked. "Someone other than Lord Bainbridge?"

"Then that will be someone I want to talk to," said Sparks.

He knocked on the door first, waited for a respectful interval, then knocked again. There was no answer. He took a deep breath and turned the key in the lock.

The door opened onto a foyer, which in turn led to a small dining room. The table had a linen damask cloth, embroidered with fanciful versions of African plains with scenes of lions and cheetahs hunting impalas, gazelles, and other beasts. Two pairs of silver candlesticks were set on it, but it was otherwise not laid out for a meal. The wallpaper had more of a jungle theme, clearly done from illustrations rather than actual experience on the continent. A stuffed antelope's head surveyed the scene from the center of the wall at one end.

"Hello?" called Henri.

There was no answer.

"Right," said Sparks. "I suppose you'll want to remain while I search."

"Unfortunately, I must. Will you be long?"

Sparks didn't respond, choosing instead to pull on a pair of black leather gloves from her bag.

There was a sitting area, with a sofa and a pair of armchairs surrounding a low table. There were copies of *The Telegraph* stacked on one end. She glanced at the dates. The last one was from Thursday, so someone had been bringing them in. Lord Bainbridge himself? Or someone else?

There was a small kitchen. The pantry was fully stocked. The refrigerator held a quart bottle of milk that was half-full. She opened the cap and sniffed it. It was still fresh. There was a stick of butter and a bottle of porter, but nothing else.

There were two bedrooms. Here was where the themed opulence of the dining room gave way to something more voluptuous in the decoration. Rich, transparent silks surrounded the four-poster bed in the first room she entered. There were small, metal rings set into the posts. Those she remembered from her visits with Carlos.

And there was mosquito netting rolled into the canopy, for those who wanted to pretend they were back in Africa.

The bed was made. She leaned over and sniffed at the pillows, but no scents triggered anything. She methodically went through the drawers in the dresser and night tables, then the bureau. There was nothing to be found. She ran her hands under and around the mattress, to no avail.

"Immaculate," she said. "And not your doing?"

"He requested no housekeeping service," said Henri, watching uncomfortably from the doorway.

"Let's see the other room," she said.

The second bedroom was identical to the first, nothing in the drawers or bureau, the bed made up neatly.

Except it looked different somehow. Sparks couldn't place what it was.

"Be right back," she said.

She went back to the first bedroom and stared at it for a time. Then she returned to the second.

It was how the bed was made up. The quilted coverlet sat differently. Slightly lower. She grasped the edge by the pillows and pulled it back, revealing the printed sheet underneath.

She went back to the first bedroom and repeated the experiment, revealing a light blue blanket. Under that were printed sheets similar to the first.

She went back into the second bedroom, Henri following her, his body language indicating his weariness with the constant pendulum that was Sparks on the prowl.

"Shouldn't this bed have a blanket?" she asked him, pulling back the coverlet to show him.

"I suppose it should," said Henri.

She opened the bureau, the top of which contained extra bedding. No blanket.

"Where is it, then?" she asked.

"I have no idea," he said.

Anyhow, he wasn't killed here. Someone wrapped his body in a blanket and dumped it after the fact.

"I do," she said grimly.

She went back into the dining room, looking around more closely. One of the high-backed chairs for the dining table was placed against the wall rather than at the table with the other three. She moved it away.

There was a round hole in the wall, with gouge marks at the bottom. The wall immediately around it was slightly lighter in colour than the portions further away. She ran one gloved finger around it. The area around the hole was clean. She tried the farther portions, and her fingertip came away with a light residue of dust. She took her torch from her bag and shone it inside the hole.

"You've got another crime scene here, Henri," she said, peering inside. "They did a nice job of cleaning it up after, but they didn't patch the hole after they dug the bullet out. They must have wiped up the blood as well."

"And the blanket?"

"Used to carry the body out."

"The man in the alley."

"That's my guess. If the blanket matches, that would be proof."

"Why dump him there? Why not leave him in the room?"

"So the police wouldn't immediately connect it to the person who took the suite," said Sparks, shutting off her torch and turning. "Whoever killed him may not have known whether housekeeping would be coming in or not. They needed to buy time. They cleared everything out of here that could be traced to whoever was staying here."

"But Lord Bainbridge wasn't spending his nights here."

"He did Sunday," said Sparks. "After that, I'm guessing it was the dead man up through sometime Thursday or early Friday morning."

"What do we do?"

"You call the police," said Sparks. "Detective Superintendent Parham or Detective Sergeant Kinsey. But do me a favour."

"What?"

"Call them tomorrow."

"Why? There is a murderer on the loose. It might even be Lord Bainbridge."

"It might be," she agreed. "But there are other lives at stake. I need twenty-four hours."

"Why should I do that for you? For whomever you work for?"

She grabbed him by the arm and pulled him into the bedroom. Then she held up one of the metal rings on the bedpost.

"Because I know what really goes on in the special guest rooms," she said. "And you don't want the public to know about that, do you?"

"I only work here," he said.

"And you and everyone else who works here will be out on their ears if they shut this place down," said Sparks. "Twenty-four hours, Henri. Do we have a deal?"

"Yes, Miss McTague."

She walked out of the bedroom, giving the dining room one more perusal.

Something small and yellow under the table caught her eye. She knelt down and picked it up. It was a bit of broken crayon, the letters "AT" visible on the paper.

Atlas, she thought.

She put it back where it had lain.

Let the police make of that what they will, she thought. She had disturbed the scene enough.

Sorry, Mike.

On the other hand, you never would have found it without my help.

CHAPTER 13

What makes you think I have anything to do with that man?" asked Lord Bainbridge.

"You come back from your extended sojourn in Africa, and instead of reuniting with your family, you spend every evening at your club," said Gwen. "That isn't normal. You speak of keeping up appearances, yet you do exactly the opposite. You've been lashing out at everyone in the household, both family and staff. Even poor Ronnie—the way you treated his gift to you was heartless."

"So I'm heartless," said Lord Bainbridge.

"But I don't think you are," said Gwen. "You've been damaged by your life. Disappointed that you couldn't live out your youth exploring. Your adventurous spirit was quashed by your father's wishes, and it seems as if you're repeating his errors out of, shall we call it vengeance?"

"These are suppositions you've learned from your therapist," he said. "They don't mean anything."

"Then a man is found murdered outside your club."

"Coincidence. You're equating proximity with connection."

"Oh, it certainly could be a coincidence," agreed Gwen. "People die all the time in the most inconvenient of places. But your reaction to that news at the dinner table Friday made me realise two things."

"Which were?"

"It wasn't just lurid gossip to you. You were too upset to be discussing it."

"And the other thing?"

"That you were involved with him in some way."

"Pure fancy."

"I saw it in your face, Harold. I heard it in your voice. This man meant something to you. What was it?"

"Merely my distaste for the waste of human life."

"Said the man who lives off the sweat of men he sends into mines."

"As I said, you've turned socialist."

"Well, won't that be fun when I finally take my place at the table in the boardroom? But there's another reason why I believe you know more about him than you say."

"Which is?"

"You knew he wasn't one of the staff. Why would you know that? You're only a member of the club, not someone involved with its day-to-day operation, especially after being away for six months. Yet you immediately declared the dead man a nonemployee, and you spoke from personal knowledge. So I ask you again, Harold: what is your connection to him?"

"None. This is the product of your current plight exacerbated by your mental illness."

"On the contrary, I've had almost a full day of bed rest," she said. "As a working mother of a small child, this has practically been a vacation. Let's see, what else can my disordered mind come up with? Oh, of course! The kidnapping, only two days after the murder of the man you don't know. The kidnapping, which took place on the way to the Livingstone Club! Another major crime with proximity in time and place to the first."

"Nonsense."

"And with proximity to you," she said. "I am going to ponder that for a while. Do me the great favour of not talking."

"Ponder what? What do you mean?"

"I mean shut up, Harold. I'm thinking."

Albert pulled in behind the house, then got out and opened Iris's door for her.

"I have to go meet them at the church," he said, looking at his watch.

"That's fine," said Iris. "I'll be holed up in Lord Bainbridge's office. Let Percival know. And thanks, Albert."

He nodded brusquely, then got back in the car and backed down the driveway.

She let herself in and made her way to the office unobserved. She made sure to lock the door behind her, then turned her attention to the rolltop desk, smiling as she saw Ronnie's green rocks guarding it.

The lock was a simple one. I could force it easily enough, she thought. Or pick it.

She pulled the leather pouch containing her lock picks from her bag, glancing at the clock to see how much time she might have. Something about it piqued her interest.

Or, she thought, maybe I could unlock it without leaving behind any telltales.

She went to the clock, opened the concealed drawer from where she had seen Percival retrieve the key, and felt inside.

There were two keys in the drawer.

She held them up. One was short and made of brass, with an ornate curlicue design in the bow that echoed the decorations on the clock. The other was made of steel with a simple looped bow, suitable for putting on a key ring. Its long shank culminated in a short oblong bit.

She inserted the steel key in the desk lock and turned it. She was rewarded with the sound of tumblers sliding into place. She rolled the cover into its receptacle, then sat down and peered at the revealed contents.

The first thing that met her eye was a small framed picture of Ronnie Senior in the full-dress uniform of a Fusilier. Behind it, the desk was stuffed full of folders, ledgers, and stacks of correspondence tied with red twine.

This could take days, she thought glumly.

The ledger on top of the pile looked new, its blue cloth cover unfaded, unlike the others. She pulled it out, swept the rocks to one side, and opened it.

On the first page was the handwritten title, *Bainbridge, Limited. Mopani Acquisition and Development.*

She had no idea where Mopani was.

The succeeding pages were ruled in a double-entry format, but the ones directly following the title page were a journal of sorts, kept in the same handwriting as the title.

Made contact with guides in Chililabombwe. First foray to site postponed as advised roads unreliable. Arranged purchase of mules and wagons, along with supplies.

Details of the purchases were duly noted, along with payments to the guides.

There was a four-day journey. At some point, the notation *End of road* came up, but they carried on.

Arrival at village, she read. *They speak Lunda here, but a few of them understand my Bemba well enough.*

He actually took the trouble to learn the local language, thought Iris, impressed.

They showed me a pair of rocks. Split one open. Green veins throughout, don't know if malachite or annabergite without further testing, but green! Had them show me where found. Preliminary dig yielded more of same.

Asked if any other white men have been sniffing around. Cagey in their response. Pegged area for preliminary claim. Negotiated initial price. They wanted livestock and grain. Money no good this far out. Agreed to arrange for all.

The return trip to Chililabombwe occupied one ledger line. Then an entry was made for the price of a lab test on the rock samples. A single word was written, underscored three times: *MALACHITE!!!*

She skimmed through pages and pages as finances took over. Miners, equipment, supplies, food. The numbers became a blur after a while.

Gwen should see this, she thought. She'll figure out what's what.

One very large number jumped out at her. *Loan arranged from X. Thirty-seven thousand pounds.*

Why doesn't X have a name? she wondered. And why, looking at the big picture, is this ledger here and not at Bainbridge, Limited? Could the thirty-seven thousand borrowed now become forty-five thousand due?

Or overdue, hence the ransom demand?

Could X be Prendergast?

She read on. More expenses, interrupted by occasional jottings about mining progress.

No personal details, she noticed. He doesn't even put his own name anywhere.

She flipped through one of the bundles of letters, found one signed by Lord Bainbridge. The handwriting did appear to be the same as that in the ledger. Satisfied, she flipped over to the next page.

A photograph fell onto the floor.

She picked it up. It showed a medium brown–skinned woman, possibly in her mid-twenties, standing by a small boy, somewhat lighter in complexion. Both were dressed in British-style clothes. They were standing in front of the same large brick mansion that provided the backdrop for the photograph of Lord Bainbridge posing with his household staff. She went over to examine that one again.

The woman and child were not in it.

Interesting, thought Iris.

Iris riffled though the remaining pages of the ledger. The entries came to a halt a week before Lord Bainbridge began his return to London. The final notation read: *X recalcitrant. Must renegotiate terms.*

She returned the ledger to the top of the stack, then closed and locked the desk. She put the key back in its hiding place in the clock, making sure to put the clock key on top of it so Percival wouldn't suspect anything. She stared at the photograph some more, then tucked it in her bag.

I have seen you before, she thought. And a family resemblance is a family resemblance.

Archie Spelling was wearing his Sunday finest, his best charcoal grey suit with a wide red tie that would have brought on a curfew violation if the war was still going. But it wasn't. London was getting back on its feet, it was Sunday, and the zoo was open for business.

He used the south entrance, off the Broad Walk. He paid his fee and walked through the turnstiles, unique amongst the crowd going through in that he was alone. Children swarmed about once he came inside, screaming at the tops of their lungs, imitating beasts and birds, no doubt to the irritation of the beasts and birds being imitated.

Bad enough being put on display in a cage without the brats making fun of how you talk, thought Archie.

A bored, pretty young zoo attendant walked by, yanking at a leash, the other end of which was around the neck of an equally bored-looking llama, a small, terrified child sitting on its back while several more rode in a cart behind. A young dad was scampering alongside them with a Brownie camera, yelling, "Smile, sweetie! Smile for Daddums! One for Gram!"

Archie passed by the okapi, giving it a glance for cover's sake, then made a wide path around the children jostling one another for the best view at the Penguin Pool. One urchin dashing about fetched up against Archie's legs and looked up at him, startled.

"Watch where you're going, son," Archie admonished him.

"Sorry, mister," said the boy. Then he dropped his voice. "'E's already there. Got two blokes watching 'im."

"Good lad," said Archie, handing him a coin. "Go buy yourself a sweet."

The boy took it and dashed off. Archie was tempted to check to see if his wallet was still in his pocket, but the boy belonged to his gang, so he figured he knew better.

The big cat enclosure was past the penguins. He stopped before reaching it to tie his shoe. Next to him, a young mum was fussing with a baby in a carriage.

"'E's by Rota," she muttered. "One man by the tiger cage, the other smoking by the second bench."

"Gotcher," said Archie.

Rota was a lion, the chief draw for the zoo. His completely inappropriate name came from Rotaprint, the company owned by the man who initially raised him as a pet in Middlesex after winning him in a bet. Archie, knowing the story, often wondered what the other stakes were in that particular game. Rota, with his suburban upbringing, was one of the tamest specimens of his kind in the world, but his symbolic value as a British lion was such that the zoo had "given" him to Churchill during the war, and the Prime Minister had been known to visit him publicly and feed him raw steaks with British Pathé cameras in close attendance. Now he paced his cage waiting for his next meal, eyeing his audience with unleonine benevolence.

A more dangerous creature stood on two legs in front of Rota's cage, observing him with professional interest. The man wore a black suit, beautifully tailored, probably from Italy before the war and kept immaculately through it. He wore a white carnation in his buttonhole, and the kindness of his smile as he let some children step in front of him was in sharp contrast to the malevolent look in his eyes as he saw Archie walk up next to him.

"I always wonder how he can stand it," the man said, nodding at the lion. "Moving from that posh house to this. Like going to jail, if you ask me."

"At least 'e gets fed regular," said Archie. "Not enough coupons in the world if you 'ave one of these lying around the 'ouse. 'E'd start considering you as a ration if 'e got 'ungry enough. 'E's better off 'ere, and 'e knows it."

"Is he your favourite?" asked Manfred.

"Nah," said Archie. "I like the zebra best."

"Why is that?" asked Manfred.

"'E's the only one 'oo ever escaped," said Archie. "Made a break for it when 'is cage took a bomb. They caught him after a night on the town."

"Too bad he was wearing prison stripes," said Manfred. "Made it obvious. Although, given the shortages, he was lucky he wasn't eaten. Shall we walk?"

"Let's."

They strolled about, letting the crowd noise cover their conversation.

"I see you're using women and children to guard you," said Manfred.

"If I was meeting someone I was actually worried about, I'd 'ave brought a bloke," said Archie. "But seeing how this is meant to be a peaceable conversation, I left the boys behind."

"I appreciate your trust," said Manfred. "Why are we talking?"

"I 'eard there was a snatching done," said Archie. "Yesterday, on Marylebone Street."

"Really? Didn't see anything about it in the papers."

"Not likely to, either," said Archie.

"Who got snatched?"

"Some rich industrial feller," said Archie. "At least, 'e was the target. But they took his daughter-in-law as well."

"Did they?"

"They did."

"And what does this have to do with you or me or the price of tea in China?"

"Snatching is a special job," said Archie. "Never personally saw the profit in it. What I do is relatively low-risk, usual course of business, throw the coppers a bung, and everyone gets along fine. Snatching, on the other hand, is 'igh risk—"

"High reward," interrupted Manfred.

"Maybe," said Archie. "But it brings the coppers in full force and shines the spotlight so bright that everything else gets lit up as well. So not many go in for that line of work. I know of only two teams 'oo might. One of them works for you."

"That's as may be," said Manfred. "I'm waiting for a point to be made."

"I don't care about anyone making money off 'Is Lordship," said Archie. "But the daughter-in-law—"

"Ah, now we've come up against it," said Manfred. "What's she to you, Archie? Anything to do with that little brunette you've been sneaking about with?"

"The daughter-in-law is a blonde," said Archie.

"A blonde," mused Manfred. "I heard there was a tall blonde hanging about with the little brunette when you were celebrating a score a few weeks ago. The same?"

"The same. Mrs. Gwen Bainbridge. She was an accidental in

the snatching, not worth the ransom. Assuming she's still alive and well, I would prefer that she remain alive and well."

"And if she's not?" asked Manfred. "I'm not saying yea or nay to anything, because I don't know anything. I only wish to know the extent of your interest in the situation."

"Mrs. Bainbridge 'appens to be, and I cannot emphasise this strongly enough, a Friend of Archie."

"So is this a threat or a favour?" asked Manfred.

"It's not a threat unless something 'appens to her," said Archie. "As to favour—owing you a favour can be more dangerous than threatening you, from what I'm told. So let's not label this as anything other than me expressing my interest in the situation."

"Well, I don't know what to make of this," said Manfred. "It's all news to me. However, for the sake of charity and good feelings, I could ask about."

"That would be appreciated," said Archie.

"You mentioned two teams," said Manfred.

"Yeah, I'm off to the Monkey House next," said Archie.

"Give Mr. Clement my regards," said Manfred. "I suppose meeting me by the lions is a token of your respect."

"I respect lions more than monkeys," said Archie. "I'm off. Maybe I'll take a butcher's at the new panda while I'm 'ere."

"Always a pleasure, Archie," said Manfred, putting a finger to the brim of his hat.

He walked away, his two men joining him.

"Go all right?" asked Reg as he emerged from where he had been keeping vigil.

"Remember when the bombing started, and they 'ad to kill all the poisonous snakes here in case they got out?" asked Archie as he watched Manfred leave.

"Yeah."

"They missed one," said Archie. "Let's go."

*　*　*

I am keeping watch on a churchgoing man, thought Sally as he sipped his coffee slowly to make it last. I am keeping watch on this churchgoing man because he is a suspect churchgoing man. The churchgoing man is suspect because he was keeping watch on Gwen. So now I am keeping watch on him. Which makes me suspect, or would if anyone was keeping watch on me. Which would be easy at the moment because I am not in a church.

I wonder if anyone is watching me. I wonder if anyone is watching them in turn. Maybe . . .

Daile came out of the church, interrupting Sally's train of thought. He jumped on his motorcycle and roared off while Sally was still throwing his coffee out the window. He put his car in gear and drove after Daile, but had to brake as a family crossed the street in front of him. He accelerated the moment he had a clear path, just in time to see the motorcycle heading towards the Thames again. Then Daile turned left.

Please don't tell me you're going back home, thought Sally. Please don't tell me I've wasted all of my Sunday morning only to eliminate you as a suspect because you really are an innocent, churchgoing man.

He made the turn and picked up Daile, who was a block ahead.

And please let Gwen still be alive, Sally added fervently.

Gwen's stomach rumbled.

"There's a limit to the amount of pondering one can do without breakfast," she said. "Not to mention lunch."

"Have you come up with anything?" asked Lord Bainbridge.

"Oh, many things," she said. "I'll have to run them by Iris and get her view on all of this. She often sees things I don't."

"The two of you make quite the pair," said Lord Bainbridge.

"We do, don't we?" said Gwen. "To think that a year ago, we barely knew each other. It's unfortunate she's not looking into my abduction. I'm sure she would have freed me by now."

"That little thing?" scoffed Lord Bainbridge.

"You dismiss her at your peril," Gwen warned him. "She's—wait, someone's coming. Two someones. Quickly, one last question: Would you have stayed in Africa if your brother had lived?"

"We'll never know, will we?" he replied.

They listened as two sets of footsteps approached the door. The lock turned, the door opened, and the two drew near her.

"Rise and shine, duchess," said First Gaoler. "Time for you to be up and about."

"My apologies for not coming down to breakfast, gentlemen," said Gwen. "If there is any left, I'll take it. I wouldn't say no to one of those yummy cheese sandwiches if not."

"No more for you," he said, untying her. "Get up."

She stood, feeling dizzy from the blood rushing away from her head and the lack of food. The two men held her on either side, then one retied her hands.

In front again, she noticed.

"Where are we going?" she asked.

"It's checkout time, duchess," he said. "Say goodbye to Dad here."

"I guess this is it, Harold," she said. "Sorry for leaving the party early. I pray you make it out of here intact."

"You'll be fine, Gwen," he called as they pulled her through the doorway.

Down the hall to the right. This time she counted fifty-seven steps before they paused. She heard keys rattle, a lock turn, a door open.

"Stairs," said First Gaoler.

"Thanks for the warning," she said, feeling forward with her foot until she found them.

Fifteen steps up. Another door opened, and she felt sunlight on her face.

"From this moment, not a word from you," said First Gaoler.

"All clear," said the other man.

"Right," said First Gaoler, guiding her forward. "You're about to climb into the back of a lorry. Here's the step. Then a large one. Good."

He climbed after her and had her sit on a bench seat along the right side. She heard a thump, possibly them loading the step into the van, then the doors were closed and secured.

"We're going for a little ride," he said. "Won't be long."

Only the rest of my life, she thought.

She was shaking.

The lorry's motor came to life. Then they pulled forward, stopped, then turned left.

Driveway to street, she thought. She crooked her left pinky.

At the end of the block, the lorry made a right turn, then another. She left the fourth and middle fingers straight. They drove in that direction for about thirty seconds. There was a short bumpity-bump, followed by another a few seconds later.

Railroad tracks, she thought.

If I was going to dump a body somewhere, where would it be? The Thames was too busy during the daytime, and one would need something to weigh down the body. They hadn't wrapped any heavy chains around her, nor dipped her feet in the proverbial bucket of cement, so hopefully she could eliminate that possibility.

The lorry stopped. She heard other cars driving by. Then they made a left, then a right and the lorry picked up speed.

They were on a main road of some kind. She kept the fingers on her left locked into position.

Left, right, right, left, right so far. They went faster. She could hear the gears changing. Scents permeated the lorry—diesel fumes, coal burning on heavy rotation, even—fish? They were near the waterfront, clearly.

Maybe the Thames was back in the game for her final destination.

There was a slow rise and fall—a bridge. She tried to visualise a map of London along the Thames, but she was woefully ignorant of everything east of the City of London, even with her recent forays into the East End with Iris. Not a long bridge, so they hadn't crossed the Thames. Were they north or south of it? She had no idea.

There was another straight stretch. Then came the rushing noise of a train to the right and above. Then another to her left. Two lines coming together.

The lorry made a left at that point. She heard the echoing of the motor off the arch of a railway as they passed underneath. She was up to the thumb of her right hand now. Thumb left plus railway junction.

There was not so much of a turn as a veer to the right. Same road angling, she thought. How do I count that? Just remember it somehow. Another left, then a right.

The lorry slowed, stopped. Then it backed into something on the right side.

A road? A driveway? A loading dock? Maybe—

"End of the line, duchess," said First Gaoler. "Time to get out."

The lorry's motor kept idling as he helped her down. He guided her forward until her hands, still with her fingers bent with the simple coding of the route, came into contact with the rough brick of a wall.

He released her and stepped back. Then she heard the gun cock just behind her head.

"I have a son," she said quickly, trying not to cry. "He's six."

"And he's got every advantage, doesn't he?" said the man. "Big house, nice clothes, regular meals, bloody servants waiting on him hand and foot."

"He already lost his father. If he loses me—"

"He'll still be better off than most. I have a son, too."

"Do you? How old?"

"Old enough to maybe lose an eye, thanks to you," he said.

This is useless, she thought in despair.

"I am sorry for it," she said. "Please tell him that for me. Tell him to find a better way out than this."

"You mean he should join the aristocracy like you?" asked First Gaoler. "Yeah, I'll pass that bit of wisdom along. Sure he'll take to it like a duck to water. If it was up to me, duchess, we'd be taking an eye for an eye right now."

She felt the muzzle of the pistol press against the front of the blindfold. Absurdly, she closed her eyes underneath it.

Then the pistol withdrew.

"But it ain't up to me," he said.

She heard his footsteps retreat. Then the driver put the lorry into gear, and it pulled off.

Was he gone? Was he still there, the lorry's departure merely a ruse to lull her into—

Into doing what?

She leaned forward, feeling the wall with her hands, then resting her forehead against it. She held her breath and listened.

Boat engines, not far away. Car horns honking somewhere in the distance. Seagulls squawking overhead.

But no one else drawing breath within earshot.

She pushed up awkwardly at the blindfold, finally getting it above her eyes. She was in shadow, for which her eyes were grateful. She let herself focus on the brick in front of her, on the mortar separating it from the bricks on either side, above and below it. She stepped back, letting more and more of the wall fill her field of view. Then she took a deep breath and turned.

She stood in an alleyway, warehouses on either side of her, a narrow cobblestone street at the end.

There was no one else there.

She took a tentative step forward, then another, staggering slightly, the terror that she had spent nearly a day staving off now flooding through her. She suddenly felt faint. Her knees buck-led and she sank to the ground, breaking her fall with her bound hands, her fingers still in their positions.

The men who poured into the alley found her like that, rocking back and forth on her hands and knees, sobbing with relief.

"Blimey, look at 'er!"

"Get that rope off 'er 'ands."

"Easy now, old girl. 'Old still, we're gonna loosen those knots."

"Mrs. Bainbridge, it's all right, we 'ave you," said one.

"You know who I am?" she said as they pulled her to her feet.

"I do. It's Benny. We 'ad a nice dance together a few weeks back, remember?"

"Benny!" she cried, falling into him. "You're with Archie! You're all with Archie!"

"We are, mum," said Benny, putting his arm around her to steady her. "Welcome to Wapping."

CHAPTER 14

Daile didn't go home. He kept going east, through White-chapel, through Ratcliff, past Limehouse, then onto East India Dock Road in Poplar. The motorcycle sped up as it approached the bridge over the River Lea.

Sally kept his interval long enough behind to be unnoticed. He was beginning to worry about his petrol consumption for this little jaunt when the motorcycle turned left off Newham Way a short distance after they had crossed the river.

Canning Town. Not much to see here, thought Sally. It had been heavily bombed, and most of its inhabitants had moved out, waiting without hope for the government to rebuild their homes. The local factories hadn't restarted for the most part, so those buildings not reduced to rubble were largely abandoned.

She could easily be here, thought Sally. Take me to her, Mr. Daile. Then we shall finally do something about all this.

He patted his rucksack affectionately, feeling the hilt of his commando knife through the canvas.

Daile made a right, then stopped at an intersection, looking in both directions. Sally stayed a block behind. Then Daile turned left.

Sally quickly followed, then had to jam on the brakes. Daile was now driving slowly, his head turning back and forth as he passed each building, each lot, each ruin. He came to the next intersection, looked in both directions again, then went straight, repeating his actions.

What is he up to? wondered Sally. Is he looking for a house number? Good luck finding it around here.

The street came to a T at the next intersection. Daile made the right, still proceeding at a snail's pace, assuming the snail was capable of operating a Royal Enfield. Maybe one of the larger varieties of snail, mused Sally, with horns long enough to reach the handlebars, although seeing over the top would present a problem. No, they have eyes on stalks, don't they? Might be better suited to that mode of transportation than I thought.

Daile made the next right. Sally held back his turn until he could hear the motorcycle's engine move far enough away for him to follow it safely. Sure enough, Daile was making the same methodical search of each location.

He's looking for something, thought Sally. Maybe this has nothing to do with Gwen.

Daile straightened suddenly as a lorry crossed the intersection ahead of him. Then he gunned his engine and turned left, abandoning his house-to-house search.

Sally sped up and made the turn some ten seconds after Daile did.

There was no one visible in the street ahead.

He cursed as he jammed his foot on the accelerator, whipping his head from side to side as the buildings flew by. No motorcycle, though he thought he caught a glimpse of the lorry parked in an alley by a shut-down factory as he sped past. He continued to the next intersection and paused in the center, looking both ways.

To his right, Daile sat on his motorcycle, looking directly at him.

Slowly, he raised one hand and beckoned to his pursuer.

"You've been made, you wretched amateur," Sally muttered in chagrin. "Might as well play this out."

He drove up until his open window was parallel with Daile. The other man pointed to his handlebars.

"These do have rearview mirrors, you know," he said.

"So I see," said Sally.

"Are you with the police?" asked Daile.

"No," said Sally.

"Then why are you following me?"

"What makes you think I'm following you, old boy?"

"Your car is an unusual one. You've been on my tail all morning."

"I'm a fellow motorcycle enthusiast," said Sally. "Love the vintage Royal Enfields. I wanted to see how the old girl handled in traffic. Is she for sale?"

"Please don't treat me like an idiot," snapped Daile. "Your unusual car was also outside my home last night. Who do you work for? Are you a private detective?"

"Not as such," said Sally. "I was asked to keep an eye on you by a friend."

"What friend?"

"Not yet," said Sally. "Not until you tell me what you were looking for in this area."

"Why should I?" asked Daile.

"Because I am thinking maybe the police should be involved," said Sally. "Maybe they could clarify things for both of us."

"You have no radio in your car," said Daile, glancing at the Hornet's dashboard. "By all means, go fetch your police. By the time you find a working callbox, I will be far away from here."

"Very well, Mr. Daile," said Sally, noting the other's lack of reaction to the use of his name. "But if anything happens to Mrs. Bainbridge, you had better hope that the police catch you before I do."

Daile may not have reacted to his own name, but Mrs. Bainbridge's caused him to jerk his head up and bring his body to full attention.

"You're a friend of Mrs. Bainbridge," he said. "Are you working for her family?"

"Miss Sparks is the one who asked me to keep track of you. She's her business partner, as I'm sure you recall."

"What does Miss Sparks have to do with any of this?"

"The family asked her to assist when Gwen—when Mrs. Bainbridge and Lord Bainbridge went missing."

"Why her?"

"Because she knows people who can help."

"Like you."

"Very much like me," said Sally. "And I'm one of the nice ones."

With that, he threw open the car door and heaved himself at Daile. Daile hit the throttle, but Sally reached around his chest and simply plucked him from the seat of the motorcycle as it lurched forward. Daile struggled in the massive man's grip as the Royal Enfield rolled forward on its own, then toppled as the front wheel, deprived of human guidance, turned to the side.

"Now," said Sally calmly as the other man clawed at him, his feet dangling a foot off the road, "let's you and I have a proper conversation."

"Let me go!"

Sally walked over to the motorcycle, Daile still squirming in his arm.

"I am going to put you down, and you are going to turn off your motor," Sally informed him. "Anything other than that will make me more irritated than I already am. Are we clear on this?"

"Yes," gasped Daile. "Please, put me down!"

Sally dropped him to the street. Daile went momentarily to his hands and knees, sucking in air. Then he reached over and turned off the motor.

"You should pick it up and park it," suggested Sally. "We don't want anyone thinking there was an accident here."

Daile rolled the Royal Enfield over to the kerb. He put the kick-stand down and let the bike settle. Then he turned to face Sally, his arms folded across his chest.

"Well?" he asked.

"Is Mrs. Bainbridge safe?" asked Sally.

"I don't know," said Daile.

Then he flinched as Sally stepped towards him.

"I don't know!" he repeated. "I saw it happen. I saw them taken. I followed them, but I lost them."

"Why didn't you report it to the police?" asked Sally.

"I have my reasons."

"Share them."

Daile said nothing. Sally sighed.

"More irritated now," he said, stepping forward and grabbing Daile by his collar. "Why were you following Mrs. Bainbridge?"

"I wasn't following her!" said Daile. "I was following him."

"Him," said Sally, releasing his hold. "You were following Lord Bainbridge."

"Yes."

"Why?"

"I have—"

"You have your bloody reasons, yes, I heard that before," said Sally. "I am a large man, a strong man, and, as you have no doubt gathered by now, a violent man. What I am not at the moment is a patient man. Why were you following him?"

"He has something I need," said Daile. "I have been trying to find out where it is."

"What is it?" asked Sally.

"Something of value to my family, and that's all I will tell you," said Daile.

"Something that the police wouldn't be able to help you with?"

"No," said Daile.

"So you saw the two of them kidnapped, and you felt that your family keepsake was more important than the lives of two people?"

"Yes. Lord Bainbridge is the key to everything. I want him alive and unharmed as much as you do."

"My concern is for Gwen."

"Then we had better combine our efforts. Call Miss Sparks. If she wishes the police to be called, I will agree. If not, then we must come up with a plan of our own. What do you say?"

The telephone rang in Lord Bainbridge's office. Iris snatched the handset from its cradle before the first ring ended.

"Yes?" she answered.

"It's me," said Sally. "We may have found where they're holding her. Holding them, I should say."

"You have! Wonderful! And what do you mean by 'we'?"

"Your Mr. Daile is the one who found them. We're good friends now."

"Oh, dear," said Iris. "Is he still conscious?"

"Conscious, cooperative, and full of interesting tidbits, some of which I have pried out of him."

"When you say pry—"

"Verbal persuasion. Mostly. He saw the abduction, followed them, then lost track when they disappeared into Canning Town. He's been prowling around, searching, and spotted the lorry today. I've spied out the location. Looks to be guarded. Two men, likely armed, one by the street, one by the door."

He summarised the details of the conversation.

"That's very useful," said Iris when he concluded. "Mr. Daile has validated two separate theories of mine. I'm coming to meet you. Where are you located?"

She scribbled down the directions.

"Now, Sally, don't go barging in there on your own," she said. "If we're going to rescue Gwen, we need some subtlety."

"I am fully capable of subtlety," he protested.

"Only when you write," she said. "I'll be there as quickly as I can."

She hung up, then paused. She tiptoed to the door and pulled it open.

Ronnie stood there, looking distraught.

"Mummy needs to be rescued?" he asked.

"No, no, no, not literally," said Iris, kneeling to hug him. "That's just an expression. She's at a party where she's not having a good time, so I am going there to give her an excuse to leave without being rude."

"Oh," said Ronnie, looking dubious.

"In fact, there's a big favour you could do for me," continued Iris.

"What?"

"Do you know where your mummy keeps her shawls?"

"I think so."

"Could you run and get one for me? Something bright and colourful. She needs it for later."

"All right."

He turned and scampered off.

She sighed and pressed the button to summon Percival. He appeared a minute later.

"Yes, Miss Sparks?"

"We have a lead," she said. "Might even be a rescue mission. I'm going to need Albert and the car again."

"I will inform him. Where is he taking you?"

"To meet an informant. I don't want to say any more in case it doesn't come to anything. If you hear this telephone, take a message and tell them I'll ring them up when I return."

"Very good, Miss Sparks."

He left. A moment later, Ronnie flew in, clutching a fringed silk shawl printed with an Art Deco pattern of teal and dark blue flowers on a field of bright red.

"This one's her favourite," said Ronnie, handing it to her.

"Perfect," she said, folding it carefully, then planting a kiss on top of his head. "Thank you, darling. I will see you later, I hope."

"All right," said Ronnie. "Are you still a secret?"

"I am. Thank you for keeping it so well."

"You're welcome," he said. Then he ran off.

Percival returned.

"Albert has the car out front," he reported. "None of the servants are downstairs apart from the cook, so I'll take you out the front way."

"I'm moving up in the world," said Iris. "Thank you, Percival."

He led her to the front door.

"Good hunting, Miss Sparks," he said as he opened it for her.

"Thank you again, Percival."

She walked out to the driveway where Albert was holding open the rear door of the Daimler.

"Where are the wild geese now?" he asked.

"Canning Town," she replied as she got in. "Know it?"

"Driven through, never stopped," he said as he took his place behind the wheel. "We go through Poplar and over the Lea, as I recall."

"You're the driver," she said, settling back into her seat. "I'll direct you further once we get there."

Tony looked up from his racing form as Archie came through the front door of the warehouse.

"She's 'ere, boss," he said.

"When did that 'appen?"

"About forty-five minutes ago. Someone called in, said there's something for you in the alleyway by Number Eight. A bunch of us went, and there she was, 'ands still tied."

"They brought her 'ere," said Archie. "Into the 'eart of our turf. Bloody nerve. 'Ow does she look?"

"Took a nasty wallop to the 'ead. Wouldn't let us 'ave the doc look at it. Said she needs to talk to you."

"Yeah, well, I need to talk to 'er," said Archie.

"Then you two 'ave a nice conversation," said Tony, returning to his reading.

Archie strode to the rear of the warehouse, where a steel door in the corner led to the private club they had built. He walked through to see a group of his men gathered around the card table, peering down at its surface. Sitting in their midst was Mrs. Gwendolyn Bainbridge, looking disheveled for the first time Archie had ever seen. She was clutching an ice pack to the side of her head with one hand while the other shoveled scrambled eggs from a plate into her mouth.

She and the men were looking at a piece of paper in front of her, on which was scribbled a series of lines, connecting at different angles, with notes written at some of the junctions.

"Might be Stepney East," Benny was saying. "There's two lines coming in there."

"That would work if she was coming from east of 'ere," said Reg. "Oh, 'ello, boss. Look 'oo turned up."

"Archie!" cried Gwen in delight as she saw him.

She got up from the table and threw her arms around him.

"Thank you, thank you, thank you!" she burbled. "To think, you had just declared me a Friend of Archie the other day. I knew it would mean something to those blighters, and it did!"

"You told them you knew me?" Archie asked her.

"Of course! Isn't that what got me out?"

"Maybe," said Archie. "Maybe you're lucky you didn't get your throat cut. Come into my office. You and me got to talk."

"Yes, of course," she said, grabbing her plate. "Where did you get those sausages, by the way? They're marvelous. Mind you, I'm so hungry I could eat a horse right now."

"You might just 'ave eaten one," said Archie. "Let's go."

They went inside a small office behind the bar.

"You take the seat at the desk since you're still eating," he said.

"Thank you," she said.

"So what do you mean by them letting you go after you told them about me?" he asked. "When did you tell them?"

"Last night," she said. "I assume it took them some time to figure out what they were going to do."

"That's not 'ow it 'appened," said Archie.

"It isn't? But they dropped me outside your—well, I don't know what to call this place. Your den? Your lair?"

"My place of business, if you don't mind."

"Certainly. I didn't mean to offend," she said hastily. "If it wasn't because of me, how did you get involved, then?"

"Sparks called me last night," said Archie. "Asked for my 'elp in the matter."

"Iris called you? But how did she know?"

"'Er Ladyship brought 'er in after you got snatched."

"Carolyne called Iris," Gwen said, shaking her head in wonderment. "If that isn't the most unlikely thing, I don't know what is. Well, good for her, and good for Iris. And I cannot thank you enough, Archie. You've been a true friend in every sense. Now, I should call home and let them know I'm safe."

"No," said Archie.

Something in his tone made her look up at him with concern. His expression was bleak.

"What is it?" she asked. "What's wrong?"

"You don't know me," said Archie. "Not really. You think you do, you and Sparks, but this is just a lark for you, 'aving acquaintances in the underworld."

"It isn't like that," she protested.

"What Sparks asked me to do for you, what you got yourself into by getting yourself kidnapped—"

"That was hardly my fault."

"Nevertheless, it forced me to get involved in someone else's operation. And that isn't done. We work best by keeping the truce, each 'aving our own territory, our own specialities. You cross the line, payment will be extracted. Or payback."

"I see," said Gwen.

"I don't think you do, Mrs. Bainbridge."

The formality of the address sent a chill down her spine.

"What don't I see, Mr. Spelling?" she asked softly.

"I stepped on some very large toes to get you released," said Archie. "Most likely I'm going to 'ave to do something down the line that I don't want to do, whether it's returning a favour or starting a war. Either way, it's done, but it isn't over. And part of the agreement is that the rest of the operation goes on unobstructed."

"Unobstructed? What do you mean by that?"

"I mean that they play it through, get their ransom—or not," said Archie. "In which case, they do what they 'ave to do, and without any interference from me—or you."

"But—"

"Which means no buts," said Archie. "You are our guest until we get the all clear. But no calls to family, no police, no nothing."

"So this is because you went to some other gang's leader and negotiated for my freedom," Gwen said thoughtfully. "Well, not freedom just yet, but for my safety."

"Now you understand," said Archie. "Sorry."

"And this was because the kidnappers needed to complete their work."

"Right."

Gwen started to laugh. Archie stared at her, nonplussed.

"What joke am I missing?" he asked.

"Archie, my friend," she said, wiping her eyes on her sleeve. "You've been snookered."

The telephone in Lord Bainbridge's office rang several times before Percival was able to make his way there. He grabbed it with unbutler-like haste.

"Lord Bainbridge's office," he said.

"Where's Sparks?" came a man's voice.

"To whom am I speaking?" asked Percival.

"Listen close, you plummy-voiced berk, I need to speak to Sparks, and I need to speak to 'er now."

"Miss Sparks is presently unavailable," said Percival. "I shall be happy to take your number and have her ring you when she returns. I shall relay the message in my plummiest of tones."

"Look, you—"

He stopped, and Percival heard a muffled conversation in the background. Suddenly, a woman's voice came on the line.

"Percival, is that you?" asked Gwen.

"Mrs. Bainbridge! Thank Heavens!" exclaimed Percival. "Are you all right?"

"As well as can be expected, Percival."

"My goodness, I had no idea Miss Sparks would be successful so quickly," said Percival.

"What? What are you talking about?"

"The rescue mission. How did she manage it? And what about Lord Bainbridge?"

"Iris is on her way to rescue me? When did she leave? Where is she going?"

"She can't have been gone more than half an hour," said Percival, glancing at the clock. "And I regret to say that she neglected to tell me the destination."

"How was she getting there?"

"Albert was taking her in the Daimler."

"Oh, dear. I wish she had waited," said Gwen. "Percival, how many in the house know about what happened?"

"Lady Bainbridge, Albert, and myself," said Percival.

"Good. Keep it that way, and don't tell Lady Bainbridge I'm free yet. And if this continues through tomorrow, tell her I said not to pay one farthing in ransom."

"But Mrs. Bainbridge—"

"Percival, things are very much in flux, and I don't want anyone to get killed."

"Killed? Good Lord, is that a possibility?"

"It just became one. Above all, make sure Ronnie knows nothing about it. Will you do that for me, Percival?"

"I will. When should I expect to hear from you again?"

"In a few hours, if all goes well."

"And if it doesn't?"

"Then I expect it will be spread across the front of tomorrow's papers," she said grimly. "Goodbye for now, Percival."

Gwen hung up and looked at Archie.

"Iris has set off on a rescue mission," she said. "She left half an hour ago."

"Bloody 'ell," said Archie.

"We have to stop her," said Gwen. "We have to figure out where they were holding us."

"'Old on," said Archie. "Assuming we do, what exactly are we supposed to do about it?"

"No idea," said Gwen, walking out of the office.

The men were still poring over the paper on which she had drawn her route.

"How is it going, gents?" she asked.

"Take a look, mum," said Reg, pointing to a street map of London they had laid out by her drawing. "We think Benny was on the money when he said Stepney East. So if you was coming a long straight way west before turning left at the station, you probably came through Poplar on East India Dock Road."

"Makes sense," said Gwen, looking at where he was pointing.

"And you've got a bridge marked 'ere," said Benny, pointing where she had drawn a long line. "Said it wasn't a big bridge, so not crossing the Thames, right?"

"Right," said Gwen.

"Then it 'ad to be the Lea," said Benny. "And the lorry turned onto the road just before the bridge?"

"I believe so. A right turn."

"That puts us 'ere," said Benny, pointing back at the bus map. "Canning Town."

"Whose turf would that be?" Gwen asked, looking at Archie.

"No-man's-land at the moment," said Archie. "Nothing there worth the taking since the war."

"Left out of a driveway or alley, two rights, and a left before turning right onto the bridge," remembered Gwen. She looked at the map. "So reverse it. Come off the bridge, go left, which would be north, take a right, two lefts, and a right to a driveway. Somewhere in this section here. Shall we be off?"

"I'll get a car," offered Reg.

"Aren't you all forgetting something?" asked Archie.

"What's that, boss?" asked Reg.

"Repeat the last word you just said, and think about its meaning for a moment," said Archie.

"Car?" repeated Reg with a puzzled look.

"Boss," said Benny. "You said, 'What's that, boss?'"

"Yeah, because 'e's the boss," said Reg. "Why wouldn't— Oh. Sorry, boss. I guess we all got carried away with the treasure 'unt and all. But we ain't doing nothing without your say-so. So what's the plan, boss?"

"The plan is we are going to try to intercept Sparks before she gets 'erself killed or starts a war between us and them," said Archie. "We take two cars, split up when we get there. You see 'er, you tell 'er to stop until we all meet up again. We don't go inside, we don't give a damn what 'appens to 'is Lordship. What kind of car is she in?"

"A black Daimler with a chauffeur," said Gwen. "It shouldn't be hard to spot. Which car am I going to be in?"

"And 'oo says you're coming?"

"It's better if I do, don't you think?" she replied. "I know the chauffeur and you don't. It will smooth things over if he sees me with you. And I might recognise the lorry they used if it's still there."

"All right," said Archie reluctantly. "But you 'ang back otherwise. I didn't go to all this trouble springing you only to 'ave you take a bullet after."

"I will cower behind all of you, I promise," said Gwen.

"Then you're with me," said Archie. "Let's go."

"We're crossing the bridge now, Miss Sparks," said Albert. "Which way?"

"Take the next left, please," said Sparks, consulting her directions. "And the third right."

"What exactly are you going to do when you get there?"

"Rescue them, of course."

"By yourself?"

"Are you offering to join the expedition?"

"Above my pay grade, miss," he said.

He slowed the car to a halt.

"What are you doing?" asked Sparks. "We haven't got there yet."

"I'm sorry, miss," said Albert, reaching under the dashboard. "But I can't let you go through with this."

Then he stopped, puzzled as his hand found nothing.

"Looking for this?" asked Sparks as she put a gun to his neck.

"Careful now, Miss Sparks," he said, stiffening. "A lady like you shouldn't be fooling with things you're not familiar with."

"A lady like me is familiar with the Webley-Fosbery automatic," she said. "Thirty-eight calibre, eight shots. I took the liberty of removing it this morning before we went out. Not a fan, personally. It's a fussy gun with a nasty tendency to go off accidentally. I would hate to splatter your brains all over this lovely car. Do I have your complete attention, Albert?"

He nodded.

"Now, we are going to continue to our destination. You are to drive slowly and carefully, and keep your hand away from the horn. Understood?"

"Yes, miss," he said.

He put the car in gear. They drove a few blocks.

"Over there," she said. "Behind the Hornet."

Albert pulled over and parked.

"Turn off the engine and hand me the keys," she instructed him.

When he did, she leaned out the window and whistled a sharp blast between her teeth.

Sally and Mr. Daile emerged from a nearby alley.

"Afternoon, Sparks," said Sally. "Are we hijacking cars now? Didn't have the fare for the cab again?"

"Hello, Sally. And hello, Mr. Daile. This is Albert, the Bainbridges' chauffeur."

"What's up, mate?" Sally asked him. "Did you try to get fresh?"

"Albert is a coconspirator in all of this," said Sparks. "Aren't you?"

"I don't know what you're talking about," said Albert. "The woman is insane."

"Quickest route from the house to the Livingstone Club is the one you took me on this morning," said Sparks. "Skirt the southern end of the park, keep on going until you get to Charing Cross, then north. I'm sure that's how you took Lord Bainbridge to the club, isn't it? Every single time. Except for yesterday, when you took the long way through to Marylebone Road, which happened to be a perfect location to stage a kidnapping."

"Traffic was better."

"On a Saturday? Mr. Daile, you've been following Lord Bainbridge all week, haven't you?"

"Yes, Miss Sparks," said Daile as Albert shot him a surprised look.

"Did anyone else tail him when he left the house on Saturday?"

"No, Miss Sparks. They came out of nowhere after he reached Marylebone Road."

"So they couldn't have known that change in route unless it had been prearranged. Am I right, Albert?"

The chauffeur said nothing.

"How many men are in there?" asked Sparks. "Where are they holding Mrs. Bainbridge?"

He remained mute.

"I can get it out of him," offered Sally.

"No," said Sparks. "There may not be enough time. We'll have to improvise. Mr. Daile, would you be so kind as to take my place with the gun?"

"I want to go with you," said Daile.

"Someone needs to keep an eye on Albert," said Sparks. "I need Sally for obvious reasons. That means you stay here. No point in arguing with me."

"Never is, in my experience," said Sally. "Do what she says."

"Very well, Miss Sparks," said Daile.

Sparks got out, holding Gwen's shawl. She handed Daile the gun, then leaned towards his ear.

"The safety's on," she whispered. "Keep it that way."

"Yes, Miss Sparks," he replied.

He got into the Daimler behind Albert.

"Let's go," said Sparks to Sally.

"About time," he replied. "Let me get my kit."

He reached into the Hornet and removed his rucksack.

"Are you sure you wouldn't rather take that pistol?" he asked.

"We're not going to kill anyone," said Sparks.

"Are you sure?"

"I am," she said. "Make certain that you are as well, Sally. I don't want you to lose control here."

"What are you saying?"

"I'm saying we use nonhomicidal means to secure the guards. Agreed?"

"That's so much more difficult than simply killing them," he said. "Fine, we'll do it your way. Follow me."

He led her down the block. A concrete wall blocked their view until they reached the corner. Sally stopped her short of the intersection.

"Guard number one is visible from here," he said. "Guard number two is not, so he's the danger."

"Can you get behind him?"

"There's a connecting wall on the other side, and another in the rear. I could try to get over one of them."

"How much time?"

"Six minutes," he said.

"Fine," she said. "Lend me your flask."

"Why?"

"Verisimilitude."

"You're always inventing new ways of cadging whisky from me," he said, pulling a flask from his coat pocket and handing it to her.

"Thanks," she said, looking at her wristwatch. "On my mark, we'll—Sally?"

He was already gone, running at a speed that belied his bulk.

"So we'll count it from now, shall we?" she muttered.

She uncapped the flask, took a sip of whisky, and swirled it around in her mouth before spitting it out. She replaced the cap, put the flask in her bag, then unfolded Gwen's shawl and draped it around her shoulders. She unpinned her hair, shook it loose, then ran her fingers through it several times until it looked extra messy. Then she glanced at her watch again and waited.

Mervyn leaned against the corner of the wall abutting the alley-way, idly scanning the street in each direction. He was bored. The scary part of the day was carting that woman to Wapping and dumping her without getting caught, but they pulled that off and scarpered without raising so much as a peep from the local spar-rows. He didn't see why they couldn't wait until everything was over, or just bump her off and tip her body into a rubbish bin, but orders was orders, and he knew better than to squawk.

He lit a cigarette. Guarding seemed a waste of time to him, but the no-squawking rule persisted. Only signs of life he had seen were the black fellow on the motorcycle when they were pulling the lorry in, then that Hornet driving by, but the black fellow didn't give them a second glance, while the driver of the Hornet was go-ing too fast to take notice of them, or so Mervyn figured. And that had been an hour ago, so so much for them.

His interest in his surroundings increased when the bird hove into view. Good-looking brunette, nice set of pins, albeit a bit wob-bly at the moment. Her hair was a tangle. Looks like the morning after has stretched into the afternoon, he thought. She was walking in his direction, so he watched her, which wasn't a burden at all, considering. She looked around uncertainly, paused to take a flask out of her bag, then saw him eyeing her.

She walked towards him unsteadily, brushing an errant clump of hair out of her face.

"'Allo," she said as she came up to him.

"'Allo yourself," he replied. "What's up, love?"

"This is embarrassing," she said, "but could I ask you where I am and where the nearest station is?"

"You're in Canning Town."

"Canning Town," she repeated in a tone of wonder. "'Ow the bloody 'ell did I wind up in Canning Town?"

"Where'd you start out?" he asked, grinning at her.

"I was at a pub in Limehouse," she said, a yawn abruptly escaping her. "Sorry, rude of me. There was a lad named Billy 'oo was buying me drinks, and then we were going to a party, and then I woke up 'ere."

"Lucky Billy," said Mervyn with a leer.

"It wasn't Billy I woke up next to," she said ruefully. "I din't know 'oo it was, and din't want to find out."

She took a sip from the flask, then held it out to him.

"No thanks," he said, shaking his head reluctantly. "Working."

"Really? On a Sunday? That's awful," she said, putting the flask in her bag, her hand resting inside.

Then her eyes grew wide as she looked past Mervyn to see Sally looming behind the guard by the factory door, his knife raised.

"Hey!" she cried. "I said no killing!"

"What?" exclaimed the second guard.

"What?" echoed Mervyn as he turned to see Sally slam the haft of the knife into his mate's temple.

Mervyn had time for two thoughts. The first was that the man with the knife was the biggest bloke he had ever seen.

The second was that he probably shouldn't have turned his back on the bird.

Sparks's sap slammed into the back of his skull, precluding the formation of any third thought, however profound it might have been. Relieved of the need to support any further conscious activity, Mervyn's body slumped to the ground.

Sally pulled out some short lengths of rope from his rucksack and quickly trussed up his victim. He stuffed a gag into the guard's mouth, then picked him up and tossed him into the back of the lorry. He looked up to see Sparks laboriously dragging her man towards him.

"Allow me," he said.

He picked him up easily and slung him over his shoulder. He dumped him into the lorry, then secured him to the other guard.

"Two down," he said as they walked towards the door. "How many left, do you think?"

Before she could answer, the door opened. Sally ducked behind it.

"Oi, Tim," said a man coming out. "Boss says to take a break. Oh! Who are you?"

"I'm Tim's girl," said Sparks, smiling. "Din't 'e tell you?"

"He shouldn't be having girls here," he said, stepping towards her. "Where is he?"

Sally stepped behind the man, picked him up, and banged his head against the building wall one time. The man sagged in his arms.

"You're right," said Sally to Sparks. "That wasn't very subtle."

"Tie him up," said Sparks, yanking a key ring from the third man's belt. "I'm going in before anyone misses him."

"Behind you in a minute," said Sally.

Sparks entered the factory. There was a desk to her right where a security man might have sat if the place was still in business. Ahead of her was her first choice to be made: a hall leading into the main rooms, and a stairwell going down.

She could see the indistinct shapes of machinery and conveyor belts in the darkness ahead. The stairwell, on the other hand, was lit.

She chose the stairwell.

She emerged on a long hallway, broken on one side by doors marked with stenciled titles—BOILER, JANITORIAL, and so forth. She opened those that she could, but her purloined keys only worked on a few of them, and those gave her nothing.

Finally, a door on her left gave way to a room with two cots, one on each side. The one on the left had a pile of rope on it. The other was empty.

She went inside. Both cots looked like they had been in use. She examined the one with the ropes, then leaned down and sniffed the thin sheet. She smelled a faint perfume on the sheets, one she had encountered many times at the office.

Gwen had lain here.

Where was she now? What had they done with her?

Was she still alive?

She sensed rather than heard someone behind her and whirled, feet shuffling into position. Sally stood in the doorway, a finger to his lips. He glanced at the bed, then at Sparks. She shook her head.

They continued down the hallway together. Ahead came the sound of men's voices, a bark of chagrin, laughter. They came to an open door. Light streamed from the other side into the hallway.

"Stay back," whispered Sparks.

Sally nodded and disappeared into a doorway, his hand at his side gripping the knife.

Four men sat around a card table, a poker game in progress. There was a kitchen set up to the right along with a pantry and a refrigerator. One of the men was scooping up a pile of toothpicks from the center of the table. Butt-filled ashtrays and half-empty tumblers were scattered across it.

The men looked up at Sparks as she walked in with expressions ranging from surprise to open hostility. She returned their looks with disdain, then pulled an empty chair from the table and sat down.

"Hello, boys," she said. "Deal me in."

CHAPTER 15

Archie's team traveled in two cars. The first, driven by Benny, had Archie himself in the rear, with Gwen in the middle, Reg on her right, and another spiv she didn't know in front. Gwen clutched her hand-drawn route, more for comfort than for use.

She closed her eyes as they crossed the River Lea, trying to feel if it was the same bridge, though reversed. The cars slowed as they reached Canning Town and turned left.

They took the next right, then stopped. The driver from the other car pulled up next to Archie's car.

"You take the first left, we'll take the second," said Archie. "We stop at the next intersection and wait until we see each other, then move onto the next block. If you don't see us, that means we found her, so come running. We'll do the same with you."

"Right, boss," said the other driver.

"Have you done this sort of thing before?" asked Gwen.

"We've done all sorts of things before," said Archie.

They took the second left and proceeded up the block. No Daimlers were to be seen. They came to the intersection and paused. The other car came into view. The drivers exchanged waves, and they continued.

At the second intersection, Gwen glanced to the right, then let out a cry.

"There!" she said. "Parked halfway up."

The driver paused until he saw the other car, then motioned for it to follow. They pulled up behind the Daimler and got out. Gwen dashed over to it before the others could stop her, then pulled up short, amazement lighting up her face.

"Mr. Daile!" she exclaimed. "Whatever are you doing here? And in our car? Oh, and there's Albert! Hello, Albert, I cannot tell you how happy—"

She stopped, then looked back and forth at the two men, both of whom were regarding her with astonishment matching her own.

"Mr. Daile," she said severely. "Why are you pointing a gun at Albert?"

"Miss Sparks told me to," replied Daile.

"Oh," said Gwen, considering. "Yes, I see now. Quite right. Carry on."

"But Mrs. Bainbridge, how is it that you are free?" asked Daile.

"Long story, I'll tell it to you over tea when we're done. Where is Miss Sparks?"

"She went to rescue you," said Daile. "But you don't need rescuing."

"Which way did she go?" asked Gwen.

"Around that corner to the left," said Daile, pointing with the gun in a way that made the surrounding gangsters nervous. "There's an alleyway with a lorry parked in it, next to the side door of a factory."

"Good," said Gwen. "Let's go."

"Wait," said Archie. "'Ow long ago was this?"

"Maybe ten minutes before you arrived," replied Daile.

"Go take a look around the corner," Archie said to Reg. "Tell me if you see anyone."

Reg trotted to the corner, peered around the wall, then turned back, shaking his head.

"We're too late," said Archie.

"But she's gone in!" said Gwen. "We have to stop her."

"No," said Archie. "The time to stop 'er was before she went in. Bad enough if they recognise her as my girl, but if I take a team of my lads in after 'er, then the war starts for real, and it won't end 'ere and now. I won't be losing any men for a girl. Any girl."

"But it's Iris!" said Gwen. "Our Iris! She's risking her life for me, and she's taking on that gang all alone."

"She's not alone," said Daile.

"That's kind of you to say, Mr. Daile, and it's lovely of you to help out with the pistol and all, but Iris—"

"Miss Sparks is not alone," said Daile. "She has this very large man with her."

"Sally? Sally's here?"

"She called him that. I thought that was a woman's name."

"Well, I guess there's no need to send in your team," Gwen said to Archie. "She already has one."

Sparks looked around the table.

"Well?" she asked. "Isn't someone going to stake me?"

The man sitting directly opposite pulled a gun from inside his jacket and pointed it at her.

"Who the hell are you?" he asked.

"I'm the woman who found you and walked in here despite your guards," said Sparks. "That makes me either very clever or very dangerous. I'm both, in fact. What I am not is with the police."

"How do we know that?"

"Ask your boss," said Sparks. "He knows who I am."

"I am the boss," said the man, bristling.

"No, you're not," said Sparks, nodding to the man sitting to his right. "Hello, Lord Bainbridge. Mind if I call you Harold? The title's too long, and I'm not feeling all that respectful. Where is Mrs. Bainbridge?"

"You insolent little—" Lord Bainbridge growled.

"Careful now!" snapped Sparks. "Just because I'm not with the police doesn't mean I came alone. We've got three of your men tied up in the back of your lorry."

"I don't believe you," said the man holding the gun.

"One of them is named Tim. Another had these."

She held up the key ring. The three gangsters glanced at each other.

"Who are you?" asked the man with the gun. "Do you work for Spelling?"

"Who?" asked Sparks.

He pointed the gun at her head and cocked it.

"We can substitute hostages," he said.

"Silly idea," she replied. "Nobody wants me badly enough, which saddens me some lonely nights. Since you ask, I was brought in by Lady Bainbridge, initially to help both her husband and Gwen. Where is Gwen, Harold?"

"She's safe," said Lord Bainbridge.

"Safe? How do you mean 'safe'? Where did you put her?"

"She was turned over to Archie Spelling," said the gangster. "And I guess if you were working for him, you'd have known that. So what's your story, lady?"

"Put the gun away, and we'll parley," suggested Sparks. "And someone stake me. What's the game?"

"Five-card draw," said the gangster as he holstered his gun.

He took ten toothpicks and tossed them in front of her.

"You want to deal?" he asked.

"No, thanks," she said, smiling sweetly. "I'd rather keep my hands free. Who's the sharper in the room?"

"That'd be Dex," he said, nodding to the man on his left.

"Then let him deal," she said. "I'd like to see a pro in action."

Dex picked the deck up and shuffled, throwing a few tricks into it.

"Bravo!" applauded Sparks.

"What are you doing?" asked Lord Bainbridge.

"Playing cards," said Sparks. "For toothpicks. Things of no value for most situations, then absolutely vital when one gets a bit of filbert wedged between one's molars. Ante up, everyone."

"Would you like to cut the deck, miss?" asked Dex as they each tossed a toothpick onto the center of the table.

"Will it matter?"

"Let's say it does," said Dex.

Sparks cut the deck, then did it again for luck.

"Well, Harold, what have you got to say for yourself?" asked Sparks as Dex dealt five hands around the table.

"I was abducted by these men, along with Gwen," he said. "She was released earlier. My abductors and I have come to an understanding, so they have allowed me to spend the remainder of my captivity in relative comfort."

"Does the understanding cost extra?" asked Sparks. "I'm asking in case I go into the kidnapping business."

The man between Dex and Sparks tossed two toothpicks into the pile.

"See you and raise one," said Sparks, throwing three in. "Your answer was a complete fabrication, Harold. I thought you'd do better."

"Why don't you tell me what my answer is?" suggested Lord Bainbridge, matching her raise as he did. "Maybe it will be one where you could walk away with something for your troubles."

"And there's the bribe," said Sparks. "I thought you'd hold that back until the end. Two cards, please."

Dex dealt, apparently from the top of the deck.

"That looked positively legitimate," said Sparks, taking her cards. "You're setting me up nicely."

"Unless it's an honest game," said the man opposite her as Lord Bainbridge took one card and he took three. Dex took one, looked at it, and grimaced dramatically. The man next to Sparks threw his cards down and watched her.

"Honest or dishonest, it was a game from the start," said Sparks. "I knew that the moment Albert showed me where it happened. We've got him secured, too, by the way."

"Albert? Is he all right?" asked Lord Bainbridge.

"We didn't do him any damage," said Sparks. "Unlike you lot. Raise one. He must be very loyal indeed to take a blow like that, but God knows it made him look like a genuine victim."

"So you thought he was involved?" asked Lord Bainbridge, throwing in another toothpick.

"Right away," said Sparks. "But his loyalty to you, his years of service—those seemed genuine to me, which was confusing at first. It all made sense when I considered the idea that you had faked your own kidnapping, in which case Albert would be the most devoted coconspirator one could possibly ask for."

"I raise two," said Dex.

"Naturally," said Sparks. "I'll call. Harold?"

"Raise one," said Lord Bainbridge. "Why would I fake my own kidnapping?"

"For the money, of course."

"You do know I'm rich, don't you?"

"You're worth an enormous amount," said Sparks. "On paper."

"I'm out," said the man opposite her.

"But something I've learned in the time I've become the co-owner and operator of a small business concern is that there is a difference between book value and paying cash on the nail. At the end of the day, all of your worth means nothing if the note's due and you've got everything tied up in new paint and furniture. Or in a blue ledger in a rolltop desk."

Lord Bainbridge's eyes narrowed.

"Fold," said Dex.

"The sharper has folded," observed Sparks. "Lovely! Done to make me think he might have dealt the cards honestly for a change out of courtesy to the lady present."

"I don't see no lady here," said Dex.

"No, you don't," agreed Sparks. "Now, that play might reassure the lady if she thought Dex was playing only for himself. But in a serious con, he would be setting up someone else at the table to take advantage of the poor little innocent female. So here I am with a nice hand in front of me, getting overconfident. And there's you, Harold, looking uncomfortable. Is that due to your hand, or what I said about the ledger?"

"Make your point and be done with it," he said wearily.

"Come, Harold, poker is a dull game unless you play for something," she said. "Even something as insignificant as toothpicks, as long as you imbue them with enough value."

She tossed her remaining toothpicks onto the pile.

"I am betting everything I have on a hand that I am going to lose to you, Harold," she said. "That's what I think. And do you know something?" She picked up a toothpick and snapped it between her fingers. "If you take something that seems valuable, and reveal it for the worthless thing it actually is, then the game no longer matters. You were never the target of this kidnapping scheme. Your wife was. You needed a large sum of money fast to pay off a large debt. So you arranged all of this to get her to fork over cash which she had on hand and you didn't. Only Gwen unfortunately blundered into it, so what was never a kidnapping accidentally became one. Are you calling, Harold? I'm already all in."

"If I needed money from my wife that badly, why wouldn't I just borrow it from her directly?" he asked as he threw in enough toothpicks to match her bet. "The mining game is a gamble on a vast scale. I've been up and down many times. She knows that."

"Show me your hand, Harold," said Sparks.

"Flush," he said, laying five clubs on the table.

"You win, of course," said Sparks. "As you were meant to. And I was meant to get excited because I had three queens. Queens for the lady, no less! An appeal to my feminine vanity. The reason you couldn't tell Lady Bainbridge why you needed the cash was because the debt had less to do with mine investments than for something that would cause her to lock her fortune away from you forever. So you needed to force the issue with the kidnapping. Well, let's take a look at these lovely lasses."

She slapped them down in front of him, one at a time.

"Queen of spades, queen of clubs, queen of diamonds," she chanted. "Oh, wait. Here's a fourth lass to join them."

She slapped her hand on the table one last time, then lifted it up again.

The picture from inside the ledger lay before Lord Bainbridge, the faces of the woman and boy looking up at him.

"Have you seen this child?" Sparks asked softly.

He reeled back from the table, his chair clattering to the floor behind.

"What are you worth, Harold?" she asked, snatching the photo from the table and holding it up before her. "As a kidnap victim, you're worth forty-five thousand pounds to your long-suffering wife. As a scheming, heartless adulterer, you're worth nothing."

"You stupid, reckless woman!" he roared, his face turning a deep red. "You've ruined everything!"

He stopped abruptly, staring at her, one hand rising towards his chest.

Then he collapsed.

"Oh, bloody hell," muttered the man next to him.

* * *

Sally lurked in the doorway down the hall, picking up snatches of the conversation. Then he heard a crash and a man yelling, followed by a commotion.

"Sally!" Sparks yelled.

In a flash, he burst into the room. Then he saw Sparks kneeling by a man on the floor while three others stood by, watching uselessly. They looked up as Sally loomed over them, knife poised to strike.

"Jaysus," one said, his hand moving towards his waistband.

Sally shook his head, and the hand stopped.

"What precisely am I supposed to be doing right now?" asked Sally.

"Lord Bainbridge collapsed," said Sparks. "He's still breathing, but I think it may be his heart. Run and fetch the Daimler. It's the fastest car we have right now."

"What about them?" he asked, nodding towards the trio.

"They don't matter anymore," she said.

"Where's Gwen?"

"Safe. I'll explain. Please, Sally, we have to move. Oh, you'll need these."

She tossed him the keys to the Daimler.

"Get him to the alley," he said, catching them. "I'll be back in two minutes."

He ran down the hall, up the stairs, and out of the building. He never broke stride until he turned the corner and saw Gwen in all of her radiant glory in the center of a pack of spivs.

"Sally!" she shouted, waving to him, and he wanted nothing more than to pick her up and hold her in his arms until he died an old, contented man.

But there was another man dying in the building behind him.

He ran to the group.

"I won't ask how you got here," he said. "I need the Daimler. Lord Bainbridge needs to get to a hospital immediately."

"What happened? Is Iris all right?"

"Heart attack, we think, and yes, she's fine."

The lorry roared through the intersection behind him.

"And there goes the gang, I expect. Come on."

"Wait," said Archie. "Let Benny drive."

"Why?" asked Sally.

"It's what 'e does," said Archie.

"Go," said Sally, tossing him the keys.

Albert was yanked from the driver's seat while Daile got out on his own. Benny slid behind the wheel as Sally folded himself into the rear.

"I should go, too," said Gwen. "I'm family. He'll need me."

"Get in," said Sally.

Benny had the car in gear and moving before she had the door closed. He peeled around the corner, then screeched to a halt in front of the alleyway where Sparks stood waiting.

"Benny?" she exclaimed as she saw him. "Gwen! But how— Never mind. Sally, help me."

The gangsters had carried Lord Bainbridge up in one last gesture of loyalty before making their getaway. He sat against the wall, eyes closed, his breathing shallow. Sally got out, picked him up, and put him in the seat next to Gwen.

"You go," he said to Sparks. "I'll catch up. Which hospital are you taking him to?"

"London Hospital in Whitechapel," said Benny.

"That's a fifteen-minute drive," said Sally.

"Eight," said Benny. "Shut the door."

"I think if he hadn't already had a heart attack, Benny's driving would have given him one," said Gwen as they sat in the waiting room.

"What about you?" asked Iris with concern. "You don't look one hundred percent chipper."

"I took a knock to the head," said Gwen. "I'm still alive."

"You are going to get it looked at," said Iris. "Right now."

"Not until Carolyne gets here," said Gwen. "Then I will, I promise. So, you came to rescue me."

"Yes," said Iris. "Then you came to rescue me from rescuing you."

"Something like that," said Gwen.

She reached for Iris's hand and squeezed it.

"We have a complicated friendship, don't we?" she said.

"We do indeed."

"Now, I have many questions for you," said Gwen. "The first being: Is that my shawl you're wearing?"

"Ah. Yes, it is," said Iris, taking it off and folding it neatly.

"Why are you wearing it?"

"Part of my brilliant disguise. I wanted to look more dissolute."

"I bought that shawl at Broussard's in Paris when I was fifteen," said Gwen. "It's still the height of fashion. How did you expect it to make you look dissolute?"

"I figured your average spiv wouldn't be privy to high fashion. Sorry, I was improvising."

"Well, at least you didn't get blood on it," said Gwen, inspecting it.

"You still haven't forgiven me for the cape, have you?"

"I have not," said Gwen.

"So when did you figure out that your father-in-law faked his own kidnapping?" asked Iris.

"Not long after I came to," said Gwen. "They had me bound and blindfolded, so there was some initial panic, followed by lots more panic, so my thinking wasn't at its peak."

"And the blow to your head didn't help, either."

"No. But what occurred to me after my heart rate settled down was that when I asked Harold what time it was, he knew. Which meant he could see his watch. And I thought, Oh! He's not blind-

folded. Why not? And then when I had to use the lav, the gentlemen who escorted me had to unlock the door, but I never heard
them relock it after I came out of the room, and I thought, Oh! They
aren't worried about keeping him secured. Why not? And then I
remembered when I first got into the car at the house to confront
him, he and Albert were both antsy about getting somewhere on
time, and why would that matter if it was just another evening at
the club? I realised that it was all a sham, only it became real when
I inserted myself into the charade."

"You think better after being knocked unconscious than most
people do with their brains intact," said Iris.

"One of the benefits of having had my brains scrambled before.
I'm better at reassembling them now."

"What else did you figure out?"

"I think it all has something to do with that man who was killed
by the club. I don't know what Harold's connection is to him, but
he knew something. Knows something, I mean. I'm trying to be
hopeful."

"I think you're on the right track," said Iris. "I was hoping to
get more out of him when his ticker interrupted the conversation."

"What caused that, do you think?"

"This," said Iris, pulling the photograph from her bag.

Gwen looked at it, her brows furrowing.

"I've never seen them before," she said. "Yet they both look so
familiar somehow, especially the boy. Where did you find this?"

"Inside a ledger inside a locked rolltop desk in Harold's private
office. I want you to look at the ledger when you get back."

"The boy," said Gwen. "He's lighter skinned than the woman."

"Yes," said Iris.

"He— Oh Lord."

"Say it," Iris urged her.

"He looks like Harold."

"I think so, too," said Iris. "And I've seen him before."

"Where?"

"On a flyer in the window of a shop in Soho. He's gone missing. There's more— Wait, here come Archie and Sally."

Archie and Sally came in together. Iris immediately got up and went to Archie, her arms poised for an embrace, but he stopped her in her tracks with a gesture.

"What?" she asked.

"We'll 'ave to talk when this is all done," he said.

"Oh," said Iris, her voice small, her arms falling to her sides.

"What's the word?" asked Sally.

"None yet," said Gwen. "Lady Bainbridge has been notified. She should be here shortly."

"Where is Mr. Daile?" asked Iris.

"He went into the factory," said Sally. "He was looking for something."

"I don't think he'll find him there," said Iris.

"Him? Who are you talking about?"

"A boy," said Iris. "I think Lord Bainbridge did all of this for him."

"What are we talking about?" asked Sally.

"Family business, I think," said Gwen. "And here comes the family's most terrifying member."

Percival came through the door, then held it for Lady Bainbridge. She strode through, then stopped when she saw Gwen and Iris. Her expression on seeing Gwen was one of relief, if not enthusiasm. She nodded at Iris, and looked at the others with puzzlement.

"Where is he?" she demanded as she came up to them.

"In treatment," said Iris. "We're waiting for the doctor."

"What are they doing to him?"

"What they can, Carolyne," said Gwen, taking her mother-in-law's hands in her own. "All we can do is pray."

"I'm not sure what I'm praying for," said Lady Bainbridge.

Abruptly, she burst into tears.

"Sit, please," urged Iris, guiding her to a bench.

"Who are these two?" asked Lady Bainbridge.

"These are our friends, Salvatore Danielli and Archie Spelling," said Gwen. "They all helped with the rescue mission."

"Your rescue mission may have killed my husband," said Lady Bainbridge. "No, I'm not being fair. The abduction must have placed enormous strain on his heart."

"Actually," Iris began, then she looked at Gwen who nodded. "We should talk about that. We've uncovered some information. It won't make you any happier, I'm afraid."

Lady Bainbridge looked back and forth between the two of them. Then her shoulders sagged.

"Very well," she said. "Must it be in front of these others?"

"Not at all," said Sally. "That corner over there is empty. We'll stay here and wait for the doctor."

"Come, Carolyne," said Gwen, standing and offering her a hand.

The three women walked away, leaving Percival with Sally and Archie. He glanced at the latter with disdain.

"Are you the Chicken Man?" he asked.

"Not my preferred name," said Archie, turning towards him.

"I believe we spoke on the telephone earlier," said Percival. "I'm the plummy-voiced berk."

Archie smiled.

"Nice to meetcher," he said. "You sounded shorter on the phone."

"I understand you had something to do with rescuing Mrs. Bainbridge and His Lordship."

"I did."

"Then I won't slap that lower-class East End smile off your face," said Percival. "This time."

He walked away and stood, keeping an eye on the ladies.

"'E's all right," said Archie.

"Yes, he is," said Sally.

Lady Bainbridge looked at Iris in disbelief.

"This was all done to get money from me?" she said.

"Yes," said Iris. "There was no kidnapping."

"I was kidnapped," protested Gwen.

"Fine. Gwen was kidnapped, but as an afterthought."

"My head hurts just the same," muttered Gwen.

"Why did he need money so badly?" asked Lady Bainbridge. "We aren't poor. Or are we? Has something happened to the company that I don't know about? Do I need to start taking in washing?"

"I think Lord Bainbridge's wealth may be tied up in something nonliquid," said Iris. "But there's something else, and I need to speak to Mr. Daile to confirm it and see what can be done."

"Who is this Mr. Daile?" asked Lady Bainbridge.

"He's the man who's been following Harold," said Gwen. "He was posing as a gardener down the street, then tailing him when he went out to the club each night. We have him to thank for locating where they were holed up."

"Why? Does this have something to do with Harold's last trip to Africa?"

"That's a likely bet," said Iris.

"Your Ladyship," said Percival, coming over to interrupt. "I believe the doctor wants to see you."

A nurse was with him.

"Are you family?" she asked Lady Bainbridge.

"Yes," she replied. "I'm Lady Carolyne Bainbridge, his wife."

"Any others with you?"

"My daughter-in-law, Mrs. Gwendolyn Bainbridge," she said, indicating Gwen. "I should like her to accompany me."

"Of course. Come this way."

She led them through the emergency room doors, then down

a hallway to the right to a door with the name CHRISTOPHER BARING, M.D. on an engraved bronze plate mounted on it. The nurse knocked, then opened the door.

"Lady Bainbridge and Mrs. Bainbridge," she said, motioning for the two women to enter.

The doctor looked like he couldn't have been more than thirty-five, although he was haggard around the eyes. He stood and came around his desk as they came in, shook their hands, then waved them to a pair of seats.

"Right, let's get straight to it," he said. "Your husband had a myocardial infarction. It was not severe, fortunately. The lungs are clear, there's no cyanosis—"

"What is that?" asked Lady Bainbridge.

"Sorry, it means that there is enough oxygen getting into his blood. We injected him with digitalis immediately, then administered papaverine to relieve the spasms. We've put him on oxygen and a morphine drip and will be giving him heparin as an anticoagulant. No history of heart troubles before this, I take it?"

"I was unaware he even had a heart until now," said Lady Bainbridge.

The doctor broke into a momentary grin, then recovered himself and resumed his professional manner.

"As of now, he's awake and resting," he continued. "Bed rest for the near future, as undisturbed as he can possibly be. We've moved him to the Quiet Ward. I'll be checking on him through the night. We'll have a better idea of his prognosis in the morning, but I'm cautiously optimistic."

"I want to see him," said Lady Bainbridge.

"I'm sorry, but he cannot be agitated right now."

"But I'm his wife!" she protested.

"He specifically stated that no family members should be allowed to visit," said Dr. Baring. "We are obligated to respect his wishes."

"We should let him rest, Carolyne," said Gwen, patting Lady Bainbridge on the arm. "There will be ample time to agitate him when he's recovered."

"Quite right, Mrs. Bainbridge," said Dr. Baring. Then he looked at her quizzically. "I say, I don't mean to presume, but is anything the matter with your health?"

"I received a nasty bump to the head recently," said Mrs. Bainbridge. "I was going to have it checked."

He took a penlight, came over to her, and shined it into each of her eyes.

"You had better let us take a look at you," he said. "I think an X-ray may very well be in your future."

"Can you find your way back to the waiting room by yourself, Carolyne?" asked Gwen as she stood up.

"Don't be silly, child," said Lady Bainbridge. "I'm coming with you."

"You're angry with me," said Iris.

"You're damn right, I'm angry," said Archie. "After everything I've said about stirring things up, after asking me to go against common sense and get involved, which I did—"

"And I want to thank you for it."

"Yeah, you don't know the 'alf of it, who I 'ad to kowtow to so I could get 'er sprung, and then you charge off into battle anyway—"

"I got a lead. I was pursuing it."

"Then you should've called me first," said Archie.

"That's why you're angry? Because I didn't tell you what I was doing?"

"I 'ad two cars out looking for you."

"Archie, I didn't call you because you let me know in no uncertain terms that I had already asked too much of you. I didn't want you to jeopardise your men on my behalf. Two cars? You had that many men looking for me?"

"Considering it was you and Gwen, the lads were lining up to 'elp."

"How did Gwen persuade you?"

"She made me realise we'd all been played for fools with this fake kidnapping. I 'ad put myself out to curry favour with two different gangs to spring her, and it was just a con."

"She may have been in real danger, Archie. We couldn't know at the time."

"Yeah, I figured that, too. We're gonna 'ave to do some smoothing over when all is said and done. 'Ere comes the Battling Butler. Wonder if there's news."

"What's going on, Percival?" asked Iris.

"I just conferred with Her Ladyship," said Percival. "Lord Bainbridge is alive and resting under observation. Mrs. Bainbridge has been taken for X-rays. Lady Bainbridge is with her."

"So far, so good," said Iris.

"There is one other thing, Miss Sparks."

"Yes?"

"I telephoned the house to let the staff know what is going on. Mrs. Peek, the housekeeper, told me that the police had been by the house. They wanted to speak to His Lordship. She informed him that he was here. They're on their way."

"Oh, dear," said Iris. "Did they say why they wanted to speak to him?"

"They want him for murder."

CHAPTER 16

Henri must have jumped the gun," said Iris.

"I don't know who that is or what he has to do with anything," said Sally.

"And I don't care," said Archie. "But it sounds like this would be a good time to find some woodwork to fade into."

"And so say all of us," said Iris. "Percival, I'm going back to the house. The Daimler is parked around the corner to the left. Here are the keys."

"Where is Albert?" asked Percival.

"A very good question," said Iris, turning to Archie. "Where is Albert?"

"Last I saw, on foot in Canning Town," said Archie.

"I hope he has bus fare," said Iris. "It will be a long walk otherwise. And Percival—if he does find his way back to the house, take my advice and give him the sack."

"Very good, Miss Sparks. What shall I tell the ladies about the police?"

"Tell them to keep them away from Lord Bainbridge. He didn't kill anyone."

"I am relieved to hear it, Miss Sparks."

"And tell Gwen I'll meet her in Lord Eainbridge's office in the morning if her head is up to it."

"I will, Miss Sparks."

The three hurried out. Benny was waiting with Reg in the car. Archie turned to Iris.

"We'll talk when this is over," he said.

"You are not breaking up with me, Archie Spelling," said Iris. "I won't have it."

"Can't break what isn't there," said Archie. "We'll talk."

He got into the car. Benny peeled off immediately.

"Better come with me, then," said Sally.

She followed him to the Hornet. He held the door for her, then got in behind the wheel. He rested his forehead against it for a moment.

"Long day," he said.

"For all of us," said Iris, leaning against his side. "You've been the best friend a girl could possibly have today. Thank you, Sally."

"Anytime, Sparks," he said. "But not tomorrow, if it's all right with you."

"Unless Gwen needs you."

He turned his head towards her, still resting it on the steering wheel.

"I was trained to withstand all manner of interrogation and torture during the war," he said. "Yet between Mrs. Billington last night and you tonight, I feel compelled to reveal my innermost secrets like a weepy schoolgirl."

"Schoolgirls are tougher than you think."

"I suppose," he said, sitting up and turning on the motor.

"You should tell her."

"No," he said. "As long as I don't, I don't have to face the rejection. And the look of pity for the lovesick monster. That would be the worst part. I'll just keep mooning about, if it's all right with you."

"What a pair we make," said Iris. "Maybe it's for the best that we don't find mates. Let the generations of breeding miserable humans end with us."

"Hear, hear," said Sally.

They drove off as a pair of police cars screeched to a halt in front of the hospital.

Percival must have alerted Prudence to Iris's return, because when she emerged from Sally's Hornet, the cook opened the kitchen door for her.

"Have you had anything to eat?" she asked.

"Come to think of it, nothing since breakfast," said Iris.

"Sit," directed the cook. "I'll warm up some stew for you."

It might have been chicken, or it might have been pigeon. It didn't matter. It was late, Iris was starving, and it was delicious.

She made her way to her room unattended, stripped down, and plummeted headlong onto the bed.

She woke to hear voices from the ground floor. She held her watch up to the small bit of moonlight slipping through the shutters. It was four in the morning.

She threw on her clothes hurriedly and came down the stairs, still barefoot, to find Gwen and Lady Bainbridge in the entry hall. Gwen had a dressing plastered to the side of her head, dried blood speckling her blond hair.

"Hey," Iris said softly. "How's the noggin?"

"More or less intact," said Gwen. "No fracture. A concussion, though, and a couple of stitches. I'm afraid I won't be able to come into work for a few days."

"That's half the family on bed rest," said Lady Bainbridge. "When do I get my turn?"

"What happened with the police?" asked Iris.

"Harold is under suspicion for murder," said Lady Bainbridge.

"The man who was found near his club was killed in a room that Harold had rented."

"That's not enough to prove he did it," said Iris.

"That's exactly what I told them," said Lady Bainbridge. "And a few other things as well."

"You should have seen her," said Gwen. "She was magnificent. All the Furies rolled into one."

"On behalf of a man I now despise," said Lady Bainbridge. "Still, appearances must be maintained. That doctor proved invaluable. His authority trumped theirs in the end. Harold must not be disturbed, so saith Medicine."

"Never thought it would be lucky for a man to have a heart attack, but it's proving to be remarkably convenient," said Iris.

"They'll have a constable on guard around the clock until he's well enough to be arrested," said Gwen.

"Then we still have time to sort this all out," said Iris.

"Not right now," said Gwen. "I need sleep, I smell horrid, my head is swimming from whatever they gave me at the hospital, and I've been wearing the same outfit for nearly two days straight. I don't know if I've ever done that before."

I have, thought Iris. More times than I care to remember.

"Of course, darling," she said. "Come find me in the morning. I still need what's left of your brain added to mine if we want to save anyone."

"Do we want to save him?" asked Lady Bainbridge.

"There may be someone else who needs saving," said Iris. "Get some sleep, the both of you. We're not done with this yet."

She awoke at seven thirty when she heard a noise outside her door. She opened it to find breakfast on a tray again.

I could get used to this, she thought as she carried it in. I could have had it if I had gone through with that first engagement.

And how dreary my life would have been if I had. There is not enough breakfast in the world to make me trade that existence for my current one.

What does Archie do for breakfast? she wondered. Never thought about that before. Raw meat and whisky mixed with the blood of his enemies, she supposed.

Then she remembered his parting words, and wondered if she'd ever get to have that breakfast with him.

She finished, washed, dressed, and did her face. Her hair, already messy from her performance in Canning Town, was three quarters to Medusa after a night tossing and turning. She brushed it hastily, then coiled it into an uneven bun and pinned it as best she could.

She saw Percival when she came downstairs. His appearance was as impeccable as it had been on Friday, she noted with envy.

"Good morning, Miss Sparks," he said.

"Good morning, Percival. How is the patient?"

"Awake, and having breakfast in her room."

"Up to receiving visitors yet?"

"Millie has gone in to attend to her. I would suggest waiting half an hour."

"Thank you, Percival. I shall be in Lord Bainbridge's office should anyone ask."

She went to the office and dialed The Right Sort. Mrs. Billington answered on the first ring.

"It's Sparks, Saundra," said Iris.

"Is everything all right?" Mrs. Billington asked immediately.

"Everything is at sixes and sevens," said Iris. "Mrs. Bainbridge is temporarily out of commission with a concussion. I'm at the house, helping out. Oh, and Lord Bainbridge had a heart attack and is wanted for murder."

"Good heavens! Your sixes and sevens are other people's catastrophes, aren't they? And it's only Monday."

"I'm hoping to make it in tomorrow, but cancel and deflect everyone who's on today. Oh, if Mr. Daile calls, tell him to come meet us at the house."

"No need. He won't be calling."

"What makes you say that?"

"Because he's sitting right here. Should I be worried?"

"No. Put him on."

His voice came through a moment later.

"What is going on?" he asked.

"I think you should come to the house," she said. "We need to puzzle this out, and you hold some of the pieces."

"Very well," he said. "I will be there in twenty minutes. And I have something to give you."

"I'll let them know you're coming."

She hung up, then took the desk key from its hiding place, unlocked and opened the rolltop, and removed the blue-covered ledger.

She ran up the main staircase to Gwen's bedroom just as Millie, one of the maids, was leaving. She looked at Iris with surprise.

"Miss Sparks!" she exclaimed. "I didn't know you were visiting."

Then her eyes took in the state of Iris's hair.

"You need me," she said.

"I need a miracle," said Iris.

"I can work a miracle in ten minutes," said Millie, opening Gwen's door. "Get in."

Gwen was sitting up in her bed, a blue floral silk robe wrapped around her. She had a scarlet turban covering her hair. There was a half-eaten piece of toast and a cup of tea on a tray next to the bed, presided over by the silver-framed photograph of Ronnie, Senior, in his Royal Fusiliers dress uniform.

"What do you think?" asked Gwen, pointing to the turban. "Are these back in fashion, or should I chuck it all in and set up shop as a fortune-teller?"

"It covers a multitude of sins," said Iris.

"And one dressing," added Millie. "Sit down, Miss Sparks, and let me get to work."

Iris tossed the ledger onto the bed.

"Some light reading for you," she said as she sat in front of Gwen's dressing table.

Gwen picked it up and opened it while Millie unpinned Iris's hair, clucking sympathetically as it fell in tangles.

"Harold's handwriting," said Gwen as she began skimming through it. "So this is what he was up to. He said nothing about it in his letters."

"What do you make about the expenditures?"

"There do seem to be a lot of them," said Gwen. "What strikes me is that none of them came from Bainbridge, Limited. If I read this correctly, he was spending his own money."

"That seems reckless."

"Extremely. Did he not want the company involved, or was he doing this without their approval?"

"He wouldn't have needed it if he controlled your shares."

"Yes, but this may have gone beyond his powers. There may have been clauses minority shareholders could have invoked to stop him. Ronnie said something about that once after coming home from a particularly argumentative board meeting."

"What did they argue about when he was there?"

"Harold wanted to explore more. The others used to scoff at him. Lord Morrison kept saying he was trying to recapture his lost youth."

She read further.

"Lord Morrison may not have been wrong," she commented. "There is more passion and excitement in some of these entries than I ever saw in any of Harold's letters. Or heard from him in person. I almost feel guilty looking at it. It's like stealing a friend's diary at school and reading it."

"You did that?" exclaimed Iris in horror.

"No, no, no," said Gwen, colouring. "I was just making an analogy. Shut up and let me read."

Millie finished brushing out Iris's hair. Then her hands flew about Iris's head, braiding and coiling. She grabbed a handful of pins and secured everything, then stepped back to admire her handiwork.

"Nine minutes and forty-two seconds," said Iris, looking at her watch, then in appreciation at the mirror. "A new record for miracles in my book. Thank you, Millie."

"My pleasure, Miss Sparks," said Millie. "Ring if you need anything."

She left. Iris glanced over at Gwen, who was thoroughly engrossed in the ledger.

"I'll leave you to it," said Iris. "I'm going to—"

There was a screeching of brakes outside. Then another, and another.

"What's all that about?" asked Gwen.

There was a commotion from downstairs. Then Millie poked her head through the doorway.

"It's the police!" she cried. "They've come to search the house!"

She disappeared to tell the rest of the household.

"Search for what?" wondered Gwen.

"The nonexistent murder weapon," guessed Iris. "Do you keep any guns in the place?"

"Not that I know of," said Gwen. "The usual collection out in the country estate, of course, but other than Albert—"

"Blast!" exclaimed Iris. "I forgot about Albert's gun. Mr. Daile said he had something to give me. I'll bet that's it. He's going to walk right into the arms of the police, and we need to talk to him before they do. I'm going to intercept him. Keep reading. I'll be back."

She forced herself to walk unhurriedly down the stairs, observing constables swarming through the ground floor, opening cabinets and closets, upending cushions. The staff stood by and watched in dismay.

Standing in the entryway coordinating the chaos was Mike Kinsey. Detective Ex. She sighed, then walked towards him.

"Sparks," he said wearily as he saw her. "You're everywhere of late."

"You know I work with Mrs. Bainbridge, Mike," she said.

"But why are you in their home?"

"She was feeling under the weather, so I dropped by. Thought we could get some work done here, but it doesn't seem likely what with you lot stomping about the premises."

"First you're walking by the scene of a murder, next you're in the house of the prime suspect," he said. "I don't believe in coincidence when it comes to you."

"Believe whatever you like," she said. "I want to take a walk so I can get my thoughts in order. Any reason I can't?"

"Can't think of any."

"Good," she said. Then she fixed him with a lewd grin. "Like to frisk me, just to be safe? For old times' sake?"

"Get out of here, Sparks," said Kinsey.

She sauntered by him and out the front door. She nodded at the constable in front keeping the neighbours at bay, then kept going until she reached the corner.

Please let him be coming this way, she prayed.

She had guessed Daile's route correctly. She heard the motorcycle before she saw it. She flagged him down. He pulled up by her and lifted his goggles.

"Before you say anything else, have you still got Albert's gun?" she asked.

He nodded towards the basket in the rear.

"I was afraid of that," she said. "We have half of CID searching the Bainbridge house for firearms. Take off, wait an hour, then call this number. I'll let you know if it's safe to return."

She scribbled the office number on a piece of paper and handed it to him.

"Oh, one more thing," she said. She took out the photograph and showed it to him. "That's who you're looking for?"

"Yes," he said. "Do you know where he is?"

"Not yet," she said. "But we're on the same side. You have to trust me on that."

"I do," he said, putting his goggles back over his eyes. "One hour."

He roared off.

She walked the long way around until she came back to the house. The constable recognised her and let her back in.

The constables had moved to the second floor. Ronnie was on the landing with Agnes, watching them with fascination. He waved when he saw her.

"Hello, Iris!" he called. "Isn't this exciting?"

"It is indeed," said Iris. "Is your mummy still in her room?"

"She went down to Grandfather's office."

"Thank you, Ronnie."

Gwen was sitting at Lord Bainbridge's desk, still reading the ledger.

"They are going through every bedroom now," she said disconsolately. "I tried to look all fluttery and helpless when they came in, but they were having none of it. I'm glad I had my robe on. I'm not accustomed to gendarmes invading my boudoir when I am en déshabillé."

"How goes the ledger?"

"'Loan arranged from X,'" she read. "'Thirty-seven thousand pounds.' That's what you wanted me to see?"

"That's the one that jumped out," said Iris. "Let's say you borrowed short term from someone who wasn't a bank. They could set whatever conditions they wanted. The interest could have been extremely exorbitant. Enough to make the payoff—"

"Equivalent to a ransom of forty-five thousand pounds," finished Gwen. "Or something close to it plus whatever he was paying the gang and Albert to make this happen. But how does this connect to that photograph?"

"I'll explain, but I want to have Mr. Daile here to fill in some gaps. He should be calling in half an hour. Sounds like they're starting to clear out. If you're up to it, throw on something suitable for receiving a gentleman client."

"We should have Carolyne join us," said Gwen. "It concerns her more than anyone."

"She's taken in a lot already in the last twenty-four hours."

"She's strong," said Gwen. "She's had to be strong for a long time in this marriage. It's made her into a terrible person in many ways, but I'll give her that."

"And if she can't handle it, there's more whisky in the house somewhere," said Iris.

She poked her head out the door. The constables were filing out. One carried a long box, which he opened and showed to Kinsey. The detective sergeant reached in and pulled out a pair of flintlock pistols, then sniffed at their muzzles.

"We'll duel at dawn," said Iris. "Have your seconds call mine."

"I doubt that they've been fired in over a century," said Kinsey. "But we'll take them along for comparison. So here's something interesting. We got onto Bainbridge because we got a tip from the maître d' at the Livingstone Club to check out a suite His Lordship had taken. We think it's where the man was killed before his body was dumped in the alley."

He brought up one of the pistols and leveled it at her head. She met his gaze without flinching.

"The maître d' told us he got onto it because some woman from Special Operations popped in and made him show her the suite," he said. "Short brunette, very pushy."

"Sounds like just your type, Mike," said Iris.

"I don't suppose you'd want to come down to the club to have him identify you, would you?"

"I'd love to, but I'm busy."

"Then I guess we're done here for now."

"Lord Bainbridge didn't kill that man, Mike."

"And I suppose you're going to tell me who did," said Kinsey.

"I thought I'd let you have a go at this one," said Iris. "I'm tired of doing all your work for you."

He lowered the pistol and put it in the case with its companion.

"Stop showing up at crime scenes, Sparks," he said. "You're starting to unnerve the dead."

He turned and left. Around her, the staff began to put the house back in order. Behind her, the telephone rang in Lord Bainbridge's office.

"One second, I'll ask," Gwen was saying as she walked back in. She looked up at Iris. "Is the coast clear?"

Iris nodded.

"Yes, it's safe to come in," said Gwen. "Fifteen minutes will be fine."

She hung up.

"You can get dressed in fifteen minutes?" asked Iris.

"Amazing how quick it is when one doesn't have to fuss with one's hair," said Gwen, patting her turban.

Iris heard the motorcycle approach. Then the sound of the motor continued to the rear of the house. A minute later, Percival appeared.

"He's here," he said. "Where shall I bring him?"

"What's the best place for a private conversation?" asked Iris.

Percival hesitated.

"What is it?"

"I normally would suggest the library but—" He stopped, looking the most uncomfortable she had seen him in their brief acquaintance.

The penny dropped.

"But he's black and Lady Bainbridge would not like him there," said Iris.

"Unfortunately, that is the case."

"Lady Bainbridge is not going to like much of what she's about to learn," said Iris. "Would it be better to have her screaming where all the neighbors can overhear?"

"It would not," said Percival. "I will bring him to the library."

Iris picked up the ledger and walked down the hall. She was the first to enter the library. The books were shelved unevenly, having been shoved around by some particularly thorough constables in search of the missing weapon.

The coppers and the copper magnate, thought Iris. There's the headline if this all goes wrong.

There was a knock, then Percival opened the door to admit Mr. Daile. He nodded to Iris, then looked about the room.

"Impressive," he said. "Do you think the Bainbridges have read all these pretty books?"

"Lady Bainbridge may surprise you in that regard," said Iris. "But I wouldn't make it our first topic of conversation."

"I doubt that we'll get to a second topic," he said. "Oh, and let me give you this. It presents too much of a danger for me to keep it. Don't worry, I unloaded it."

He pulled the gun from his jacket, then a handful of cartridges from his pocket, and gave them to her. She put them on the mantelpiece over the fireplace.

The door opened, and Gwen and Lady Bainbridge came through together. Gwen smiled immediately upon seeing their visitor.

"Mr. Daile, I haven't thanked you properly for your role in rescuing us," she said, coming forward to shake his hand. "I am eternally grateful."

"I am glad I could help, Mrs. Bainbridge," he said. Then he

stepped forward and made a brief bow. 'Lady Bainbridge, I am honoured to make your acquaintance. My name is Simon Daile."

"What is he doing in my house?" asked Lady Bainbridge, ignoring him. "Why is he in this room?"

"Because he is part of all this, and we need him," said Gwen. "He is my guest, Carolyne, so I expect you to show some manners. For appearance's sake, if nothing else."

"Hmph," said Lady Bainbridge, walking past them to take her seat by the fireplace. "Let's get this over with."

"Carolyne, what did you know about Harold's most recent trip to Africa?" asked Gwen, taking the ledger from Iris.

"He was going to inspect the holdings of Bainbridge, Limited," said Lady Bainbridge. "Visit the plantations in Nyasaland, the mining operations and the smelters in the Rhodesias, and so forth."

"Did he say anything about exploring? Prospecting for new mining locations?"

"He wouldn't do that," she said. "He knew how much it would worry me."

"Yet that seems to be what he was doing," said Gwen, opening the ledger. "It's quite involved. And it ended up being rather expensive. He had to borrow money to keep it going. A considerable amount."

"How could he—" Lady Bainbridge started. Then she closed her eyes and sighed. "He could never sit still. Not for a moment. Being a rich man in England was never what he wanted. He wanted to be out there, making his name into the legend he thought he should be. So, he owes someone money. Who?"

"Someone who was willing to take drastic action if he wasn't paid," said Iris. "To threaten the one person Harold cared about more than anyone else."

"Not me, clearly," said Lady Bainbridge. "Who?"

"His son, Lady Bainbridge," said Iris.

"His son? His son is dead!" said Lady Bainbridge, her voice rising.

"Ronnie is dead," said Iris. "But he had another son. One born in another world."

She took the photograph from her bag and placed it on the small table in front of her. Lady Bainbridge glanced at it, then slowly picked it up to look at it more closely.

"Who is she?" she said, her voice shaking. "Who is this—this young woman?"

"Her name was Bayenkhu," said Mr. Daile. "She was my sister. The boy's name is John. My sister's son—and your husband's."

He reached into his wallet and pulled out a smaller photograph. It was the same boy, slightly younger, smiling.

"That's the photograph that you used for the missing child flyer at Moroni's," said Iris.

"Yes. How did you know it was mine?"

"The telephone number. It stuck with me for some reason. I finally remembered it was the same one you had given us."

"You used the past tense to refer to your sister," said Gwen. "What happened?"

"There was a boat—no, that is the end of the story," he said. "We grew up in a small village in Nyasaland. She was older than me by two years. She would tease me all the time because all I wanted to do was to read and study so I could leave our village and better myself. Ten years ago, she left to work as a housekeeper on a great coffee plantation. One owned by Bainbridge, Limited. We didn't want her to leave, but our father had died and our older brother had joined the military, so there was no one to tell her to stay but my mother, and Bayenkhu was too strong-willed to listen to her. She left, and all we would get was the occasional letter with some money inside. My mother would weep, and use the money for me to go to the mission school.

"This was before the war. Lord Bainbridge would come once a year. There was a great dinner each time, with music, dancing. Everyone was invited, and he would preside over it like a great king. And he saw my sister.

"I don't know the details. I wouldn't reveal them if I did. All that matters is that they had a son together."

"When was he born?" asked Gwen.

"In 1939. Lord Bainbridge was there, and from all accounts was delighted with him and with her. They named him John Nathan Daile."

"This is some blackmail scheme," said Lady Bainbridge hotly. "You have no proof."

"I have a copy of the birth certificate," said Mr. Daile. "Your husband is listed as the father."

"That means nothing. A birth certificate from some African—"

"And there are letters," said Mr. Daile. "But I am not here for blackmail, Lady Bainbridge. We don't want your money. We wanted to bring John home to his mother."

"What made you believe he was in England?" asked Iris.

"Lord Bainbridge had visited his child and, let's be frank, my sister on every one of his travels to Nyasaland. There was a long period where he was unable to come because of the war, but his support and correspondence continued. Then, on his recent trip, he proposed taking his son to see the workings in Rhodesia. Bay-enkhu agreed. She wanted John to spend time with his father. But they didn't come back. She received a letter from Lord Bainbridge stating that he intended to take his son to England, where he would receive the appropriate education and upbringing.

"She was frantic, but had no way of finding or intercepting them. She left the plantation and contacted our brother, who wrote me to do what I could from this end. I postponed my re-entry to my school and came to London. I took a job as a gardener to watch your house for his return, but when he appeared here without my nephew, I took the next step and came to The Right Sort posing as a customer. I hoped to somehow find my way into the inner circles of the family and find where he was keeping John. Then came a letter from my brother. They had taken a steamship across Lake Nyasa. There was an accident. Many drowned, including Bayenkhu."

"I am so sorry, Mr. Daile," said Gwen, taking his hand in hers.

"But if the boy's mother is dead, what claim do you have on him?" asked Lady Bainbridge, speaking to him directly for the first time.

"The claim of family," he said. "Which is outweighed by Lord Bainbridge's rights as a father, but only if he acknowledges John's paternity in England."

"Where is the child?" asked Lady Bainbridge.

"That, I do not know," said Mr. Daile. "I suspected that Lord Bainbridge's nightly visits to the Livingstone Club were a ruse, but each time he went in, he stayed for a few hours, then emerged. I befriended one of the staff there and asked if there was a child staying anywhere in the club, but he said there was none. I watched the rear alley, but he never sneaked out that way. As far as I could tell, Lord Bainbridge only visited his club for social purposes."

"I may have an answer as to that," said Iris. "At least partly. There is—"

She stopped and glanced at Lady Bainbridge.

"Go ahead," she said.

"There is a building on the other side of the alley," said Iris. "Connected to the club by a tunnel in the basement. There are rooms there."

"What sort of rooms?"

"Places to stay. Places to live. Places to keep secrets."

"I see," said Lady Bainbridge. "I am not surprised to find that you know about them."

"Think what you like," said Iris, shrugging. "Yesterday morning, I went into a suite there that had been taken by Lord Bainbridge since last Sunday."

"Sunday?" interrupted Lady Bainbridge. "But he arrived home Monday."

"I'm afraid not. He came home Sunday, went to the club, and rented that suite. It had two bedrooms in it. The place had been emptied out when I was in there, but I found two things that struck me. One was a bullet hole in the wall. The other was a bit of crayon under the table. The same brand as the ones Ronnie uses."

"Crayon," said Gwen. "John was kept there."

"Until someone came and took him away," said Iris. "My guess is the dead man was a caretaker your husband brought home to watch him until further arrangements could be made."

"Are you saying that the child was kidnapped?" Lady Bainbridge said with horror.

"I suspect it. I believe that the man who loaned your husband the money for his mining adventure decided to force the issue, only the caretaker resisted and was shot for his troubles."

"Then by disrupting the fake kidnapping, we may have doomed that poor boy," said Gwen. "Harold must have been devastated. No wonder his heart gave out."

"Maybe my nephew is still alive," said Mr. Daile. "Do you know who was behind this?"

"Someone who was at the dinner party here," said Iris.

"What makes you think that?" asked Gwen.

"Your son," replied Iris. "He's developed a taste for listening in on the conversations of grown-ups. I did the same when I was his age."

"So did I," said Lady Bainbridge. "What did he overhear?"

"A man arguing with your husband over a debt," said Iris. "Ronnie heard the other man say 'Nothing happens to the boy as long as you do what you're told. When the company is mine, we'll be quits.' Ronnie naturally thought they were referring to him."

"Prendergast," said Gwen. "It has to be him. He loaned money to the company. He said he was considering trying to take an interest in it, even a controlling interest. Oh my God—even when he was pursuing me, he had that poor little boy locked up somewhere? How cruel!"

"He was pursuing you?" asked Lady Bainbridge. "When was this?"

"Saturday morning at the office. That craven, manipulative, calculating—"

The litany was interrupted by a knock on the door.

"Yes?" called Lady Bainbridge.

Percival entered, holding a silver tray with a card on it.

"I beg pardon, Lady Bainbridge, but there is a visitor for Mrs. Bainbridge."

"This really isn't a very good time," said Gwen, taking the card. "I'm— Oh!"

"What?" asked Iris.

"It's Prendergast. He's here!"

CHAPTER 17

W hat do we do?" asked Gwen. "Should we call the police?"

"And tell them what?" responded Iris. "All we have is speculation at this point."

"I have an idea," said Daile, glancing at the gun on the mantelpiece.

"No," said Iris. "Look, he may know that Lord Bainbridge is in hospital, but he can't know if he's talked or not. He must be here to find out what the police have learned. Go and speak with him, Gwen. I'll be with you in a minute. I need to arrange something."

"But what shall I ask him?"

"Make small talk, don't give anything away until I join you."

"And me?" asked Lady Bainbridge.

"You two stay here," said Iris as she went out the door.

"Talk to each other," advised Gwen as she followed. "You have more in common than you know."

She closed the door behind her. Lady Bainbridge looked at the man standing before her, his face impassive.

"Will you sit?" she asked, indicating the chair opposite her. "I have more questions to ask. I'll ring for tea."

"Thank you, ma'am," he said, sitting. "Tea would be most welcome."

* * *

Prendergast was gazing out the front window when Percival announced Gwen.

"Mrs. Bainbridge, thank you for seeing me," he said, turning and coming to offer her his hand.

She hesitated, then took it.

"Good morning, Mr. Prendergast," she said, shaking it firmly. "This is an unexpected visit. Will you take a seat?"

"Thank you," he said, sitting on a sofa.

She took the high-backed chair in front of the portrait of her in-laws, hoping their stern glares would give her added protection.

"Place is in a bit of a shambles today," Prendergast observed, looking at the maids scurrying about, putting the house back in order after its roughing up by the police.

"Lady Bainbridge mislaid a brooch," said Gwen. "All hell has broken loose."

"Unfortunate to have that on top of everything else," he said. "I just learned about Lord Bainbridge. I came first to see if there is any assistance I may provide."

"Thank you, we're coping," said Gwen. "How did you find out?"

"I went to Bainbridge, Limited, this morning."

"Why?"

"That's the other thing I wanted to tell you," he said. "I have made my decision as far as the loan goes. I went there and accepted the full payment with the interest. No renewal, no insistence on shares. My relationship with the company is now terminated, and I am free to pursue other interests."

"Meaning me?"

"No, Mrs. Bainbridge, and that is something for which I wish to apologise. I told you that I like to know everything about a situation before I make my decision, and I was precipitate in advancing my—my courtship, if my clumsy efforts could be labeled as such. I should have looked into the obvious reason for your unwillingness to consider any approach from me."

"What reason is that?" asked Gwen.

"Hello, hello," said Iris, bouncing into the room. "Sorry to be late. How do you do, Mr. Prendergast? You may not recognise me when I'm not covered with paint, but we met on Saturday."

"Miss Sparks," he said, rising to greet her. "I remember you, of course. I'm sorry, but we were speaking of personal matters."

"Miss Sparks is my confidante in all things," said Gwen as Iris sat by the fireplace where she could watch them both. "You may speak freely. You were about to tell me why I was reluctant to accept your invitation to dine."

"Your son," said Prendergast. "That's the source of the conflict between you and Bainbridge. He seized custody while you were recovering. I cannot think how painful that must have been for you, and there I was, piling on to it when it was so blindingly obvious. I cannot forgive myself for that, but I am asking you to do so."

"Who told you about that?" asked Gwen.

"I spoke to Morrison when we were finalising the payment. He's acting head of the company with Bainbridge out. He's the one who told me about the heart attack. In any case, I will cease my efforts until you've succeeded in yours. And if there is any assistance that I may provide to you, whether to help defray the legal expenses, or—"

"Thank you, but I would prefer to handle this on my own," said Gwen.

"Of course, of course," said Prendergast, quickly getting to his feet. "Then I should be leaving."

"Wait, please," said Gwen. "I need to ask you something. You make such a point about knowing everything about a situation that I feel I should do the same."

"Anything I can answer, I will," he said, sitting again.

"Since I am a principal shareholder, I should know how much

the loan was, and why it was taken in the first place," said Gwen. "Is the company in trouble?"

"Not immediately," he said. "Bainbridge's munitions division went into heavy production during the war, of course. Remuneration for government contracts was irregular, and payments were not always forthcoming when they should have been. Workers and suppliers still have to be paid on time, though, so the company needed an emergency sum to tide them over. They approached me."

"How much was this sum?"

"A hundred twenty-five thousand pounds. I mentioned the terms previously."

"Two percent over market," she said, glancing at Iris. "Yes, I remember. With the options to take payment in shares. How is it that they, or should I say we, were able to pay you now?"

"The British government received a rather massive loan from the States. Many contractors were paid, including Bainbridge."

"How much did you investigate their holdings before you made this loan?" asked Iris.

"I hardly see how it's any business of yours, Miss Sparks," he said, looking at her in surprise.

"Consider her questions my own," said Gwen. "We are two businesswomen who are learning the ropes."

"Well, as I said, I like to acquire a thorough knowledge of the entire company before I make any move."

"Then you are familiar with their holdings in Africa?" asked Iris.

"I am."

"Do you know if the company has any operations in Mopani?"

"I've never heard of Mopani. Where is it?"

"In Northern Rhodesia, four days' journey north of Chililabombwe."

"I know of no activity by Bainbridge anywhere in that region. Are you saying there is some?"

"I'll let you know when I do," said Gwen, standing. "Mr. Prendergast, I would like to thank you for clarifying things. And for being honest with me."

She walked forward to offer her hand, this time with confidence. He stood and held it.

"I hope that everything works out favourably for you," he said.

"Thank you."

"And I hope that you will contact me when it does," he said.

"I promise that I shall study the situation until I understand it thoroughly," she said, smiling at him for the first time.

"I cannot ask for more than that," he said, smiling back. "Miss Sparks, good day."

"Goodbye, Mr. Prendergast," said Iris.

He left. They watched as he walked down the front walk to a waiting cab and drove off.

"He was telling the truth," said Gwen. "He's not Mr. X. The loan amount was different, and he was dealing directly with the company."

"And he's not the man Ronnie heard arguing with Harold," said Iris.

"How do you know that?" asked Gwen.

"Ronnie!" called Iris.

Ronnie stepped from outside the doorway to the parlour, a guilty look on his face.

"Were you listening in?" asked Gwen sternly.

"Yes," said Ronnie.

"Because I asked him to," added Iris. "We needed to know if that was the voice or not. Was that the man, Ronnie?"

"No," said Ronnie. "He had a much gruffer voice than the arguing man."

"How long were you listening?" asked Gwen.

"From before Iris went into the parlour."

"Oh, dear," said Gwen, glaring at Iris. "Ronnie, I expect you heard us say many things you didn't understand. Do you want to ask Mummy any questions?"

"What does 'custody' mean?" he asked immediately.

Iris looked stricken.

Gwen knelt down so she could look her son directly in the eyes.

"Custody is about who in a family gets to raise a child," she said. "Sometimes mummies and daddies have fights and separate, and the one who the child lives with is the one who has custody."

"But you and Daddy didn't separate," said Ronnie. "Daddy was killed in the war."

"Yes, my darling boy," said Gwen. "And you remember how sad Mummy became when that happened? So sad that she became sick and had to go away to get better. So while she was away, your grandparents had custody of you. Do you understand what the word means now?"

"Yes," said Ronnie. "But you're all better now. You're home with me."

"I am home with you," said Gwen, sweeping him into her arms for a prolonged hug. "And I'm all better. It's only that your grandfather loves you so much that he didn't want to give you back to me."

"But if he loves me, why did he go away to Africa?" asked Ronnie. "And why has he been so mean to everyone?"

"Your grandfather is a very complicated man," said Gwen. "No one always understands the reasons why he does the things he does. But we're trying to figure them out, and what you did just now was very helpful. All right?"

"All right," he said dubiously. "I have to have my lessons with Agnes. May I go, please?"

"Not until you give Mummy a kiss," said Gwen.

He put his lips to her cheek. She returned it, then quickly rubbed the lipstick off.

"Run to Agnes," she said. "I love you!"

"Love you, too!" he cried, disappearing. "Bye, Iris!"

They heard him clatter up the steps. Gwen turned to Iris.

"I don't like what you did," said Gwen sharply. "You should not have involved him without asking me."

"Things were happening quickly," said Iris. "I had to move fast to get him into position, and I didn't want anyone getting suspicious."

"Including me."

"Including you, for the moment of this conversation. And in my defense, I didn't know the custody question would come up. I suggested you make small talk. That was a large topic."

"You could have taken twenty seconds to clear it with me beforehand."

"And what would you have said?"

Gwen was silent.

"I thought so," said Iris, sighing. "I'm sorry, darling. There was another child's life at stake, and I made some decisions on the fly. And all we ended up doing was ruling out our only suspect."

"No," said Gwen. "Not our only one. Let's regroup and talk it out."

They went back to the library. As Gwen reached for the door handle, she heard voices from within. Peaceful, happy voices. She looked at Iris in wonder.

"Beats me," said Iris.

Gwen opened the door to see Lady Bainbridge and Mr. Daile chatting away, holding their teacups in front of them.

". . . and two parts vinegar?" said Lady Bainbridge. "That will be effective?"

"I guarantee it will work better than any chemical poison you can get, and will do less harm to your nervous system," he replied. "Ah, they are back."

"Mr. Daile has been consulting with me on my roses," said Lady Bainbridge. "He is very knowledgeable. They turn out smart men at Harper Adams, I see. How did it go with Prendergast?"

"He isn't our man," reported Gwen.

"So we're back to square one," added Iris gloomily.

"Not quite," said Gwen. "If it wasn't Mr. Prendergast who threatened Harold here on Friday night, then it must have been someone else at the party."

"Someone on the board?" exclaimed Lady Bainbridge. "But we've known them all for years."

"Nevertheless, someone loaned Harold the money and threatened harm to a boy," said Gwen. "And we can narrow it down further."

"How?" asked Iris.

"It had to have been someone who knew about John beforehand, and knew he was staying at the Livingstone Club."

"Not just the club," said Iris. "It had to be someone who knew about the special guest rooms."

"How does one become a member of that club?" asked Mr. Daile.

"You have to have spent time living in or exploring some part of Africa," said Iris. "Harold qualified, of course."

"So did Lord Morrison," said Lady Bainbridge. "They were there together. But he's Harold's closest friend. I can't imagine him betraying him like this."

"For money and control of the company?" asked Iris. "I think every man has his price."

"Not him," said Lady Bainbridge firmly.

"Wait," said Gwen. "I've thought of something. And we may need to move fast now. Who knows how long it will be before the police move in on Harold?"

A taxi drove through the arches at the entryway to New Scotland Yard and pulled up in front of the new building. Mr. Otis Burleigh paid the driver and got out, looking around him curiously. Then he went through the door where a constable was manning a security desk.

"May I help you?" he asked.

"I have an appointment with Detective Superintendent Parham," said Burleigh.

"Of course, sir. He's with Homicide and Serious Crime Command. Take the lift to the third storey."

A directory was on the wall opposite the lift when he got out. He followed the arrows until he reached a cluster of offices. One of them had DETECTIVE SUPERINTENDENT PHILIP PARHAM stenciled on the frosted glass of the door. He knocked. A young woman called, "Come in."

He entered to see Morrison, Birch, and Phillips seated inside. They looked at him morosely.

"Good Lord, you as well?" he exclaimed. "Where's McIntyre?"

"On his way," said Lord Morrison. "Any idea what this is about?"

"None."

There was a young, blond secretary typing at a desk. He went over to her.

"You're Mr. Burleigh?" she asked without looking up.

"Yes."

"He wants to talk to you first," she said. "He'll be right with you."

She picked up a telephone and pressed a button. Burleigh heard a tinny voice respond.

"Mr. Burleigh is here now, sir," she said. "Yes, sir. Right away."

She hung up, then stood, opened a door at the far end of the room, and indicated for him to go in. She closed the door after him.

Parham was retrieving a brown wool jacket from a coat tree in the corner when Burleigh came in. The detective was in his late forties, of medium height, the grey at his temples matching the grey in his mustache. On his desk lay a half-eaten sandwich on a piece of wax paper next to a cup of tea.

"Mr. Burleigh, is it?" he said as he put on the jacket. "Philip Parham."

He came over to shake Burleigh's hand, then directed him to a chair in front of his desk.

"I apologise for the mess," he said, sitting behind the desk. "I was grabbing a quick bite, lost track of time, and here you are. Thank you for coming in."

"Not at all," said Burleigh. "What's it about?"

"You know about Lord Bainbridge's heart attack, I take it?" asked Parham, taking a bite from his sandwich.

"I heard about it this morning, of course, but how is that a police matter?"

"We're investigating him for the murder of a man named Rawson Mulenga."

"Good Lord! Harold? A murderer? I don't believe it."

"It seems to be a shock to all who know him. His wife has been a virtual harridan since we showed up at the hospital. Unfortunately, we can't get to him until the doctor gives us the go-ahead, so we are pursuing other lines of investigation until then."

"I will be happy to assist in any way I can," said Burleigh. "But I doubt that I have anything of use to you."

"Mr. Mulenga's body was found in the alleyway behind the Livingstone Club. Did you happen to hear about that?"

"Yes, as a matter of fact, although we didn't know his name at the time. Someone brought it up at dinner at the Bainbridge place Friday night."

"Did they?" asked Parham. "That may be of importance. Do you happen to recall who brought it up?"

"Let me think," said Burleigh, frowning. "It may have been Birch. Sandy Birch. Alexander, rather, but everyone calls him Sandy."

"And he's on the board of . . . ?" asked Parham, reaching for his pen and knocking it off the desk. "Blast, hold that thought."

He bent under the desk to retrieve it, then emerged holding it triumphantly.

"Right," he said, uncapping it. "Alexander Birch, known as Sandy. And he's on the board of Bainbridge, Limited?"

"Yes," said Burleigh. "As am I, as well as the others you have waiting outside."

"We'll get to them," said Parham. "It's going to be a long morning. Blast again."

This was in response to his telephone ringing. He picked it up.

"Parham," he said. "Yes? Yes, that's fine. Go ahead. Call me when you're done."

He hung up, shaking his head.

"It's a wonder I can have a complete thought nowadays," he grumbled. "So how did Lord Bainbridge react to the introduction of this unpleasant news?"

"He was quite upset by it, as I recall," said Burleigh.

"Was he? Was he indeed?" said Parham, writing the word "upset" in his notes. "Good, good, sounds like we're getting somewhere. What I would like you to do, in as much detail as you can recall, is to tell me everything you saw and heard that evening."

"Well, I arrived with my son, Stephen, sometime before seven o'clock," he began.

His account continued uninterrupted for a good ten minutes, Parham pausing him only to replenish his fountain pen or start another sheet of paper. Then the telephone rang again. Parham held up his hand to stop Burleigh's narrative and answered it.

"Parham," he said. "Yes. Good, tell me. They did. And his condition? Excellent. What else? Really? That's fine. Should be enough for now. Thank you."

He hung up, then smiled at Burleigh.

"Good news?" asked Burleigh.

"Always good to hear about a successful police operation, Mr. Burleigh," said Parham. "Unless you're the subject of it, of course. Which, I'm afraid, you are."

"Excuse me?" said Burleigh.

"While you were wearing out my writing hand with your account, two teams of police officers under my command executed raids on your home as well as another house that you maintain in Islington."

"You had no right—" Burleigh began.

"We had every right," said Parham. "In the Islington house, my men found a young boy being held against his will. His name is John Nathan Daile. You are hereby arrested and charged with kidnapping him and holding him for ransom."

"That's nonsense!" protested Burleigh.

"You've also been identified as the man who used the boy's abduction as a threat to Lord Bainbridge at his home on Friday evening."

"But that's impossible!"

"And my men have recovered a pistol believed to have been used in the abduction, as well as a key to a building connected to the Livingstone Club. A key, as you know very well, being a member, only available to those who take rooms there. You took a room there for a few days while the boy and Rawson Mulenga were staying in a room taken by Lord Bainbridge."

"I returned that key!" said Burleigh.

"Yes, you did," agreed Parham. "The one we recovered was a copy you had made. Gentlemen, please come in!"

Two police constables entered the office and took positions on either side of Burleigh.

"Two men were arrested at the Islington house," said Parham. "We'll find out which one of them pulled the trigger, or if it was you. One of them will talk, it doesn't matter which. The boy will be able to tell us what happened, and we'll get a match for the gun. It was clever of you to remove the bullet from the wall, but Mr. Mulenga was shot twice, and the second bullet remained in his body. I expect that the task of digging it out was too time-consuming."

"I want my solicitor!" shouted Burleigh as one of the constables handcuffed him. "You said someone identified me! That's impossible!"

They dragged him away. Parham watched for a moment, then pulled his chair back from his desk and peered under it.

Ronnie Bainbridge looked back up at him from underneath where he had been sitting.

"All clear?" he asked.

"All clear, young man," said Parham, holding his hand to pull the boy out from under and to his feet. "Well done. Very well done indeed. Let's go find your mother."

The other members of the board had already been sent away. Parham took Ronnie to a waiting room one storey up where Gwen, Iris, Agnes, Lady Bainbridge, and Mr. Daile sat.

"You were right," said Parham. "Burleigh was the culprit. And a member of the Livingstone Club."

"I thought so," said Gwen. "A big-game hunter like him would have been eligible. Ronnie, are you all right?"

"I helped catch him!" burbled Ronnie. "Didn't I, Mr. Parham?"

"I couldn't have done it without you," said Parham. "I'd offer you a treat, but we can't be bribing witnesses, now can we?"

"How did you have Ronnie do it?" asked Iris.

"I put him under my desk," said Parham. "Once he had enough time to hear Burleigh speak, I dropped my pen so I could see him and get the nod."

"And I gave him the nod!" said Ronnie excitedly.

"After that, a prearranged telephone call from Kinsey allowed me to give the go-ahead for the raids."

"All right, young man, let's get you cleaned up," Agnes said to Ronnie. "And then we'll get a snack somewhere."

She led him out of the waiting room, dusting off his trousers.

"And my nephew?" said Mr. Daile. "Is he all right?"

"He was found in good health, Mr. Daile," said Parham. "I'm

sure it was a terrible experience. It wouldn't surprise me if there are nightmares to come."

"I have to tell him about his mother," said Mr. Daile sadly.

"Once we've had him checked over by a doctor, we'll return him to you," said Parham.

"Thank you," said Mr. Daile.

"No," said Lady Bainbridge.

The others turned to look at her. Her expression was mournful, but determined.

"What is it, Carolyne?" asked Gwen.

"He shouldn't go back to Mr. Daile," said Lady Bainbridge. "He should live with his father."

There was a collective stunned silence in the room. Gwen was the first to break it.

"Do you mean with us, Carolyne?" she asked. "Or are you going to divorce Harold?'

"Divorce him?" snorted Lady Bainbridge. "I'm praying that he recovers well enough for me to make the rest of his life a living hell. But that punishment shouldn't be visited upon the child. Harold is his father. He has to take responsibility."

"But what about appearances being kept up?" asked Iris. "There will be a scandal when this comes out."

"We will tell those who ask that he is our ward," said Lady Bainbridge. "That Harold brought home an impoverished boy from Nyasaland to give him a better chance and a proper English education. I would say values, but the word chokes me at the moment. Will that be acceptable to you, Mr. Daile?"

"As long as I have contact with him, Lady Bainbridge," he replied. "He should know about our side of his family. And someone should keep his Chitumbuka proficient."

"You do understand that the Bainbridge title will never be his," she said stiffly. "It only passes through legitimate issue. Ronald remains the heir."

"I have no quarrel with that, Lady Bainbridge."

"Then you will let us know when we may receive the child, Detective Superintendent."

"Of course, ma'am," he said, a bemused smile on his face.

"Very well. I am going to the car."

"We'll catch up," said Gwen.

Lady Bainbridge nodded, then stalked out of the room.

"That surprised me, I admit it," said Parham. "I take it you'll want to keep the boy's paternity on the QT?"

"As much as possible, Detective Superintendent," said Gwen. "Thank you."

"Then if you will excuse me, I have work to do. Mrs. Bainbridge, Miss Sparks, Mr. Daile, good day."

He exited, leaving the three of them together.

"Looks like your son has a new playmate," said Iris. "Unless he's still going to St. Frideswide's."

"We still have to win that battle," said Gwen. "Mr. Daile, given what we now know about you, I feel that The Right Sort should refund your five pounds."

"Would it be strange of me to ask you to keep me on as your client?" he asked shyly. "It looks like I will be staying in England longer than I had anticipated."

"As we said before, we currently don't have any female candidates of African descent," said Gwen. "We can look, certainly, but you should know that."

"I am willing to broaden my horizons," he said. "Perhaps you could reinterview me now that all need for subterfuge has passed."

"A splendid idea," said Iris. "Once Mrs. Bainbridge's brain is in full working order, we shall have you back at the office."

"I have the utmost admiration for the quality of Mrs. Bainbridge's brain," he said. "I look forward to seeing it in full health."

"As do I," said Gwen. "I've been trying to figure out all of the relations now. John is my husband's half brother, so that makes him Ronnie's half uncle, even though they're a year apart. And you're John's uncle, of course. So what does that make us?"

"Simple," said Mr. Daile, smiling. "We're family."

CHAPTER 18

The new chauffeur's name was Nigel. He had driven members of the General Staff during the war, so was able to remain unperturbed in the presence of Lady Bainbridge. He sounded the Wraith's horn as he turned onto the street where the Bainbridge house was located, so by the time he pulled into the driveway, the greeting party was in place.

They had kept it small, wanting to avoid overwhelming the latest addition to the household. Nigel stopped the car in the driveway in front of the house, turned off the engine, then came around to open the rear door.

Lady Bainbridge emerged, then turned and beckoned to the other occupant of the rear seat. A boy of seven exited the car, looking around at the house and the neighbouring houses with unease.

Percival came out of the house, walked up to the two of them, and bowed.

"Good afternoon, Percival," said Lady Bainbridge. "This is Master John Nathan Daile. He will be staying with us. John, this is Percival, our butler."

"Master John, welcome to Kensington," said Percival, holding out his hand. "We are delighted to have you with us. Please, let me show you inside."

John looked up at Lady Bainbridge. She nodded at him with a smile that was meant to be comforting, but was no less terrifying than most of her public expressions. John turned back to Percival and shook his hand. Percival smiled, then turned and walked back to the front door. After a moment's hesitation, John followed him with Lady Bainbridge at his heels.

Percival held the door for them. Waiting by the foot of the stairs were Ronnie, Gwen, and Agnes. John stared at them suspiciously.

Harold's expression, thought all of the adults immediately.

Before anyone could say anything, Ronnie darted forward, his hand out.

"Hello," he said. "My name's Ronnie. Do you like to draw?"

"Yes," said John, accepting the proffered hand. "I like it very much."

"Come on up, I've got lots of crayons," said Ronnie. "It's this way."

And before anyone could say anything, the two boys dashed up the stairs.

"I should go after them," said Agnes.

"Please," said Gwen. "We'll do more introductions later."

Ralph was coming out of the Tender Arms, his regular haunt, when a dark red Lancaster pulled up by him and Carlton poked his head out the driver's window.

"Manfred wants to see you," he said.

"When?" asked Ralph.

"Do you see me holding his appointment book? Get in."

Ralph was not at all happy about the sudden invitation, even less so when he saw the two large blokes in the back seat. One of them got out, holding the door. Ralph considered making a break for it then and there, but rejected it in favour of seeing if he could talk his way out of whatever trouble he was in.

He got into the car, sandwiched tightly in between the blokes who took advantage of their positioning to pat him down thoroughly.

"Any idea what this is about?" he asked as the car pulled away.

"Yeah," said Carlton.

Ralph waited expectantly, but that turned out to be the extent of the conversation until they reached Manfred's headquarters.

"You know the way," said Carlton as they got out.

"I do," said Ralph.

One of the blokes opened the door for him. He went down a long corridor towards a doorway at the end with light coming from it. He went through it to see Manfred sitting at the head of a long table, which didn't surprise him. What did was seeing Archie Spelling sitting to Manfred's left, and next to him . . .

"What the hell is she doing here?" he exclaimed.

"Hello," said Mrs. Bainbridge. "I recognise your voice. So nice to put a face to it at last."

Manfred smiled and pointed to the chair across from her. Ralph went to it, trying to figure the situation. Then he gave up and sat down.

"How's the head feeling?" he asked.

"Improving, thank you for asking," she replied. "How is the young man's eye? I understand there is some hope he'll regain his sight."

"Yeah, there is," said Ralph. "Apart from his dad, none of us holds that against you."

"How very big of you," said Gwen. "I suppose I should thank you for not treating me worse than you did. You weren't expecting to have an actual hostage to look after, were you?"

"What's going on here, duchess?"

"You will address her as Mrs. Bainbridge," said Manfred. "Call her anything else, and I will teach you a lesson in etiquette myself."

"My apologies, Mrs. Bainbridge," Ralph said hastily.

"Accepted," she said. "In answer to your question, I am here on behalf of the Bainbridge family. You may know about some of the circumstances surrounding my father-in-law since you and your men fled the scene."

"We heard a few things," said Ralph.

"What you haven't heard is anything about a kidnapping."

"It wasn't really—"

He stopped as she glared at him like his gran used to when she caught him stealing a biscuit.

"No, Mrs. Bainbridge, we haven't heard about any kidnapping," he said.

"Nor will you, as long as you agree to certain conditions," she said. "My understanding is that you were to be paid five thousand pounds by my father-in-law for your part in his attempted swindle of my mother-in-law. Is that correct?"

He nodded. She reached into her bag and pulled out a thick manila envelope.

"We expect you to keep mum about everything you know," she said. "Mr. Willoughby here has assured us that he will guarantee your silence, but I want to hear it from you."

"You have my word, Mrs. Bainbridge," he said, glancing at Manfred.

She held the envelope across the table. As he reached for it, she pulled it back.

"One more thing," she said.

"Yes?"

"You were sloppy. The young man let me disrupt things. I was one second away from getting his gun and turning Marylebone Street into the Wild West."

"You telling us we should be better at our jobs, Mrs. Bainbridge?" he asked.

"No," she said, handing him the envelope. "I'm telling you that I'm going to be better at mine."

She held her bag open long enough for him to see the butt of a gun inside.

"If I ever see you, that young man, or anyone from your gang anywhere near our house, our car, or any member of my family, I won't hesitate to use this," she said. "Do I make myself clear?"

"Perfectly clear, Mrs. Bainbridge," said Ralph. "We have an understanding."

"Good," she said.

She rose from her seat. Manfred and Archie got up as well, as did Ralph a quick moment later.

"Thank you, Mr. Willoughby," said Mrs. Bainbridge, offering her hand. "You have been most accommodating."

"A pleasure to meet you, Mrs. Bainbridge," said Manfred, shaking it. "May the next time be under more pleasant circumstances. Archie, a word before you go."

"Wait for me in the 'all," said Archie.

Mrs. Bainbridge nodded, then walked out.

"This squares us," said Archie.

"Agreed," said Manfred. "She's quite the lady, isn't she?"

"Far above our ability to judge," said Archie. "So we're done. Good luck to the both of you."

He left without shaking hands.

"And now I know all about you, Archie Spelling," said Manfred. "Right, you. Hand it over."

Ralph, who had been counting the money in the envelope, pulled out a thousand and gave it to him. Manfred shook his head.

"It's going to be more," he said. "You made me go to the damn zoo on this one. That will cost you another five hundred."

"Think that will keep them away?" asked Gwen.

"I don't think the Bainbridges will be considered worth the trouble," said Archie. "I'll need the gun back."

"Of course," she said, pulling it out of her bag and handing it to him. "Thank you for setting up the meeting. And for everything."

"Thanks for going through with it," said Archie. "Worth doing to find out 'ow afraid 'e was of me. I never figured 'im for that until you told me 'ow 'is lads reacted to my name. We're all so scared about 'anging on to our little kingdoms that we forget the other side is just as scared. And that's 'ow wars get started."

"You're quite the philosopher when you want to be," said Gwen.

"Don't spread it about," he said. "Where shall I drop you?"

"London Hospital, please, if it's not out of your way."

Harold had asked to see her. Her, of all the possible people he could admit to his isolation, although he had spoken to his solicitor by telephone. Still, when Percival had approached her with the request, her first thought was, Why not Carolyne?

Then she thought about letting Carolyne loose in the Quiet Ward in her current mood, and approved of the decision.

The station nurse directed Gwen to his room. When she entered, he was lying on his bed with his eyes closed, an opened copy of the *Financial Times* resting on his stomach. She pulled up a chair next to the bed and sat. The noise woke him.

"Sorry," she said.

"Don't be. You shouldn't have to sit around watching an old man sleep," he said, trying to sit up.

"Let me help," she said, arranging the pillows behind him until he was comfortable.

"I didn't think you would come," he said. "Did you bring the books?"

"It's one book, and yes, I did," she said.

She pulled a ledger from her bag. It was bound in good paper coloured the same light green as her office walls. THE RIGHT SORT MARRIAGE BUREAU was printed in large black letters on the cover.

"May I?" he asked.

She handed it to him, then sat back and watched as he went through it.

"This is mostly your handwriting," he observed.

"Iris's abilities exceed mine in many areas," said Gwen. "But maths aren't among them. I would also say my financial acumen is superior to hers."

"You certainly married better," he commented.

"I married superbly," she said. "So did my husband."

"Yes."

"So did you, if you had only realised it."

He winced, but kept on reading.

"Where did you learn how to keep books?" he asked.

"From books about keeping books," she said. "And we had an accountant friend take a look at what I was doing just to make sure I had the hang of it."

"It appears that you did," he said. "It took awhile to get your business up to speed."

"We had to accumulate clients. We couldn't simply pair the first people who signed up. The whole point was for us to put some thought and effort into it."

"What's your success rate?"

"About fifteen percent of our clientele is married now. That will be going up, we expect."

He kept reading, then stabbed his finger at an entry.

"You've been getting five pounds from each new client," he said. "Forty as a combined bounty for a wedding. What's this ninety-pound fee about?"

"We were asked to vet a potential spouse for a wealthy client," said Gwen.

"Who?"

"Sorry, can't tell you."

"Then there's this entry ten days later. Rather a hefty sum."

"The client was pleased with our work," said Gwen. "There was an investment of sorts."

"What were the terms?"

"Generous, and that's all I'll say about it."

"And that enabled you to expand."

"Yes."

He closed the book and returned it to her.

"It's exciting, isn't it?" he asked. "Starting with nothing, making it into something."

"It is," she agreed. "It may not be prospecting for copper in Africa, but it certainly has been an adventure. More dangerous than we anticipated."

"What would you say to me investing in it?" he asked, glancing at her slyly.

"I would say no."

"You could use the money."

"Not your money," she said. "Do you have any left after Mopani? Your wife had to cough up the five thousand to pay off your gang of rented abductors."

"Why did you do that?" he asked. "They failed. They ran."

"They met their end of the bargain. We didn't want a group of dangerous men running about feeling that you owed them money. And you still owe a debt to Burleigh."

"Burleigh's in jail."

"But his son is not. Poor Stephen—he's been forced to take over his disgraced father's holdings, including his place on the board at Bainbridge, Limited. He may wish he was back in the prison camp after a few meetings. So, how are you going to pay off the Burleighs, Harold? All of your money is in a nonexistent mine in Mopani."

"It exists," he said. "The preliminary shafts have been sunk. I was right. It's a rich deposit. A profit will be made."

"In time," she said. "Why did you go it alone? Why not bring the company in?"

"Because I wasn't doing it for them," he said. "I was doing it for my son."

"Tell me," she urged him. "What was this all about?"

He was silent. Then, looking out at some point past her, he began to speak.

"You went crazy when Ronald was killed," he said. "You weren't the only one. All I could think was my son and heir was dead. All I had given up in my life to build Bainbridge into something he could take over was for nothing."

"There was your grandson," said Gwen.

"There was Little Ronnie, of course. But he wasn't my son. He wasn't the best part of me the way his father was. That's neither kind nor rational, I know, but all I could think about was that I had another son, and there had to be something I could do for him that would be ours and ours alone. I didn't know how much time I had left. I'm nearing the age when my father died, and I've long outlived my brother. I had to go back to Africa and make something I could give to John, even if he couldn't carry the Bainbridge name.

"I went to Africa to dig a hole to bury myself in."

"But you lived," she said. "You brought John here. You took him away from his mother, Harold. How could you do that?"

"I wanted to bring her here," he said. "She wouldn't agree to it, so I thought if I forced the issue, she would have to come join him after."

"Only she died first," said Gwen.

"Oh, God," he said, starting to weep.

In all the years she had known him, she had never seen him cry.

"I can never go back there," he said. "The doctors say I can't travel anymore."

"Then you'll have to live your life here," she said. "With your family."

"Does John know?" he asked, wiping his eyes on his pajama sleeve. "About his mother?"

"Not yet," said Gwen. "We wanted to give him a chance to get used to his new surroundings. Then we'll let his uncle break the news to him."

"His uncle? One of Bayenkhu's brothers is here?"

"Yes. Simon Daile. An absolutely wonderful man. Carolyne is pulling every string she can to help him transfer to Royal Ag so he can visit more easily on the weekends."

"How does John like the house?"

"It's all very strange and upsetting to him, especially given what he went through. Fortunately, we have a great ally in your grandson. They took to each other right away. Ronnie decided he would be the one to introduce John to all the staff. 'Priscilla, Nell, this is my new friend, John! He's going to stay with us! Isn't that wonderful?'"

"If only it were that easy for everyone," he said.

"Yes," she said. "Ronnie has been a lifesaver. It's too bad he has to go away to St. Frideswide's so soon."

He looked at her. She smiled at him.

"That was well played," he said.

"Thank you."

He thought for a few minutes. She sat quietly, watching him.

"How about this?" he asked finally. "You let me continue voting your shares on the board, and I won't contest your having full custody of Ronnie."

"I'm sorry, Harold," she said sweetly, "but did you just offer to sell me my own child?"

"I suppose I did," he said. "It doesn't sound all that appropriate when you put it in those terms."

"No, it doesn't."

"What is your counteroffer?"

"Simple," she said. "I go before the court and petition to have myself declared competent. I regain full custody of Ronnie and full rights in my inheritance from my husband, including my seat at the board of Bainbridge, Limited, and all that that entails. That is my alternative."

"I will fight you," he said.

"You will lose," she replied. "Especially if we bring up everything you've done recently."

"Very well. St. Frideswide's is out. Ronnie stays in London for school. Will that do for now? Let me recover before we discuss the rest."

"I'll think about it. You should know, by the way, that Carolyne is considering taking legal action concerning you."

"Divorce? She would never dare!"

"Not divorce, Harold. But given your poor health, she's thinking of applying to the court to have herself appointed your guardian. Wouldn't that be fun?"

"Good God, woman. When did you become so ruthless?"

"I've had to be, living with you. I could try to talk her out of it."

"What would I owe you for that?"

"Owe me?" she said. "You already owe me. You owe me for twenty-four hours of captivity, humiliation, and terror. How will you repay me for that?"

"I thought you figured out that it was a scheme early on."

"And I was a threat to that scheme, not to mention a legal inconvenience standing between you and control of Bainbridge for the rest of your remaining years. There I lay, helpless but posing a danger to you and some very dangerous men. Did the thought ever cross your mind that it would simplify matters to have me killed?"

"No," he said immediately. "Not once."

"Really? Because it crossed my mind more than once that my

life might be in even more danger with you involved than if it had only been a kidnapping."

"They brought it up," he said reluctantly. "I insisted upon your safety. That sentimentality was the ruin of everything, as it turned out."

She looked at him, then leaned forward and patted his hand.

"I believe you, Harold," she said, standing up to leave. "Now, you rest up. Take your time. By the time you get home, the boys will be in school and I will be an emancipated woman. I look forward to learning the business."

"What about Carolyne?"

"What about her?"

"Are you going to talk her out of becoming my guardian?"

"Maybe, maybe not. It depends on how you make things up to her."

"That may be impossible," he said.

She paused in the doorway and looked back at him.

"Try," she said.

Iris heard the knock on the door. She checked her makeup in the hall mirror, then opened it.

"Hello, Archie," she said.

"'Allo, Sparks," he said.

"Come in, please."

He entered, taking his trilby off and depositing it on the coat tree.

"How did it go with Gwen and your counterpart?" she asked, sitting on her sofa and patting the seat next to her.

"Peace was made," he said as he sat. "For now."

"Good," she said. "I'm glad. So, you have that 'we should talk' expression on your face."

"Right," he said reluctantly. "It's not that I don't like you, Sparks. It's just that 'aving you and Gwen around is 'aving a disruptive effect on our business. Watching the lads around 'er at the table, I've never seen the like. She took a passel of 'ardened criminals and turned them into puppies. We 'ad to turn men away for that rescue mission."

"She does have that effect on people," said Iris.

"As do you, Sparks. At least, when it comes to me."

"Careful, Archie," she said. "That sounded almost like an endearment."

"Yeah, that's the problem, innit? We ain't the Lost Boys, Sparks, and we don't need a pair of Wendys 'anging about to darn our socks and tuck us into bed at night. What we do is illegal, and sometimes dangerous, and I don't want you caught up in it."

"Maybe I like being caught up in it," said Iris. "Maybe danger is what I need in my life."

"I don't want anything to 'appen to you because you've become my girl," he said. "I can't 'ave that on my conscience. I don't even like thinking I 'ave a conscience."

"Archie, it's my choice to take the risk. And honestly, the chances of Gwen and me getting involved in what you do again are ridiculously low."

"They've been as regular as the moon so far."

"Granted, but that can't keep happening. We run a marriage bureau, no more, no less."

"Murders, kidnappings, blackmail—"

"Those aren't our lives," insisted Sparks. "What I want—"

She hesitated.

"What do you want, Sparks?" he asked, looking directly at her.

"What I want is you, Archie Spelling," she said. "Broken nose, wide ties, troubles, and all. Don't even think you can scare me away."

"I know three little words that would do exactly that," he said.

She got up, grabbed him by his lapels, and pulled him to his feet.

"I know those words," she said. "I've said them to three men in my life, and each time things went horribly wrong. So yes, they make me gun-shy, and not even guns do that."

"Then don't say the words, Sparks," said Archie as she dragged him to her bedroom. "We'll manage fine."

A week later, Millie put the finishing touches on Gwen's coiffure.

"It's growing back nicely where the stitches were," she said. "But we'll keep this part pinned over until it does."

"Thank you, Millie," said Gwen.

"Excited to be going back to work?"

"I am. And it will be quieter there than it is here."

"I think it's lovely to have two boys running about," said Millie. "Oh, Mr. Percival has something he wants to show you before you go."

"Oh? Where is he?"

"In the playroom."

"How odd. Very well, Millie."

She walked down the hall to the playroom, opened the door, then smiled.

Percival was standing next to Ronnie's heavy bag, which was suspended from its old hook.

"Did you lug that all the way down from the attic, Percival?" she asked.

"I did, Mrs. Bainbridge. Since you'll be resuming your lessons, I thought we should have it in its original setting. And if you would be amenable, I thought I would take it upon myself to give the young men some rudimentary lessons in boxing."

Her late husband didn't like boxing, she remembered. But he wasn't here. She was, and there were dangerous people in the world.

"Yes, Percival, I would appreciate that very much," she said.

"Gracious," said Lady Bainbridge from behind her. "I didn't know we still had that thing."

She went up to it and gave it a tentative poke.

"I'm taking a ladies' self-defense course, Carolyne," said Gwen. "I'd be delighted to have you join me. It does relieve a great deal of tension."

"Perhaps I shall, Gwendolyn," she said. "Now, go match some loveless people."

They met beforehand on Old Compton Street in front of Moroni's.

"Is that the place?" asked Gwen.

"That's the place," said Iris. "Have you got the new flyer?"

"I have."

They went inside and spoke to the owner. Then Gwen carefully pinned the flyer to the bulletin board, where its bright green colour made it stand out. They went outside and looked at it together.

"'Looking for love? Searching for happiness?'" read Gwen.

"'Come to The Right Sort Marriage Bureau and let us sort you out,'" continued Iris.

"'All races and all nationalities welcome,'" finished Gwen. "Will that drum up business or turn customers away?"

"I don't know," said Iris. "But it's worth a try. The world must be peopled!"

"The world must be peopled!" echoed Gwen. "Let's get to work, partner."

THE HAUNTING OF THE DESKS

A BONUS SPARKS & BAINBRIDGE STORY

ALLISON MONTCLAIR

Angus MacPherson leaned upon his mop, lost in thought. That's what he liked to call it, although the usual meanings of the phrase—to be meditative, ruminative, absorbed in the contemplation of a topic—were not strictly applicable to his state of mind. It was more along the lines of his habit of starting to think about one thing, then go wandering down a branch off that particular path, and another subbranch from that, and so on, until all memory of the original inspiration had vanished, leaving him disoriented, rambling through the mental thickets with no discernible way forward or back.

It had started with the mop, he thought. Mopping was a frequent cause of his distraction, which is why he resisted doing it, or at least that's what he told himself when it came time to do the floors of the four-storey office building for which he had been the custodian for nigh on thirty-five years apart from his time in the Royal Army. He had a vague notion that the tangle of wet, grey strings clinging to the worn wooden pole had put him in mind of the hair of someone he once knew, and he was trying to remember who, exactly. Some old woman—or was it an old man? Lived near the stables in the town where he grew up before he came to London. Something to do with horses, then, which in turn reminded him of the time he took a girl on a carriage ride after he came home from the Great War, when everyone was celebrating and any lad in a uniform could get at least one girl to ride in a carriage with him at least once. He was trying to remember her name, but kept hearing a man's voice saying, "MacPherson! MacPherson!" over and over again, which was his name, not hers.

Why would he be thinking about his own name? And in that voice, which wasn't his?

He finally sorted out that it meant someone was calling him, and he looked up from where the mop was slowly dampening a small portion of the floor in an irregular, ever-widening circle to see Mr. Maxwell the younger staring at him in irritation.

"I'm sorry, am I interrupting something?" asked Mr. Maxwell. "Something important? I've been looking all over the bloody building for you."

"I was here," said Mr. MacPherson, in a tone that suggested he himself had just been apprised of that information.

He looked at the implement in his hands.

"Mopping," he concluded.

"You do have a mop," observed Mr. Maxwell. "And if it had in fact been put into some form of motion, I might even have agreed that you were mopping, which would equate to you working, which is what we pay you to do."

"It is," said Mr. MacPherson.

"But it was not in motion when I arrived here," said Mr. Maxwell. "It and you were the very epitome of stillness. You could have been posing for a statue. You could have actually been a statue. We could have had you and the mop bronzed on the spot, titled it Torpidity, and mounted it in an exhibition devoted to the general subject of Uselessness in Society. You weren't mopping, MacPherson, you were moping. And we don't pay you for that."

Mr. MacPherson, taking the man's point, shoved the mop back and forth a few times.

"Now you're getting the hang of it," said Mr. Maxwell. "At the rate you're going, you might finish the job before Christmas."

"Why are you here, exactly?" asked Mr. MacPherson.

"I do own the building, MacPherson. I'm bound to pop in once in a while. It does do my heart good to see it being kept in such a pristine condition."

"It isn't your building," said Mr. MacPherson. "It's your father's building."

"It belongs to and is managed by the firm of Maxwell and Son," said Mr. Maxwell, bristling. "It technically may be held in my father's name, but I am the Son of Maxwell and Son, and as such, if I say this is my building in a manner of speaking, then it's my building. In any case, as much as I enjoy bandying legal concepts and figures of speech with a lethargic custodian, I happen to be here not just to check up on the superb quality of your work, but to ask you to do something specific."

"All right then," said Mr. MacPherson.

"Do you want to know what the specific task is?" asked Mr. Maxwell.

"Yes," said Mr. MacPherson, after a few moments' consideration.

"Four oh seven, MacPherson. You know it?"

"Next to the marriage bureau ladies."

"That's the one. The marriage bureau ladies, The Right Sort Marriage Bureau, to give them their official name, have leased four oh seven in addition to their old office. They are expanding, Mac-Pherson. Imagine that. When they showed up last spring and told me what they were about and took four oh five, I gave them six months before they went under."

"You gave them four months," remembered Mr. MacPherson.

"Did I? Well, in any case, those two girls have made a go of it, so good on them. And now they're expanding. They have leased the office next to theirs—"

"Four oh seven," said Mr. MacPherson. "The old Cooper and Lyons place."

"Yes, that's the one."

"I don't like going in there. Not after what happened."

"That was fifteen years ago."

"And nought's been in there since. It's a cursed place. I don't know why you let the ladies have it."

"Yes, well, we needn't mention anything about that to them, right?"

"The names are still on the door."

"Then scrape the bloody names off the door, MacPherson. That should have been done years ago. Why wasn't it done?"

"Didn't have anyone moving into the place," said Mr. MacPherson. "There weren't no hurry."

"I should like to see you in a hurry, MacPherson," said Mr. Maxwell. "Just once before I die, so I could go to my Maker and report, 'Yes, Lord. I did see a miracle on this glorious world You created: I saw MacPherson hurry to accomplish something.' And the Almighty would shake his grey locks in amazement and say, 'Even I cannot fathom such a thing. It just goes to show you.'"

He and MacPherson looked at each other for a long moment, Maxwell smirking in his self-congratulatory way and MacPherson waiting to determine if Maxwell was done ridiculing him. After enough time had elapsed, he ventured to ask, "So scraping the name off the door is the specific task?"

"No, MacPherson. The task is to get the entirety of four oh seven in shape for immediate occupancy. Sweep, dust, give the floors a decent polishing, clean the windows, scrape however many years of pigeon droppings are on the sills, and get the Right Sort ladies the keys to the place. Oh, that reminds me—they have expressed a concern about the security here."

"What about it?"

"They said you kept all of the office keys on hooks in your office downstairs, and that you generally leave your office unlocked. They're worried about people being able to break into their office."

"Why would anyone break in there?" wondered Mr. MacPherson. "Is there someone out there stealing husbands?"

"I highly doubt it, MacPherson, but they said they did have one break-in already, and they think it was done with your keys. So make them secure, would you?"

"The keys or the ladies?"

"The one should lead to the other, I should expect. Start with the keys, MacPherson."

"How?"

"My dear fellow, you are the custodian of this building, and I am the owner."

"Your father—"

"We're not repeating that portion of the conversation, MacPherson," said Mr. Maxwell. "I have, as the owner of the building and employer of your services, pointed out a problem that I wish to have solved. You, as the subordinate with, we hope to God, the necessary skills to do so, must find the solution. Am I understood?"

"Generally speaking, you are," said Mr. MacPherson.

"Fine," said Mr. Maxwell.

He turned to leave, and Mr. MacPherson resumed his mopping. The sound of the water sloshing around stopped Mr. Maxwell in his tracks. He turned back to watch Mr. MacPherson with astonishment.

"MacPherson," he said. "You're mopping."

"Yes," said Mr. MacPherson. "It's my job."

"Yet I distinctly remember telling you to clean up four oh seven."

"You wanted me to do that first?"

"Yes, MacPherson."

"Because I was in the middle of the mopping."

"I am worried that you will continue with your mopping, and it will drive every thought of cleaning up four oh seven out of your head."

"You want me to do that first, then."

"Yes, MacPherson."

"And then continue with the mopping?"

"MacPherson, if you somehow manage to recollect your sacred quest of moppery when you are done with four oh seven, I will renounce all of my worldly goods, particularly this building, and become a hermit, providing the Church of England has a comfortable hermitage with a well-stocked wine cellar somewhere. I must look into that. I will leave you to it, MacPherson. Good day."

Mr. MacPherson watched as Mr. Maxwell the younger receded from view. Then he sighed, a long, multitoned exhalation containing within it the full-bodied flavour of long-standing aggrievement, a nose of resentment, hints of bitterness and self-pity, and a finish of resignation to his fate. Then he deposited the mop into the rolling bucket and trundled it into the storage closet for the third storey.

He was halfway up the stairs to the fourth when it occurred to him that he was going to need the keys to get into 407. He cast a baleful glance at the remainder of the stairs, then made his way down the several flights that culminated in the subterranean domain where he held sway. He walked to his office, stopping to wipe a tiny bit of soot that had dared affix itself to the brass plaque on the door that was the only item that gleamed down there. The one that he had made up to proclaim to one and all, "Angus MacPherson, Senior Custodian."

He reached for the keys at his belt to unlock the door only to find that he had left it unlocked.

Or had he? He thought he had locked it, but there it was, the cylinder already turned anticlockwise as far as it could go, the door swinging open on the first touch.

He hoped nobody had taken anything.

He stepped inside and flicked on the light switch. There was no visible disturbance in the normal disorder of the room. He glanced across the rows of keys dangling unprotected from the hooks driven into the wall.

Ripe for the taking, he thought. Mr. Maxwell was right.

He stood in front of them, contemplating possible solutions. Some cabinet with a lock on it, with the keys inside. Seemed simple enough. Where to put it, though?

He scanned the rest of the walls, his gaze passing over the odds and ends he had stuck up over the years, things he had scavenged from the wastepaper baskets he had emptied from office to office or clipped from discarded magazines. Pinup girls, an aviator calendar from 1926, adverts for dental appliances, postcards written by people he never knew from places he'd never go, showing beaches, ski slopes, racing cars, elephants (elephants! He loved elephants), cancan dancers, all mingling in a giant collage of detritus.

His eyes rested upon the elephants. Elephants had good memories, he thought. There was something he was supposed to be remembering. Nothing to do with elephants, though.

"Mr. MacPherson?" came a woman's voice from behind him.

He turned.

It was the tall one from The Right Sort, the blonde.

"Yes, Mrs. Bainbridge?" he replied. "Is there something you need?"

"I was wondering if Mr. Maxwell spoke to you," she said.

"He did," said Mr. MacPherson, now remembering what it was he was supposed to do. "You're taking over four oh seven. I was just fetching the keys so I could tidy up the place."

"Ah, good," she said. The decorations caught her eye. "My goodness. That's almost a work of art you have going there."

"Art?" he said, turning to look at it in a new light. "Don't think so. It's only things I like to look at. Although I suppose that's what art is, ain't it?"

"I suppose it is," said Mrs. Bainbridge. "If it isn't too much of a chore, could Miss Sparks and I get into the office now? We'd like to make some measurements."

"That's fine, Mrs. Bainbridge," he said, grabbing the set for 407 from the hook. "Let's go up."

He waited for her to go through, then followed her, this time remembering to lock the door behind him. She gave him a look of approval as he did, and he found himself thinking she was another thing he liked to look at. A work of art if ever there was one. Outclassed him by a considerable margin, of course, but she was always pleasant to him and her smile, when it happened, was gorgeous.

He sometimes tried to think what it would be like to be with a woman who looked and smiled like Mrs. Bainbridge, but when he did, his mind immediately shifted to the girl who rode out in the carriage with him that time. Who let him kiss her. What was her name?

"Mr. MacPherson, are you all right?" asked Mrs. Bainbridge with a look of concern.

"Sorry, I was somewhere else for a moment," he said.

"Come back to us, Mr. MacPherson," she said. "And stay this time."

They climbed the steps. She was in front of him the entire time. There were worse views than that for certain, he thought.

"Marriage business doing all right, then?" he asked.

"It's picking up," she said. "We're quite happy with it."

"How does it work, exactly?" he asked. "How do you match them up?"

"There is an art to it," she said. "Miss Sparks and I each have instincts for putting people together. Different, but complementary instincts. Between us, we've been finding—"

"The Right Sort," he said, completing the thought.

"Yes," she said. "And the more people we have, the more prospects there are. It's an accumulative effect."

"Think you could match me up?" he asked suddenly.

She turned in surprise, stopping mid-step.

"If you're interested, by all means come in and sign up," she said. "I never thought—"

She hesitated.

"Never thought what?"

"Never thought you had much interest in finding a wife," she said. "All this time we've been here, you've never mentioned it."

"All the time you've been here, how many times have you asked me about anything about me?" he asked.

"We've had conversations."

"You say hello. You occasionally ask me to fix things. You asked me for the keys to four oh seven so you could look at it."

"Granted, these are not the best starters," said Mrs. Bainbridge. "I had no idea you had any interest in talking to us further."

"Maybe I do, maybe I don't," he said. "Won't know until I try. So, think you can find me a wife?"

"We won't know until you try," she said. "We would be happy to have you sign up for our service."

"What's that cost, and what's it get me?"

"It costs five pounds to become our client, and that gets you our professional efforts to find you a wife," she said.

"But no guarantees."

"No guarantees," she said. "Not in love, not in life."

"Well, I'll think on it," he said. "I don't do much without thinking on it."

"I can see that," she said.

He looked at her suspiciously, and she coloured.

"I mean to say, you seem to be a deliberative person," she said, stammering slightly in her haste. "Ah, here we are!"

They stood side by side, contemplating the door with its frosted glass upper, the once proud title of "Cooper and Lyons, Chartered Public Accountants" still emblazoned on it in bronze letters.

"You'll want those letters off, then," he said.

"We are not Cooper and Lyons," said Mrs. Bainbridge. "Nor are we chartered public accountants. Think how disappointed their customers would be if they saw us sitting there instead."

"They haven't had a customer in fifteen years," said Mr. Mac-Pherson.

"Could you give us a key for it, then? Two, preferably."

He looked down at the ones in his hand, dangling from a small metal tag stamped "407."

"I only got two," he said, half to himself. "That's odd. Thought there were three."

"There were two when I borrowed them to look at the office last week," she said. "Has one gone missing?"

"Doubt that," he said. "I keep them safe in my office."

She looked dubious.

"Tell you what," he said, detaching one and handing it to her. "You can have one for now. I'll get going on the cleaning, and I'll go by the locksmith after I'm done and get him to work up a couple more. He's open late."

"Very well," she said.

He unlocked the door and pushed it open. Then he peered cautiously into the room.

"Everything all right?" asked Mrs. Bainbridge, trying not to be impatient with him.

"I don't like going in here," he said.

"Why not?"

"I just don't," he said, remembering Maxwell's admonition not to say anything about the office's history.

He stepped in and turned on the light.

The office was fifteen feet wide and eighteen deep, its only occupants a pair of massive mahogany partners' desks that stood side by side, each backed by a curtainless window. These desks had stood in those exact spots ever since Mr. MacPherson had come to work here, when Cooper and Lyons were the old Cooper and Lyons, the fathers of the business. Five and a half feet across, three and a half feet deep, two and a half feet tall, with thick square pedestals holding drawers front and back. Desks of the Gods, young

Cooper had called them when the two fathers retired jointly and handed the keys over to their sons.

For a brief moment, Mr. MacPherson could see the elder Cooper and Lyons sitting behind the desks, glowering at the unexpected intrusion. Then he blinked, and all there was was a pair of old, empty desks.

There was no other furniture in the office. The paint on the walls was once a soothing cream colour, but was cracked and peeling now.

There was something odd about the desks that caught his eye. He stepped closer to inspect them.

"Look at that," he said, pointing to the one on the left.

"Look at what?" asked Mrs. Bainbridge.

"The top of the desk. The other one's dusty. This one isn't it. Someone dusted it."

"That was me," said Mrs. Bainbridge quickly. "When we were looking at the office. I wanted to see what shape the desks were in, so I cleaned that one up. You said we could take them with the office if we wanted, and we decided to keep them."

"Oh," said Mr. MacPherson. "I thought it might be—"

"Yes?"

"Nothing," he said.

"You don't think it's haunted, do you, Mr. MacPherson?" asked Mrs. Bainbridge, giving in to an impish impulse.

"Empty offices are always haunted," he said. "And this one's been empty a long time. But I don't think ghosts are inclined to dusting."

"Not to my knowledge," said Mrs. Bainbridge. "More's the pity. I'm going to fetch Miss Sparks. Be right back."

She walked out. He took one more look at the desks, then went down the hall to the janitor's closet.

The desks that currently supported the business of The Right Sort were not as magnificent as the two in their newly acquired office.

They were of a more recent vintage but, due to the cheapness of their construction, were already showing signs of falling apart. Gwen's was missing part of one leg, the improvised prosthesis being a copy of *The Forsyte Saga*. Iris's, while visibly complete, had developed a slight wobble of late, giving her the appearance as she pounded away on her trusty Bar-Let typewriter of a clerk on a ship swaying in rough seas. Gwen frequently worried that the entire structure, the short brunette included, would someday collapse together in an inextricable tangle of bruised limbs, bent lead, and splintered wood. The partners' desks next door, on the other hand, were quite capable of taking whatever the two ladies dished out.

Iris looked up as her partner came in, holding the key up in triumph.

"We have four oh seven!" Gwen crowed. "Three cheers for expansion!"

"Huzzah," said Iris. "Only one key?"

"That's all he had to spare," said Gwen. "There may be one missing. We might want to spring for a new lock down the line."

"I'll add that to the list," said Iris. "Let's see how much we have available after we buy paint and furniture."

"You haven't by any chance 'borrowed' the other key, have you?" asked Gwen.

"Stolen it, you mean?" replied Iris as she picked up a notepad and a measuring tape from her desk. "Not this time. How is Mr. MacPherson?"

Gwen took a quick peek outside, then closed the door to their office.

"Odd," she said.

"He's always odd."

"Odder than usual," clarified Gwen. "Iris, he was asking about The Right Sort. I think he's considering signing up."

"My word," said Iris. "He would definitely present a challenge. How old do you think he is?"

"Somewhere in his late fifties," guessed Gwen. "Maybe early sixties. He's well preserved. I think it's because he lives by a slower clock than the rest of us. Anyone we find for a bride would run rings around him. Although he did notice I had dusted off one of the desks next door."

"Really? I didn't think he was the noticing type. Good thing he didn't notice the man we had tied up in there last week."

"That would have been awkward to explain," said Gwen. "Let's not make a habit of that."

"Agreed," said Iris. "We'll leave the tying of the knots to the clergy."

Mr. MacPherson returned from the supply closet with a handful of rags and a bottle of window cleaner clutched in one hand, the other dragging a vacuum cleaner behind him. He stopped in the doorway to stare at Miss Sparks, who was standing on the right-hand windowsill, stretching the measuring tape across the frame.

"Are you daft?" he exclaimed. "It's four storeys to the ground!"

"Which is why I'm standing on this side of the glass," said Sparks. "Toss me a ukulele and I'll sing a chorus of 'When I'm Cleaning Windows' while I'm up here. Don't worry, Mr. MacPherson, I'm just measuring for curtains. Looks like there used to be a curtain rod here. There's still one on the other side. Do you have any to match down in storage?"

"I'll look," he said. "Would you mind getting down from there, Miss Sparks? You're making me nervous."

"She does have that effect on people," said Mrs. Bainbridge, holding her hand out to her partner.

Sparks took it and jumped down, then jotted down the measurement on her notepad.

"I wonder why there's a curtain rod on the other window, and none here," she said. "Do you know, Mr. MacPherson?"

"It broke," he said. "Years ago."

"And you never replaced it?"

"No need," he said. "The tenants were gone, and we didn't have anyone come in until the two of you."

"It broke when Cooper and Lyons left?"

"Something like that," he said reluctantly.

Mrs. Bainbridge took one end of the measuring tape.

"Let's get the back wall," she said, moving to the left.

"Right," said Sparks, holding her end against the right corner. "So that's fifteen feet across, minus the two windows which are three feet each. Same for the front wall, minus the door, and the two side walls are fifteen by eighteen. Two coats of the green we used in the other office, white for the ceiling. White for the sills and frames?"

"I think so," said Mrs. Bainbridge. "How soon will you be done with the cleaning and the floor polishing, Mr. MacPherson?"

"Your lease starts the first of the month?"

"It does, but Mr. Maxwell said we could paint before that."

Mr. MacPherson put his hand on one of the desks and gave it a small, experimental shove. It didn't budge.

"I'll have to get my mate Charlie in to help move these if I'm gonna polish," he said. "And I'll have to let the polish dry before I put them back, so that's a two-day job by itself."

"It's Tuesday," said Mrs. Bainbridge. "We'd like to paint on Saturday. Do you think you could have everything done by then?"

"I think so," said Mr. MacPherson.

"Wonderful. We also have to arrange for the telephone and intercom to be installed. And we'll be interviewing secretaries, so you might see more traffic than normal."

"Makes no difference to me," said Mr. MacPherson.

Sparks was crouching behind the right desk, testing the drawers. Three of them were locked.

"Mr. MacPherson, you don't happen to have any keys to these desks, do you?" she asked.

"They ain't my desks. They don't belong to the building. Why would I have the keys?"

"It would be nice if we could unlock and lock the drawers," she said, straightening. "Might they still be in the possession of Cooper and Lyons themselves?"

"Who knows?" he asked. "They've been gone—"

"Fifteen years, yes, we know," said Sparks. "Both died, I think you told me once."

"Yes."

"Maybe they had heirs?"

"No," he said. "No kids. Neither of them. Each was the last one."

"Iris, the desks came from Harrods," said Mrs. Bainbridge. "Maybe they keep spare keys."

"Really? After all this time?"

"For desks like these, they might. And those are serial numbers on the plates there."

"So they are," said Sparks, jotting them down. "Then I think we have everything we need. Thanks, Mr. MacPherson."

"And drop by anytime you'd like to talk about signing up," added Mrs. Bainbridge. "Or just to say hello."

"Right," said Mr. MacPherson. "I have to think on it first."

"You do that," said Mrs. Bainbridge. "Goodbye for now."

They left. He suddenly realised he was alone in the office. He shivered for a second, then slowly began wiping the dust and grime from the windowsills.

"Why didn't you pick the lock if you wanted to see what was in there?" asked Gwen when they were back inside The Right Sort. "You're always picking locks. There are days when I have to hold you back from picking locks, yet today, with some locks that were eminently pickable, you refrained."

"I was tempted," admitted Iris. "But there were two things weighing against it. First, those are really nice desks, and I didn't want to put scratches on them. More important, they are now our desks, and I want to be a responsible property owner."

"Your socialist tendencies vanish into smoke the moment you get your hands on a good piece of mahogany."

"You're the one who went swoony when we first saw them in there," Iris pointed out. "Anyhow, it's nearly four. What say we knock off for the afternoon and make an expedition to Harrods? We could find out if they can come up with some desk keys."

"Why not? It's on the way home for me anyway," said Gwen, fetching their hats and tossing Iris's to her.

They locked The Right Sort behind them, then tiptoed over to 407 to peer in. Mr. MacPherson was staring down at the surface of the undusted desk, a cloth in his hand.

"Goodbye, Mr. MacPherson," called Mrs. Bainbridge, startling him into a fit of activity. "We're leaving early to see about the desk keys. Don't forget to make copies of the office key for us."

"I won't," he said. "Goodbye."

"Tuppence says he forgets," said Iris as they walked down the stairs.

"No bet," said Gwen.

It was a twenty-minute walk from their office to Knightsbridge. The familiar dome of the department store came into view, and soon they were walking alongside what one commentator referred to as its "exuberant Baroque" style.

"I haven't been here in ages," said Gwen. "I think the last time was shopping for baby clothes for Little Ronnie when I was at eight months. I looked like a dirigible going up the escalators. That was right before we evacuated."

"I used to come here with my mother," said Iris. "She could never walk by the displays without telling me, 'That's the window that Emmeline Pankhurst broke for women's suffrage in 1912!' All I wanted was to go to the toy department. She stopped repeating it when I threatened to break one myself. 'But Mummy, it's for suffrage! You said it was a good thing!'"

They entered, then paused on the first-floor landing before the four tablets commemorating the Harrods employees who died in the Great War.

"They haven't got one for the recent war yet," said Gwen sombrely. "Still gathering the names, I suppose."

"'Harrodians Who Died For Their Country,'" Iris read. "I always liked how they listed the departments they worked for. 'Arthur Miles, Grenadier Guards, Antique.' It reminds you that these were men with real lives and real jobs before they gave them up to join. I sometimes imagined them interchanged in the reports. 'The brave men of the Fifth Bedding Unit fought gallantly at the First Battle of the Marne, shoulder to shoulder with the fierce lads of the Fighting Furniture Porters.'"

"Once, when I was a girl, my mother brought my older brother and me here," said Gwen. "He looked at the tablet and scoffed, 'Harrodians. Like they thought they were Etonians.' And my mother turned to him and said in a voice that was nearly a slap, 'They fought and died just the same. You give them their due.'"

They took a lift to the third floor. The doors opened onto the Furniture Department, where a salesman immediately stepped from behind a Jacobean-style cupboard to greet them.

"Good afternoon, ladies," he said. "How may I be of assistance? We have a lovely collection of vanities with rose marble tops that would be just the thing on which to lay your bottles of perfume and your jars of cream."

"We've come to inquire about some desks," began Mrs. Bainbridge.

"Ah, for the writing of exquisite invitations to elegant soirées," he said, closing his eyes and inhaling deeply, imagining the aromas of the hors d'oeuvres as they passed through his mind's nostrils. "Or," he continued, giving them a glance that bordered on the roguish, "for the composition perhaps of some sweet billets-doux?"

"I promise you'll be first on my list," said Sparks. "But we would like to speak to someone who could advise us on the provenance of some desks we already own."

"We want your best desk man," said Mrs. Bainbridge.

"The one in charge of the Desk Desk," added Sparks.

"Then Mr. Lancaster is the one for you," said the salesman. "Allow me to escort you to him."

No Lord Chamberlain at Windsor could have led them with more pomp as they threaded their way through imposing assemblages of teak and ebony. He brought them through a showroom featuring several fully furnished bedrooms, turned right through Office, Hall, and Library and down the Great Hall of Secondhand.

"I am forced to take you the long way round, I'm afraid," he informed them. "We've been going through some renovations. The Ministry of War requisitioned the Hans Road side of the floor during the war. We thought they would have been out by now, but once an occupying army has taken over a place, they become terribly difficult to dislodge. Light Oak and Modern are moving to one of the Brompton Road rooms and, between you and me, Bureau and Hall are at their last gasp."

"Poor Bureau and Hall," said Sparks with as much empathy as she could muster for a roomful of furniture.

They came to an unobtrusive door hidden behind a Georgian-style armoire that could have concealed most of a regiment. Their guide knocked lightly. A voice answered, and he opened it.

"Mr. Lancaster," he announced. "A pair of ladies seek enlightenment on the subject of desks. I could think of no better man in England on the topic."

"Thank you, Mr. Purefoy," said an older man inside, rising as they entered. "Good afternoon, ladies. Daniel Lancaster, Assistant Manager, Furniture Department. How may I be of assistance?"

He was in his late fifties, his black hair pomaded back, his temples white as snow. His mustache was a thick, sturdy brush-

THE HAUNTING OF THE DESKS

like affair, and his body powerfully built. From his pocket, a gold watch chain made a perfectly symmetrical hanging arc to his lapel.

The office was small and crammed from floor to ceiling with cabinets, many containing stacks of drawers the size of filing cards. A calendar showing the last Derby winner was on the wall.

"Good afternoon, Mr. Lancaster," said Mrs. Bainbridge. "I am Mrs. Bainbridge, and this is my partner, Miss Sparks. We hope we aren't troubling you."

"Not at all, not at all, ladies," he said. "I was brushing up on tonight's debate topic."

"Are you a debater?" asked Sparks.

"I am," he said. "A longtime member of the Harrodian Brains, Trust, and Debating Club. We meet twice a month. Tonight's topic is 'The Advance of Electricity in the Modern Kitchen,' if you fancy an evening's entertainment."

"Alas, we are previously engaged," said Mrs. Bainbridge. "To the matter at hand. We have come into possession of a marvelous pair of Harrods partners' desks."

"Really? How fortunate for you!" he said, his pride apparent.

"Unfortunately, the original keys appear not to have accompanied them," said Sparks. "We were wondering if Harrods either kept copies or could make new ones."

She handed him the piece of paper on which she had copied the serial numbers. He put on a pair of pince-nez spectacles and looked at it.

"Hmm, these go back," he said. "Partners' desks, you said. Mahogany with brass fittings? Tooled burgundy leather inserts?"

"Yes," said Mrs. Bainbridge.

"I wonder, I wonder," he said. "Sounds like the Gillows models, which were quite beautiful. Let me look."

He turned in his chair, stood, and let his hand follow the columns of small file drawers, tracing them back towards the farthest corner of the room. The moving hand stopped abruptly. He pulled out the drawer and thumbed through the cards until he found what he was looking for. He pulled it out. With it was a small felt drawstring bag.

"I was right," he said triumphantly. "A matched pair of Gillows, delivered on March 18, 1904, to the accounting firm of—oh! Cooper and Lyons."

"Yes!" cried the two women.

"My, my," he said softly, glancing at them curiously. "So those desks survived."

"They did," said Sparks.

"Unlike Cooper and Lyons," he said. "Remarkable. This is the old office on _____ Street in Mayfair? Room four oh seven?"

"It is," said Mrs. Bainbridge. "Are those spare keys in that bag?"

He loosened the drawstring and spilled two brass keys into his hand.

"We use these to make copies," he said. "Say a pound for the pair. Does that sound fair?"

"More than fair," said Sparks, placing a note on his desk.

"And I assume you'll want them with tassels?"

"What would a Harrods key be without a tassel?" said Mrs. Bainbridge.

"What, indeed? Provide me with your address, ladies, and I'll send a delivery boy over tomorrow," he said.

"Same as Cooper and Lyons," said Mrs. Bainbridge. "We're currently in room four oh five next door. The Right Sort Marriage Bureau. How marvelous that you've kept the spares all this time!"

"We are Harrods, after all," he said. "Buy a Gillows desk, and we're with you for life. I can only hope you have better luck with them than did the previous owners."

"What happened to them, exactly?" asked Sparks.

"You don't know the story?" he exclaimed. "Well, I suppose you were too young, now that I think about it. It's rather a lurid tale for young ears."

"Our ears are of age, I can assure you," said Sparks. "Is it juicy?"

"Bloody, I'm afraid," he said, lowering his voice. "You might find it distressing."

"We might," said Sparks, shooting a glance at Mrs. Bainbridge, who smiled. "Then again, we might know some stories of our own. Dish away, my good man, and we'll keep the smelling salts handy."

"It may surprise you that those desks you've acquired and I have a long relationship," he began. "I started working here as a furniture porter when I was a strapping lad of sixteen. One of the first jobs I had was to deliver those very same desks to Cooper and Lyons."

"Remarkable!" exclaimed Mrs. Bainbridge. "You mean you've been here for over forty years?"

"Apart from my time in the Great War, I have," he said. "Rising through the ranks, learning the trade as I went along, ascending to the lofty heights where now you see me. Yet I remember that delivery clear as day. Those desks each came in three sections, which had to be assembled on site. Two of us, old McMurtry and myself, made six trips up and down those flights of stairs, lugging each massive piece. Thought I would break my back by the time we got to the last. I was seriously rethinking my career choice, but then old Lyons tipped me a half crown, and suddenly manual labour was looking up again.

"So I had a soft spot in my heart for Cooper and Lyons from then on, and on those rare occasions when they appeared in the business section of the papers, I would think about that day. I read when they jointly retired and passed the firm on to their sons, and I read about their sons."

He stopped and shook his head sadly.

"I read about the sons too often," he continued. "They unfortunately made the news more than a proper accountancy firm should. They were well-to-do from the start, and profligate in their ways. They would show up on the society pages, running with a fast crowd."

"Which crowd did they run with?" asked Mrs. Bainbridge.

"Gamblers, gents who'd bet on the most outrageous stunts.

They'd devise outlandish challenges for each other, wagering absurd amounts on the outcomes. Which duck would swim under a footbridge first in the Serpentine, how many high kicks a chorus girl could do without stopping. They fell in with the Bentley Boys—"

"Oh!" interjected Mrs. Bainbridge. "I know about the Bentley Boys. My brother was on their fringes."

"Then you know the sort I'm talking about, Mrs. Bainbridge," he said. "So many of them came to an early death, frequently in flames."

"The younger Cooper and Lyons raced?"

"Among other things, yes. And racing is expensive, and gambling leads to debt, and expenses and debts are to an accounting firm corrupters of the worst kind. The word was they embezzled from one of their principal clients, Malachi Selvyn. He ended up going under, and when the authorities began to investigate, the firm, shall we say, dissolved quickly. Only not quickly enough."

"What happened to them?" asked Sparks.

"Lyons fled to the Continent," said Mr. Lancaster. "With the money. And Cooper, left behind with nowhere to go, killed himself."

"No!"

"How?" asked Sparks. "Was it at the office?"

"I'm afraid it was, Miss Sparks," said Mr. Lancaster sadly. "Four storeys up, police on their way, only one other way out."

"The window," said Mrs. Bainbridge. "Poor fellow."

"Poor fellow, my foot," said Mr. Lancaster. "He brought it upon himself."

"What happened to Lyons?"

"He carried on doing what he had been, racing cars, gambling, drinking. Then, maybe a month or so later, he crashed his auto while running from the police in Trieste, and that was the end of him."

"And we've just taken over their office," said Sparks. "No wonder Mr. MacPherson thinks it's haunted."

"Who is he?"

"The custodian of the building. He believes in ghosts, but he's the spookiest thing there."

"Well, ladies, I have no doubt that your loveliness will exorcise any spirits lingering about," said Mr. Lancaster.

"Thank you, Mr. Lancaster," said Mrs. Bainbridge. "You have been most helpful."

"And very entertaining," added Sparks. "Good luck with your debate, and come visit the desks and us when we have everything set up."

"You know, I will," he said. "I should like to see them again before I retire. And while I'm still fit enough to walk up those stairs."

He shook their hands, then brought them to the lift.

"Our desks have a past," commented Gwen when they emerged from the store. "Quite the story."

"Who were the Bentley Boys?" asked Iris.

"Oh, a pack of men who lived to race Bentleys and brag about it after," said Gwen. "Woolf Barnato's lot. I think he even bought the company at one point, but he lost it in the Crash. Diana Barnato's father. You know Diana, don't you? She flew planes for the ATA during the war."

"And your brother knew them?"

"He was obsessed with automobile racing for a while. He persuaded Daddy to take him to Le Mans once, and came home talking nonstop about Bugattis and Bentleys and such. I was at a few parties in the thirties where the Barnatos came along with a crowd of aging man-boys. I remember one weaving up to me, tumbler in hand, and saying, 'Hello, gorgeous. Do you know I hold records in both speed and endurance?' I was sixteen, for God's sake, and quite repulsed."

"No doubt," said Iris, with a shudder. "I must say that story has whetted my curiosity. I think I'll swing by the library on the way home and see what I can find out."

"What on earth for?"

"Why not? I don't have a date tonight, I'll be wondering about the rest of the story every time I sit at my dead man's desk, and my only alternative is the Harrodian Brains, Trust, and Debating Club. Libraries are my refuges against the world, Gwen. You know that."

"I do," said Gwen. "I'll see you tomorrow. Don't get so absorbed that you get locked in overnight."

"That lock I will pick," promised Iris. "See you at the office tomorrow, my dear. The world must be peopled!"

"The world must be peopled," echoed Gwen with a wave and a smile.

Gwen arrived at The Right Sort the next morning at eight forty-five. Iris wasn't there yet. She unlocked the office, turned on the light and hung up her hat, then decided to take a look in 407 to see what progress Mr. MacPherson had made.

She put her key in the lock to find, to her irritation, it wasn't locked. She opened the door to see a man standing behind the right-hand desk. He was in his forties, wearing a shabby, solid brown two-piece suit with a drab dark green tie loosely knotted around his neck. He had a malnourished look to him—the wrists poking through the frayed cuffs were alarmingly skinny. He swallowed nervously as she looked at him, her eyes narrowing.

"Hello," she said suspiciously.

Then she remembered her conversation from the previous day with Mr. MacPherson.

"Are you Charlie?" she asked.

"Yes, ma'am," he said, removing his hat quickly.

"I'm so sorry to startle you like that," she said coming forward to offer her hand. "I'm Mrs. Bainbridge with The Right Sort. We're the ones taking the office."

"You're taking the office?" he repeated, blinking rapidly.

"Yes. Didn't Mr. MacPherson tell you?"

"He didn't say what was going on," said Charlie.

"I don't suppose it was of much importance," said Mrs. Bainbridge, looking around. "Looks like he got it cleaned up well enough. Pardon me."

She stepped around him and ran her fingertip across the windowsill, then glanced up at the panes.

"Better than I had hoped for," she pronounced. "So you're helping him with the desks?"

"The desks," he repeated. "Yes. I was just looking at them."

"Marvelous, aren't they?" she said, turning to him with a smile. "But rather massive. I'm so glad you're pitching in. He can't possibly move them by himself. He should be here shortly."

"Will he?" said Charlie. "Good. I'm going to step out to the landing for a smoke until he does. Nice meeting you, Mrs. Bainbridge."

"You too, Charlie," she replied.

He walked out. Gwen looked back out the window, which faced the rear of the building, overlooking an empty lot where another office building had once stood until the Luftwaffe had reduced it to rubble. She glanced down, imagining where Cooper had fallen.

It would have been an alley then, she thought. He died alone in an alley between the backs of two office buildings. Not the longest of drops, either.

She found herself hoping he died immediately.

"Rest, rest, perturbed spirit!" said Iris, watching from the doorway.

Gwen gave a guilty start, then laughed in embarrassment.

"Do you sense it, too?" she asked.

"The haunting of the desks?" replied Iris. "No, of course not. Though if ever a desk was haunted, it would be this one. Wait until you've heard what I've found out."

"Could we go back into our office?" asked Gwen. "I have a feeling I should be sitting down for this."

She walked into the hallway, locking the office door behind her, then glanced at the landing below.

"Oh, he's gone," she said.

"Who's gone?"

"That Charlie fellow who was going to help Mr. MacPherson move the desks."

"He was here?" asked Iris.

"Yes. He said he was going to have a cigarette while he was waiting."

"I saw no one when I came up," said Iris. "Nor do I smell any smoke."

"Neither do I, now that you mention it. Maybe he went outside."

"And he was in four oh seven?" asked Iris.

"Yes. When I came in."

"Do me a favour," said Iris. "Open it up again."

Gwen, puzzled, unlocked the door. Iris went in.

"Where did you see him?" she asked, looking around.

"Behind the desk on the right."

Iris stood behind it, looking up where the curtain rod once was, then at the desk itself.

"This was Cooper's desk," she said, half to herself.

"Oh, God!" said Gwen. "You don't suppose that was Cooper's ghost I saw just now."

"Don't be silly," said Iris as she squatted down and examined it. "Here. Come look at this."

Gwen joined her somewhat hesitantly.

"Remember how I didn't want to get any scratches on the locks?" asked Iris.

"Yes?"

"It looks like someone lacked my reticence. Those weren't there yesterday."

Gwen looked where Iris was pointing. There were fresh scratches on one of the locks.

"And ghosts, being incorporeal, don't need to pick locks," concluded Iris.

She tugged at the drawer. It stayed shut.

"I guess that wasn't Charlie I was speaking to," said Gwen.

"Did he say he was Charlie?"

"I asked him if he was Charlie," recalled Gwen. "He said yes. I wonder what he wanted."

"Something in this desk," said Iris.

"After all this time? Cooper and Lyons vacated the office fifteen years ago. By different exits."

"He might have hidden something here since then," speculated Iris.

"But if he was able to lock something inside, why wouldn't he be able to unlock it now?"

"People lose keys all the time," said Iris. "Well, we'll know soon enough when our keys are delivered."

"You're not going to pick it?" asked Gwen. "Now that we know there's something in there worth burgling?"

"After all the trouble we went to at Harrods? No, I'll wait."

"I can't believe you're that patient. I'll be on tenterhooks the entire time."

They went back to 405, locking 407 behind them. At one point, they heard someone coming up the stairs. They looked out to see Mr. MacPherson.

"I've got you the keys," he said, waving a pair of them. "One more plus a spare."

"Thank you, Mr. MacPherson," said Mrs. Bainbridge, taking them. "There is a problem, however. Did you lock four oh seven after you left last night?"

"Of course," he said. "Why?"

"Because there was a man in there when I looked in this morning. He said he was Charlie."

"Charlie isn't supposed to come until tomorrow," said Mr. MacPherson. "What did he look like?"

She described him. Mr. MacPherson started shaking his head before she got halfway through.

"That wasn't Charlie," he said. "And he was inside?"

"He was."

"That accounts for the missing key. That's bad. That's bad, all right. I'll have to get a new lock put in."

"That's the building's responsibility, not ours," said Mrs. Bainbridge sternly.

"I'll have to tell Mr. Maxwell," said Mr. MacPherson sorrowfully. "All right, I'll get that done. Probably tomorrow before the locksmith can come in, but you haven't moved in yet. Don't know why anyone would be in there. There's nought worth stealing."

"It is curious," said Sparks. "Very well. Thank you, Mr. MacPherson."

They went back inside The Right Sort, shutting the door behind them.

"Sit," ordered Iris. "I have a tale to tell."

"Will there be ghosts in it?" asked Gwen.

"There will not. What we heard from Mr. Lancaster was the bare bones. Yes, the younger Cooper and Lyons went gadding about, best friends, gambling buddies, and partners in crime. But it turns out that there was also a woman involved."

"Ah, a proper story at last," said Gwen. "Before it was just men, money, and cars."

"Her name was Gladys Llewellyn, a minor socialite with major ambition. She attached herself to the Bentley Boys like a lamprey, but was discarded by the upper echelon. She wound up marrying Cooper, but from all reports was bitter about her treatment. The police believed she was the one who encouraged the embezzlement. Selvyn went under, and since he was one of the major investors in Bentley Motors, the whole lot eventually collapsed. Then, when exposure was imminent, the Coopers prepared to vamoose—only she ran off with Lyons instead!"

"No!" exclaimed Gwen. "No wonder Cooper killed himself."

"Lost his wife, his best friend, his fortune, and his reputation in one fell swoop," said Iris. "He tried to brazen it out for a month or so, but the walls were closing in. He should have held out—it was only embezzlement, after all, not a capital crime. The firm's junior partner, a man named Forlingen, was convicted as part of it and sent to prison."

"And what happened to the widow Cooper?"

"She was in the car with Lyons when he crashed. She died with him."

"One can become too attached to the wrong man," said Gwen with a sigh. "It's too bad we weren't in business then. We could have saved them."

"Not likely," said Iris. "There's one more curious thing—the case was investigated by our old friend Detective Superintendent Parham."

"Really? They thought it was murder?"

"No, but Parham was in the fraud unit then. Remember, this was fifteen years ago. He was a promising young up-and-comer then."

"It's hard to imagine him as a young man," said Gwen. "What connection do you suppose this has with Not Charlie, the burglar?"

"No idea," said Iris. "We'll have to ask him if he comes back."

"Do you suppose he will?"

"I would."

"You, as always, are my guide to the criminal mind," said Gwen. "We should try to get some work done until those keys show up."

They came up with three potential matches and prepared letters to be sent out. Around eleven, an energetic series of footsteps rose towards them. A moment later, a young man in a Harrods delivery uniform knocked on the doorway.

"Are you Miss Sparks and Mrs. Bainbridge?" he asked.

"We are," said Sparks.

"Mr. Lancaster sends his regards," said the young man. "I am supposed to wait until you try out the keys."

"Let's go next door," said Mrs. Bainbridge.

The young man stood back as the two trotted back to 407.

"Do you know, I'm actually excited about this," said Mrs. Bainbridge as she unlocked it.

She opened the door for the others. The deliveryman stopped in his tracks when he saw the desks.

"Blimey," he said admiringly. "Those are a couple of real beauts! I thought Mr. Lancaster was puffing them up, but I see what he was talking about. They don't make them like that anymore."

"You clearly have the right bent for your department," said Sparks. "Which key goes with which?"

"They have the numbers on the tags," he said, handing her a small cardboard box.

She opened it and pulled out a pair of brass keys, each with a red tassel hanging from it. She went behind Cooper's desk, compared the tag to the number on the plate, then handed the other key to Mrs. Bainbridge, who took up a position behind Lyons's.

"On three," said Sparks. "One, two, three."

They inserted their keys into the locks on the centre drawers and turned. There was a pair of clicks, and the drawers slid open.

"Hooray!" said Mrs. Bainbridge.

"Try locking them," advised the deliveryman.

They did.

"Our thanks and compliments to Mr. Lancaster," said Mrs. Bainbridge, giving him tuppence. "Did he tell you that he was one of the men who carried these up here?"

"Mr. Lancaster is a legend in Furniture," said the young man quite solemnly. "Good day, ladies."

He left, and the two immediately went to work, opening each drawer, front and back.

"Nothing," reported Gwen, "but he was at your desk."

"I'm on the last one," said Iris, unlocking the lowest right-hand drawer.

She pulled it open. There was a small, scattered pile of postcards in it. She pulled them out and laid them on the desk.

"Not exactly a treasure map," commented Gwen, coming over to look at them.

They were pictures of racing cars, fifteen in all. Bugattis, Lorraine-Dietrichs, Alfa Romeos, Bentleys, some in action, some posed proudly in pits, their drivers and crews standing by them, goggles atop helmets, pennants frozen in mid-flutter behind.

"The things he loved most were with him to the end," said Iris.

"He must have saved them from races he had gone to," said Gwen. She flipped one over.

"Or," she said, "they were sent to him. By Lyons. Look."

Iris picked it up.

"'Still on the hunt?'" she read. "'I'm disappointed, old boy. I'd say Gladys sends her best, but I think she's saved her best for me, based on how it's been going.' Nasty piece of work, wasn't he?"

"On the hunt for what?" wondered Gwen.

She flipped over the rest of the cards. Each had the same handwriting.

"This one's the oldest," she said, picking it up. "Addressed from Paris. 'Dear Ken, Awfully unsporting of me to leave you to face the music, but there it is. Let's make it interesting—I have put your share somewhere safe, and am going to send a series of clues as to where it is. If you can figure it out within thirty days of the thirtieth card, come and get it. If not, I'll keep it for myself. Best of luck, old friend! Ogden. P.S. Gladys says hello!' Where was that other one from?"

"Le Mans," said Iris, holding it up so Gwen could see the postmark.

"Thirty cards," said Gwen. "There are only fifteen here."

She perused the rest of them. They all contained children's riddles.

"'Kings and queens may cling to power and the jester's got his call,'" Iris read aloud. "'But, as you may all discover, the common one outranks them all.'"

"An ace in a pack of cards," said Gwen promptly.

"You're quick."

"I have a six-year-old son and a book of riddles. I may have it memorised by now."

"Try this," said Iris, picking up another one. "'Every dawn begins with me, and daybreak couldn't come without. What am I?'"

"The letter 'D,'" said Gwen wearily. "These can't be the clues. They're too childish."

"Maybe one has to put the whole sequence together," said Iris. "Ace, 'D'—a word beginning with 'AD'?"

"But we've only got half of them," Gwen pointed out. "And the order—well, it must be in the order they were mailed. Check the postmarks—each came a day later."

"The first four from Paris, then they move on," said Iris. "Lyons was certainly a meticulous tormentor."

"Were these what Not Charlie was after?" Gwen asked. "Why now? It's been fifteen years. What could keep him from looking for fifteen—oh!"

They looked at each other.

"What's the prison term for embezzlement?" asked Gwen.

"I don't know," said Iris. "But fifteen years sounds eminently plausible. The junior partner, Forlingen. Could he have just finished his sentence and come back?"

"We should ask Parham," said Gwen. "It was his case. He would know."

"Let's give him a call," said Iris. "And let's put these postcards in our strongbox for now."

She scooped them up. They left 407 and returned to The Right Sort, where Iris bent under her desk, opened the panel concealing their strongbox, and locked the postcards inside next to the petty cash.

Gwen pulled her address book from her bag, looked up a number, then dialed.

"Detective Superintendent Parham, please," she said. "Mrs. Gwendolyn Bainbridge calling. Hello, Detective Superintendent, how are you? Yes, it hasn't been very long. No, not a new murder—an old case of yours. The Cooper and Lyons case. Yes, I'm not surprised. Miss Sparks and I are taking over their old office, and we learned about them in the process. Would you happen to have some time free to speak with us about it? No, not idle curiosity—we've come across something you might find interesting. Yes? Two o'clock would be fine."

Iris waved at her. Gwen put her hand over the mouthpiece and looked at her quizzically.

"Ask if he could pull the case file," she whispered.

"And Miss Sparks is requesting that you have the case file handy," continued Gwen. "Yes, she is very much that. Thank you, Detective Superintendent."

She hung up.

"I'm very much what?" asked Iris.

Gwen merely smiled in response.

"He actually recognised us," said Iris as they passed by the constable at the entryway to the Homicide and Serious Crime Command.

"We've been here often enough," said Gwen.

"We should have earned a complimentary set of dishes by now," commented Iris.

Parham's secretary looked up from her typing as they came into the anteroom.

"One moment, please," she said, picking up her telephone and pressing a button. "Sir, the ladies from The Right Sort are here."

They heard a response. The secretary hung up the telephone, then got up and opened the door for them.

Detective Superintendent Philip Parham came from around his desk to shake their hands.

"Well, ladies, it seems we can't spend enough time together," he said, showing them to a pair of chairs. "I had no idea you had grown so fond of me."

"What is amazing to us," said Mrs. Bainbridge as they sat, "is that from the first time you burst into our office until now you've never mentioned having investigated a case in the office right next to ours."

"It had nothing to do with why I was seeing you," he said. "As for after, I did not want to distress you unduly. Some people don't like being at the scene of a homicide."

"Homicide," said Sparks. "So not necessarily a suicide. That struck me about the news reports. There was never a final coroner's verdict. Is it still officially a homicide pending investigation?"

"Tell me why this concerns you," said Parham.

"When you investigated Mr. Cooper's death, did you happen to find any postcards with racing cars on them?" asked Mrs. Bainbridge. "Written to him by Mr. Lyons?"

"That was never released to the public," said Parham. "How on earth did you know?"

"We've taken over their office," said Mrs. Bainbridge. "Including the original desks. We found a pile of the postcards in a locked drawer."

"I'm surprised the police didn't take them," said Sparks.

"I wasn't with this bureau then," said Parham. "I pushed for it to be handled as a murder, but the detective in charge concluded suicide and couldn't be bothered. The scene was not gone over as much as I would have liked."

"You kept pushing the matter, didn't you?" asked Sparks.

"I did."

"May we see the postcard?" asked Mrs. Bainbridge.

He reached into a large accordion file lying on his desk, pulled out a postcard, and handed it to her. It showed a photograph of a group of men clustered around a Bentley Speed Six, the car filled with bouquets from a recent victory.

"That's identical to two of the ones we found," said Mrs. Bainbridge. She turned it over. "Postmarked from Trieste, twenty-nine days after the first one."

"Trieste was where Lyons was before he was killed in the crash," said Sparks.

"You've done your homework," observed Parham.

"'I'm disappointed, old friend,'" read Mrs. Bainbridge. "'Your problem is that you've always been a two-dimensional thinker in a three-dimensional world. Too bad you couldn't put it all together. This is my last message to you.' And the postmark—how long after this was Cooper's death?"

"A week from when it was mailed. It would have taken that long to arrive, so Cooper's death must have been shortly after."

"He died, Lyons died," said Mrs. Bainbridge. "The junior partner, Forlingen, went to jail. How long was his sentence?"

"Fourteen years," said Parham.

"He was convicted in '32," said Sparks. "He would have got out sometime this year."

"He got out three years ago," said Parham. "Feet first. In a coffin. He died in prison."

"Oh!" exclaimed Mrs. Bainbridge. "Then he couldn't have been—" She stopped.

"Couldn't have been what, Mrs. Bainbridge?" asked Parham.

"There was a man poking around the office this morning," she said. "We thought he might have been Forlingen, trying to track down the embezzled fortune."

"Most of it is still unaccounted for," said Parham. "We assume Lyons stashed it, and the location died with him."

"Where was this found?" asked Mrs. Bainbridge, holding up the postcard.

"Inside Cooper's jacket pocket," said Parham. "Which he was wearing when he died."

"No suicide note?" asked Sparks.

"None," he said, one eyebrow moving up slightly.

"But there was something else, wasn't there?" she asked, looking at him intently.

In reply, he upended the file. A pair of long, thin pieces of wood clattered onto his desk. Each culminated in jagged ends that looked as if they could have been joined together evenly.

The two halves of a broken curtain rod.

"Oh, you clever, clever man," said Sparks admiringly.

A few minutes after five, the two women came out of the office building, chattering away. He watched them from inside his car as they walked towards Oxford Street and vanished. The tall blonde he had already met—Mrs. Bainbridge, she had said, and her first name, Gwendolyn, he got from the placard for The Right Sort at the entryway to the building. So the short brunette must be Miss Iris Sparks, he thought.

He continued to watch as other occupants of the building exited. He had to time it right—go in too early, and he might run into someone asking questions, maybe even that oblivious custodian; go in too late, and the front door would be locked.

He gave it another ten minutes, then got out of his car and walked briskly to the door as if he had business inside.

Which he did, of course.

He went up the four flights of stairs swiftly and silently until he reached the fourth storey. He glanced over at The Right Sort Marriage Bureau. There were no lights on the other side of the frosted glass, and he knew it was the only occupant of that floor.

He reached into the pocket of his overcoat and pulled out three items: the key to 407 that he had nicked from the custodian's office, a torch, and a small, steel jimmy.

He unlocked the door and flicked on the torch. The desks stood where they always stood, mute witnesses to a pair of good old men and another pair of perfidious younger ones. He strode towards the one on the right, jimmy raised to do some serious damage.

Then the ceiling light came on. He spun to see the blonde standing in the doorway, her hand still on the switch.

"I saw you come out the front door," he said.

"You did," said Mrs. Bainbridge. "But you didn't see me return through the back door. I've been watching the stairs from the third floor for you to show up."

"Why?"

"I didn't want you to do any more damage to that perfectly lovely desk," she said. "And I wanted to apologise."

"For what?"

"For thinking of you as a burglar," she said. "It turns out I was wrong. I've been told on good authority that it's only a burglary if it happens at night, and if it's a dwelling."

"Is that right?" he said, gripping the jimmy in both hands. "So what does that make me?"

"Well, that depends on why you're here," she said. "Hang on, I wrote it down."

She reached into her bag, pulled out a notepad, and flipped it open.

"What sounded closest is something called Housebreaking with Intent to Commit Felony," she said, consulting her notes.

"This isn't a house."

"Yes, but the definitions are more expansive. 'Every person who,' and this is the key point, 'with intent to commit any felony therein,' and I'm going to skip over a few sections—"

"Please do," said the man.

"'Breaks and enters any' and there is a long list of places including countinghouse, which arguably this once was—"

"It was, but it isn't anymore," he said.

"No, but the list also includes office, which it still is," she said, closing the notepad and putting it away. "So we're back to your intent, and that's what, quite frankly, aroused our curiosity. If you are who we think you are, we might be in a position to help you."

"Why would you do that?" he asked.

"Justice," she said, with a determined look in her eye.

"Justice for whom?" he asked.

"For you, for a start," she said. "Now, put down the jimmy and we can talk properly."

He looked at her for a long moment, then put it down on the desk.

"I wasn't going to do anything to you with it," he said.

"I'm relieved to hear that," said Mrs. Bainbridge. "Let's go into our office where there are actually chairs. Would you like a cup of tea?"

"If you're offering, that would be nice," he said.

"I am offering, Mister—well, you haven't told me your name, have you?" she asked.

"It's Selvyn," he said. "Malachi Selvyn."

"Which makes sense," she said. "Would you mind leaving the office key you stole on the desk as well? I assure you that there is no longer anything of any interest in here to tempt you to further felonious activities."

"You have them, then?" he asked as he deposited the key on the desk next to the jimmy.

"That's a test, isn't it?" she asked as she led him into The Right Sort. "I admit to knowledge of what the 'them' is in your question. I have a teakettle on the hot plate ready for you. We only have oolong. Will that be all right?"

"Fine, Mrs. Bainbridge," he said, bemused.

He sat and watched her as she busied herself with the teakettle.

"Where did you serve?" she asked as she poured.

"In India," he replied. "Fourteenth Army. I was demobbed in June and came home three weeks ago."

"Welcome back," she said, placing a cup and saucer on Sparks's desk in front of him. "I saved you a biscuit. I'm sorry I can't give you anything more. You look like you haven't been eating well."

"Thank you," he said, taking the cup and sipping from it. "That's extraordinarily kind of you under the circumstances."

She put another cup by Sparks's typewriter, then sat behind her desk.

"If you don't mind, Miss Sparks, my partner, will be here shortly," she said. "I know she'll want to hear your story."

"I'm coming!" called Sparks as she bounded up the stairs.

She strode into the office, hand extended.

"Hello, hello," she said. "How do you do? I'm Iris Sparks. And you must be our office ghost."

"Hardly that," said Mrs. Bainbridge. "This is Mr. Malachi Selvyn."

"Ah, the true victim in all of this," said Sparks as she took her seat. "Cooper and Lyon took you for everything, didn't they?"

"You know about it," he said.

"We know the public story," said Sparks. "And you've come back thinking you could find where the money went. What took you so long?"

"I never knew it could still be around," he said. "I was ruined by those two, and brought my friends down with me. I couldn't show my face in society anymore. I couldn't afford to be in society anymore. So I signed on to a freighter, jumped ship in India, and there I stayed."

"Until?" prompted Mrs. Bainbridge.

"A letter came," he said. "From Forlingen, maybe three years ago. He was dying, and he wanted to make amends. He told me about Lyons abandoning Cooper, then sending him postcards with riddles containing keys to the location of the money they stole. I was in the army by then, and couldn't do anything about it, of course. But once I got out, I came back."

"How could you possibly have believed they were still here?" asked Mrs. Bainbridge.

"I had a friend in London. I wrote to him without telling him everything. He found out that no one had taken the office since then. And, most importantly, that the desks were still here."

He laughed abruptly.

"I thought it was a bloody miracle," he said. "That God had

kept me alive and kept those postcards intact all this time just so I could be made right again. And then I got here, and you two were taking over the office."

"You could have asked us," said Sparks.

"With this story?" he said. "How could I know you'd believe me? Or let me have the postcards?"

"Did Forlingen know how to solve the riddles?" asked Mrs. Bainbridge.

"No," said Selwyn, but there was a momentary shift in his eyes when he said it.

"Well, we are happy to help you," said Sparks. "But there's a problem. We only have half the cards."

"What?" he said, his face turning ashen. "How can—no. No, no, no, not after I've—half?"

"There were supposed to be thirty," said Mrs. Bainbridge. "We found the first fifteen in the desk, and the police have the last one, but the rest are unaccounted for."

He stood and started walking rapidly about the little office, turning and shaking his hands.

"What did he do with them?" he shouted. "That wretched, evil man! It wasn't enough to swindle me once when he was alive, but to do it again from the grave!"

He stopped, his arms falling limp at his sides, then turned to face them.

"I apologise, ladies," he said hoarsely. "I have caused you undue distress and, as it turns out, for nothing. All I can do is thank you for your understanding. And for not going to the police."

"Trying to break into a desk is hardly worth bothering them about," said Mrs. Bainbridge.

"I am glad you think so," he said, collapsing onto his chair.

"Murder, on the other hand," said Sparks, "that's worth having them here."

"Murder?" exclaimed Selwyn. "What murder?"

"Cooper's murder, Mr. Selwyn," said Sparks.

"He killed himself," said Selwyn. "He jumped out the window."

"That's what it looked like," said Sparks. "To most people. But not to me, and not to one of the detectives on the case. There was a curtain rod on that window. Holding up curtains, no doubt. And it was broken when the police went into that office the day he died. I thought that was strange. Why would Cooper go to the trouble of standing on the windowsill, breaking the curtain rod, then jumping out the window after?"

"I have no idea," said Selvyn. "Desperate men do irrational things, I suppose."

"I suppose they do," said Sparks. "But this was so odd. I mean, what could he have had against that curtain rod? What could a curtain rod do? Other than hang things?"

He looked at her sharply.

"Let's say someone wanted to make it look like Cooper committed suicide," Sparks continued. "Let's say the first attempt was to hang him. Bop him on the head, put a noose around his neck, then tie the other end around the curtain rod and watch him die. Only you didn't reckon on the curtain rod being on the cheap side and snapping like a twig. So you followed up with the simple expedient of shoving Cooper out the window."

"Maybe Cooper tried to hang himself first," muttered Selwyn.

"Then the rope would have been left behind," said Mrs. Bainbridge. "But it wasn't."

"How do you know that?"

"Because we saw the police reports this afternoon," said Mrs. Bainbridge. "It was never ruled a suicide. And God knows you had reason enough to hate the man."

"I had more than enough reason," he said, sipping his tea. "But that doesn't mean it happened like that. It's too far-fetched, and even if it did happen, you can't connect me to it."

"We couldn't before," said Parham, standing at the doorway, another man behind him. "But we can now."

Selwyn turned to look at him.

"You're the detective they bothered about this, I take it," he said.

"It was no bother," said Parham. "Ladies, you remember PC Godfrey."

"A woman never forgets the first man who ever fingerprinted her," said Mrs. Bainbridge. "Good to see you again, Constable."

"You as well, Mrs. Bainbridge," said Godfrey.

"Tell them what you found, Godfrey," said Parham.

"I was able get a couple of decent prints off the jimmy, a partial off the key, and several off the drawers of that desk next door," he said. "I did a preliminary comparison with a photograph of the ones we got from the original scene. I'll leave the final conclusion to Mr. Harvey, who's the main bloke back at the Yard for prints, but I'd say it's a match."

"A match? From where?" asked Selwyn.

"From the curtain rod," said Parham. "Extremely difficult place to leave fingerprints. Unless, of course, one is hanging something from it. But I'm sure you'll come up with an explanation for that. Come along, Mr. Selwyn. We have a car waiting for you."

"May I finish my tea first?" he asked.

Parham nodded. Selwyn, with a nod to Mrs. Bainbridge, drained his cup, then placed it on the saucer.

"I think I'll save the biscuit for later," he said, putting it in his pocket. "Good night, ladies."

He stepped into the hallway, where a pair of constables were waiting.

"You may want to take his cup with you," suggested Sparks. "I'm sure it will give you a clear set of prints."

"Will do, Miss Sparks," said Godfrey, producing a paper bag from his kit and scooping the cup into it. "Nice seeing you all."

"Detective Superintendent, would you stay behind for a few minutes?" asked Mrs. Bainbridge.

"Certainly," said Parham.

They waited for the rest of his party to get out of earshot.

"Thank you," he said when they were gone. "This one has been gnawing at me for fifteen years."

"Our pleasure," said Sparks. "It's a pity the embezzled funds couldn't be recovered."

"I think they can be," said Mrs. Bainbridge.

"How?" asked Sparks. "We're still missing nearly half the cards. And we don't know how to piece together the riddles."

"I think it's time we put our cards on the table," said Mrs. Bainbridge. "Or desk, as the case may be."

"You've been saving that one, haven't you?" observed Parham.

"I have," said Mrs. Bainbridge happily. "Iris, would you get them out of the strongbox, please?"

"I already have them," said Sparks, taking them from her bag and spreading them out on her desk, picture sides up.

"Here's my paltry contribution," said Parham, adding the one from the case file.

"On the contrary, yours is the key," said Mrs. Bainbridge. "Now, you both figured out the significance of the curtain rod, and I didn't, so well done."

"This is where she is going to one-up us and be smug for a month," said Sparks to Parham.

"Maybe two," said Mrs. Bainbridge.

She reached into her bag and pulled out a handful of postcards, which she spread out below the ones already there. They were photographs of racing cars, identical to those in the first group.

"Are those from Lyons?" asked Sparks.

"They are."

"Where did you get them?" asked Sparks, looking at her in disbelief.

"Mr. MacPherson. He turns out to be a bit of a scavenger, among other things. I noticed he had a wall of postcards he's plucked from baskets and bins over the years. Among them were these. He told me that Cooper discarded them. I guess he became frustrated with Lyons's riddles after a while."

"There are only ten," said Sparks. "We're still missing a few."

"We don't need them," said Mrs. Bainbridge.

"But the riddles—"

"Are a distraction," said Mrs. Bainbridge. "Look at the postmarks. The first four are from Paris, but then they hit the road. Lyons mailed one every day. But all the postcards are from the same set. Why wouldn't he buy new ones in each place he came to instead of carrying these around with him?"

"Something about the race cars," guessed Parham. "Something with which to taunt Cooper."

"Or the cars themselves are a code?" speculated Sparks.

"No," said Mrs. Bainbridge. "'Your problem is that you've always been a two-dimensional thinker in a three-dimensional world.' Let's take the first one sent. A postcard would seem to be a two-dimensional object."

She picked up the first of the Parisian cards and held it in front of her, picture side forward.

"Only it isn't," she said, turning it on its side. "It has depth. Not much, of course."

"There's something on the edge," said Sparks, peering at it. "A smudge—no, several smudges."

"Which is true of all of them," said Mrs. Bainbridge. "'Too bad you couldn't put it all together,' to quote from the last one."

She stood before the desk, picked up the cards in chronological order, and assembled them in a neat stack.

"And thus do two-dimensional objects become three," she said, pressing them together so that the sides were uniform.

The smudges weren't smudges. They were fragments. Reassembled, even with the few missing members, they produced a series of perfectly legible letters and numbers that ran around the edges of the stack.

"'UBS Gen,'" read Mrs. Bainbridge. "Union de Banques Suisses in Geneva, I should think. The rest appears to be an account number and other information needed to withdraw whatever is in there. Lyons bought the entire set so he could write on the sides. Then each day he mailed the top one until they were gone."

"Ingenious," said Parham.

"Him or Mrs. Bainbridge?" asked Sparks.

"Both. And you, of course. May I have those?"

"What will happen to the money?" asked Mrs. Bainbridge, handing him the stack.

"We will demand its return as stolen property," said Parham. "Then it will be given to the victim."

"So Selvyn will get it back after all," said Sparks.

"Yes," said Parham. "He can afford a decent barrister now. Good evening, ladies. Call me if you solve any more of my cases."

Mr. MacPherson stared at the rows of keys on the wall in his office. A cabinet, he decided. A cabinet with small pigeonholes for each set of keys. Four rows high, and a lid that can swing down and be padlocked. He'd have to get a carpenter to make it, but that shouldn't be a problem.

Carpenter, he thought. Something about a carpenter.

There was a light knock on the door. He turned to see Mrs. Bainbridge standing there.

"Hello," he said. "Have you brought my postcards back?"

"Oddly enough, the police require them as evidence in a murder case," she said.

"Murder? What have my postcards have to do with a murder?"

"It's a long story," she said. "But Miss Sparks and I would be glad to tell it to you. We would like to invite you to take tea with us tomorrow afternoon while we tell it. It would provide you with a break from the polishing the floor in four oh seven."

"Could I bring Charlie?"

"Of course," she replied. "And here's some good news. We recovered the missing key."

She came forward to hand it to him.

"How did you do that?" he asked.

"It's all part of the story," she said.

"I'm looking forward to hearing it," he said.

"Have you given any further thought about applying to The Right Sort?" she asked.

"Well," he began.

Carpenter, he thought.

"You know, there's something I want to try first," he said. "If it doesn't work out, maybe I'll fork out the five pounds."

"That's fine," she said. "We'll see you tomorrow at teatime."

She left.

Carpenter, he thought. The girl he kissed in the carriage. Her name was Jenny Carpenter. Maybe he could find her again. Worth trying.

Jenny Carpenter.

Better write it down.

The author gratefully acknowledges the help provided by Sophie Denman, Archive Executive, Harrods Company Archive.

Read on for a sneak peek at Allison Montclair's new novel

The Unkept Woman

Available Summer 2022

PROLOGUE

The black Wolesley roared down Welbeck Street and came screeching to a halt behind the two patrol cars double-parked at Number 51. Cavendish and Myrick got out of the front seat while Keller got out the back, pulling his camera from his case as he did.

There was a constable standing at the entrance. He glanced cursorily at the detectives' idents, then jerked his head towards the entrance.

"Flat thirty-one," he said.

"Thanks," said Cavendish. "Medical examiner's on his way. Any word on Godfrey?"

"Dispatcher said he's coming back from another job, so they'll turn him around straightaway."

"Good. Send him up the moment he gets here."

There was a flash from behind him as Keller took a shot of the doorway.

Cavendish went in, followed by the others. He stopped by the mailboxes, pulling out his notebook as he scanned the names.

"Thirty-one belongs to Anthony Rigby," he said. "Ian, call that name in, then meet me at the flat."

Myrick nodded and went outside in search of a callbox.

Another constable stood in front of Number 31 on the third storey.

"Cavendish, Homicide and Serious Crime Command," said Cavndish. "You're PC Peterson?"

"Yes, sir," said the constable. "I was first on the scene."

"Talk to me."

"A Miss Jennifer Pelton in thirty-two called it in," said Peterson. "She was coming home about six, saw the door partly open, peeked in, and saw the body. She called from her flat. I got here at ten after. I went inside, ascertained that the woman was dead, and did a quick look around the flat to make sure no one else was hanging about. Then I secured it. I was careful not to step in any blood, sir. I recommend you stay to the right when you go in."

"Good," said Cavendish. "Stay here. Don't let anyone inside until I've done my walk-through."

"Yes, sir."

Cavendish slowly pushed the door open. The body of a young woman was immediately evident, lying in the entrance hall about eight feet from the door. There was a spray of blood droplets on the floor and lower part of the wall to the left.

"Get some shots of those," he said, pointing them out to Keller.

He stepped gingerly into the hallway, staying to the right to avoid treading through the evidence. More blood drops made a trail from the initial group to where the woman had fallen. He had to edge around an umbrella stand on the right, noting a cricket bat nestled between two umbrellas.

The woman lay on her stomach. She was wearing a light blue blouse which set off a small amount of blood surrounding a bullet hole in the upper middle of her back. Her arms were awkwardly bent, so she must have been dead before she hit the floor, he thought. There was a small pool of blood below her left shoulder. He stepped around her, then carefully lifted the shoulder up. There was a second bullet hole in the right side of her chest. No exit wound on the other side.

He glanced about the apartment. There was a small kitchenette next to them. A vase holding a spray of lilacs sat on the window sill. They were starting to wilt.

Did Mr. Rigby give you those? he wondered.

The hall opened into a sitting room. There was a door to the right which he assumed led to a bedroom. He looked at the wall opposite. No bullet holes visible.

He turned back to the woman, squatted down and looked at her face. Late twenties, he guessed. Brunette, petite. Eyes still open, her last expression one of shock and pain.

"Quite the looker," commented Keller as he turned his lens towards her.

"Certainly was," agreed Cavendish, straightening.

He looked around for a handbag, saw none.

"Peterson," he called. "Did you see a bag or anything with her ident?"

"No, sir," replied Peterson. "I thought it might be a robbery. I saw some letters and bills on the table in the sitting room."

"Thanks," said Cavendish.

He stepped into the sitting room. There was a small table, large enough for an intimate dinner for two, with a stack of letters on it. He picked up the top one.

"Miss Iris Sparks," he read.

He replaced it in the stack, then looked back at the woman.

Hello, Miss Sparks, he thought. My name is Nyle Cavendish. I'm going to find the man who killed you.

ABOUT THE AUTHOR

ALLISON MONTCLAIR grew up devouring hand-me-down Agatha Christie paperbacks and James Bond movies. As a result of this deplorable upbringing, Montclair became addicted to tales of crime, intrigue, and espionage. Montclair now spends their spare time poking through the corners, nooks, and crannies of history, searching for the odd mysterious bits and transforming them into novels.